This one's for David.

ACKNOWLEDGMENTS

Thanks to the many people who contributed, in some way, to this effort: Jonathan Frakes, Mitchell Ryan, Gene Roddenberry, and everyone who made *Star Trek* the phenomenon that it is; Marco Palmieri, Keith DeCandido, and the gang at the *Star Trek* editorial office; Paula Block; Ted Adams; Howard Morhaim; Lauren Murdoch; and my usual support network, Chris, Scott, Nancy, Shoshana, Tara, Jack, and my family.

HISTORIAN'S NOTE

This story commences in 2355, sixty-one years after the presumed death of Captain James T. Kirk aboard the *U.S.S. Enterprise*-B in *Star Trek Generations*. It concludes in 2357, seven years before the launch of the *Enterprise*-D in "Encounter at Farpoint."

PART ONE
JUNE 2355

Chapter 1

He put one foot in front of the other. That was all it took, one foot, then the next, occasionally a swerve or a sudden stop to dodge the other pedestrians who traversed San Francisco's sidewalks, and then, one cluster of citizens or another averted, he continued on toward his destination. In some spots where the streets of days gone by remained, he could easily have walked in those, thereby avoiding most of the foot traffic, but the idea didn't occur to him. His name was William Hall, he was a yeoman second class currently assigned to Starfleet Headquarters in San Francisco, and he was on a mission.

He did not let his mind drift toward the nature of his mission. His mind didn't drift much at all, for that matter; it was consumed with the process and not functioning much beyond that. One foot in front of the next. Turn left at that corner, up three blocks, cross the street. He came from Pine Bluff, Arkansas, which could have fit inside San Francisco a hundred times over. He'd been to other planets, he'd seen the stars, up close, but a San Francisco street was still, to him, alien and not a little intimidating, filled as it was with members of dozens of races, from planets almost beyond counting.

One foot.

Most of the other pedestrians were civilians; he wore one

of the few uniforms he had seen since he started out on this mission.

One foot.

As he walked, the sun dipped behind tall buildings, throwing the busy streets into shadow. His destination loomed ahead, one of those same tall buildings. He noted it, and then his mind slipped back into its routine. One more clutch of pedestrians to bypass, gazes to avoid. He made a graceful sidestep to get around them: a family, nicely dressed, heading out to a restaurant for dinner, perhaps, or a play. Two boys and a girl, two older ones who must have been parents. He had parents, back in Pine Bluff.

At the building, he stood in front of the door. The door surveyed him for a moment, noting his uniform, his professional demeanor, scanning his retina and maybe, depending on how up-to-date the security system here was, his DNA. After a moment, an electronic voice asked him, *"What is your business here?"*

"Official Starfleet business," Petty Officer William Hall said. "Urgent and classified." The door didn't open. Very up-to-date, then. He held a small electronic tag up toward where the door's camera eyed him. He'd been told not to use this unless it was necessary, but it seemed that it was. Like a lot of things about this mission, he had been left in the dark about why he shouldn't use it frivolously.

But he didn't let his mind wander there, either. The door opened for the tag, as he'd been told it would, and he walked inside. There was a live guard in the lobby, middle-aged but fit, with a heavy mustache hiding his mouth, sitting behind a high counter and regarding him with curiosity. But William just showed him the tag and the guard gave a half-smile, a twitch of the bushy mustache, really, and then turned back to his monitors. When William reached the elevator, it opened for him, and he stepped inside. He told the elevator to take him to the nineteenth floor, and the doors closed and then they opened again a moment later and he was there. He stepped out.

The apartment number was 1907, he knew that much. The rest, he had been assured, would become clear when he needed to know it. He found 1907. It would be empty now.

In the corridor, he waited.

"Most people," Kyle Riker said, "achieve enlightenment, if at all, through living. Through the process of life, going through it, you know, a day at a time. That's most people. Me, I achieved it all at once, through surviving. That's all. Nothing to do with me, just the luck of the draw. But I survived, and what wisdom I have . . ."

He let the sentence trail off there. It didn't matter. The man he'd been talking to—talking at, running off at the mouth toward, he decided—had ceased to listen and was leaning toward the bartender, signaling for another Alvanian brandy. Kyle, drinking instead a sixty-year-old single malt from right there on Earth, recognized that he had probably reached his own limit. His limits were stricter these days than they had once been, and he was better about enforcing them. Had to be. He gripped the bar with both hands as he lowered himself from the stool, and with a wave at Inis, the shapely Deltan bartender who was two-thirds of the reason Kyle came here in the first place, he headed for the door.

You sound like an old fool, he mentally chided himself as he went. The bar was thirty-five stories up, with floor to ceiling windows facing west, and the sun, he could see as he walked out, was an enormous red ball sinking into the sea on the far side of the Golden Gate Bridge. *It's sunset,* he thought, *that's the problem.* There had been a time when he'd liked sunsets, but that had been before Starbase 311. As he went to the elevator that would take him down to the twentieth floor, from which he could tube across the street to his own building, he remembered another sunset when he'd had virtually the same conversation. He'd stopped himself, on that occasion, at about the same moment, and said, self-pityingly, "This is the kind of story a man should tell his son. If he had, you know, a son he could talk to. Because a boy needs to hear that his dad—"

"Kyle, dear," Katherine Pulaski had said then, interrupting him, "shut up." She had taken away his drink.

Too many painful memories associated with sunsets, he thought. But the wounds had been fresher then, the scars more raw. He was better now. Obviously not whole—*you don't jabber at strangers in bars like you were doing if you're whole.* But better, nonetheless.

When he rounded the bend toward his door, he saw a uniformed Starfleet officer, young and well-scrubbed but with a strangely vacant look in his pale green eyes, standing outside his apartment. A yeoman in a red duty uniform. Kyle had been drinking, but not really that much, and seeing this unexpected sight brought him around to sobriety fast. The yeoman started toward him.

"Are you Kyle Riker?" he asked. His voice sounded odd, as if he were distracted by something even as he voiced the question.

"Yes," Kyle said. Most of his work was for Starfleet. Maybe the young man was a messenger. But he didn't see a parcel, and couldn't imagine any message that would have to be delivered in person. Anyway, he had just been at headquarters before heading home—*well, heading for the bar on the way to heading home,* he admitted. If anyone had needed to tell him anything they could have done it there.

"I need to see you for a moment, Mr. Riker," the yeoman went on. His expression—*or lack of one, to be more accurate,* Kyle thought—didn't change. He didn't even blink. "Can we go inside?"

"I . . . sure, come on in." Kyle pressed his hand against

the door and it swung open for him. "Can I ask what this is about?"

The yeoman nodded but didn't verbalize a response as he followed Kyle into the apartment. For a moment Kyle thought this was all the setup for some kind of elaborate practical joke. Friends would pop out from hiding places and wish him a happy birthday. Except that it wasn't his birthday, nowhere near it, and he didn't have friends with that kind of sense of humor. *He* didn't have that kind of sense of humor. That was something else he'd left on Starbase 311.

The yeoman came into his apartment and the door swung shut behind him. "I'd really like to know who you are, young man, and what this is all about," Kyle said, more forcefully than before. "Now, before we go any further."

He waited for an answer. But the man's face didn't change, and he didn't speak. Instead, he drew a phaser type-2 from a holster on his belt. Kyle threw himself to the floor, behind a couch, thinking, *That's some message.*

The yeoman fired, and the phaser's beam struck the wall in front of which Kyle had been standing a moment before, blowing a hole in it. Sparks flew, and a cloud of smoke roiled in the air. "*Unauthorized weapons discharge,*" the apartment's computer said in its toneless robot voice.

Kyle rolled to the side and tucked his feet underneath himself, preparing to spring. "I know," he told the computer through clenched teeth.

The yeoman turned stiffly toward him, phaser still at the ready. Kyle jumped toward the young man, slamming into him with all the strength he could muster. They both went down, crashing onto a low table, and then the table tipped over and they rolled to the floor. Kyle caught the man's wrist and twisted, aiming the phaser anywhere but at himself.

As he did—panting from the exertion, blinking back sweat—he noticed that the yeoman's blank expression still had not changed. He could have been waiting for a transport, or watching a singularly unexciting game of chess. Kyle pounded the man's wrist against the edge of the overturned table, once, twice, again; and finally the phaser went flying from his hand. The man gave a soft grunt of pain, but that was the first sound he had made since they had come into the apartment.

"*I am alerting the authorities,*" the computer said.

"Fine," Kyle barked back. He made the mistake of turning away from his opponent for a brief moment, and the man took advantage of the opportunity to reach out with his other hand, locking it around Kyle's throat. Kyle released the now-empty phaser hand and brought both his arms up, hard and fast, knocking the choking hand away. Regaining his feet, he waited for the yeoman to try to rise. When the man did so, his face still empty, Kyle shot out with a right jab to his chin, then a left hook, and another right that cut the flesh above his eye. The man took the blows, air puffing out of him, but showing no evidence of pain or fear.

Then, without warning, he blinked three times in rapid succession. His eyes seemed to focus suddenly, and he looked around, turning his head from left to right quickly. "What . . . ?" he started to ask, and then he stopped, blinked once more, and pitched forward. Kyle stepped back as the man landed in a heap at his feet.

He didn't move. Kyle hesitated a moment, in case it was a trick, then knelt and touched his fingers to the guy's neck. He could find no pulse.

"You alerted the authorities?" Kyle asked the computer.

"*They are on the way,*" was the response.

"Cancel them. Get Starfleet Security, not civilian authorities."

The computer didn't answer, but he knew it was already complying with his demand.

Carefully avoiding the dead man, Kyle sat down on his couch and waited.

His wait was not especially long. Starfleet sent four officers to his apartment, arriving less than fifteen minutes after the yeoman had fallen. They checked the body and confirmed what Kyle already knew. The young man was dead. One of the security officers, a seasoned human lieutenant with hair almost as silver as Kyle's own and heavy, hooded eyes, sat down on the couch next to Kyle while another called for a removal team to come for the body. He had introduced himself as Lieutenant Dugan.

"There'll be a hearing, I expect," he said. "But it looks as if the case for self-defense is pretty strong. Guy was in your house, discharged his phaser. I should arrest you, but given who you are, sir, I feel confident that you'll surrender yourself if I ask you to."

"Of course." It had gradually dawned on Kyle that this was probably coming. He was innocent, of course, of any misdeed. But until a thorough investigation proved that, he would be under some degree of suspicion, even though his story made sense. As they spoke, the other security officers were busying themselves around the apartment, checking the central computer, inspecting the wall that had been damaged, trying to recreate, as best they could, the sequence of events as Kyle had described it. While they worked, a coroner's team arrived to take the body, closing it into a kind of sled that then hovered waist-high so they could guide it from the apartment and out to a transport. They were quietly efficient. It was possible that Kyle's neighbors didn't even know what had happened.

An hour later they were all gone, and Kyle was left alone. He ordered the computer to repair the wall now that the forensic team was done examining it.

Lieutenant Dugan had recommended that he get some sleep, but Kyle knew that was impossible. Every time he closed his eyes he was back on 311. He could hear the emergency Klaxons, see the flashing red alert lights, taste the adrenaline and fear that had been in his mouth as he scram-

bled from room to room. No, sleep was the last thing he
wanted to try just now. Instead he went to his bookshelves
and withdrew a biography of Napoleon he'd been meaning
to get to, then sat back on the couch to wait for daylight.

At the Starfleet Command plaza station, Kyle disembarked from the monorail and took the stair-lift down to
plaza level. There, he had to pass through a security station
where two alert-looking security officers scanned him. Instead of going to his own office, as he normally would have,
he headed for the office to which Lieutenant Dugan had
asked him to report. The office was in the main Headquarters building, seventh floor, on a long hallway lined with
closed, numbered doors.

He was, he had to admit, a little relieved to find that the
room really was just an office, and not a cell or a hearing
chamber. Dugan sat behind an orderly desk, speaking to his
computer, and he looked up when Kyle came in. "Mr.
Riker," he said with a friendly tone. "Thanks for coming.
Have a seat."

Kyle sat. The office, he noted, was sparely furnished, as if
Dugan didn't really spend much time in it. Beside Dugan's
desk there was a credenza with globes on it, depicting Earth,
Jupiter, and Saturn, and two visitor's chairs. Holoimages
hung on the walls—landscapes of planets Kyle couldn't
identify but which clearly weren't Earth. The images
changed as Kyle watched them, one planetscape dissolving
into another in random sequence. "If I were to guess, Lieutenant Dugan, I'd say you were not all that happy about
being chained to a desk. You seem to be a man who'd rather
be in deep space."

"I've spent some time on a starship," Dugan admitted.
"It's always fascinating. But there's nothing wrong with good
old momma Earth, either."

"That's my attitude too," Kyle said. "Our own planet is almost infinite in its variety. I like a little trip off-world as much as the next guy, but I'm always glad to see her in the forward viewscreen when I come home."

Dugan glanced at a screen that Kyle couldn't see, and when he looked up again his expression was more serious. "Mr. Riker," he began. "I have a little more information now than I did last night, at your apartment."

"It'd be hard to have less."

Dugan chuckled. "That's true. The man who attacked you was named Yeoman Second Class William Hall. He was assigned here, at Headquarters. His primary duty was as an assistant clerk in Vice Admiral Bonner's command. The vice admiral's office has notified his next of kin, family back in Arkansas, I gather. Do you know Bonner?"

Kyle tried to picture him, and came up with a vague impression of a severe man in his fifties, with thick black hair and a pinched face. "I believe I've met him once or twice, but I don't really know him."

"He's very loyal to those in his command," Dugan said. "My impression is that he barely knew Yeoman Hall, but he's very concerned about what happened to him."

"So am I," Kyle confessed. "Do we know the cause of death?"

Dugan hesitated before answering, as if he needed to decide how much to reveal. "An autopsy was conducted last night. There's evidence of brain damage—some kind of interference with the operation of his brain's limbic system. More specifically, the hippocampus."

"Caused by what?"

"That we don't know," Dugan replied. "He's still being examined to see if that can be determined."

"And that could have killed him?" Kyle asked. "That damage?"

"Not by itself, no. But the force of your blows, in combination with the preexisting condition, possibly might have."

Kyle looked at the floor, carpeted in institutional blue. "So I did kill him."

"It's quite possible that you did, yes. Or contributed to his death, which would probably be more accurate. I'm sorry."

"So am I," Kyle said sadly. "I'd like to be able to contact his next of kin, if that's possible, to express my deep regret."

"I'll try to get you that information, sir. In the meantime, we've checked your computer's memory, and it confirms your version of events."

"I could have faked that," Kyle suggested.

"You could have," Dugan agreed, his narrow, hooded eyes fixed on Kyle's face. "But you would have had to work fast. We were there shortly after everything started happening. And the computer was recording events the whole time—it would have been pretty tricky of you to fake the record without any gaps in the real-time log."

Kyle had intentionally kept the computer recording everything, just for that reason. Once the authorities had been notified, he knew one of their first priorities would be to investigate what the computer had observed from the first phaser discharge on.

"Did Mr. Hall have any genuine reason for coming to see me?" Kyle asked. "Was he bringing a message from Bonner, or anyone else in the command?"

"Not that we've been able to determine," Dugan responded. "He went off duty at eighteen hundred hours, and last anyone knew he was headed to his home in Daly City. There seems to have been no Starfleet-related reason for him to even have still been in uniform, much less passing himself off as on official business. That's how he got through the door of your building, by the way. And he had a Starfleet keytag to make it seem on the level. It wasn't activated—wouldn't have got past a first-year cadet—but it was good enough to get into a century-old civilian apartment building."

Kyle felt defensive. "It's a nice place," he said quickly. "Lots of atmosphere."

"I'm sure," Dugan replied. "And substandard security."

"Which is normally not a problem," Kyle countered. "I've been living there for years. This is the first time I've been attacked. So statistically, it's still a good bet."

"Statistically, most people only get killed once," Dugan pointed out. "We're not charging you with anything, sir. And we'll keep investigating Yeoman Hall, to see if we can figure out what he was doing there. But if I were you, I'd be a little careful." He looked away, wordlessly dismissing Kyle.

"I will," Kyle assured him. "And thanks."

His own office on the twenty-third floor of the Headquarters skyscraper tower was, Kyle thought, a good deal more "lived-in"-looking than Lieutenant Dugan's. As he kept books at home, he also had a cabinet full of them here. One wall was entirely covered in old-fashioned paper maps. Some were antiques—a map of the battleground at Antietam, from the American Civil War, in which one of his ancestors had distinguished himself, for instance, and a map of San Francisco from the twentieth century. Others were nautical charts of the world's oceans, and still others two-dimensional printouts of stellar cartography—not especially practical, but he still enjoyed looking at them. He liked being able to see the lines on his maps and visualize himself at a particular point in time and space.

Just now, though, Kyle sat at his desk, chair turned away from it, looking at a shadowbox frame above the bookshelf in which there were some other items with a deeply personal meaning to him: his wife's wedding ring, the key to the first house they'd lived in, up in Alaska, and a holoimage of her outside that house, holding their baby boy, Will, in her arms. She had been standing in the shadow of a tall fir, but the sun's rays had fallen on her as if cast there by one of the ancient Dutch masters, picking her and the baby out and limning them clearly against the dark backdrop. Her hair was golden in that light, reminding Kyle of a honey jar in a window with the sun beaming through it, and her smile had been equally radiant.

Less than two years later, Annie was dead, leaving Kyle and young Will on their own.

Kyle turned away, suddenly. That was not why he'd come in here, he knew. He had to figure out why someone would want to kill him, not lose himself in a past that could never be reclaimed.

Starfleet was primarily a scientific, exploratory, and diplomatic agency, not a military one, but there were always conflicts brewing at various points around known space, and therefore always something to which Kyle should be paying attention. Recently, the U.S.S. *Stargazer* had found itself in some difficulty in the Maxia Zeta System, for instance. The ship had been nearly destroyed, but her crew had survived, drifting in a shuttlecraft for a few weeks until being rescued. Kyle was trying to draw together all the information he could on the attack in hopes of learning who had done it, and what its captain, one Jean-Luc Picard, might have done differently in its defense.

Could the attack have had something to do with that? Kyle wondered. The *Stargazer*'s assailants were still unknown, and maybe they preferred to stay that way. Of course, Kyle Riker wasn't the only person working on that mystery, not by a long shot. He wasn't even the most high-profile. *Why would they come after me?* he asked himself. *I'm the least of their worries.*

Well, not the least, he mentally amended. He was good at what he did, and if—when—he found out who was behind the attack on the *Stargazer*, whoever had done it would be sorry they had survived. But even granting that, it still seemed unlikely that Yeoman Hall had been responsible for an attack so far away, or would have any connection to the mystery attackers.

Still, he noted "Maxia Zeta," down on his padd, and then turned his mind toward his next priority. But before he could continue, his office door tweedled at him.

"Come in," he said.

The door opened and two security officers—not Lieutenant Dugan—stood outside. Chief Petty Officer Maxwell Hsu, an aide to Admiral Owen Paris, stepped in, looking more than a little uncomfortable. "Mr. Riker, sir . . . the admiral would like to see you," he said haltingly.

"He normally just calls when he wants to see me. What makes this time different?" Kyle knew his directness would take the aide off guard, which was why he did it.

Maxwell cleared his throat and examined his feet. "I . . . I don't know the answer to that, sir," he said. "I just know that he asked me—" here he raised his hands slightly, as if to indicate the security officers waiting in the corridor. "—us . . . to come and escort you to him."

Kyle pushed his chair back, pressed his palms flat against the surface of his desk, and rose to his feet. "Well, then," he said with forced affability, "I guess we'd better find out what he wants."

They walked briskly through the halls, the security officers a couple of strides behind Kyle at all times, as if they thought he might make a break for it. He didn't know what it was about, but he knew he didn't like the feeling. First, that someone had tried to kill him, compounded by the fact that he had actually, albeit in self-defense, killed his assailant. And now this, being escorted through Starfleet Headquarters as if he were little more than a common criminal. It was infuriating.

And not a little terrifying.

Instead of Admiral Paris's office, they led him to a nearby conference room. Hsu motioned for Kyle to stay put while he poked his head inside. A moment later, he emerged and gestured Kyle in with a halfhearted smile. Kyle walked in, completely at a loss as to what he should expect.

If he'd had hours to think about it, he still would not have expected what he saw.

At the end of a long, oval table polished to a high gloss, Admiral Owen Paris sat rigidly upright, giving him an avuncular, sympathetic smile. To his right, on the table's side, Vice Admiral Bonner eyed him appraisingly. To Bonner's right, an assortment of Starfleet brass, human and non-, most known at least in passing to Kyle. Charlie Bender, F'lo'kith Smeth, Teresa Santangelo, and two others Kyle couldn't put names to.

Admiral Paris half-rose from his chair and swept his arm toward an empty chair, looking very lonely all by itself on the near side of the table. "Come in, Kyle, please," he said, his voice familiarly gruff. "I'm sorry for all the formality."

"I'm sure there's a good reason," Kyle offered, generously, he thought. He took a seat in the suggested chair.

"Do you know everyone?" Paris asked.

Kyle looked at the two strangers. "Almost," he replied. "I haven't had the pleasure."

"Right, sorry," Paris said. With appropriate arm movements, he added, "Captain Sistek and Captain Munro. Kyle Riker."

"Pleasure," Kyle muttered, convinced that it would not be.

The conference room was anonymously Starfleet—lots of gray and silver, with no windows and mostly undecorated walls. The wall behind Owen Paris had a large reproduction of Starfleet's arrowhead symbol mounted on it, and the wall Kyle faced had a holoimage of the old NCC-1701 *Enterprise* soaring through space. It looked like a room meant to emphasize that what was discussed in it was more important than the surroundings.

"The reason we've brought you here, Kyle," Paris began, "with all these people and all the special treatment, is that an accusation has been made against you. An accusation that, should it be true—and let me say at the outset that I don't believe it to be—but if I'm wrong and it were true, would be a very serious matter indeed."

"Does this have something to do with last night?" Kyle asked. "Because if it does—"

Owen Paris waved away his question. "No, not at all," he said. "I'm sure you had a terrible night because of that, and I guarantee we'll get to the bottom of it. But this is a completely separate matter."

"Okay, then," Kyle said. "Please excuse the interruption."

"Feel free to speak at any time," Paris told him. "This is not a formal hearing of any kind, just a—well, let's say a casual meeting to make you aware of what's going on."

"If I'm being accused of something, that doesn't sound very casual," Kyle pointed out.

"That may have been a poor word choice," Paris admitted. "There has been an accusation made, to Vice Admiral Bonner, but so far no evidence has been presented to support it. We're not at the stage of bringing formal charges, or doing anything other than launching an investigation that I suspect will be fruitless. But the matter, having been raised, can't be dropped without the investigation."

Kyle, not having slept to begin with, was beginning to lose patience with the way Paris was dancing around the issue. "So what's the accusation?" he asked.

Owen Paris looked at the others, as if wishing someone else would take the lead. No one did. Vice Admiral Bonner shifted uncomfortably in his seat, and the others remained still, looking at either Kyle or Owen and waiting for the admiral to continue.

Owen cleared his throat before going on. "The attack on Starbase 311," he said. "It's been theorized that you, being the only survivor, might have had something to do with it. That you were somehow in league with the Tholians."

Kyle couldn't believe what he was hearing. "I almost died in that attack!" he exclaimed. "I've had nearly two years of therapy. I still see those Tholians in my dreams, and sometimes when I'm awake, hunting me down, chasing me from room to room, killing with utter brutality."

"And yet, here you are," Vice Admiral Horace Bonner said. His voice was calm and even, with a musical ring to it. A *tenor's voice*, Kyle thought. Bonner had black hair, neatly cut and combed to the rear off his high forehead. His eyes were small but glimmered with intelligence, and his mouth, set now in a sort of half-frown, seemed extraordinarily wide for his narrow head. A strange-looking man, Kyle assessed, but not necessarily unpleasantly so.

"I'm sure you've heard the story," Kyle said impatiently. "If not, I'd be happy to tell it again. What's thirty thousand times, between friends?"

"We're all familiar with it," Owen assured him. "That's not at issue here."

"It sure sounds like it is," Kyle shot back. "Because in my version there is no part where I conspire with the Tholians to kill everyone on the base."

"It does seem odd, however, that you would have been spared," Bonner observed. "The Tholians went room to room, as you've said. They dismantled equipment, checked ventilation ducts and Jefferies tubes, even went so far as to blast holes in walls to make sure they weren't missing anyone. And yet, they left you alive."

"They thought I was dead," Kyle objected. "Hell, I thought I was dead. Take a look at my medical records. Ask Dr. Pulaski what shape I was in when she started working on me."

"Hardly an impartial witness," Captain Sistek put in. She was a Vulcan, with typical Vulcan features—straight black hair, slanted eyebrows, pointed ears. The only thing Kyle found unique about her was her nose, which was long and aquiline. She spoke with her head tilted back a little, giving the impression that she was sighting down it, as if it were some kind of weapon.

"My . . . relationship with Katherine began when I was in therapy," Kyle insisted. "Not before. I was hardly in any position to romance her when they took me off the starbase, unless she has an odd attraction to jellyfish. I was near-dead, more than half the bones in my body were broken, I had lost enormous amounts of blood. Katherine herself said that she had never seen anyone so badly injured. If I was in cahoots with the Tholians, they sure are lousy allies."

" 'With friends like that,' eh?" Owen quoted.

"Exactly," Kyle said. "I'd like to know just who is making this charge."

"Should it ever go beyond this stage, to a formal complaint, you will have that opportunity," Owen promised him. "But for now, that person's identity will remain confidential."

He kept up a strong front, but inside, Kyle was shaken. The attack the night before had been one thing—the threat of physical violence was unpleasant, but he had survived violence before. A body could be mended. But this threatened to attack his career, the very thing that had carried him through those bad days after the destruction of 311. Kyle had, for most of his adult life, defined himself through his career. He was an asset to Starfleet, an important cog in the big wheel that kept the peace and explored the galaxy. Without Starfleet, he would be lost.

And it could get worse yet. There could be prison time, if he were found guilty of treason. Starfleet justice was fair but firm. If whoever was behind this had somehow trumped up evidence against him, then he could be looking at a hard fall.

"So," Kyle said, working to keep his concern out of his voice. "Where do we go from here?"

"As I said, there'll be an investigation," Owen replied crisply. "I'll keep you informed of its progress as we go. If formal charges are to be brought, I'll let you know that as well. Kyle, this is not a railroad job, and no one is out to get you. But we need to follow procedure. I'm sure you can understand that."

"I understand," Kyle said. Something else had been nagging at him, and suddenly he realized what it was. He decided not to bring it up now, though, but to hold back in case it was something he could use later on. Vice Admiral Bonner had seemingly known details that he had never reported—at least, that he didn't remember having told anyone, though his first few weeks in therapy were pretty fuzzy in his mind—about the attack. He had described the Tholians looking into the ventilation units and Jefferies tubes, but he was pretty sure he had never shared the fact that they had torn apart equipment and walls looking for more victims. That meant that Bonner's source, whoever it was, had some good information—information no one alive should have had.

His future was looking more bleak by the minute.

"We're dismissed, then," Owen said. "Thank you for your cooperation, Kyle."

The meeting broke up, and Kyle started back toward his office, without escorts and without a backward glance. But Owen Paris caught up to him before he'd gotten very far from the conference room. He tried on a wan smile, but it didn't fit well and he dropped it. "Kyle," he said, taking Kyle's arm in his hand. "I want you to know I feel terrible about this."

Kyle nodded. He just wanted to close his eyes and drift off to sleep right there. He wouldn't go back to his own office after all, he decided, but he'd go home and get some sleep, if he could. If the Tholians in his brain let him. "I know, Owen," he said. "You have to do what you have to do."

"That's right." Owen sounded gratified to be let off the hook so easily. "Say, Kyle. Today's Father's Day. Have you heard from Will? I saw him in class yesterday. He's a terrific lad."

"Will?" Kyle asked. He recognized the sound of his own son's name, but was so tired, so distracted that he almost didn't make the connection. "No. He's in town?"

"Of course he is," Owen answered with a chuckle. "You have had a bad night, I see. Will's at the Academy. Second year. He's in my survival class."

"That's right," Kyle said, trying to cover. "You're right, Owen, I'm exhausted. I'm surprised I know my own name. I'm sure Will's much too busy to remember something like Father's Day, anyway. Boy's got much more important things on his mind."

"Well, he's swamped with work, I can tell you that," Owen said. "Second-year students don't have much free time." He released Kyle's arm and started back up the hall, then stopped again. "You take care, Kyle. If there's anything I can do for you, just let me know."

"I'll do that, Owen. Thank you. And give my best to Thomas."

"I'm on my way home to spend some time with him now," Owen replied. His son Tom was about ten years younger than Will, Kyle remembered.

Kyle continued down the corridor then, mentally berating himself for his ignorance. *You should have known Will was at the Academy,* he thought. *Or you should have remembered, if you did know.* He thought maybe he'd heard something about it before, and just forgotten. But the last couple of years had been hard ones for him, and most everything that wasn't immediately crucial to his survival had gone by the wayside in favor of the physical and emotional therapy he had needed to get back on track.

Anyway, Kyle Riker had long ago fallen into the habit of compartmentalizing his life. Recovery was in one compartment, work in another. Family was in another one, by itself. And that one, he didn't go into often.

Not often at all.

Chapter 2

"You might want to do some strategizing," Admiral Paris told the class. "No cheating, no going into the city ahead of time and planting supplies or anything. It won't help anyway, because you won't know what you're looking for until tomorrow morning, when you get out there. But you can talk amongst yourselves, figure out how you're going to approach the teamwork aspect of the project. As an away team on a starship, you would prep for a mission in that way before you left the relative safety of the ship. And, of course, you would gather as much intelligence as you could about your destination. In this case, we're assuming that intelligence is very limited. So that's your assignment for tonight—think strategy."

He turned away from the class and returned to the podium in the front of the room, his standard signal that the lecture was over for today. Will Riker quickly scanned the notes he'd typed into his padd, making sure he had caught all the major points and could understand his own shorthand. Dennis Haynes, whose room neighbored Will's, tossed him a cheerful grin. "This sounds like fun, doesn't it? At least, it resembles fun more than most assignments do."

Will was already almost to the classroom door, but he paused to let Dennis catch up. Before his friend reached him, Admiral Paris wagged a finger at him. "Mr. Riker, if you don't mind, I'd like a word with you before you go."

Dennis shrugged and Will said, "I'll see you a little later." Felicia Mendoza, another member of their Zeta Squadron, had joined Dennis for the trek across campus, back to their quarters. Will cast a brief, longing glance at their retreating forms, then turned back to the admiral.

"Yes, sir?"

Admiral Paris leaned against the podium. Will hoped that didn't mean he was making himself comfortable for a long conversation—he really wanted to get back to his room and get started on some of the homework. It seemed to get more and more difficult as the year went on. He was only in his second year at the Academy, which meant he still had a lot of struggling to look forward to. "I saw your father earlier, Will," the admiral said. His tone was sympathetic, not accusatory, Will noted. "Have you talked to him lately?"

"Not real recently, no sir."

"I get the impression that you two aren't particularly close."

"Not terribly, sir."

"Nonetheless, today, as you might be aware, is Father's Day. It's a custom on this planet, a day on which people honor their fathers, without whom they wouldn't be here. You've heard of it?"

"Yes, sir." Will shifted his weight from one foot to the other. *Where's the anvil?* he wondered. This felt like one of those times, as in the old Earth cartoons his squadron member Estresor Fil watched incessantly, when an anvil was surely going to fall on his head.

"So I thought that perhaps it would be a good idea for you to maybe go see him, give him a call. You know. Honor your father."

"Yes, sir," Will said again. "I'll try to do that, sir."

The expression on Admiral Paris's face showed that he understood just how little truth there was in Will's promise. He even started to shake his head sadly, but then caught himself and turned it into some other head motion, as if he were looking around the room to see if any of the cadets had forgotten anything.

I guess that's the anvil, Will thought. *The old man's disapproval. I can live with that.*

"Is there anything else, sir?" he asked.

"That's it, Mr. Riker. Good day."

"Thank you, sir." Will turned and hurried from the room, which had become suddenly hot and oppressive.

Will didn't talk to Kyle Riker. He didn't, on those rare occasions when he thought of him at all, think of him with any special fondness, and he certainly didn't think of him as "Dad" or "Pop" or any of the other endearing nicknames people had for their fathers. Kyle Riker was a person his mom had known once, a genetic donor, a man with whom he'd shared a few pleasant moments of his childhood, and a whole lot of stiff, awkward times. When he thought about those days, he thought mostly of the long silences, or of times when Kyle Riker would stare at him, as if trying to fathom how his young brain worked. The connection between them was biological, not emotional.

Father's Day. Will let out a bitter laugh, then glanced about quickly to see if anyone in the spectacular garden had noticed. Coast clear, though. There were a couple of cadets coming toward him, but they were engaged in conversation, and far enough away that they probably couldn't have heard him.

Kyle Riker had raised Will from infancy, if "raised" was the word for it. Will tended to doubt it. "Tolerated," maybe. Certainly, he had fed and sheltered the boy. But he was never cut out for parenthood. Having to do it by himself, after Will's mother had died during his second year, had proven far too difficult a task for him. Finally, during Will's fifteenth year, he had given up altogether. His work for Starfleet had been taking him away more and more anyway, and at that point he took an extended off-world posting, leaving Will behind for good.

So Father's Day, while it might mean something to others, was pretty much a nonoccasion to Will. There had been times when he'd even considered losing the Riker name. He'd decided against that—what else would he call himself? He'd have to make something up, and that wasn't the kind of thing he believed himself to be good at. *If raising myself taught me anything,* he'd tell people, *it's pragmatism. I don't like to waste my time with a lot of foolish nonsense.*

Ignoring the sky overhead, pink bruising into indigo, ignoring the fresh, sweet scent of dozens of trees, grasses, and flowering plants, ignoring even the gentle breeze that blew in off the bay, fluttering leaves and flags alike, Will Riker turned his focus away from all extraneous distractions and headed for home. Tomorrow was his final project in Admiral Paris's survival class, and it would be demanding, challenging, and crucial. The whole squadron succeeded or failed together. And there were plenty of stresses in the squadron that would work against them if they weren't careful. Paris was right; strategy would be key. Strategy and teamwork.

When he got back to the dorm, he went to Dennis's room. The redheaded, ruddy-faced cadet kept a worktable and chairs directly in front of his bay window, and he and Felicia Mendoza were sitting in them. On the couch sat Estresor Fil, a petite green Zimonian female, about the color of a fir tree, who barely passed the minimum height and weight requirements for Starfleet duty. Boon, a Coridanian, the lanky, laconic son of two miners from that underpopulated world, squatted on the floor at the foot of the couch. His skin color, common among some Coridanians, always reminded Will of an old brick storefront he had seen in Valdez, during his youth, both in texture and color. McGill's Hardware, he remembered. He'd loved the smell inside there.

"Come on in, Will," Dennis Haynes said. He was a gregarious fellow, every bit as sociable as Will was reserved. They seemed, at a glance, like polar opposites in almost every way, but had become fast friends in spite of that. Or because of it—Will had never been able to decide for sure.

"Sorry if I'm late," Will said, entering the room and helping himself to one of the chairs scooted up near the worktable. The sky had gone dark outside, and the lights of the Academy grounds and the city beyond twinkled in the distance.

"How could you be late?" Estresor Fil asked. "There was no particular meeting time scheduled."

The Zimonian seemed to Will to take everything said to her with the same degree of seriousness, as if mentioning that the day was warm or a dog was cute carried the exact same weight as a warning of a poisonous insect or a Romulan with a phaser. Add to that no sense of humor at all and a tendency to lecture rather than discuss, and you had Estresor Fil, who was Will's least favorite member of Zeta Squadron, by far. She was so formal that she insisted both her names be used at all times.

She was also, he had to admit, brilliant.

Most of the work a cadet did at the Academy was done solo, but for those occasions when group efforts were needed, cadets were formed into five-person squadrons, and Zeta was his. Any Starfleet assignment was likely to be a team situation, so the cadets broke into their squadrons fairly often. There were good points and bad to this arrangement, of course. The starship atmosphere was fairly authentic, because most everyone on a starship worked with others. But it also meant relying on other people. Will was none too comfortable with that—he liked to have his fate in his own hands.

Once Will was seated, Boon looked at the group and took command, as he had a tendency to do. He was, he had told them often, grooming himself for a captaincy, and sooner would be better than later. Will thought his personal style was at odds with his ambition—he never liked to speak in public, for instance, and didn't believe in using three words if one would do even in private. But in spite of his reticence, he was a good student and was seemingly driven by an urge that not even Will, who was plenty ambitious himself, could comprehend. "Okay, folks," he said. "We have a challenge ahead of us tomorrow. Everybody ready?"

"Since we really can't prepare," Felicia replied, her dark eyes flashing as she tossed out a smile, "we're probably as ready as we're going to be."

"There's always preparation to be done, right?" Estresor Fil argued. "Admiral Paris told us enough to begin our planning. We know where we'll be, and we know what our goal is. We might as well get started on whatever we can, while we have some time. Besides, he told us to, and that's good enough for me."

"In the abstract," Will pointed out. "But not with any specifics."

"That's true," Dennis added. "We know we'll be in San Francisco. But we don't know what part—or even if we'll all be together."

"I think we have to assume that we won't be together, at first," Felicia said. "We'll need to find each other. Without using combadges."

"Why don't we go over what we do know?" Estresor Fil suggested. "And then we'll have a more definitive sense of what we don't know."

Will nodded. " 'Know your enemy and know yourself; in a hundred battles you will never be in peril.' "

"Is that more of your ancient Chinese wisdom, Will?" Felicia asked. Her accent was vaguely Latin American, and Will liked the way she pronounced certain words. She was as tall as Will, half again the height of the diminutive Estresor Fil, with an athletic, sculpted body. When she spoke, it was usually with a forthrightness Will admired, and in any physical effort she was likely to excel.

"Sun Tzu," Will answered with a nod. He'd been reading a lot of the military strategists of Earth's past, including Sun Tzu, Epameinondas, Carl von Clausewitz, Antoine Henri Jomini, and others.

Boon blew out an exasperated sigh and began a speech as long as any Will had ever heard from him. "If we could stick to the matter at hand," he said. "Estresor Fil is right, as is Sun Tzu, I suppose. We'll have very little information until we actually start, so there's only so much we can plan ahead. But we know these things, I think. We're going on an urban survival test. We will be spending a week in San Francisco. We aren't allowed to identify ourselves as cadets, we'll be out of uniform and incognito. We can't break any laws. We'll be following clues which will lead us to other clues, in a sort of scavenger hunt, to demonstrate our ability to infiltrate, for example, an enemy alien city."

"Should be a piece of cake," Dennis said.

"But that's where what we don't know comes in," Will countered. "We don't know if we'll be transported into the city together, or separately, so we might need to track each other down. We don't know precisely what sorts of clues we'll be looking for, or how we'll know the first one when we see it. We don't know if there will be other obstacles planted in our path, although knowing Admiral Paris, I think we should count on it. We don't even know exactly how the project ends—if we solve all the clues and find whatever it is we're supposed to find, do we come in early? Or do we still wait out the week?"

"At least we can't do worse than Captain Kirk," Dennis said with a laugh. " 'Do you still use money?' " Some seventy years back, the legendary Kirk and his bridge crew, which included Ambassador Spock, had traveled back in time to the late twentieth century and had to survive in a San Francisco three hundred years removed from their own experiences. That very mission was the inspiration for this particular Academy exercise.

"They survived, didn't they?" Estresor Fil shot back. "And they saved the world. And your whales. I would certainly consider that a success by any reckoning."

"You're right," Dennis agreed, still chuckling. "They pulled it off. And we don't even have to travel back into the past to do it, so I'm sure we'll be just fine."

"Who's in command?" Boon asked. Even though the others had voted him Squadron Leader, when they faced group activities they rotated command positions so that everyone got a fair chance to lead.

"It's our final project," Felicia Mendoza pointed out. "I thought you'd be champing at the bit. Are you suggesting otherwise?"

"I'm not suggesting anything," Boon said. "Certainly I'm the best qualified. But if somebody else has a particular interest in the job, that's fine too."

There was a moment of silence as all the cadets in the room glanced around at one another. Will felt a number of eyes on him and thought that maybe he should challenge Boon for the leadership position this time. Boon generally believed that he was born to lead, and took that role whenever the opportunity came up. But Will was convinced that on a starship, anyone could be thrust by circumstance into the captain's chair, and no one who graduated from Starfleet Academy should be unfamiliar with the demands of the job.

"I think it should be Dennis," he said at last, breaking the silence. The look on Boon's face was one for the books—crestfallen and amazement battling for supremacy, with fury threatening to break through at any time. He actually bit his lower lip, trying to control his expression.

"Dennis?" Boon asked, unable to keep the disbelief from his voice. "Why?"

"Because he hasn't been in charge on any of our group projects to date," Will said. "And this is the last group project before the end of the year. Everyone needs to get a taste of leadership, and this will be his last chance with this squadron." What he didn't add was that he knew Dennis would never have nominated himself for the position. He was a get-along, go-along kind of guy, never wanting to make waves, always content to be in the back of the pack as long as he was included. Starfleet needed people like that, of course—there were a lot of crew members to every captain, and a lot of captains to every admiral—but every crew member would perform better if he or she understood the captain's position too.

"Will, I don't know—" Dennis began, but Felicia cut him off.

"I second the nomination," she said. "Will's right. It really is your turn, Dennis."

Dennis's cheeks flushed, but he went silent. Estresor Fil was the next to speak. "Dennis can do the job as well as anyone else," she insisted.

Boon looked defeated. "If that's what you guys think, well, it's fine with me." His tone indicated that it wasn't fine, but that he wasn't about to make a big deal about it this time. "Just keep in mind, it's the final project of the year, and it's Admiral Paris's pet project. So it's going to be a big part of our grades in his class."

The others expressed their assent, so finally Dennis, cheeks crimsoning until they almost matched Boon's, accepted. "Okay," he said enthusiastically. "I'll do it. With all of us working together, I think this one will be a breeze."

I wouldn't be so sure, Will thought, thinking about stories he'd heard of past years. There seemed to be a lot that could go wrong with these missions. He wasn't going to say anything that might undermine Dennis's confidence, though. Especially since he was the one who had put Dennis's abilities on the line by nominating him.

But I guess we'll find out tomorrow.

Chapter 3

He knows. Kyle Riker knows now that he is a target. In some ways, that will make the rest of it easier. So far, we've had to operate in absolute secrecy, to make our moves slowly and quietly, keeping everything under wraps until the timing was right. But now, everything can be done in the open. Riker can be made to suffer—has to be made to suffer—as others have suffered on his account.

And now that he knows, the real joy can begin. Watching Riker fall apart—watching him withdraw from everyone and everything, watching him desperately trying to protect himself from unknown dangers, will be the greatest pleasure we have known.

But what if he—?

He won't. He can't. He can only react, becoming more and more fearful and uncertain, until we allow him to die.

To die. We do like the sound of that.

Yes, we do.

Engineer Lars Gunnarson was sleepy. He knew, of course, what his shift was, and that it required him to work during the night when most of the people he knew were sleeping. But knowing it didn't make sleeping during the day a whole lot easier. There was light outside, and noise, and things going on that he wanted to be part of. So he got what sleep he could, and often came to work more tired than he should have.

But, he rationalized, *it's not like the transporter is often used during my shift anyway. I have to keep it maintained and running, and on those rare occasions when it's needed I have to operate it.* He thought he could live up to those requirements on an abbreviated sleeping schedule, at least until he rotated back to days, which he greatly preferred.

And he was glad that he was here on Earth, at Starfleet Command, instead of out on a starship, where who knew what kinds of demands might be made of him.

But he had received one reprimand for dozing off on the job. Another would get him booted down a rank and lose him this assignment, which came with a certain amount of autonomy that he enjoyed. So he struggled to stay awake and aware, just in case. He was doing that, on this occasion, by poring over a manual for impulse engines, which he had not yet had the dubious pleasure of working on. The material was dense and, obviously, quite technical, and when he heard footsteps just outside the transporter room, he was in the middle of a very difficult paragraph. When the door whooshed open, he still hadn't made it to the end, and he was trying to grasp the concepts firmly in his mind. "Be right with you," he said, battling to maintain his focus on the page.

Suddenly the thought that whoever had entered might be an officer swept into his head, and he began to turn, ready to offer a salute and an apology if necessary. But he had barely begun to spin around when he caught a flash of a red uniform sleeve coming toward him. He tried to raise a hand to dodge but he was too late. An impact, a bright flash of light, and then Lars Gunnarson's world went dark.

Sleep, in the weeks and months after the attack on Starbase 311, had been a virtual stranger to Kyle Riker. When exhaustion finally overtook him and he succumbed, dreams almost invariably followed—nightmares that left him thrashing about and screaming, waking up in a bed drenched in cold sweat, heart hammering, throat dry. Then another extended period of wakefulness would occur, when closing his eyes and drifting off seemed almost as terrifying as being back on the starbase during the assault. Finally, the cycle would repeat; sleep would come, and with it the dreams.

Under the skillful care of Kate Pulaski, his physical injuries were healed, bones knitted, internal organs mended on a cellular level. Meters of damaged veins had been replaced by synthetic ones, and one ruined kidney was removed, with an artificial one substituted in its place. The body, Kate had explained, is basically a complex machine, and machines can be fixed. Sometimes they were better than they had been, when all their parts were strictly organic.

But the mind, she had said, is a different story altogether. Certainly there were specific physical repairs that could be made to the brain, but there were limits to what those could accomplish. And Kyle fought against some of those. Memories of the most terrible parts of the Tholian attack, for instance, could have been wiped from his memory by careful surgical manipulation of his brain. Kyle had refused. He was a military strategist, and the lessons learned from the Tholian attack—and the disastrous, limited defense—on Starbase 311, were not lessons he wanted to forget. He would, he insisted, learn to live with the memories, but he would not lose them.

And he was right. It took time, and a hellish amount of hard work, with Kate and a whole team of counselors and therapists, but he eventually made a kind of peace with his own inner turmoil and as he did, the bad dreams became more and more rare. He learned, once again, to welcome sleep, to accept it as a refuge from the demands of the day, and to consider dreams a kind of nightly vacation from real life and concerns. Some nights, still, it was harder to achieve sleep than others, and some nights the nightmares returned. But they were unusual, now, and not the norm.

This night, because of the stresses of the day, Kyle had suspected that it might be hard to let go and allow sleep to come, and he'd been correct. But it had come, finally, and he had slipped into a solid slumber, without dreams. When he heard the familiar hum of a transporter beam, he thought at first that it was a dream. He was groggy and thickheaded, and he tried to just roll over in his bed, away from the sound.

But his eyes flickered open as he did, and he saw the glow reflected on the wall near his bed. Instantly awake, he shot up and looked toward where the beam was just fading away, expecting to see another attacker coming at him. The room was empty, though. Maybe it had just been a dream, after all. He blinked a couple of times, trying to see through the darkness of the beam's aftermath.

Not empty, after all. Where the beam had been, there was something on the floor. He couldn't make out the details, in the dark room, but what he could see was a low, flat disk, just a little smaller than the holographic target in a game of velocity. Unlike a velocity disk, though, this one wasn't floating through the air, but sitting on his floor with solidity and some kind of purpose.

What purpose it might have struck Kyle, and he leapt from the bed, running for the open door of his bedroom. Beyond the door was a short hallway, with a bathroom and a room that he used as an office, and then leading into his large living room. He had just cleared the bathroom door, heading for the living room, calling out to the apartment's computer, when the bomb went off.

The first thing Kyle noticed was a flash of light and his own shadow cast before him, stark and hard-edged against the suddenly bright room ahead. The flash was succeeded simultaneously by a deafening roar and a shock wave that lifted him off the floor and hurled him against the living room's far wall. He slammed into it hard, just about where his shadow had been, trying to turn to hit it shoulder-first but without enough time. Instead, his left arm and the left side of his face made contact, and then he fell off the wall and onto the floor. Finally, a wave of searing heat struck him, burning his right side.

The apartment's computer took over then. A sprinkler came on in the bedroom, extinguishing the fire, and a force field contained the worst of the heat there. The computer informed him that authorities had been notified, for the second time in two nights. This time, Kyle didn't argue with it. He lay on the floor, bleeding and burned, until they arrived.

"You're a lucky man, Mr. Riker."

He sat up in the biobed and looked at the doctor, who was just putting away his dermal regenerator after having used it on Kyle's burns. "Every time somebody tells me that, I'm lying in an infirmary somewhere," Kyle said with a bitter grin. "I'm beginning to think luck isn't all it's cracked up to be."

Dr. Trbovich smiled back at him. He was a kindly looking, slightly stout, avuncular fellow with a shock of white hair and an infectious grin. His blue coat was snug around the waist and ribs. "You had a bomb go off in your apartment. You didn't suffer any broken bones. You had some cuts and burns, all of which were easy enough to fix up. You'll be sore for a few days, probably, but you're still here to complain about it. If you hadn't woken up, you'd be much worse off than you are. I count that as pretty fortunate."

"I suppose," Kyle agreed, wincing at a stabbing pain in his ribs as he reached for his shirt. One of the emergency medical technicians who had brought him in had been kind enough to grab a fresh jumpsuit and a padd from his office for him, since his clothes had been torched in the fire and the pajamas he'd worn had needed to be cut from his body. "But more fortunate still are all those people who slept through the night without anyone trying to blow them up."

"Well, yeah," the doctor said. "I can't disagree with that. You'll be fine, though. You should rest here for another couple of hours, just so I can monitor your progress. Then you should take it easy for a few days. I'd like to see you again in a week so I can check your progress, okay?"

"Got it," Kyle assured him. He pushed his hands through his sleeves and then sat on the biobed until the doctor left the room to go check on other patients.

What he hadn't told the doctor was that, in the bomb's aftermath and in the ambulance shuttle that brought him to Starfleet Command from his ruined apartment, his mind had been full of horrific images. Tholians, intense heat barely contained within their shielded suits, features completely hidden, bizarre sticklike weapons emitting fuzzy red rays that spread death and destruction everywhere. For a moment, in the shuttle, Kyle had been convinced that the medic sitting next to him would turn and reveal a red, crystalline face glowing with heat, and he'd felt about himself for a weapon he could use in his own defense. The moment had passed, though, and reason had returned.

Now, though, he didn't think himself capable of simply sitting calmly in the infirmary. His mind was racing. The bomb, combined with all the other stressors of the past couple of days, had brought back the flashbacks. Kyle knew this was a danger signal. But it wasn't something he wanted to talk about with a strange doctor, someone he didn't know. Especially given the threat to his career from whatever trumped-up charges he might be facing on the starbase attack—if his credibility was to be questioned, the idea that he was seeing perfectly innocent medics as Tholian killers wouldn't be advantageous.

He didn't want to sit around the infirmary, and he couldn't help thinking of himself as a target there anyway. A bomb had been transported into his apartment. Certainly, there were transporters in civilian hands, and in the hands of enemy alien races. But the majority of transporter technology in and around San Francisco belonged to Starfleet. Add to that the fact that the assassin who had visited his home the other night had been from Starfleet, and he had to be concerned about his safety, even right here in the middle of the Starfleet Headquarters complex.

Maybe *especially* here.

With the friendly doctor examining another patient, Kyle finished dressing and hurried from the room. The hallways carried the same slightly sweet, antiseptic odor as infirmaries everywhere—and Kyle had been in enough over the past couple of years to become very accustomed to it. Doctors and nurses strolled through the hallways, talking and laughing, but there didn't seem to be much sense of urgency. This time of night, Kyle figured, most people—with the exception of cases like his, of course—were either sound asleep at home or in their biobeds, and emergencies were rare.

He turned a corner, hoping to put more distance between himself and Dr. Trbovich, when he saw a familiar figure virtually blocking the entire hallway. The man was large, with broad shoulders and a muscular neck. Close-cropped, wiry hair clung to his head. He wore the gold uniform of engineering, and even from behind, Kyle could recognize Benjamin Sisko.

"Ben?" he asked, incredulous at seeing the man here. Ben Sisko had just graduated from the Academy a year ago. Ben was a protégé of Curzon Dax; the ambassador had introduced him to Kyle on the *Livingston* a few months back.

The man turned and, in fact, it was Ben Sisko, who wore an ensign's single gold collar pip. But he looked terrible—his face drawn and sallow. If he hadn't had rich brown skin, Kyle thought he'd have looked positively green.

"Mr. Riker," Ben said. His voice sounded as shaky as Kyle's legs felt. "What are you doing here?" He indicated a bandage over Kyle's left eye. "Are you okay?"

"A little misunderstanding with an explosive device," Kyle explained. "Nothing too serious. What about you? Aren't you still posted to the *Livingston?*"

"Yes," Ben said, tugging at his uniform collar. He flashed white teeth in a quick smile. "But they let me come back for this. Jennifer just had our baby."

"You're kidding," Kyle said, sharing Ben's grin. He put out a hand, which Ben enveloped with his own, and they shook hard. "Congratulations, Ben, that's great!"

"Yeah," Ben said. "It's a boy. We're calling him Jake."

"That's a fine name."

"Thanks. I can't sleep, though—Jennifer was in labor for almost twenty hours, and now she's snoozing but I'm just too excited."

"I don't blame you a bit," Kyle said.

Ben looked at the floor. "Do you—do you want to see him?" He spoke almost shyly, though with his deep voice the effect was a little odd.

Kyle realized that this was the first time since the bomb went off that he'd stopped thinking about his own problems, and was glad to continue that trend for a while longer. "Sure," he said gladly. "I'd love to."

Ben started down the hall. "They're right in here," he said, stopping at the door to a private room. He said "Open," and the door obeyed. Inside, the room was mostly dark, with a soft glow coming from one light in a corner. Kyle followed Ben Sisko in.

Jennifer Sisko slept soundly in a comfortable bed, her baby snuggled up on her chest, wrapped in a blanket. All Kyle could see of the boy was a dark circle of a face, but he seemed to be a handsome baby—not that Kyle would have expected anything less than that from the union of Ben and Jennifer, as attractive a couple as one could hope for.

Ben's face was in shadows as he stood with his back to the light, spine straight despite his exhaustion, and hands clasped behind his back, looking down at his wife and son, but in it Kyle could see a range of powerful feelings. *Love, gratitude, relief, and respect,* he thought. Then he remembered what Admiral Paris had told him, what seemed ages ago now. "What time was he born?"

Ben looked at a chronometer on the wall as if it had recorded the moment. "Twenty-three fifty-four," he said.

"So, yesterday. Just. Congratulations, Ben. Your son was born on Father's Day."

Ben broke into a broad smile. "I guess you're right."

"It really is a kind of miracle, Ben," Kyle said.

Benjamin Sisko nodded gravely. "Yes. Definitely a miracle. I just . . . I can't even begin to find the words that describe what I'm feeling right now."

"You don't need to, Ben. I've been in your shoes."

Ben nodded again and they stood in silence for a few moments, watching the mother and child sleep. But while they observed quietly, Kyle heard voices out in the hall. The one that caught his attention belonged to Dr. Trbovich, but instead of his usually folksy self, his voice was raised in something like alarm.

"Surely this can wait," he said insistently. "The patient is resting after a very serious incident. I don't want him disturbed."

Kyle glanced up at Ben, catching his eye. Ben shrugged but both men kept quiet, listening.

"I'm sorry, Doctor," another voice said firmly. "We need to take custody immediately. We have medical facilities in the brig if he's still in need of treatment."

The brig? Kyle wondered. *Why . . . ?*

"You can't just walk in and take away one of my patients," Dr. Trbovich declared. "I won't have it."

"This warrant says we can," a third voice chimed in. "Now, where is Kyle Riker?"

Chapter 4

Ben Sisko walked over to the room's doorway, and Kyle's heart jumped in his chest. The man was going to turn him in! But instead, Ben spoke in a soft voice. "Close."

The door slid shut, and Ben turned to Kyle, his expression curious. "What's this all about, Mr. Riker?" he asked in an anxious whisper.

Kyle blew out the breath he'd been holding. "I'm not sure, Ben. There's some sort of . . . it seems ridiculous to say 'conspiracy,' but that's what it's looking like . . . against me. A couple of nights ago a Starfleet crewman tried to kill me in my apartment. Ridiculous charges have been leveled against me by some anonymous source, who went straight to the admiralty. And tonight someone beamed a bomb into my place, nearly finishing the job. I know I haven't done anything to merit being arrested by Starfleet Security, so I have to believe that if I let those men in the hall take me away, I won't be coming back."

"But . . . that's crazy," Ben said. "Starfleet doesn't just make people disappear. There are rules, procedures. Due process."

"Normally, I'd agree with you," Kyle told him. "This isn't normal, though. There's something going on, something that isn't right. I don't know what it is or who's behind it. But whoever it is wants my head."

He watched Ben carefully as the younger man processed this data. Out in the hall, they could still faintly hear the security officers arguing with Dr. Trbovich.

"Ben, you don't know me that well, but I hope you know I'm an honest man," Kyle pleaded. "I just want to stay free of all this until I can figure out what's going on. Even if they don't kill me, if they lock me up I won't have a chance to defend my name. But since there have been two attempts on my life in the past two nights, both seemingly with Starfleet participation, I think killing me is the likeliest outcome."

Ben glanced at the door. The voices had faded away down the corridor. He looked back at Kyle and nodded his head. "You're right, Mr. Riker. I don't know you that well. But Curzon has spoken highly of you, and I've learned to trust the old man. So I'll give you the benefit of the doubt here."

Kyle let out the breath he hadn't realized he was holding.

He'd only met the Trill ambassador a few times, and was now very grateful that he had left a good impression on him.

"It sounds like you're being railroaded," Ben continued, "and I can't go along with that. I'll do what I can to get you out of here, and then you're on your own. Fair?"

"More than I could ask for, Ben. I won't forget it."

"I have temporary quarters nearby," Ben said. "I'll grab you a uniform from there. Then together we can walk out, and maybe you won't be spotted. Just wait in here till I get back—no one's going to disturb a sleeping mother and baby."

"I'll be here."

Ben turned and went out the door, leaving Kyle alone with Jennifer and young Jake Sisko. He turned down the light, so that anyone who peeked in would have a harder time seeing the unexpected visitor inside. As he waited, he watched Jennifer Sisko sleep, her arms gently cradling her son, even in sleep her maternal instinct to cherish and protect kicking in.

He had felt like that, in the days after Will had been born. The delivery had been hard on Annie, Kyle's wife, and for the first several days after the boy's birth Kyle had needed to take care of both of them. He had risen to the task, though, tending to everyone's needs, throwing himself into the job wholeheartedly. Even after Annie was feeling better, he stayed home with them, happy just to be in their company. Nobody got much sleep those first few weeks, but he didn't care. Even the cries of his son had been magical to him. Kyle watched young Will carefully, not wanting to miss a moment of his development, as the boy became able to sit up, then to crawl, and finally to take a few steps on his own. He had exulted in his son's first words, and then his first attempts at whole sentences.

But as time wore on—especially after Annie got sick again, and Kyle's primary focus had to be on caring for her— the luster of having a new son faded. Daily life got in the way,

Kyle had decided. He still loved his son, but other parts of life kept interfering, and that pure paternal bliss was diluted somehow. He wondered, now, how that happened. How the sheer joy of looking at his son's face changed, through familiarity, into something different, something lesser.

He wondered if it happened to all fathers, or if it was just a failing in him.

He had not reached any conclusions when Ben Sisko returned with a bundle in his hands. As soon as he was inside with the door closed, he tossed it to Kyle. "They're still out there," he said. "Scurrying around the corridors looking for you. The doctors aren't helping them, but they aren't stopping them anymore, either. I ran into one of the nurses, and told her I was bringing Jennifer some spare clothes. I think she bought it."

Kyle looked at Ben, and then down at his own body. Ben was considerably larger than he was. Instead of taking off his own dun-colored jumpsuit, he pulled on the uniform over his clothing. "I appreciate this, Ben," he said, tugging the oversized tunic down over his head and shoulders. "I really do."

"I know," Ben said confidently. "And I want you to do one thing for me in return."

"Name it," Kyle said.

"Let me know how this works out. When you've got it all settled, I mean."

"I will," Kyle assured him. "Hopefully it'll be all cleared up before you're a captain someplace."

Ben laughed. It was a sound that, under other circumstances, Kyle thought, might be very intimidating. "I don't know if there's any big hurry, then," he said, "but we'll call it a deal."

With Kyle fully dressed in Ben's spare uniform, Ben opened the door and the two of them strode confidently into the hallway, as if leaving a conference room or an officer's lounge instead of a recovery room. A nurse passed them in the hall without a second glance, even though, to Kyle, the bad fit of the uniform seemed like a beacon.

They didn't slow when they reached the corner, but instead made a sharp right turn and kept going. When they passed another intersection, Kyle caught a glimpse of the two security officers coming toward them. He tensed, felt himself sweating beneath the extra layers of fabric. But he kept Sisko's bulk between himself and them and continued on. The security team didn't seem to think twice about them. But then, they knew Kyle Riker was a civilian, so two officers in uniform would not raise a flag.

One turbolift and two minutes later, and the two men were outside the building in the cool night air. A gentle breeze felt good on Kyle's flushed face. "There you go," Ben said. "I'd better get back to my family."

"You do that," Kyle agreed. "Keep them close, always." He fingered the uniform's collar. "I'll, uhh . . . send this back to you."

"Take your time."

Ben put out his hand and Kyle took it in both of his. "Thank you, Ben. You made the right call."

"Curzon's a pretty good judge of character, Mr. Riker," Ben replied. "I already knew that."

He turned on his heel and went back inside. Kyle was alone, with who knew how many enemies around him.

Very much alone, he thought.

They came for him on the air tram. This time of night, the car was empty except for him, and there were only a couple of other passengers on the transport at all. He wasn't sure where he would go; he just wanted to put some distance between himself and Starfleet Command. He closed his eyes, willing his body to relax after the tension back at the infirmary. But after riding for about twenty minutes, he heard it—the familiar hiss of breathing apparatus that allowed them to function in an M-Class atmosphere. He snapped to attention and saw three of them boarding his car, their suits disguising superheated crystalline bodies, multicolored masks hiding their hideous faces. They pointed long, crooked sticks at him and he knew they were about to fire.

Panicked, he dove from his seat, hitting the floor and rolling beneath a seat farther down the aisle and hunched there, breathing heavily, waiting for the worst. The red rays he expected didn't come, though. After a few moments, he dared to open his eyes. Two elderly civilians, both human, both somewhat astonished, stared at him with concern etching their features. "Are you okay, son?" one of them asked. Both of them kept their distance, Kyle noted, as if afraid to come too close.

"I don't . . . the Tholians . . ." Kyle was dumfounded.

"Haven't seen any Tholians around here," the other one said with a chuckle. "I think we'd notice if there were any."

"I expect so," Kyle agreed. Humiliated, he crawled out from under the seat. Not that it would have provided him with any protection, he thought, studying it so he didn't have to look at the people who assumed he'd gone completely insane. Not against those weapons they carried. He remembered those weapons, and the fierce damage they could do, entirely too well.

Realizing that he was still badly dressed in Ben Sisko's uniform, he jumped off the transport at the next station rather than let the old couple get a longer look at him. He wasn't sure where he was, but that was for the best. *They're starting again*, he knew. *The flashbacks*.

He needed medical attention, or psychiatric help. But they were looking for him at the infirmary. Starfleet Command wasn't a safe place for him now. No place was safe, really—at least, no place that Starfleet controlled, or where they had operatives. As he exited the station on a stair-lift to the street, he felt a stab of fear. What might be waiting on the street? A Starfleet assassin? A force of Tholian warriors? Something else, equally deadly, that he didn't even know to watch for?

When he reached the street, which was dark and empty, he realized he was still carrying his padd, and it suddenly occurred to him that each padd had global positioning technology built in. A user could immediately locate his own coordinates via satellite. But conversely, that meant that someone else—someone at Starfleet, for instance, with access to the satellite, could locate the user. The mouth of an alley gaped ahead, and Kyle turned down it, looked all around to be sure he wasn't observed, and then raised his padd, intending to hurl it full force into a blank brick wall.

He stopped his arm at the peak of his motion, though, when a different idea dawned on him. Instead of throwing the thing he sat down in the alley, back against one of the high walls, and spent a few minutes reprogramming it. When he was finished, instead of accurately signaling its position, it would send signals to satellites chosen at random, in orbit all around the world. Anyone who tried to track it would find themselves hopelessly confused. Satisfied then that his padd would no longer give away his location, he tucked it into a pocket and hurried away from the alley.

As he walked quickly through the city's nighttime streets, Kyle hoped that whoever was looking for him developed a massive migraine from trying to use his own padd against him. Once he had figured out who was after him, and why, he hoped to give them a much worse headache.

At the very least.

Chapter 5

A sharp knock at Will's door woke him from a sound sleep. He glanced at the chron near his bed. Four-forty in the morning. Who . . . ?

"Yes?" he called, hoping his animosity was clear in his voice.

"Will Riker?"

"That's right." He spoke these words defiantly. Anyone who would be rude enough to come around at this hour—especially today, of all days, when he was about to embark on his final project for Admiral Paris's survival class—was going to be told off, Riker style. "Who's there?"

"Starfleet security, cadet. Please open the door."

"Come in," Riker called, the vocal command unlocking the door. Two gold-shirted officers pulled down the old-fashioned handle to open the door and enter. One of them looked at Will, his hand resting on the butt of his phaser pistol, while the other glanced about the room. "Looking for something?" Will asked, sitting up on the edge of his bed.

"We're looking for your father, Cadet. Mr. Kyle Riker. Have you seen him recently?"

Will couldn't restrain the laugh. "That depends. What's recent to you?" he asked. "Five years?"

The security officer looked surprised. "He's your father. He works here at Starfleet Headquarters."

"And your point is . . . ?"

The second security officer, the one giving Will's small quarters the once over, seemed satisfied by his search. "He's not here."

"I told you that," Will said. "He's never been here."

"Have you heard from him? Tonight?"

Will shook his head vigorously. "You don't seem to get the point," he said. "We don't talk. At all."

"So you'd have no idea where he is right now?"

Will glanced at the chron, as if for emphasis. "Since he's not crazy, as far as I know, I would guess he's home in bed. Wherever that is."

"He's not there," the security man said.

"Well, I wouldn't know anything about that."

"Do you know where he might go? Any favorite places, anyone he'd turn to in an emergency?"

These guys just don't have a clue, Will thought. *And they're supposed to be providing security?* "I have no idea," he said. "Listen to me—Kyle Riker and I haven't seen or spoken to each other in five years. I don't know who his friends are, I don't know where he spends his time. I just don't know. The last time I saw him was in Alaska, if that helps."

The second security officer touched the first one on the arm. "Come on, he's got nothing."

The first one paused, as if unwilling to admit defeat, but then he gave a little shrug and turned away. "If you hear from him, contact security immediately," he called over his shoulder as they left the room.

Yeah, Will thought. *Because that's likely to happen.*

He looked at his bunk again, and he looked at the time. Almost o-five hundred. They were to report to the Academy's transporter room by six-thirty. Other squadrons were being transported into the city at different times during the morning. It was foolish to think he'd get back to sleep now, and even if he did he'd have to get up soon anyway. Instead of trying, he went into his bathroom for a hot shower. It might, he knew, be his last for a while.

At the appointed hour—stifling a yawn, his eyes burning from lack of sleep—Will met his squadron mates in the transporter room. Estresor Fil looked excited, for her: her eyes open wide and sparkling with some inner light, her lips parted in something that looked like a smile-in-training. Boon lounged against an operator console, apparently as barely awake as Will himself, although with Boon that was more or less his natural state. Felicia and Dennis chatted happily between themselves, in low tones.

He had thought that perhaps Admiral Paris would be here to see them off, but he wasn't. Instead, there were only a pair of engineers and a security officer. The campus had been buzzing with word of an attack on a lone engineer in a Starfleet Command transporter room late the night before. Will had missed most of the rumors, his mind on other things, and intentionally made an effort not to listen to them because he was already overtired and knew that he needed to be able to devote all his attention to the mission at hand. But he figured it explained the extra precautions in this room, on this morning.

Felicia looked up from her hushed conversation with Dennis and noticed Will in the doorway. She smiled at him and beckoned him over. Dennis turned, too, at Felicia's gesture, tossing Will a friendly grin of his own. "Glad you could join us, Will," he said, sarcasm leavened by good-natured humor.

"I seem to be developing a bad habit," Will said. "I never used to be late to everything."

"You're not late," Felicia assured him. "We're early. Just too excited about the project, I guess."

Will bit back another yawn. He was excited too, and should have been early, but everything had taken extra effort this morning, from getting his breakfast, to dressing, to making his way here to the transporter room. He didn't want to have to explain why, though. If the old man had gotten himself into some kind of trouble, it was no concern of Will's. The last thing he wanted was for his squadron to think that he would be distracted by his father's problems, whatever they may be.

"As long as I didn't hold anything up," he said. He recognized that much of his concern was due to his own impatience. Just this last project stood between him and summer break, which would be followed by his penultimate Academy year. Two more, and after that he could sign onto a starship and get off this planet for a while.

"Not at all," Dennis assured him. "But now that we're all here . . ." He addressed the pair of engineers. "We're ready, I guess. Whenever you are."

One of the engineers, a Bolian with an unusual fringe of brown hair around the back of his blue, bifurcated head, stepped forward then and examined the cadets. "No phasers, no tricorders, no padds, no combadges. You aren't hiding anything from me, are you?"

"Not at all," Dennis assured them. Boon, Will noted, hadn't changed his position or his slumped posture, as if the whole process was so boring he could barely stay awake.

"Then I have one thing for you." The Bolian handed Dennis a sealed envelope.

"Paper," Estresor Fil noted. "How . . . antiquated."

"You won't have instruments with which to read anything else," the engineer explained.

"We're supposed to consider ourselves crash-landed in hostile territory," Dennis added. "Without our technology to rely on."

"That's what they tell us," the other engineer, a human female with swept-up blond hair, said. "Step onto the pads, please."

The five cadets did as instructed. Boon was the last one in place. Will thought he seemed reluctant, maybe even resentful. *Because we put Dennis in charge?* he wondered. *Maybe I shouldn't have done that—it's Boon's last chance to lead this squadron, and I took it away from him.* But it had been the squadron's tradition to do so from time to time, so it shouldn't have been entirely unexpected. And Boon himself had brought it up.

Will didn't have a chance to worry about it any longer, though. As soon as Boon was in position, the engineers began their process. "Coordinates locked," said the human, and the Bolian, nodding, touched his keypad.

"Good luck," the Bolian said. As he did, he began to fade from view, and Will realized that the annular confinement beam was surrounding him, beginning the process of converting his molecules into energy that could be sent to a specific, predetermined point. He had aced his transporter theory class last year, and he had been transported numerous times. But that experience hadn't quite soothed his concerns. He knew full well that the technology was safe and time-tested, but at the same time there was something just a bit wrong about it that he wasn't able to get used to.

He didn't have time to worry about it for more than a few seconds, though, before he found himself rematerializing someplace else. After a perfunctory self-examination to make sure all his parts had shown up when he did, he glanced about, looking for any of his squadron mates. But there were no transporter beams evident, and no one around. He was alone.

Dennis Haynes recognized his location, and, if it hadn't been too much like a bad joke, he would have described the sensation in his gut as a sinking feeling. He was looking across water—a lot of water—toward Fisherman's Wharf and the Embarcadero. Which could only mean that he'd been beamed to Alcatraz.

And Alcatraz was an island. An island that had formerly been used as a prison, at that. It had, of course, been a prison because it was difficult to get from there to the mainland without a boat.

Sadly, Dennis hadn't been able to bring one with him.

What he did have with him was a paper envelope. He sat on the jagged rocks at the island's edge and tore it open, appreciating the forethought that had gone into using such an old-fashioned technology. They'd been correct—he wouldn't have been able to read anything except paper, here.

Of course, if he couldn't get off the island, it wouldn't matter much what the words on the paper said. He'd be unable to communicate with his squadron, and they'd all fail the project—and the class. He looked toward the mainland again. He could swim it, maybe. But it'd be bitter cold, and he figured the chances were fifty-fifty that he'd drown in the effort. That, he decided, would be a last resort.

Seriously last. The more he contemplated it, the laster it got.

Tearing his gaze away from the waves, he removed a sheet of paper from inside the envelope. A stiff breeze from off the water tore at it, threatening to yank it from his grip. But the paper—really, he knew, a polymer with many of the same characteristics as the old-fashioned stuff, whose name this material shared out of convenience—held firm against the wind's worst efforts. Written on it was a single sentence. "At the feet of these twins, find your first checkpoint."

Short, sweet, and almost completely unhelpful, Dennis thought. He knew from the reports of previous years that finding the checkpoints was often the most difficult part of the assignment. And it wouldn't have helped if he'd been given coordinates and a map, if he couldn't get off this damn rock. The squadron had agreed to meet at the peak of Nob Hill, as quickly as possible after being transported into the city, because it was a more or less central location. Already, Dennis was sure, the others would be rushing to the meeting point. But he, their leader for this project, wouldn't be there.

Well, he thought, forcing himself to his feet and casting his gaze about the rocky outcrop. *Things certainly look bad, but I'm not ready to admit defeat quite yet.*

* * *

I might as well have walked here, Estresor Fil thought with mild disappointment. She had beamed in at the near end of the Golden Gate Bridge, which was barely a stone's throw from the Academy itself. She hadn't been sent far at all, but she had a good distance ahead of her to get to the meeting point. Cutting through Academy grounds would shorten the trip, though of course she couldn't do that. She was in civilian clothes and carried no Starfleet identification, and stepping onto Academy or Starfleet Command grounds was cause for instant disqualification.

Even the nearest tram station was the Academy stop, so she couldn't catch a transport there. She started walking, giving the Academy a wide berth, toward the nearest public station. With her short legs, it would take her a good while to get there. But at least the project was under way.

"Hey! Watch it!"

Felicia Mendoza spun around. She had materialized on a busy sidewalk, and a small knot of pedestrians had to part, like a river flowing around a rock, to get around her as she gathered her bearings. One of the men fixed her with an angry glare, as if it had been her fault where she wound up. Not that he'd have any way of knowing it wasn't, of course.

But she wasn't sure what her location was. She was in an urban canyon, with towers of steel around her, but there were many places in San Francisco that could be so described. Felicia wasn't very familiar with the city—she came from El Salvador, and had moved here only to attend the Academy. She had spent one summer interning at Jupiter Station, and knew that distant locale far better than she did this earthly one.

Getting her bearings wouldn't be an insurmountable problem, she knew. San Francisco was a temporary home to many tourists and out-of-towners, and the city's heads took great pains to make it a comfortable place to visit. Kiosks located every few blocks showed transit information, complete with maps and schedules. All she had to do was find the nearest one and she'd be on her way to the meeting point. She was anxious to hear where everyone else had landed, and what their first goal was.

So far, this whole thing seemed like a great deal of fun. She didn't necessarily expect that it would stay that way. But it might. Being an ordinarily optimistic type anyway, she was willing to accept that small chance.

With a smile on her lips and a spring in her step, she started up the block.

Boon's feet were soaked. He found this extremely annoying, because it meant that someone had entered coordinates wrong, or there had been a transporter malfunction, or the transporter crew was just plain trying to make life difficult for him. The first two scenarios could have resulted in death or horrific injury, so all things considered, finding himself standing up to his ankles in the freezing surf of the Pacific Ocean wasn't really as bad as it might have been. But he didn't think it was either of those two problems—great care was always taken with transporter use, and the crew would not have been haphazard about where they sent a cadet on an Academy project.

Which meant that it was intentional. That ticked him off no end. He didn't know if it was because he was a Coridanian, or if they simply chose random cadets to harass, just because they could, but the motive didn't matter to him. He tried to remember their names, so he could make life miserable for them once he was a senior officer, but the names wouldn't come to him.

He waded ashore. The beach was a dozen or so meters of rocky sand, and he trudged across it, water streaming from his legs and a scowl on his brick-red face.

When this is over, he thought, *I'm going to have a serious talk with a certain transporter crew.*

*   *   *

Will thought for a moment that a mistake had been made. They were all supposed to be beamed into San Francisco, but he was in a deep forest somewhere. Early sunlight slanted between trunks and leaves, highlighting dust motes and the last traces of morning fog. The air had a rich, fecund aroma he had been used to, in his youth, but had almost forgotten—the tang of pines, the dusky dry smell of summer grass in an arid clime. Tall trees surrounded him and the brush was so thick he couldn't even see through it. Branches scratching at his hands and tugging at his clothing, he forced his way through the heaviest of it.

A few minutes of working his way out of the tangle brought him to a clearing and an explanation. Thick grass and low shrubs had grown over an old road here, splitting the roadway and hiding it until Will was literally standing on top of it. He looked at the sweep of the road as it curved out of sight, and it brought back half-remembered pictures he'd seen. He was, he believed, deep inside Golden Gate Park, which had been closed to vehicles for more than a century and allowed to grow wild.

He was alone here, so the question of whether they would all beam in together had been answered. Picking a meeting place had been the simplest precaution, but he was glad they had made the effort. A good portion of this first day might be spent by the squadron members trying to find their way to the Nob Hill location. And for all he knew, others might be even farther away than he was, or in more remote locations. Nob Hill would be a good hike, for him, but not too difficult.

He noted the position of the morning sun, and then started east, toward it, following the broken, overgrown road away from the ocean and into the city.

Chapter 6

Another failure. That Riker has more lives than a damned Antillean feenetchluk.

And how many is that? How much longer do we have to play this game?

The feenetchluk has eleven redundant nervous and circulatory systems that reconfigure themselves in the event of serious injury. You think you've killed one but it just shuts down for a few moments, and then comes back at you, scared and angry but not dead. Hence the saying.

Maybe it is just dumb luck, though. Maybe he should be playing dabo someplace, since he seems to survive every attack we throw at him, not by effort of will or any particular ability, but through simple twists of fortune.

Or by simply refusing to concede.

Perhaps. Luck or lives, it doesn't matter. What matters is that he's scared now. Fearing for his life, his safety, his career. That means he's off balance, and therefore right where we want him. He'll start making mistakes. We can keep this up indefinitely, playing him, making him suffer.

As we have suffered.

Exactly. In the end, that's better than killing him right away. His suffering is so delicious, so . . . right. And we know that he can't run from us. He can't hide, not for long. No matter where he goes, we will have our pleasure.

Yes . . . that's the perfect word to describe it. Our pleasure is Riker's pain, and his death our ultimate release.

San Francisco's civilian spaceport, at the edge of the bay, never slept. All day and all night transport vehicles from all across the planet rumbled into the port, laden with goods destined for distant planets, and those same vehicles, equally bur-

dened, left with imported goods for markets on Earth. Lights
burned through the dark of night, engines roared, the voices
of working men and women mixed with the clatter and whine
of the servos and gears of robotic helpers. Cargo and tourists
alike left from this port, ferried to orbital platforms from
which the big ships, the deep spacefaring craft, would launch.

Kyle made his way here by a roundabout path, taking underground transport part of the distance, then getting off and
walking for a while, then catching an air tram for another
segment. If anyone's gaze fell on him for more than a few
moments he changed course or mode of travel. A few times,
he thought Tholians had spotted him, but he managed to
both avoid them and convince himself that he was merely
seeing things, that there were no Tholians trying to kill him,
here on Earth. Although plenty of humans were doing their
best to make up for that shortage, it seemed.

Finally, as the eastern sky turned from slate gray to pale
blue, he approached the great port, thrilling a little as he always did to the rhythmic bustle of enterprise and the stirring
adventure of people traveling to the farthest reaches of the
universe. He loved his home planet, but his work had taken
him off it enough times that he was comfortable in space or
on good old terra firma, and the idea of travel always held
the promise of the new and unexpected.

This time, though, he wasn't traveling for fun or business,
but for survival. Since it seemed certain that whoever was
after him—for whatever reason he couldn't fathom—had access to Starfleet technology and personnel, then no place in
San Francisco was safe for him. With Starfleet headquar-
tered here, its influence was everywhere. For that matter,
there were precious few places on Earth where he'd be beyond their grasp. Alaska beckoned, since that state still contained untamed places where a man might hide. But that
would probably be the first place they'd look for him once
they realized he'd slipped their noose here, and he might

not even make it to the back country before they found him
again.

You've become paranoid, he told himself. *Convinced that
you're the focal point of a massive Starfleet conspiracy. It's
crazy.*

But crazy or not, it seemed that the evidence pointed toward the truth of his fears. Maybe the conspiracy wasn't as
far-reaching as he thought. Its size didn't matter—he would
be equally dead if there were one person after him or a thousand, if they were allowed to catch him. And his fears were
paranoia only to a point—perhaps there weren't Tholians
tracking him through the city's streets, but the attempts on
his life were continuing. Surrendering to Starfleet authority
would be, he had to believe, tantamount to suicide.

No, if he was going to stay safe long enough to figure out
who was trying to kill him, he would have to be off the
planet. He was certain of that. His only safety lay in a combination of distance and anonymity, neither of which could be
long achieved Earthside. The rankest beginner to military
strategy learned that you had to know the strength of your
enemy. An ounce of intelligence was worth a pound of lead,
to use the archaic analogy of tacticians of old. Starfleet, Kyle
knew, was plenty strong, but he wasn't yet convinced that it
was all of Starfleet after him. Just some of it, person or per-
sons unknown. Until he could reason out who was his
enemy, and why, though, he had to assume that all Starfleet
personnel were dangerous.

Even at the civilian spaceport there were Starfleet officers
to avoid, he discovered. New recruits came through here, as
did Starfleet personnel traveling on personal business, or vacation. Starfleet inspectors examined cargo and kept track of
the coming and going of ships, alongside the civilian authorities. It seemed that everywhere Kyle looked, he saw uniforms. Dodging them all was patently impossible, so Kyle
inserted himself into the middle of a large group of tourists,

laughing and joking among themselves, headed for an out-
bound shuttle. Hidden in the center of the group, he made
his way past a small cluster of Security officers. Once he was
beyond them and through the doors of the vast passenger
terminal, he slipped away from the jovial crowd and headed
quickly down a side corridor, where the people weren't so
well dressed or so loud. Here, even the lights seemed dim-
mer, and the sound of his own footsteps echoed in the emp-
tier space. Freight deals were made down this hallway, cargo
consigned, but those were usually deals done quietly, between the interested parties. No crowds of spacefaring
tourists came down this way, and Kyle felt exposed as he
wandered, trying to move with purpose even though he
didn't know precisely where he was going.

Down this side hall there were several offices, mostly just
glorified counters over which deals were made, some decorated with holoimages of ships in flight or extraterrestrial
landscapes. Humans staffed some of these offices, but not all.
At this hour, most negotiations had long since been done,
and the real action was out at the loading docks, so humans
and aliens alike sat on stools or chairs, staring at the walls and
waiting for shift changes. With no particular knowledge or
experience to draw from, Kyle picked one more or less at random. It was a company he had never heard of, which was exactly the kind he had been looking for. The sign on the wall
above the counter said INTAGLIO SHIPPING AND FREIGHT, and
the man leaning on the counter looked as if he was giving up
on the struggle to stay awake. His skin was a prunelike color,
so dark it could have been brown or a deep purple, his hair a
startlingly canary yellow against that skin, and his eyes were
small and hooded. Kyle suspected he was part human and
part something else that he couldn't even guess at.

"Help you?" the man asked sleepily. He barely glanced at
Kyle.

"I need to take a trip," Kyle told him.

"We're a freight mover, not a travel agency."

"I'm not looking for scenery," Kyle said flatly. "Or companionship. Just distance."

The man straightened now, taking his elbow off the counter. "That a fact?"

"That's right. In fact, the fewer fellow passengers the better. Surely you've got a berth on something, going somewhere."

"Well," the man said with a yellow-toothed smile, "if you're going to be picky . . ."

"I can be demanding," Kyle said. "I demand discretion and privacy. But those are my only nonnegotiable needs. Beyond that, you'll find I'm very flexible."

The man hummed a couple of times, looking Kyle up and down as if expecting him to metamorphose into something else right before his eyes. All he would see, Kyle knew, was a fit, square-jawed man whose once-dark hair, now mostly well on its way toward gray, was undoubtedly somewhat mussed from the night's activity, dressed in a civilian jumpsuit, who hadn't had nearly enough sleep in the past couple of nights. Finally, apparently satisfied with his examination, the man clasped his hands together. "I happen to know a ship's captain," he said, "for whom discretion is practically a religion. This same captain is about to embark on a long voyage, and might, I suppose, have some space on her ship for an unexpected passenger. But this particular captain, I'm afraid, has a bit of a gambling problem. She is well recompensed for her labors, but somehow can always seem to use a few more credits than she has."

Kyle had expected nothing less. "I can pay," he declared. In fact, this was what he had hoped for. The Federation had largely evolved beyond such things as greed and bribery. The fact that this ship's captain was amenable to both implied that she was outside the Federation mainstream, maybe not from a member world at all.

The man's smile broadened at Kyle's willingness. "Then we should talk further," he said. "By all means."

Chapter 7

For a moment, Will thought he was the first one to reach the rendezvous point at the corners of Sacramento and Jones. This city, like Paris and Vienna and New York, had been laid out with an efficiency and a consideration of the landscape that had made their plans virtually unchanging over the centuries. While the buildings themselves sometimes came down and new ones went up, the basic grids of the streets had been the same since the days when horse-drawn carriages were the only vehicular traffic. These days, the traffic on the streets was virtually all pedestrian, with only the rarest vehicles passing by.

From this intersection, Will could look down the hill in four directions and see for what seemed like kilometers in each one, could see the rising and falling of the city's many hills, the homes and businesses crowding the streets, tall skyscrapers claiming extra height by virtue of being built on the crests. A gentle breeze from the west seemed to carry the scent of the sea to him, though he thought that was probably an illusion. More likely there was a seafood restaurant down the block preparing some lunchtime fare.

After standing there for a few minutes, turning to admire the view and also search for his squadron-mates, he realized that Estresor Fil watched him from a shadowed doorway alcove, a serious expression on her small green face. Since she didn't seem interested in coming to meet him, he went to her.

"Been waiting long?" he asked when he reached her position.

"Twenty-eight minutes, eleven seconds," she replied. She hadn't had to consult a timepiece of any kind to know that.

He gestured at the doorway. "Are you, ahh, hiding from someone?"

"This is supposed to be a survival exercise," she explained. "We've been instructed to remain unobtrusive. Standing out there gawking hardly seems unobtrusive to me."

Will shrugged. "I don't know," he said. "It seems a little more natural than hiding in a doorway. Don't you think it's a pretty great view?"

"I hadn't given it any thought at all," she told him. "It's a view. I don't see how one would judge any given view as greater or lesser than any other."

"Unless it was a view from which you could see what's-his-name, that sailor. Popeye, or something, right?"

"That's different," Estresor Fil said quickly. "That's a cultural study, not simply an empty aesthetic enterprise. If you were studying the view to scout for dangers, perhaps, or landmarks, then I could understand you. But just admiring it because you can see a long way? I'm sorry, I just can't comprehend."

"Are you sure you're not part Vulcan?" he asked with a grin.

"Absolutely certain," she replied, as stone-faced as ever. Her expression—eyes wide, narrow lips pressed firmly together in a straight line, tiny nub of a nose barely more than a pinch of flesh—rarely seemed to change, even though Will knew he had seen her happy and sad and worried. It wasn't that she didn't feel strong emotions, but her face didn't seem to be up to the job of showing them. "Why do you ask?"

He decided to drop it. Vulcans believed in logic, but that didn't mean that humor was completely alien to them. "No reason. Have you seen any of the others since you've been skulking in the doorway?"

"I have not. We're the first."

"I wish we could use combadges," Will sighed.

"That would contradict the point of the project," Estresor Fil argued. "We're supposed to be in a hostile city, relying on just our wits and what we've learned of urban survival, not our technology."

"But if we really were infiltrating a hostile city we'd still have our combadges, our padds, and our phasers," Will insisted. "Right?"

"We might," Estresor Fil relented. "But there might be some technology that jammed our combadges, or would allow the enemy to locate us when we used them. By the same token, our weapons might have been removed from us during capture, and we've just broken free. We need to follow the admiral's rules."

Will gave up and nodded. Admiral Paris had already been over all this, of course, and Will had expected nothing different. But he could complain about it nonetheless. Admiral Paris was a nut for the Prime Directive, as well, and Will knew that it was his philosophy that if an away team had landed in a primitive city of some kind, the use of any technology beyond the level of which the locals had attained would be forbidden. So really, there was no way combadges would be allowed on this project. They'd just have to wait until the others showed up, no matter how long that might be.

But with only Estresor Fil for company, he hoped it was soon.

Dennis Haynes made his way around the cold, abandoned island, sticking to the rugged coastline as well as he could. The old prison still dominated the interior, its thick walls crumbling now with age but still somehow sinister in appearance. Struts sticking up like grasping fingers indicated a tower of some kind, long since fallen. He couldn't help being made a little nervous by the idea of so many desperate and dangerous people being kept behind those walls, even though it had happened a long time ago. And he couldn't shake the disturbing knowledge that the prison had been built here because getting back to the city from this spot was no simple matter. He couldn't remember if Alcatraz was a prison from which there had been no escapes, or just not many.

Either way, it didn't bode well for him.

He had made nearly a complete circuit when he spotted the boat. It was an ancient contraption, made of real wood, it seemed, and it had been dragged onto a gravelly stretch of beach, leaving a furrowed path to the waterline behind it. No footprints led away from it, though, so there was no way of knowing how long it had been sitting in that spot. A day, a year, a decade? On closer examination he saw that its oarlocks were rusted. He touched one, to see if it would still swivel, but as he turned it the wood around it broke away, rotten and soft. Even if the thing would still float, then, he couldn't control it and it would be unlikely to support his weight. He'd sink before he even got started. He felt even more dejected than before. The sun was rising high into the sky and he couldn't get to his friends.

Trying to shrug off despair, he continued his journey. Around the bend from where he'd found the boat, his spirits lifted when he saw a dock, modern and in good repair. *Of course, you idiot,* he berated himself. *You can still take a tour to Alcatraz, so there must be some way of getting to the island.* He didn't know how often the tours came, though he seemed to remember that they were at least daily, if not several in a day. All he needed to do, then, was to join the next one that came when it returned to the city.

Of course, how was he to explain how he'd wound up here, without breaking the rules of the assignment?

The only answer was, he couldn't. He'd have to do what so many prisoners in times past had failed to do—he'd have to break out of Alcatraz.

But to do that, he'd first have to get inside. Casting an eye

toward the city, he saw the familiar profile of a tourist skimmer heading toward the island. *Not much time, then,* he
thought. Swallowing his anxiety, he started up the hill toward those forbidding walls.

The path from the dock into the prison was clear and un-
barred, since it was traveled only by tour groups on organized
outings. That made getting inside the facility easy enough.
The outer wall, topped by a tall fence corroded and torn by
wind and weather, stood open for him. Chunks of stone were
piled against the wall where they had fallen under the relent-
less pressure of the elements on this exposed outcrop, but the
wall itself was still impressively thick. Beyond this wall, which
encircled the facility—he had passed another building, closer
to the shore, which had seemed to be administrative rather
than confining—the prison itself reared up, solid and grim,
with narrow windows set into the aged concrete.

He continued into the prison itself. Here, too, the doors
were open, and he passed through into a semi-contained
space. Sky showed through holes in the ceiling and walls, but
he could still get a sense of how imposing the place must have
been in its heyday. *Or either of its heydays,* he mentally corrected himself. He knew the prison had been closed sometime
in the mid-twentieth century, but then reopened again for a
time late in the twenty-first, in the hard times after the war.

As he explored, the quiet outside was broken by the
buzzing sound of the skimmer approaching the island. He
had to hurry, had to find a place where he could hide. The
first section of the prison seemed to be a processing area,
where prisoners were booked into the system. The cells were
farther back, beyond more sets of doors and bars. But a quick
look around the cells proved to Dennis that there was no hiding there—anyone walking down the hallways between cells
could see every inch of them, bunks and sinks and toilets,
mold-encrusted walls still showing graffiti from ages gone by.

Which only made sense, he realized. Surely the guards

would have needed clear sightlines throughout the cells. He turned back, his anxiety building. From outside he could hear voices already, as the tour guide led the group toward the prison. Once at the processing area, he passed through an open door and ducked down behind a chest-high counter, pressing himself up against the far side. As long as no one came through the door into this area, he would be safe, but there was no place to hide if the group decided to check out the office. The floor here was filthy, caked with years of refuse, bird droppings, and neglect, and it stank. But he could take it if he didn't have to wait too long, he figured. And really, how long could a tour of this place take? There wasn't really so much to see inside.

He could barely make out the guide's words, so hard was his heart pounding in his ears as the tour came through. He worked to still his breathing, willing himself to become as invisible as he possibly could. The guide's voice turned into a pleasant drone as she led her group through this section and into the cell block, and when they were gone, Dennis allowed himself to relax a bit.

But the hard part, he knew, was still ahead.

After thirty minutes or so, he heard voices approaching again, and he resumed his hiding position. Now was when he most risked discovery, he feared. They'd been through the cells, they were more casual about being here, and the chance that someone might decide to step away from the tour and come behind the counter was increased. Once again, when they came near he slowed his breathing. He trembled from fear of discovery, and clenched his fists between his knees to keep his limbs from rapping against the floor or the side of the counter.

This time, the guide's voice was quiet, as she'd already explained the function of this part of the prison. But the tourists were talking loudly, certainly drowning out any noises Dennis might have made. He stayed where he was

until their voices began to fade, as the group made its way
back outside, and then he cautiously raised his head above
the protective counter. He saw people—humans and aliens,
as well—walking from the inside's dimness into bright light,
blinking and shading their eyes. But no one turned back to
look behind them, so he slipped from his hiding spot and
hurried to the door, taking up the back of the line as they
headed down the slope to the waiting skimmer. As they approached the dock, he moved up, nodding casually to those
who caught his eye, pretending he had been with them all
along. If anyone thought different, no one mentioned it.

On the skimmer, he took a seat on a long plastisteel bench.
His worst moment came when the guide looked out at the
group and asked, "Are we all here? We wouldn't want to leave
anyone behind." He was afraid she might count heads, in
which case he'd be found out. But she accepted the murmurs
of affirmation that came from the crowd, and the skimmer
pulled out, skipping across the choppy surf like a cast stone,
the city growing ever larger in the front viewscreen.

Dennis started to calm down, finally, as the craft neared
the port on the San Francisco side of the bay. The beginning
of this project had been inauspicious, he thought, but it was
getting better all the time.

He had escaped from Alcatraz.

Waiting for the others in their chosen alcove, Will began
to get into the spirit of the mission. No one went in or out
the doorway—Estresor Fil had chosen well; the corner storefront had windows chemically opaqued and appeared to be
an empty space—but some of the passersby glared at him
and Estresor Fil with suspicion. He couldn't blame them—
anyone who had been past more than once would realize
that they'd been hanging around for a long time, without
leaving or apparently having any real reason to be there.
After an hour of it he was starting to feel as if they really were

in a hostile city where his life could be in genuine danger.

But the meeting place they'd agreed on was this intersection. They could cross the street to a different corner, but the other corners were even busier, with open businesses where they would be in the way. Here, at least, they were out of the sun and shielded from casual view to some degree.

Just a few minutes past the hour, he saw Felicia Mendoza, strolling languidly up the other side of Jones Street wearing a loose royal blue top with black pants and boots, looking as if she didn't have a care in the world. He started to say something to Estresor Fil about it, but then realized that she fit right in with those around her, whereas if she'd been moving with definite purpose she would have stood out among the crowd. He had realized that at first glance he'd thought she was a strikingly attractive woman, but it hadn't sunk in that she was Felicia until he looked more closely.

She hadn't seen them, and was crossing Sacramento. She knew this was the meeting point, so she would surely come back this way, he hoped. But when he stepped out of the alcove to look for her, she was out of sight, already over the crest of the hill. He caught Estresor Fil's wide-eyed, unchanging but somehow accusatory gaze, and went after Felicia.

When he caught up with her, she had crossed Jones and was heading back up Sacramento, toward him. "Felicia," he said. "I'm glad I caught you."

She smiled, her big brown eyes seeming to twinkle at him. " 'Caught' me?" she echoed. "I was coming to you."

"So you saw us?" he asked.

"In your oh-so-secret doorway hideout? Of course. Did you think I was going to dash across the street straight to you? We're supposed to be exercising some discretion, right?"

He turned around so they were both walking the right direction, back toward Estresor Fil. "Well, yes," he said. "Which you did, very nicely."

She looked sideways at him, her rich black hair falling

across her cheek. Seeing her like this, in civilian clothes, acting the part of a casual San Franciscan instead of the frequently harried cadet she really was, Will decided he had never quite realized just how lovely she was. "Thank you," she said, and her voice was as clear and pure as a ringing bell.

By the time they got back to Estresor Fil's alcove, Boon had arrived and was lounging against the wall as if he didn't have the strength to stand up. This was just Boon's typical posture, though, except when he was in uniform and required to stand straight and tall. After a while, most cadets learned to hold their correct posture all the time, but for Boon it was only an obligation of service and would apparently never be a habit.

"I didn't see you when I passed by," Felicia said to him.

"Just got here."

"Where did you beam in?" Will asked him.

"Up to my ankles in the Pacific Ocean," Boon complained. "Anyone else get wet?"

"I didn't," Estresor Fil said.

"I wasn't too far away at all, as it turned out," Felicia said. "So I took a walk around the neighborhood, familiarizing myself with the local landmarks."

"So it's just me. It's always me," Boon said morosely.

"Your life is so hard," Felicia sighed.

"But we don't know where Dennis is," Will pointed out. "For all we know, he has it worse than you."

"Fat chance," Boon opined.

They waited another hour, and then some. Finally, Estresor Fil spotted Dennis on his way, and eight minutes later he reached them. After an overly long explanation of his plight and his solution to it, he produced what they'd all been waiting for—the first clue of their project.

They all looked at the document blankly. "Twins?" Boon asked. "What twins?"

Chapter 8

"That's kind of the point, isn't it?" Felicia responded. "We're supposed to figure the clues out. If it was easy, it wouldn't really be a challenge, now would it?"

Boon looked at her as if she'd lost her mind. "I don't know about you, but I'm already tired of this," he said. "It's nonsense. Running all over the place when it'd be so much easier to use transporters. Figuring out clues. I think my feet are still pruney from the water, and they hurt."

"I would suggest you quit, Boon," Estresor Fil told him. "Except that we're a squadron, and your failure would affect all of us. So perhaps you should just take it in stride and shut up."

The Coridanian looked stricken then. Will, always curious about Estresor Fil's ways and motivations, wondered if she was really just being blunt, or if she had intentionally tried to wound him, hoping, perhaps, that it would inspire him to greater effort. *And less whining,* he thought, *that would be good too.* Boon fancied himself a great leader and a starship captain in the making, but Will figured that any captain who bitched and moaned as much as Boon did would be begging for mutiny, probably within the first few days of his command.

He had to admit that while the complaining was annoying, Boon really did have a lot of good qualities—he was smart, made decisions fast and well, could think on his feet, and could inspire the loyalty of those around him. Until the sour attitude took over, and then all that loyalty was gone. Perhaps if Boon had been chosen as the leader of this final project, he'd have stowed the negativity and would already be leading them toward their objective. Dennis, obviously worn out from his ordeal so far, wasn't exactly taking the helm and inspiring confidence, so maybe Boon would have been the better choice. But Will didn't want to let Dennis's chance at leadership vanish. He decided to spur his friend on. "Do you have any ideas, Dennis? You've had the clue the longest."

Dennis, sitting on the ground in the doorway headquarters, shook his head sadly. "I tried to come up with something, but at the same time I was trying to figure out how to get off the island. I thought that should take precedence, since if I couldn't do that none of you would get a shot at the clue either. So I didn't really make much progress, I'm afraid."

"Are you sure there's not more to it?" Boon asked. "How do we find the right pair of twins in a city this size? Must be crawling with twins."

Felicia flashed her smile again, the one that Will was finding more intriguing all the time. "Maybe it's not human twins," she suggested. "There are maps every few blocks. If the twins are a natural feature, or one of the main city attractions, they'll be on there."

"Worth a look, anyway," Dennis agreed. He forced himself wearily to his feet. "You guys have been waiting around here for long enough as it is. Let's find us one of those maps and see if we can locate some twins."

A kiosk three blocks down Jones Street had city maps and transport schedules for the whole region. When Dennis entered "twins" on the keypad, nothing came up. But when Estresor Fil called up a city overview, the twins were suddenly apparent to all. Twin Peaks were two round-topped, still undeveloped hills—two of the tallest points in the city, it turned out, even higher than Nob Hill. Will requested a history of them, in case it would help identify where at the feet of the twins they might expect to find the checkpoint, and learned that one of the hills—there were actually more than two, all in the same vicinity, though the two called Twin Peaks were the tallest—had once held a broadcasting tower from which signals could be sent through the air to homes all over the San

Francisco Bay Area, and that on clear days the view from the Peaks was considered one of the best in the region. None of which helped a bit when it came to locating their checkpoint.

They had all done enough walking, except for Estresor Fil, who had been standing more or less in one place for hours now. But majority ruled and they hopped an underground transport to the Twin Peaks area. They would have, Will suspected, plenty of walking ahead of them yet, especially if they had to circumnavigate the base of the hills in order to find the spot they needed.

He, for one, was more than happy to sit down for a while.

As the map had indicated, the burnished brown hillsides of Twin Peaks were undeveloped, left open for hikers and view seekers to enjoy, Estresor Fil's opinion on the latter notwithstanding. But the city came right up to its edge, with houses and commercial buildings hemming it in on all sides. In many spots, the members of Zeta Squadron couldn't even see where the hillside began because it was behind private homes, with no access to the public. They had to try to peer over fences and between narrowly spaced houses to see if they could locate anything that might be their checkpoint.

After making a complete circuit, they still had no idea what they were looking for. "Maybe we interpreted the clue wrong," Dennis said glumly. He had stopped walking and just stood on the sidewalk, holding his envelope between two fingers like it had become something unpleasant. "Maybe these are the wrong twins."

"Yeah, and maybe this is a stupid project," Boon added. "I mean, if we really were an away team in hostile territory, we wouldn't have checkpoints to look for, would we?"

"Probably not," Will agreed. "But we would have a mission of some kind. We'd be gathering information about the place, or we'd be trying to locate a contact, or something. We wouldn't just land someplace for no reason at all."

"Will's right," Felicia said. "So is Dennis—it's possible that we picked the wrong twins. But the assignment is as close to realistic as it can be, without risking whole classes of cadets by sending them to actual hostile cities."

"I guess," Boon said reluctantly.

"Perhaps we've been too literal about the clue," Estresor Fil suggested. "Maybe it means something other than the foot of the hills. Is there a cobbler or something like that nearby?"

Will considered this for a moment. She was right—it was unlikely that Admiral Paris wouldn't have worked in a twist or two. So they had to look for the less likely possibilities, even the opposite of what appeared to be the meaning. "Maybe we should be looking up," he announced.

"Up?" Boon repeated. "You're not making any sense, Riker."

"Not at first glance," Will agreed. "But 'feet' has multiple meanings, and one of them is as a unit of measurement. Once used, among other things, to indicate altitude."

"Good point, Will," Felicia said, touching his upper arm for emphasis. "I agree. We should go up."

Boon shrugged. "I guess we can't do any worse than we are down here. Except for the climbing part, I mean."

They split into two teams, Will and Felicia taking one hill, and Dennis, Boon and Estresor Fil on the other. As they climbed, the late afternoon sun bore down on them. Up here there was only stunted shrubbery, and nothing to shade them from its rays. Will commented on it, and Felicia just laughed at him. "This is nothing compared to summers at home," she said. "We have heat, humidity, bugs—this is like paradise, here."

"Climate-controlled paradise," Will reminded her. "Nothing like this in Alaska, I can tell you."

"We have cold, too, in the mountains," Felicia said. "But maybe not like in Alaska."

"Maybe not," Will agreed. He picked his way up a faint trail, sidestepping the low brush as he rose. "Valdez is in the southern part of the state, well below the Arctic Circle, and it's pretty nice this time of year. Buggy, too. Come winter, though, it's a different story. The sun comes up around ten in the morning and has set by five in the afternoon. In between, it never warms up. There's snow everywhere—you don't see the ground until the spring thaw, and then everything that was snow is mud."

"It doesn't sound like you miss it much," she said.

"I love it," Will told her. "But I couldn't wait to get away from it. Now that I'm here, I can't wait to get off the planet."

She shielded her eyes against the sun and looked across the way at the group climbing the other hill. "We're ahead," she said happily. "Maybe this summer—what are you doing for the summer?"

Will nodded eagerly. "I've already got my assignment," he said. "I'm going to Saturn. I'm so anxious to get going I could explode."

"That's great, Will," Felicia enthused. "You didn't get off-planet last summer, did you?" she asked him.

"Just for a couple of weeks, to New Berlin. But I spent most of the summer in Paris. I'm due for some time off-world, that's for sure."

"You'll love it out there," she said. "Two more years after this and you'll be assigned to a starship, and do great things."

"Unless," he pointed out, "we can't find our first checkpoint and we fail miserably at this assignment. In which case maybe they'll just give us all the boot, and I can go back to Alaska and clean fish." They were almost to the top now, and while the views were spectacular, they hadn't seen anything promising. Their boots were getting caked with brown dust, but that was all they'd accomplished.

Suddenly Felicia grabbed his arm, squeezing his biceps tightly and holding on perhaps a little longer than she had

to. He found that he didn't mind. "Look, Will!" she shouted.
He followed her pointing hand and saw what she meant. On
a flat area near the summit was a dark cylinder, obviously
not a natural feature but something left there. Or transported there, Will thought, which was more likely, especially
considering the lack of footprints around it.

He and Felicia rushed to the cylinder and found that it
had a Starfleet insignia embossed onto it. On one side was a
keypad, but otherwise its surface was blank. "What do you
think we do with it?" he asked.

"Try your ID code," Felicia suggested.

Every cadet was assigned an identity code to be used
throughout their years at the Academy. Will nodded and entered his code onto the keypad. This was met by a whirring
noise, and a previously invisible slot appeared on the cylinder. From the slot, a new strip of paper emerged.

"What does it say?" Felicia asked with excitement.

" 'Congratulations, Zeta Squadron,' " Will read. " 'You've
achieved checkpoint number one. Your next challenge will
be to span the globe to find an artist, who will direct you
from there.' "

"An artist?" Felicia frowned. "What does *that* mean?"

Will shrugged, palms up. "Beats me," he said. He
glanced over his shoulder at the other part of their team, still
climbing the second peak unaware of the discovery. "But I
guess we can tell the others to come down now. Unless you
want to let Boon hike around and grumble a while longer."

Chapter 9

The captain's office was dimly lit and suffused with a burning rubber smell that reminded Kyle of old skunk. He found

himself wanting to hold his breath, but knew that was impractical. Anyway, he'd have to get used to the odor since he was going to be on the ship for a while. The captain was a Kreel'n, he'd been told. Without that small warning he wouldn't have known what to expect, and having never met a Kreel'n—rumors, of course, but that was all—he was still barely prepared for the reality of it.

"Captain?" he asked hesitantly when he entered. He had been told to enter but he couldn't see her anywhere when he went in. Unlike the neat and tidy equivalents he had seen on Starfleet vessels, this room was barely contained chaos; seemingly a storeroom for old electronic parts, a workspace, a library, and an office all in one, with no apparent division between one function and another.

"Come in, Mr. Barrow," a voice like a rusted hinge squeaked at him. "I am here, at my desk."

Kyle tried to follow the voice through the gloom and clutter. He had chosen the pseudonym Barrow, on a whim, because it was both an Alaskan city he had visited on a few occasions and the name of one of the most infamous fugitives in American history, Clyde Barrow, better known in association with his partner Bonnie Parker. *If you're going to be on the lam,* he'd thought, *you might as well make the best of it.* So he had become Kyle Barrow, man of mystery.

Finally, he saw a flat surface—mostly buried under stacks of objects whose purposes he could only make the wildest guess at—and behind the stacks, a pair of black, lifeless eyes in an oddly shaped head. He stepped forward and more of the captain came into view. Her head most closely resembled, in Kyle's experience, a pickle or a cucumber, but larger, with a greater diameter. Her skin was a dark green, and her eyes, half a dozen of them, encircled most of her head at about three-quarters of its height. Above them were nodes and ridges running lengthwise; below the eyes some perforations that might have been aural, olfactory, or some other type of organs, and below those a definite mouth, un-lipped and toothless but with a tongue capable of speaking English, though with an unpleasant rasp.

"Welcome to the *Morning Star*, Mr. Barrow," she said, rising from her seat and extending a hand toward Kyle. "I'm Captain S'K'lee."

Kyle stepped forward and took the proffered hand, shaking and then releasing it. It had, as far as he could tell, ten fingers, maybe a dozen, all narrow and wormlike, with no apparent joints. Like her head, it was a dark green, or seemed to be in the dim light. Her uniform was a simple pale green tunic, belted at what must have been her waist, though there was only a third of her entire height below it. He couldn't see her legs, or whatever was beneath the belt, and she quickly lowered herself back down behind the desk.

"Thank you for the welcome, and for the berth," Kyle said. "I appreciate your fitting me in at short notice."

"Better to have a passenger than not have a passenger, right?" S'K'lee asked. "Especially a paying one."

Kyle was not used to such blatant discussion of finances, but he understood that, primitive as it was, some races still functioned on a monetary basis. He had already arranged the transfer of the agreed-upon number of credits, through an intermediary suggested by the agent back at the freight company to assure anonymity. "I trust the payment was satisfactory?" he asked.

"Yes, quite. If it hadn't been, you would not now be aboard my ship," she said. "You do understand that this may be quite a long trip with a number of stops?"

"I do."

"May I ask your ultimate destination?"

"You can ask," Kyle said. "But I can't answer. And I wouldn't even if I had one in mind."

"Understood," S'K'lee said quickly. "Then I suppose it would be pointless to ask what the purpose of your journey is, or if, by taking you, I am opening myself up to any possible legal actions?"

"You'd be correct," Kyle told her, "in that it would be pointless to ask. Is that a problem?"

"Not at all, not at all." S'K'lee shook her head rapidly, which had the effect of making her many black eyes seem to blur into a single oval shape. "I simply like to know where things stand."

"Of course," Kyle said. He had expected discretion, and was relieved to have his expectation confirmed.

"Have you seen your quarters?"

"Not yet," Kyle replied. "But I'm sure they'll be fine." After the shuttle had docked at the orbital platform, Kyle had arranged for some changes of clothes and personal grooming items, then had come straight to the *Morning Star*. He still held in his left hand the bundle he had acquired.

"You'll be escorted there directly," S'K'lee assured him. "Cargo areas, engineering, environmental, and tactical operations areas are off limits to passengers. The bridge is accessible to you only by special request. Otherwise, you are free to move about the ship at will."

"Thank you."

"If you'd like to disembark at any stop, simply tell a member of the crew and arrangements will be made."

"Sounds good," Kyle said. "I look forward to the trip."

"It won't be comfortable, but it'll be long," S'K'lee told him with a grating, huffing noise that he guessed was her version of laughter. When she finished, she asked, "Is there anything else you'd like to know, about the ship? About me?"

There was, in fact, but he was hesitant to bring it up. She had already evidenced her sensitivity to his privacy; he didn't want to disregard hers.

"There is one thing," she said, "that most of your kind seems to want to know about Kreel'n ships' captains. If you're curious, feel free to ask. I assure you it isn't a problem for me to talk about."

"I'm sure we will," he answered. "At a later date."

She made a grimace that he could only assume was a smile. "Very well, very well. It's a pleasure to make your acquaintance, Mr. Barrow. I trust you'll have as pleasant a voyage as is possible, under the circumstances. I need to prepare myself now—I like to pilot out of the dock myself. I'll arrange for someone to escort you to your quarters."

"Thank you, Captain S'K'lee," Kyle said. Behind him, the door shushed open and he knew he was dismissed. He stepped through it and there was already a crewman coming toward him. This was also a Kreel'n, a male he guessed, though he wasn't at all sure, with a deeper chest and broader shoulders and a head that was more squash-shaped than cucumber. He saw now that the Kreel'n did indeed have very short legs for their body size—this one was as tall as he was, but its legs were no longer than his were from the knee down.

"Right this way, Mr. Barrow," it said, sweeping its wriggling mass of fingers in the direction from which it had just waddled.

Unlike the captain—and this was what he so desperately wanted to ask her about, though he had sensed, and apparently correctly, that in spite of her invitation it was really something that ought to wait until he knew her better—this Kreel'n's eyes had the glimmer of life and intelligence in them. The stories he had heard about Kreel'n captains, which he had been unwilling to credit until just now, seemed to be true, though he couldn't imagine why it would be a good idea.

They were, so the rumors went, surgically blinded before assuming their commands. Six eyes, none of which worked.

Maybe there was some sense to it, but for the life of him Kyle couldn't fathom what it was.

* * *

His cabin was as promised—not particularly comfortable, but adequate for his very basic needs. Since the *Morning Star* was of Kreel'n design, it was probably handy that in spite of their physiological differences humans and Kreel'n were about the same size. The room had a bed, toilet facilities that would meet his requirements, and a replicator. At the end of the bed was a trunk in which he could store his few belongings. The trunk's lid was flat and could, he supposed, be used as a seat as well.

As in the captain's office, the lighting was dim when he entered, but after examining the controls for a few moments he was able to override the default setting and increase the brightness a bit. The light glowed from walls that were otherwise unadorned, instead of being concentrated in specific fixtures.

All in all, there wasn't much to entertain him on a long trip, he figured. But he hadn't even begun to see the rest of the ship. As much as he intended to keep to himself, in order to preserve his privacy, he guessed he'd be spending some amount of time in the public areas. Maybe they had a gym or a holodeck, or both. A library would be good as well. Kyle wanted a lot of time to think, to reflect. But he also wanted to stay sharp, in body and mind, for the conflict that was sure to come.

He stowed his small bundle and then turned to the replicator for a cup of coffee. It would not, he knew, be as good as the real thing he brewed back home. That was a pleasure he'd have to forgo for a while, in the interest of survival. When he withdrew his cup from the replicator, it was the right color, and the aroma was good. Steam wafted from the surface. He brought it to his lips and sampled it.

Replicator coffee, he thought, disappointed in spite of himself. *The same the universe over.* As he drank, a Klaxon blared throughout the ship, signaling its imminent departure. Kyle sat down on top of the trunk, bracing himself for any sudden jolts, especially considering the pilot's disability. But the launch was as smooth as any he'd experienced. He sat on the trunk at the end of his new bed and sipped his coffee, realizing he hadn't had any solid food in hours. Once they were well under way, he'd do something about that. For now, though, he was content to drink his java knowing that his most immediate troubles were slipping farther and farther away with every passing moment.

He needed sleep as well—it had been many hours since he'd slept, with the exception of a few fitful moments on the shuttle—but his mind was racing too fast for that to be a possibility anytime soon. Everything that had happened was still too fresh. The attacks on him were predominant in his thinking, of course, but other issues, more personal still, beat a discordant counterpoint. Running into Ben Sisko and seeing Jennifer and brand-new Jake, born on Father's Day, so soon after being reminded by Admiral Paris that his own son Will was on the Academy campus less than a kilometer away, had been surprisingly jarring. He remembered the simultaneous joy and fear at Will's birth and Annie's illness. He had fond memories of times with Will, watching the boy grow up from day to day, learning new skills, forming a personality all his own. The boy had always been bright and quick-witted, and there had been days when father and son had both collapsed into puddles of hysterical laughter at Will's antics and jokes.

But there had been dark days, too, when the pressure of Kyle's own inadequacy as a father had weighed heavily on his shoulders. Days when Will had questions Kyle could not answer, needs Kyle could not begin to meet. Sometimes he thought his son a completely alien being, unable to be understood in the least. Other times—worse times, in some cases— he thought he was raising a carbon copy of himself, having handed down to his heir his own faults and weaknesses.

You did what you could, he told himself, sipping from his

steaming mug. *Given who you were—who you are—you made your best possible effort.*

He had told himself that many times, over the years. As always, he wondered if it was true. Wasn't there something more he could have given of himself, some other heroic effort he could have made had he only thought of it? Was there some other expert to whom he could have turned for advice and guidance? If he had stayed, instead of leaving—running away, he now understood, as he was running again—during Will's fifteenth year, could they have reached some new plateau of understanding and acceptance?

Kyle shook his head fiercely. Those were questions of the past. While the past could be visited, with considerable difficulty, it could not be substantively changed, so it did no good to dwell on those matters. Kyle had never considered himself a great intellect, but he was a great problem solver. He didn't like wrestling with issues that had no solutions. Instead, he did what he always did at such times, visualized his mind as a series of boxes. He took his thoughts of young Will Riker, tucked them deep into one of those boxes, and closed the lid on them.

Chapter 10

By the time they had all come down from the hills of Twin Peaks, the sun was sinking toward the ocean and the air was getting colder. "I'm hungry," Dennis Haynes said when they met up. "What about the rest of you?"

"I could stand something to eat," Boon replied.

"Me too," Estresor Fil said. For her, food was often a matter of urgency. With her tiny size and fast metabolism, every meal was processed quickly, and she couldn't wait too long

for the next. Even as they'd made their way to Twin Peaks
she had snacked now and again. When she needed food her
patience grew short and so, Will had noticed, did her sentences. "Really hungry."

"We should eat something, and find some shelter for the
night," Dennis suggested. "We can brainstorm on the new
clue while we rest and hit it first thing in the morning."

Will was glad to see that Dennis was finally taking a leadership position. "Do you think the other squadrons are doing
one a day?" he wondered.

"That's what it should average out to, anyway," Dennis reminded him. "Five clues, five days, right?"

"That's true," Felicia said. "So we might as well pace ourselves."

"Does anyone have any ideas for a place to sleep?" Dennis asked.

"There are several public shelters," Estresor Fil pointed
out. "That we can find *after* we eat."

Dennis laughed, getting the point. "Okay, let's go feed
ourselves," he said, starting back toward the city itself. Everyone else followed.

"I think we should avoid the public shelters, though,"
Will suggested. "The other squadrons might be there."

"So?"

"So you really think they won't try to sabotage us if they
see us?"

"We could do the same to them," Boon offered.

"I'd rather try to win fairly," Felicia put in. "Without doing
anything to hurt anyone else's chances, just by being the best."

Boon pretended to stifle a yawn. "That's no fun, Felicia."

She shot him an angry glare. "You may not think so,
Boon. But it's the way I'd like to play it, and I think it's the
way Admiral Paris wants it. If you don't think so, maybe you
should reconsider a Starfleet career."

Boon stopped in the middle of the street, pulling himself

up to his considerable height, and loomed over Felicia. "Don't be so sure of yourself," he said, his voice low and rumbling. Will wondered if he should intercede, but then decided that if Boon moved from menacing to actual violence, Felicia would be able to handle him. "Sure, they talk about fair play and honor and integrity and all that stuff, but you think they really mean it? When the chips are down and it's them or you, you'd better do whatever is necessary to make sure you walk away and they don't."

"You don't know what you're talking about!" Dennis said. "Starfleet doesn't just talk about integrity; they personify it."

"They're right, Boon," Will said. "If you don't think so, you don't know much about Starfleet's history."

Boon shook his head, scoffing at the others. "Some people are so naïve," he said. "I'll tell you what, when I'm sitting in that captain's chair, I hope I don't have any dreamers like you all on my crew to worry about."

"With an attitude like that," Will replied, "I don't think you'll ever have to worry about being in the captain's chair at all." He was surprised that this side of Boon had never emerged before. But then, he hadn't know the Coridanian that long, just during this school year. And none of their group projects had forced them to spend as much time together as this one would. Any personality conflicts that were simmering beneath the surface would surely come out during the week's forced intimacy.

Boon leaned forward threateningly and Will braced himself, believing that the Coridanian was going to attack him instead of Felicia. Boon had height and reach on him, Will knew, and if it was going to be a fight it would be a brutal one that he would either win quickly or not at all.

Before either male could surrender to the testosterone that fueled them, however, Estresor Fil inserted her tiny form between them. "I need to eat," she implored. "Now."

Will held Boon's yellow eyes for a few more seconds,

then ticked his head toward the diminutive Zimonian. "She's right," he said. "We need to get her fed—all of us, really—and we need to stick together. You willing to do that?"

Boon breathed heavily, but Will could see his body relax, his fists unclench. "Yeah, okay," he said, sounding a bit reluctant to call off the fight. Will had the sense that their reckoning was merely postponed, not canceled.

With the tension dissipated, though not eliminated, they turned once again to the question of food. Finding some was not difficult—no one went hungry in San Francisco—and they ate at an outdoor table. Boon and Will sat at opposite ends, but the group kept the conversation away from the recent incident between them. Dennis steered it back toward the question of lodging for the night.

"If we're going to avoid public shelters," he said, with a furtive glance toward Boon, "then we're going to have to come up with some alternative. I don't want to spend the night on the streets, and we can't go back to our rooms at the Academy."

"Let's approach it as if we really were on a mission," Will suggested. "We'd want to stay someplace discreet, where the local authorities wouldn't notice us. We wouldn't want to interact much with the locals, if we could help it, until we had the lay of the land better. Since we spent most of today trying to meet up and then climbing mountains, we didn't really get to do that."

"I know a place," Felicia offered.

"Where?" Dennis asked her. "I hope it doesn't involve any more climbing."

"Remember that doorway that Estresor Fil found this morning? No one went in or out. The windows were all blacked over. I think it's an empty space, and obviously it's not getting much use, if any."

"You want to break in?" Dennis asked, surprised.

"Exactly. We don't have to hurt anything. We just go in, sleep, and leave in the morning."

"That's illegal," Estresor Fil pointed out.

"So?" Boon asked, the first word he'd said since he and Will had faced off on the street. "Like she said, we wouldn't hurt anything. If we were on an away mission in hostile territory, we wouldn't hesitate to break a few minor laws to save our own skins."

"I suppose," Estresor Fil said, more loquacious now that her stomach was full. "Although I don't feel very comfortable with the idea. Weren't we specifically forbidden from breaking laws?"

"There are laws and there are laws," Boon argued. "In San Francisco, anyone who doesn't have a place to sleep is entitled to go to one of the public shelters. That's why they have them. But if we don't want to do that—and if we were on a secret mission here, that would be the last place we'd want to show up—then we have to bunk someplace else. We don't want to stay in a tourist hotel, again since we're supposed to be here secretly. Either we make friends with one of the locals, in a hurry, or we go with Felicia's idea."

"We don't seem to have a lot of options," Will agreed. "And it does seem like if you're trying to hide from the authorities, going to a shelter run by those same authorities is a bad idea."

"It's hard to argue with that," Dennis admitted. "I still don't think I like the idea, but—"

"You got any better ones?" Boon interrupted.

"That's precisely the problem," Estresor Fil put in, having apparently been won over. "Either we don't break any of Admiral Paris's rules but we do the single thing that would most likely result in our capture, or we break rules judiciously and carry out our assignment."

When she finished, all eyes went to Dennis.

"I don't like it," he said at last. "But since I can't, in fact, think of anything better, I agree that it seems like the best of our limited options."

By the time they'd finished their dinner, the sky had gone dark.

They caught an underground transport back to Nob Hill, checking the route maps to see if there were any obvious clues to an artist who spanned the globe. There weren't, so they continued back to the corner at which they'd met earlier that day, and with which Will and Estresor Fil had become so familiar. At the doorway alcove, Boon took the lead in the breaking-and-entering process. He said he'd done it several times, at home on the hardrock mining planet of Coridan.

"Security might be a little better here," Dennis suggested in a nervous whisper.

"Are you calling Coridan some kind of primitive backwater?" Boon demanded.

"No, not at all," Dennis said quickly, backing away a step as if Boon's words had carried physical force.

"Look, Boon," Will said, stepping up and forgetting his earlier resolve. "I don't know if your problem is that we elected Dennis to lead the squadron on this mission, or what. But you're acting like someone with a chip on his shoulder the size of the moon. If you can't leave your personal feelings behind and carry on with the mission, then you should just tell us now so we can report back to Admiral Paris that we failed."

"You'd like that, wouldn't you, Riker?" Boon asked with a snarl. "You sabotage everything you ever do, guaranteeing you'll never succeed at anything so you won't really be tested. You'd just love to shoot a hole in this project right off the bat."

The accusation stunned Will. He had never thought of himself as self-destructive, and he doubted that Boon knew him better than he knew himself. But at the same time, he knew that sometimes others saw unpleasant traits in people that they couldn't see in themselves. He decided to shelve any further examination of the issue, to consider later. Right now, they had a building to break into.

"Never mind my psychological shortcomings, Counselor," he shot back. "Can you open that door or not?"

Boon had already turned away from the others and had the faceplate removed from the keypad. "Yeah, just give me a few minutes to reprogram this," he said. Will tried to watch but Boon blocked his view with his broad shoulders and quickly moving hands. "This one's easy. I've seen some with multiple redundant alarm systems, but this—well, I guess there's nothing in here worth taking."

"That's okay," Felicia said, sounding maybe a little nervous that she'd suggested this in the first place. "We're not taking anything. Is there a lot of crime on Coridan?"

"A fair bit," Boon said. He closed the faceplate and put his palm against the keypad, and the door irised open for him. "All that dilithium, you know, and other valuable minerals. Left us wide open for all sorts of folks to come around and take whatever they could get their hands on." He stepped to the side and bowed toward the doorway, indicating that the others should enter first. As he did so, he looked right at Felicia. "Of course, if I read you right, you were asking if I committed a lot of crime on Coridan. Which, of course, is impossible—I wouldn't have been accepted into the Academy if I'd had a criminal record, now, would I?"

Will knew, of course, that a criminal record was something you acquired only after you'd been *caught*. In the past few hours, he had learned not to underestimate Boon in any way—including, it seemed, his skills at illegal entry.

The inside of the building was primarily a single empty room, with bare walls and floor. A few support beams broke up the emptiness, but that was all. It had been, or would be, a shop of some kind, but currently it was nothing at all except temporary shelter for five Starfleet cadets, tired and excited and a little scared, all at the same time. At the back of the large vacant space they found a separate storage area with a working bathroom, which the cadets took turns with. Running water was more than Will had dared to hope for.

Since they'd come empty-handed, there were no blankets or pillows to make the bare floors more comfortable, but they were so tired from the day's events that it hardly seemed to matter. Will chose a spot at some distance from the others, with a view of the door. He could be a heavy sleeper, he knew, and if anyone came in the door he wanted to be close enough to hear it right away. He had just closed his eyes, though, when he heard someone come close to him and take a seat on the floor. He opened his eyes again, to see Felicia smiling down at him in the dim light.

"I just wanted to say I'm sorry that you got into it with Boon," she said, her voice barely above a whisper. "We need to stick together if we're going to succeed at this project."

"I'm not the one who has to be convinced of that," Will replied. As soon as he said it, he realized it might sound harsher than he had meant it to. "I'm sorry," he quickly added. "I guess I've underestimated him. I always knew he was kind of pushy and headstrong, but I didn't understand the full extent of it. I hope it doesn't come to violence, but if he insists on a fight, then he'll get one."

She put a gentle, soothing hand on his shoulder. "You've got to try to avoid that," she said. "For all our sakes. Do you think we'll get a passing grade on this project if you two pummel each other half to death? Besides," she appended, her voice softening, "I really would hate to see you get hurt. I wouldn't mind seeing Boon taken down a few pegs, I guess. He could use the lesson. But it would bother me if you were injured in the process."

In the near dark of the empty space, it was hard to tell for sure, but Will thought that her cheeks might be crimsoning with this confession. He wasn't quite sure how to respond. "I can take care of myself," he said, knowing even as he spoke that it was the wrong thing to say, too dismissive of her concerns, too tinged with self-serving braggadocio to be at all meaningful. "I mean, I would try not to do anything that could jeopardize our grades, and I kind of like myself unbruised and unbroken. Don't worry, Felicia. I'll do my best to keep things calm."

She released his shoulder now, after a final, firm squeeze. "See that you do, Mr. Riker," she commanded. "I kind of like you that way myself."

Then she moved away and Will settled in, resting his head on his shirt, thinking that all in all, it had been a pretty eventful day. Even this late in the year, his squadron mates were full of surprises—none more so than Boon and Felicia; Boon for his unexpected truculence and Felicia for her sudden attention.

He couldn't even guess at what the next days might bring, but as he drifted off to sleep he figured they'd be challenging, if nothing else.

Chapter 11

There was one other human passenger on the *Morning Star*, Kyle soon learned, He was exploring the corridors; two days out from the dock, he still barely had the hang of the huge ship's layout, and he was pretty sure he'd made at least a couple of wrong turns.

The ship was nothing but functional, and even then more for Kreel'n than humans. The corridors were narrow and low-ceilinged, with handrails for the top-heavy beings further crowding the available space. Floors, in many places, were simple gridwork, providing access to the miles of tubes and wires and circuits that kept the ship in flight. Doors were opened by a complex system of push buttons—easy for the multifingered Kreel'n, but a little tricky for Kyle.

On this particular morning, Kyle had been looking for the gym he'd been told was on the fourth deck below his—all the decks were identified by Kreel'n symbols which looked like nothing more than squiggles to him, so he had to count every time he went up or down the ladders, on which the rungs were far too close together for his long legs. The ship had no turbolifts, he learned to his surprise.

He had found the gym, but it hadn't taken long to discover that none of the equipment inside it was suitable for his physiology. He'd have to settle for the exercises he could perform in his own quarters, without equipment, supplemented by runs or walks through the long corridors.

Heading back to his quarters, he had indeed taken a wrong turn somewhere—he thought probably at one of the several points where five or six passageways converged on one another in a star pattern—and, trying to backtrack, had found himself in a part of the ship he hadn't yet seen. Here, pipes hung down from the metal ceiling, suspended by thin steel straps, and the burning rubber smell that he was already getting used to was largely obscured by a harsh oily stench. Even the air seemed thicker in this area. Kyle found himself blinking as the atmosphere stung his eyes. He turned a corner too fast and smacked his head against a low-hanging section of pipe.

"Ow!" he shouted involuntarily. He rubbed the sore spot, certain that a bump would appear before long, hoping he hadn't broken the skin so that whatever was crusting the outside of the pipe wouldn't get into his blood. He was starting to duck underneath the pipe when a door opened before him and a human man smiled at him.

"I thought that sounded like a human voice," the man said. "I'd heard rumors that there was another one of us about, but wasn't sure, given the size and design of this tub, that we'd get a chance to meet one another." His accent sounded indefinitely continental, as if he'd lived many places and spoke a plethora of languages, all of which contributed a little something to his English. "It's nice to hear once in a while." He was still standing in the doorway, hands gripping the jambs on either side of him, sort of leaning out into the hall but ready to flee back inside at a moment's notice. He was a friendly-looking fellow, Kyle thought, with a thick black beard that merged with the tufts of black chest hair visible above his open shirt. He had little hair on the upper part of his head, though, and what there was he kept cropped close to the scalp. His smiling face was broad, with a large red nose, small red eyes, and puffy, rosy cheeks. He looked to Kyle like a young, disheveled Santa Claus. The illusion carried down to his belly, which was immense. His expansive shirt was checked, red and white, and his pants were pale blue. His feet, Kyle noted, were bare.

"My name's Barrow. Kyle Barrow," Kyle lied.

"Of course it is. I'm John Abbott. Double b, double t, that's how it's spelled." The man was quite possibly the most cheerful fellow Kyle had ever seen. "You came from Earth, right?"

"Of course," Kyle confirmed. "Didn't you?"

John Abbott shook his huge head. "No, no. I mean, once I did, originally, certainly. Not recently, though. No, I've been here and there, moving about quite a bit, you know? I've been on board the *Morning Star* for quite a spell now. Quite a ways before I leave her, too."

"Where are you headed?"

John cocked his head sideways and shot Kyle an admonishing glare. "That's the first question you learn not to ask on a ship like this," he explained.

"I guess I've still got to learn the ropes," Kyle offered. "Sorry. Maybe I can buy you a drink sometime and you can tell me what else I shouldn't ask. There is a lounge someplace, isn't there?"

"There's a crew lounge," John told him. "But you

wouldn't want to go there. The Kreel'n are all very nice, to your face, but get a few of them together—especially with some spirits in them—and you'll learn what they're really like, quickly enough. Not a pleasant time, that, not at all."

"And if a couple of human guys wanted to get a drink, pass the time, where would they do that?" Kyle could barely believe he was asking the question. He'd planned to be the solitary traveler, the mystery man, keeping to himself and letting no one get close to him. But now, with just two days of solitude under his belt, he was already trying to force a connection with the first human who'd spoken more than two words to him. He was, he knew, generally a sociable person, who had made friends at bases, space stations, and taverns across the galaxies, so the enforced solitude was hard.

John Abbott looked at the ceiling as if giving considerable thought to the question. "Well, there would be your quarters. And then there would be my quarters. And that's about it. You wouldn't want to drink too much anywhere else on this blasted ship because you'd have the damndest time finding your way back to where you were supposed to be. And—as with the crew lounge—you wouldn't want to be wandering about without the fullest use of your faculties. You don't know who, or what, you might encounter."

Kyle could hardly believe what he was hearing. "Are you saying we're not safe on this ship, John?"

John gave him a big wink. "Oh, you're safe enough, I'd guess. S'K'lee has no doubt given orders to keep your hide in one piece. But there are those on the crew who hate humans, make no mistake about that, and if you should cross one of them at a time and place when he thought he could get away with it, then I wouldn't want to swear to anything."

Having said that, he stepped away from the doorway, moving with the surprising, almost dainty grace that some large men master as a way of dealing with their bulk. "Come on in, Kyle Barrow, and let's get acquainted. My replicator can whip up some twelve-year-old scotch just as unconvincingly as yours can, I'm sure."

Kyle followed him into the room, which was at least twice the size of his own quarters, but equally impersonal. Most of the extra room was just floor space, as if John Abbott might want to host large parties from time to time. He did have three chairs and a table, though, with a computer stationed at one end of it. He went to the wall-mounted replicator. "Name your poison, Kyle."

"That scotch you mentioned sounds fine," Kyle said. Even in here, the oily smell of the corridor hung on. "A little touch of home. You'll have to draw me a map back to my bunk, though."

John Abbott laughed, a booming sound that echoed in the big space. "Coming right up," he said. "As far as the map, well, don't worry, I'll make sure you get home in one piece. Home being a relative term, of course."

A minute later he brought two glasses over to the table and bade Kyle sit down. He followed suit, again impressing Kyle with his almost balletic grace. After a sip from his own drink, he leaned forward conspiratorially. "Can we talk frankly, Kyle? Because if we can't, it's going to be a damnably long voyage, that's for sure."

"Of course," Kyle said, knowing even as he did so that he'd have to watch his step. He didn't want to give away too much to a stranger, even one who seemed as friendly and unthreatening as this.

"Don't trust anyone on this vessel," he said. "S'K'lee let you on because you paid her price, but she'd sell you out to the first buyer who could top it. She's already got your credits, so there's no percentage in taking your side from now on. I don't think she'd put you in harm's way, as I said before, unless there was something in it for her. But you have only bought a ticket, not any kind of loyalty."

"It sounds like you know her pretty well," Kyle observed. "If she's so bad, why have you flown with her for so long?"

"Because I know what to expect with her," John replied. "I don't expect more than a berth on a fast ship that's largely ignored by the rest of the universe, and I get exactly what I expect. She knows I mean her no harm, and I try not to be too much trouble. I watch my step and I keep out of the way. I'd advise you to do the same."

"Still, it seems like a hard way to live."

"Isn't it what you wanted when you booked passage?" John asked, and Kyle realized the man was right. "If you had wanted companionship, you'd have gone on a tourist flight. If you wanted efficiency, a man such as yourself, I'd guess you've got Starfleet connections and you could have hitched a ride on one of their boats. No, you came for the quiet, for the privacy. And you'll get it. I'm just trying to warn you, it comes with a price that isn't paid in credits. You don't want to trust anyone with your secret, whatever it is—no, don't deny it, Kyle Barrow, I know you've got one. Well, that's good. You can't trust anyone with your secret on this ship, because here, just as much as anywhere else, your secret is safe with no one but yourself."

"I take it you have a secret too," Kyle said. "Since you're on board with me."

"I said everybody has a secret. That includes me, of course. I'm not telling you mine, no matter how long we're on this bucket of bolts together."

"I'm not asking."

"See that you don't." John's voice was serious now, almost grim, Kyle thought. He was surprised at the turn the conversation had taken so quickly. This wasn't a casual get-acquainted chat anymore, but had become a life-and-death discussion when he wasn't looking. "Let me tell you something else, too, Kyle—it is Kyle, isn't it?"

Kyle nodded. "Yes, of course."

"I thought as much. Next time you pick a name, don't use your real one."

"I didn't mean it was—" Kyle began, but John cut him off.

"I know, but I also know that it is," he said. "Don't fret, I don't know who you really are and I don't care, believe me. But I know what you were thinking when you chose it. 'If I use my real first name, then I won't have to worry about not answering when someone calls me by it. As long as I change my last name I'll be safe.' But the fact is, you've just given them—whoever 'they' are, whoever you're on this ship hiding from—half of your identity. If your real first name is Kyle then you should call yourself Met'ridunk or Bob, something completely different. Trust me, for the first few weeks you'll be so hyperconscious that you'll answer to anything, and by the time you're comfortable with it, it will have become habit. Go as far away from your real name as possible. I hope you did a better job with Barrow."

"I think so," Kyle said. He hadn't even touched his scotch yet. He thought he'd been doing pretty well, but John Abbott—or whoever he was, since that clearly wasn't his real name either—was making him feel like the rankest of amateurs.

"Well, you can remain Kyle Barrow for the duration of your time on the *Morning Star*, and have plenty of time to come up with a name for the next place," John said. "If you're willing to accept help, I can even scare up some convincing identification for whatever name you select. Of course, then I'd know your next name. If it were me, I wouldn't trust me for a second. But the offer's there, if you'd like the assistance."

"Thanks, I think," Kyle said. "I'll consider it."

"Good man. I'd pass on it too," John reiterated. "Next thing, did you tell S'K'lee where you're getting off?"

"I don't even know myself yet."

"That's fine, that's good. If you do tell her anything, be

sure you don't actually get off there. If you pick a spot and we actually go there, then you've got to stay on, even if it means renegotiating your fare. If you pick a spot that we might be headed for, you've got to find a way off before we stop there. If you're careful enough, you could be gone for days before she even knows it. It's harder with cargo, do you have any cargo on board? Don't tell me what it is."

"No, no cargo," Kyle assured him, shaking his head.

"Good, good. Travel light, it's the best way. Me, I've got cargo. Makes it a good deal more difficult to slip away unnoticed, I can tell you."

Kyle finally took a sip of the scotch, which was better than John had given him any reason to expect. He liked the warm sensation it made going down. "This is the good stuff," he said.

"Good as it gets. You live with the stink of this ship long enough, you'll find that anything that would taste remotely pleasant is just wonderful, simply because it takes you away from the odor. Do your quarters smell this bad?"

"No," Kyle replied, taking another drink. Once he had swallowed, he continued. "No, there's a bit of the smell of Kreel'n around, but nothing like this."

"I'm close to the engine room," John explained. "Kreel'n are notoriously inept mechanically, and they're some of the messiest creatures you could ever imagine. I'm surprised they can keep the ship aloft, even with the help of the other aliens they've got working for them."

"Do you socialize with the crew?" Kyle asked him. "Other than Kreel'n, I mean."

John looked shocked at the question. "You may get the idea that I don't like the Kreel'n," he said. "That's not true. Or not precisely true, anyway. In point of fact, I don't like much of anyone. The Kreel'n are okay with me in that they leave me alone and don't pry into my affairs, but you'd never see me calling one a friend. No, the last thing you'll ever see on this ship is me having a pleasant conversation with the crew. I'd sooner take a long walk out the airlock."

"What about other passengers?" Kyle pressed. "Are there any you've gotten to know?"

John laughed again. "Besides you, you mean?" When Kyle nodded, he went on with a wide smile. "We're *it*, Mr. Barrow. We are it."

Chapter 12

The days passed quickly for Will and Zeta Squadron. Boon corralled his own obstreperous nature, with only the occasional pointed reminder from his comrades. Dennis took on an ever-stronger leadership role, including delegating authority when it served the team. Will, as it turned out, showed a knack for analyzing and solving the puzzles with which they were faced, though he left it to Dennis to implement the solutions once he arrived at them. The artist spanning the globe turned out to be a museum's exhibition of a historical robot painter, mounted on a giant trackball—painted like the Earth—so it could work on multiple canvases simultaneously. Other clues led to Coit Tower on Telegraph Hill, and the understory of the two-level Bay Bridge, no longer open to vehicular traffic but left standing as a historical landmark.

The clue they had found at the bridge had seemed, at first, as incomprehensible as all the others. "Gone Fishing," it had said, and, "To bring them home means bringing yourselves home." Dennis had turned, under the latticework of shadows cast by the upper level of the bridge, to look at all the water visible from this point—water that, they all knew, surrounded San Francisco on three sides—and said, "Fish? There's nothing but fish around us!"

It was only while performing aikido moves in a heavy-grav environment inside the gym that Will had reached a breakthrough. When their workouts were done and they had showered, he gathered the others together and told them what he'd come to believe. "It's the easiest one of all if you just take it at face value," he told them excitedly. "Bringing the fish home. If you go fishing in a boat, you bring them home at a dock, right? Which narrows down our search to where there are working docks. But what if you don't do the fishing yourself, and you still want to bring some home? You go to a fish market."

"That almost seems too obvious," Dennis countered.

"Right," Will agreed. "That's the beauty of it. These other clues have been so convoluted, who'd expect us to get an easy one at this point? We could spend all day trying to figure out some ridiculously complex meaning to this one, but I think this is really where it's pointing us."

"You could be right, Will," Felicia said. "It'd be a way of throwing us off the track. Using our expectations against us."

"I don't know," Boon said. "If you're wrong we could waste a lot of time. We need to wrap this up today and get back to the Academy. First back, highest marks."

"But if you don't have any different interpretations, Boon," Estresor Fil put in, "we might as well try Will's, right?"

"I guess," Boon admitted. Will figured Boon's hesitation was just because the idea had been Will's and not his own. Not that he had contributed much during this exercise, other than wearisome negativity and the occasional judicious application of criminal tendencies. Will found himself glad that his encounters with Boon over the past year had been minimal, and that there hadn't been more extensive group projects like this one. Far from being captain material, Boon seemed like he'd be a detriment to any starship.

"Let's get moving, then," Dennis suggested. "The sooner we finish, the sooner we're home."

San Francisco's Fish Market, on the site of the city's old Fisherman's Wharf, was a massive complex where dozens of boats, hovercraft, and skimmers brought thousands of pounds of fish every day for the citizens of San Francisco. Fresh seafood had always been a tradition in the city, and remained so to this day.

Will smelled the market before he could see it. The unique and powerful odor of so many fish—dead and not—concentrated in one place created an olfactory wall that was unmistakable. A stranger, beamed into San Francisco for the first time, would have been able to find her way to the Fish Market from anyplace within a kilometer of it. When they passed the invisible barrier, Will wrinkled his nose and smiled at his comrades. "We're nearly there," he said.

"Will?" Dennis ventured. "I've been to the Fish Market before. It's huge. Do you have any idea how we'll find the checkpoint when we get there?"

Will flashed him a smile. "I have no idea. I figured we'd cross that bridge when we got to it."

"As long as there's a plan," Felicia put in. She walked next to Will almost all the time now, and had been sleeping next to him at night. She had never suggested anything further, though, and except for casual—and slightly more than casual—physical contact from time to time, they hadn't really touched in any meaningful way. A few days ago, Will had been sure he'd been reading her signals correctly, but now he wasn't as certain. He'd had a couple of girlfriends before, but they had been brief affairs, not at all serious, and having been raised in an all-male household, he sometimes thought of women as a race every bit as different from him as Andorians or Vulcans. Maybe if he'd had sisters, or at least a mother, he would have some idea of what to say and how to act around them. As it was, he had to make it all up. He definitely wanted something to happen—from the moment he'd started looking at Felicia in that light, instead of merely as an extraordinarily gifted cadet who happened to be female, he had wanted to be with her.

But where do you go from here, Will?

He didn't know the answer to that, any more than he knew where in the vast Fish Market they should look for their checkpoint.

There were, as Dennis had pointed out, hundreds of stalls in the Fish Market. Some offered only one specific type of seafood—Will saw stalls for squid, for shrimp, prawns, lobsters, roe, salmon, and many others—while others offered more variety. It seemed that every craft, or every fisher who went out to sea, had his or her own stall. The wares were displayed on metal trays so cold to the touch that Will had once thought his skin would stick or break off if he dared to finger them, only to find out later that safety regulations required that they be cold enough to keep the fish fresh but not to injure curious humans. Some stalls even had large saltwater tanks where live fish, eels, and octopuses swam and waited to be taken away by some consumer or professional chef. Around each stall, humans and aliens of virtually every description loitered, examining the day's catch—sniffing, touching, eyeing, comparing a swordfish at one with a tuna at the next.

"Dennis has a point, Will," Estresor Fil offered after they'd been walking amongst the stalls for a while. "This place is big, and crowded. Are we sure this is what the clue points to? And is there anything in it that might narrow things down more for us?"

Will had been trying to figure out that very question, but so far he'd had no luck. "I just don't know," he replied honestly. "We could hope we just get lucky and spot it, but other than that . . ."

"I've *got* it!" Felicia interrupted. "It *is* in the clue, after all. 'Bringing them home means bringing yourselves home.' We just need to look at it more precisely than we've been doing. This is where everybody in the city comes to bring fish home. But our home, for now at least, is the Academy. And aren't there a few vendors here from whom the Academy traditionally gets its seafood, for cadet and staff meals?"

"I think you're right," Dennis replied. "The Academy chefs like to work with people they know and trust. They contract with those particular vendors."

"Do you happen to remember any of their names?" Estresor Fil asked.

Felicia and Dennis searched one another's faces for a moment, as if the answer might be written there. "I guess not," Dennis finally ventured.

"Then we're right back where we were before," Boon said glumly.

"Not necessarily," Will pointed out. "At least we have something to look for. We've all seen deliveries come into the Academy. We've all seen the chefs. Instead of looking at all the fish, we need to look at the people. If we see anyone who looks familiar then we know we're getting somewhere."

"We *hope* we're getting somewhere," Boon, always the pessimist, countered.

Will was tired of arguing with Boon, who never had any better ideas to offer but nonetheless didn't hesitate to criticize others'. Ignoring the Coridanian, he turned to Felicia. "Good job," he said. "I think you've solved it."

She returned his smile with one he could feel in his gut. She looked straight into his eyes and they held that for a moment, with Will finally breaking her gaze only so they could renew their search. As they walked, she moved over toward him and let her shoulder bump against his. Once again, Will wished he knew the right thing to say, but as usual it wouldn't come to him.

Having rearranged their search parameters, it only took a

few minutes to find a familiar face. But it wasn't one of the faces they were expecting. Instead, Will saw the smoldering, dark eyes and thick crop of black hair of his friend and fellow cadet, Paul Rice. Paul was on a competing squadron, but Will had shouted out his name before he caught himself. It was only then that he noticed the rest of Omega Squadron: Hasimi Thorp, Naghmeh Zand, Ross Donaldson, and Kul Tun Osir, standing behind Paul at the booth. Paul set down the checkpoint canister he'd been holding and smiled at Will.

"Cadet Riker," he said. "Just a little behind the pack, as usual."

"Damn it," Boon muttered from behind Will.

"I guess maybe we are," Will said. He picked up the canister from where Paul had set it. Inside the stall, he thought he recognized one of the women who occasionally made deliveries to the Academy's mess hall. "We're doing the best we can, though." He started to punch his identification code into the canister's keypad.

"So how many more checkpoints do you have to make?" Paul asked him. "We've only got two to go."

Will couldn't hide the surprise that transformed his face. "Two?" he asked. He felt Felicia nudge him in the ribs, but it was too late. Anyway, he figured it didn't really matter now. "This is our last," he admitted. "We're done."

"Done?" Paul echoed. He sounded startled.

"Well, this is the last day, after all," Will said.

"Yeah, but a couple of them took us more than a day," Paul replied. "You guys must have had easy ones."

"I don't know about that," Felicia put in. "Maybe we're just better at this than you are."

"Maybe they cheat," Hasimi Thorp suggested. He was a squat, stocky native of Inferna Prime, with charcoal black skin and blazing orange eyes. He was a head taller than Estresor Fil, but at least double her weight.

"Will wouldn't cheat," Paul answered firmly. "I know

him better than that. I don't know about the others, though."

"We didn't cheat," Will said. "None of us."

"Come on," Ross chimed in. "How else could you guys be so far ahead of us?"

The two squadrons were facing one another now, and Fish Market customers stepped aside for them. Boon shouldered his way to the front of Zeta Squadron's pack. "Maybe you're just stupid," he said. "Did you consider that possibility?"

"Stupid?" Kul Tun Osir came from Quazulu VIII, where intelligence was highly valued, and he usually placed first, or nearly so, in his classes at the Academy. "I must have misheard you. You wouldn't have called us stupid, would you?"

"I think your hearing's just fine," Boon shot back.

"Boon," Dennis said, urgent warning in his tone. Boon ignored him, though.

"Anyone who thinks we cheated is blatantly stupid," Boon continued. "And anyone who's so far from done on the last day is doubly so."

Hasimi Thorp moved on Boon then, faster than anyone could prevent. Will and Paul eyed one another helplessly, both realizing at the same moment that their friendship couldn't put the brakes on what hot words had inflamed. Hasimi snatched a large frozen fish by the tail off the nearest display table and smacked Boon's face with it. Boon, stunned by the assault for a moment, gathered his wits and responded, scooping up another fish and throwing it at Hasimi. Naghmeh reacted quickly, grabbing two fish and tossing them both at Boon's head.

Chaos broke loose, as every member of both squadrons— except Will and Paul, who fruitlessly tried to bring their friends under control—started pelting one another with cold wet seafood. Felicia was cod-walloped, flounder flew, grouper and herring were hurled. Naghmeh pummeled Dennis with a sea bass, while Estresor Fil chucked fistfuls of king crab legs at her. Will recognized what was happening—stress, pressure, and all the tensions of the week exploding into insane release. He was a little worried about injury—those half-frozen fish could be hard, and already he could see blood flowing where Dennis and Ross had been cut—but he figured all in all they would have some innocent fun that would dissipate their anxieties. He was almost tempted to join in.

But that was before he saw the uniformed police officers circling them, phasers out—set to stun, Will hoped, considering the nonlethal nature of the combat. "Guys!" he shouted, and then much louder, "Zeta Squadron, attention!"

That did the trick, for his group at least. They snapped to, well trained enough to respond appropriately to the command. Their sudden surrender alerted Omega Squadron to the presence of the police, as well. Fish were returned to their rightful spots on the display tables, but the damage was done: seafood parts littered the ground, and the cadets—even Paul and Will, who had stood by without participating—were covered in scales and guts and fishy residue.

One of the police officers, who seemed to be in charge, separated herself from the pack and stepped forward, holstering her weapon. "What's going on here?" she demanded, her nose wrinkling involuntarily at the stink.

"Sir, we're cadets from Starfleet Academy," Paul explained quickly. "We're on a special project, and, well, I guess we got carried away with the competitive spirit. Obviously, we'll reimburse for any damages."

"You will at that," the police officer agreed. "And if I had my way, you'd serve some time as well. But if you're all from the Academy, I think I'll just turn you over to Starfleet Security and let them deal with you. Save me some time and trouble."

"Just wonderful," Boon muttered, but Estresor Fil silenced him by stomping down on his instep.

"You shut up, Boon," she hissed. "You got us into this."

The police officers herded both squadrons to a waiting transport vehicle. Just before leaving the Fish Market stall,

Will set down the canister he had held onto throughout the whole fish fight, and pocketed the slip of paper that had issued from it. He had already memorized its brief message: "Congratulations, Zeta Squadron, on the successful completion of your mission."

Superintendent Vyrek perused her ten charges with the keen eye of an experienced appraiser. They all stood shoulder to shoulder, at attention, in her office, feeling her gaze bore into them as she paced a slow, even circle around them. She hadn't spoken yet. The longer she dragged out the time before she did speak, Will knew, the worse it would be. And she would speak eventually, there was no question of that.

Admiral Paris, who waited in a corner of the large office, just might have a few words to say as well.

Finally, the Vulcan superintendent broke her silence. "I *am* surprised at you," she said. "Some more than others, but nonetheless, as squadrons overall, yours are among the last two I would have expected to engage in . . . would 'hijinks' be the appropriate term? . . . like these. Mr. Boon, Zeta Squadron is under your command, is it not?"

"Yes, sir, normally that is, sir," Boon answered. "But sometimes on group projects we elect a leader just for that project, so everyone gets a chance, sir. On this one, Cadet Haynes was in charge."

"Dennis Haynes?" Superintendent Vyrek asked with surprise. "You have never been involved with anything like this in your time with us. Or at your previous school, if you don't count—which I won't—that one incident when you were eleven."

Does she know everything *about us?* Will wondered. He'd heard rumors that she had a virtually eidetic memory—that she read through each cadet's file once a year, and remembered everything she saw. He had always discounted the rumors, though. Until just now.

"No, sir, I haven't," Dennis replied. "And I'm sorry that this happ—"

She cut him off mid-word. "Did I ask for a response, Mr. Haynes?"

He hesitated, as if unsure if she had this time either. "No, sir," he finally said.

"That is correct. I am merely expressing my shock and dismay at this outrageous behavior, not asking you to explain—or worse, make some feeble and doomed attempt to excuse—it."

Dennis remained silent, but his cheeks went crimson. Superintendent Vyrek continued her journey around the group, looking each cadet up and down, sometimes moving closer to peer at a fish-inflicted bruise or scrape.

"Is there anything remotely logical about battling with seafood, Admiral Paris, to your knowledge?"

Admiral Paris looked surprised to be spoken to, and Will had the impression that he wasn't much more comfortable in the superintendent's presence than the cadets were. "I confess that I don't see the logic in it, Admiral Vyrek," he replied.

"Nor do I," the Vulcan said. "And yet, it happened. These cadets—second-year cadets, not raw freshmen—engaged in it. Creating a disturbance, damaging property, wasting food—that police officer said she was tempted to charge them with incitement to riot. How does one explain such behavior?"

Will swallowed hard. "May I speak, sir?" he asked.

"Cadet Riker. If you can enlighten me, I would be delighted to have you speak. You, I am sorry to say, I am not terribly surprised to hear were involved in such an unfortunate affair, given your history of altercations with fellow students."

Those "altercations" she mentioned had been a series of fights Will had found himself having shortly after his father had abandoned him. He'd had a chip on his shoulder and a short fuse, and it had been a bad combination. But that had been well before he'd even applied to the Academy, and the fact that the superintendent knew about it gave even more credence to the eidetic memory theory. Not to mention confirming the "permanence" of permanent records.

"I don't think our behavior can be excused, sir," he said. "But it can be explained, to a certain extent. We were all under a significant amount of stress, with the end of our project looming, and the various personality conflicts that arise whenever a group of people is banded together closely for a number of days. We made a mistake, let our emotions get the better of us, and cut loose. We shouldn't have done it. Had we thought it through we never would have done it. But we weren't thinking, we were only reacting."

"That sounds correct," Superintendent Vyrek said. "Especially the fact that you were not thinking, any of you."

"Yes, sir," Will agreed.

"Interestingly, my understanding from the officer is that you were not taking part, Mr. Riker. Nor was Mr. Rice. Is this true?"

Will wanted to glance at Paul but he forced his head to remain still, eyes front. "Yes, sir. We were not fighting. However, we were apparently not doing enough to restrain our fellow cadets, either."

"Should you have done more? Was that your duty?"

"Sir, if the fight had been with deadly weapons instead of fish, then it would certainly have been an abrogation of duty to let our fellow cadets become involved. I think that the principle is the same, regardless of the weaponry."

"I have to agree with you, Mr. Riker. You and Cadet Rice are every bit as responsible as those who were flinging fish. You will all jointly work to reimburse the fishmongers whose stand you destroyed. There will, of course, be notations on your permanent records. And your summer plans will be altered—none of you will be going off-world this summer, so I hope you were not looking forward too strongly to any long trips. Admiral Paris?"

Will felt his heart sinking as the admiral stepped forward to face his students. "I won't apply any further punishment to what the superintendent has outlined," he said. "However, as Omega Squadron didn't finish the assignment, the five of you will be repeating my survival class next year. Zeta Squadron, you completed your assignment—narrowly—before the altercation started, so your grades will stand. Congratulations to you."

"Thank you, sir," Boon said on behalf of the squadron.

"Have any of you anything to add?" Superintendent Vyrek asked. When the cadets remained silent, she fixed them with her sternest glare and said, "Dismissed."

They began to file from the office, but Will, last in the line, felt Admiral Paris's firm grasp on his arm. "Will," he said. "I'd like a moment."

"Of course, sir," Will replied. The others glanced back at him, but kept going out the door. Will couldn't blame them—he felt the compulsion to flee as well, but knew that he had to see what Paris wanted. When they were gone and Superintendent Vyrek had taken her seat, the admiral fixed Will with a somber gaze.

"I understand that you and your father aren't close, Will," he said. "But I'm a little worried about him. He's been the apparent target of a couple of recent attacks. After the last one, he vanished from our infirmary and hasn't been seen since. He hasn't shown up at his office, and whenever we've checked his apartment he hasn't been there either. Have you heard anything from him?"

"No, sir," Will answered. "Before we left on the project, a couple of security officers came to my room looking for him. I told them the same thing."

"*Before* you left?" Admiral Paris echoed.

"That's right, sir. Early that morning."

"Interesting," the older man said. "And you don't have any idea where he might have gone?"

"As you said, sir, we don't talk much."

"Yes, that's right. Well, then," Admiral Paris said, "we'll keep looking for him. Try not to worry though, Will. He's a tough one, your dad. He's survived more than a few close calls in his time, and wherever he is, I'm sure he can take care of himself."

"Yes, sir," Will said.

"That's all. You're dismissed."

The door had barely closed behind Will when he heard Admiral Paris burst into gales of laughter. It sounded as if the superintendent, notwithstanding her reticent nature, was joining in. "Fish, Owen!" he heard the Vulcan say through the door. "Have you ever heard of such a thing? Fish!"

Chapter 13

As they walked away from the superintendent's office, out of the climate-controlled air and into the always-brisk San Francisco twilight, Boon grumbled and Estresor Fil expressed no emotion whatsoever and Dennis Haynes smiled, as if he'd expected the punishment to be far worse. Will, though . . . Felicia tried to put a word to the look on his face, before he'd been stopped at the door by Admiral Paris. He had looked bereft, as if a bomb had snatched away his family and friends in a single instant. She had never seen him so grim. Generally speaking, she liked his face—liked it a lot, in fact. He had sparkling, intelligent blue eyes, and a mouth that was serious but could turn funny, even goofy, in a flash, perfect cheekbones, and the cleft in his chin exuded masculinity, to her.

But in the superintendent's office, his lips had been pressed together in a tight, bloodless line, his eyes stared straight ahead blindly, and he seemed to have lost all color.

She was nearly overwhelmed by a desire to mother him, to minister to his needs and assure him that everything would be all right if only he would let her take care of him. Not that he was the dependent type—that's what made her want to do it, to play against what she knew was an independent, even solitary nature.

"We got off easy," Dennis said, his voice low as if in awe of what had occurred. "They could have expelled us."

"For getting in a fight?" Boon countered, disbelief giving his tone a harsh edge. "They'd have to expel half the student body, every year. Part of what they're teaching us to do is fight."

"When it's the right thing to do, Boon," Felicia said, feeling herself drawn into the argument in spite of herself. "As a last resort, and not just for fun."

Boon laughed. "It was fun, though, wasn't it?"

"Well, I'm glad you enjoyed yourself," she said. "Next time, spare me the pleasure."

She turned back toward the office, hoping to see Will, maybe accompany him someplace away from the others where they could talk, even make some plans for the summer now that they'd be on the same planet. But she didn't see him behind them. Felicia stopped walking, turned in a slow circle, and finally spotted him, heading away from their dorm and away from the group, over one of the low Japanese garden-style bridges.

"I think he wants to be alone," Estresor Fil noted. "It's not an uncommon response. I think I have a *Flintstones* episode that might be instructive." She had stopped too, Felicia realized, and was looking at her with those big emerald eyes. Her blank face reminded Felicia of a puppy's, to which people always seemed to impart whatever feelings they wanted to see there. She wondered suddenly if Estresor Fil had a crush on her. *Why else would she have let the other guys go on without her?*

Because she wants to make sure you're okay, stupid, she

answered herself. *It has nothing to do with a crush. Not every person's interest in every other person is romantic.*

That, she realized, glancing at Will's distant, retreating form, was a lesson she had learned many times over.

No Saturn. Will could scarcely believe the dumb luck. He'd already been tagged as a research assistant on a scientific project taking place there, and had been looking forward to it for months, and now, with the flinging of a few fish—flinging in which he hadn't even taken part—it was gone, vapor through his fingers.

He figured the rest of his squadron had already gone home by the time he was released from Superintendent Vyrek's office, but he wasn't ready to face people he knew yet. Instead, he wandered alone across the Academy campus in the dying light. Boothby, the groundskeeper, looked at him with sad eyes and slowly shook his head, wispy white hair fluttering with the motion. *So word is already out,* Will thought. *That didn't take long, did it?* Helping himself to a seat on one of the benches stationed at intervals along the paths, he watched the whirl of Academy life pass him by for a while. A cluster of cadets joked and laughed, Geordi La Forge—with his distinctive VISOR, everybody knew who Geordi was—at their center. Will knew that it was ridiculous to think he'd never be that happy again, but at this precise moment he had a hard time imagining any other fate.

He was still sitting on the bench, stewing in his own juices, as his father would have put it back in the days when they'd spoken to one another, when a first-year cadet named Arnis, a Trill female, sat down next to him. Though Arnis and Will had been friendly, they had not been especially close until both were picked for the Saturn team this coming summer. After that they'd spent a lot of time together, planning for the summer, studying the research project and the living conditions they'd face, and making guesses about their futures. She was an attractive young woman who kept her dark hair trimmed close, displaying the distinctive Trill spotting along her temples, cheeks and neck in all its glory. As she sat, she frowned at Will. "I'm so sorry, Will."

"So you've already heard, too? Is there anyone on this campus who *doesn't* know yet?"

"It's pretty much all anyone's talking about," Arnis told him. "You guys—you and Omega Squadron—are just about famous."

"Infamous, maybe," Will countered.

"Either way, it seems like everyone knows your names. You'll be signing autographs before long."

"So all you have to do to make yourself well-known is to be escorted back to campus in the custody of Starfleet Security," Will said bitterly. "After having caused property damage and wasted enough seafood to feed a large family for a month."

"Maybe it's not something to message home about," Arnis said. "Although, in your case, I guess you don't do a whole lot of messaging home to begin with. But, you know, maybe it's better to be known than not known. In time, people might forget *why* they know your name, but they won't forget your name. It could be a good thing, in the long run."

Will shrugged. "Going to Saturn would have been a good thing in the short run," he said. "Tomorrow I'll learn what my replacement posting will be, but I doubt it'll be nearly as interesting as that would have been."

"Oh, I'm sure Saturn will be boring as anything," Arnis said. Then, with a laugh, she admitted, "Okay, it won't be. But I'll pretend it is, for your sake."

He tried to smile but had a feeling it wasn't coming off quite right. "Thanks," he said. "It's just—you know, sometimes it doesn't feel like anything ever works out for me here on Earth. I don't think I was meant to be here. My destiny is out there somewhere, among the stars. Down here I'm just too landlocked."

"Will, that's not true," Arnis said sorrowfully. "You've had a rough time, I guess. But you've also got an exemplary record here at the Academy. The way you whipped that Tholian ship in the battle sim? That may go down in Academy history just as much as your little fish fray does. Okay, you got a black spot today, but overall it's still a record to be proud of. When you graduate, you'll be assigned to a starship right away, with your record, and then you're on your way."

Will knew, intellectually, that Arnis was right. But he couldn't shake the cloud of pessimism that hung over him with the near-arrest, the loss of his summer plans, and now the mystery of whatever had become of his father. It wouldn't be the first time the old man had walked away from responsibility, but Kyle Riker took his job, if nothing else, seriously, so it was odd that they hadn't heard from him. "Thanks, Arnis," he said without notable enthusiasm. "You'll keep me posted, right? Let me know what Saturn's like?"

"Of course I will," she promised. She looked out at the sky, which had grown dark while they talked, and stood up. "Hey, I'm meeting some people in the mess hall. Do you want to come with?"

Will hadn't thought about dinner, but now that she mentioned it he did notice the first stirrings of hunger. "The mess hall? Do you know what they're serving tonight?"

She hesitated for a moment. "Um . . . I think it's fish."

"I'll just get something in my room," Will said. "Thanks anyway."

Arnis gave him a half-smile and retreated to join her other friends. Zeta Squadron had scattered after the superintendent's rebuke, and Will—not for the first time in his young life—found himself feeling utterly alone.

Kyle sat on his bunk, back up against the bulkhead and his padd balanced on his lap. It wasn't very comfortable, but he was learning that nothing about the *Morning Star* had been designed for the comfort of humans. But then, there were precious few humans on the ship to be inconvenienced. He kept reminding himself that he had chosen a freighter specifically so he wouldn't have a lot of people around.

Well, he thought, *you got what you wanted. In spades.*

Ever since leaving Earth, the Starbase 311 flashbacks had lessened in frequency and severity. For that, he was profoundly grateful. But after having spent several days in no company but his own, he had decided that the best thing to do was to confront those memories in an organized way.

Someone at Starfleet, he had no doubt, was trying to ruin him at the very least, and more likely to kill him as well as ruin his reputation. He had gone over, in his own mind, all the Starfleet-related jobs he had done for the past few years, and couldn't quite make the intuitive leap from any of those to his becoming a target. That left only Starbase 311 and the Tholian massacre that had taken place there. That was the wild card, the life event that seemed most likely to have brought him to the attention of his unseen enemy.

Had the whole attack on the starbase been designed to kill him, he wondered? Was the only survivor of the assault really the target? Was someone now trying to finish the job left undone two years before? It seemed unlikely, but he had to consider every possibility. And to do that, he had to try to recall those details he had intentionally boxed away, forever, he had hoped. Somewhere in that incident the key to what was happening to him now might be buried, and if it was there he had to turn it up. So he scanned the records on his padd of his work there, and he worked on remembering.

The Tholian Assembly took the concept of territoriality to new heights. There were various theories espoused for this, but the fact was that Federation relations with the Tholians had always been marginal at best, and very little was known about their forbidding world—a Class-Y planet incapable of sustaining human life—or their culture. Tholians were believed to have very short lifespans, possibly measured in months, although there was speculation that they passed on their consciousness in some kind of crystal memory formation from one generation to the next. Whatever the psychosocial reasons, though, they didn't tend to stray far from their own territory, and they didn't like it when others encroached. That was, in fact, a huge understatement—they defended their own territory with rabid determination. As a result, most other cultures tried to keep their distance lest they raise the ire of the Tholians.

Which, given the expansive nature of the Federation, was bound to happen someday. Starbase 311, a free-floating space station, was primarily a scientific field station, in the far outreaches of the Alpha Quadrant. While its stated purposes were science and research, the fact of the matter was that it was the closest Federation outpost to Tholian space and therefore of political and possibly military significance as well. If the Tholians would accept a starbase so near Tholian space, what else might they accept? Whole regions of the Alpha Quadrant were unexplored due to the Federation's unwillingness to test the Tholian comfort zone, so 311 was intended from the outset to be somewhat of a test case.

Because of its military potential, Kyle had been assigned to the starbase to examine the situation for himself. If the Tholians permitted the starbase to function unmolested, then there might be room for further expansion, and Kyle's role was to help arrive at that determination. If, on the other hand, the Tholians objected to 311's presence, Kyle would be on the scene to help strategize a Starfleet response. Either way, his strategic expertise was needed there, and he went where he was needed.

He was there for only a couple of months, as it turned out. A couple of months—but for everyone else on the starbase, their final months. Sitting on his bunk on the Kreel'n ship, he brought up the list of those who had served on Star-

base 311 alongside him. Humans, Deltans, Rigelians, Andorians, Vulcans, Saurians . . . the sons and daughters of at least
a dozen worlds had died that day. Looking at the names
brought back flashes of memory. Li Tang, brilliant and sar-
castic; Wulthrim, whose laughter could shake the starbase
on its axis, Sul Sul Getreden, acerbic and humorless but
with an unexpected poetic streak that showed through even
on scientific reports. And so many more.

Combing the records on his padd, he noticed something
he had forgotten about completely. Most of the scientists were
fairly open about their research, and enjoyed talking about it
even with those who might not thoroughly understand their
stories. But there was a small group of scientists who claimed
their work was classified at levels even beyond that at which
Kyle was cleared, and this group remained secretive about
their experiments the whole time Kyle was on the station.
Other researchers began to suspect that they were up to something they shouldn't be—genetic engineering experiments,
strictly forbidden by Federation law, was the rumor. Now that
he thought about it, he remembered the conversation he had
with Simon Urs-Sistal, the half-Aurelian physicist who had
confided in him.

"I'm just not sure what to do about it," Simon had said to
him. They'd been sitting together at a table in the starbase's
lounge, some distance away from anyone else, hunched over
their drinks and talking in low tones. Kyle had known from
the outset that this was a conversation Simon wanted to have
in private, but he said it had to be in a public place, because
anyone's quarters might be bugged. That had piqued Kyle's
curiosity, and the story Simon told once they huddled in the
lounge had more than lived up to it.

"Report it," Kyle said simply. "What else can you do?"

"The thing is, these are only suspicions," Simon said. Au-
relians were humanoid but with a skull crest that came to a
point at the top rear of their heads, and Simon had inherited

that feature from his Aurelian mother. In times of stress—as now—he had a tendency to scratch at the base of the crest, as if to soothe an itch. "I can't prove a bit of it. What Roone and Heidl and the others are up to in there, none of us know for sure. But that in itself concerns us."

"Because the rest of you know what you're all working on?" Kyle asked.

"Exactly," Simon replied. "I'm assessing the intersection of pulse theory with superstrings—the idea that subatomic pulses can travel on the superstrings that bind all matter in the universe. Theoretically, this could give us instantaneous communication across vast distances, and possibly even, at some point, virtually unlimited transporter potential. Much faster and more efficient than subspace communication. I stress that it's all very theoretical at this point. I'm interested in pure research, not necessarily the practical applications of the research, and this is a good place to do it. But the point is that everyone knows what I'm working on. We talk, we share ideas. A biogeneticist might have a brainstorm that will help me in my work, and by the same token I might give her an idea as well."

Simon paused, scratching at his crest like he was trying to excavate it. His sunken eyes looked into Kyle's meaningfully. Kyle was silent—Simon had a lot on his mind, and he'd spill it, given time—and waited. Finally, Simon continued. "But those guys—Heidl especially, but also Roone and what's his name, Latriso Bistwinela—they're so secretive you'd think they were working for the other side. They're not, I'm sure— they came on Starfleet ships, and their research seems to have Federation support—but their attitude is such that it worries me. And then, from what little I've been able to glean by talking to other researchers, I'm not sure the Federation is precisely sure what it's supporting in that lab."

"What do you mean?" asked Kyle.

"This far from home, it's very hard for the Federation to

keep real tabs on anything. Yes, we send back reports and data, but reports can say anything we want them to, and data can be doctored. Falsified. I could say I'm working with sub-atomic pulses in deep space, while really I could be spending my days with holodeck simulations of Orion slave girls. It's unlikely that anyone at Federation headquarters under-stands much of what my data shows anyway, so they believe what I tell them, for the most part."

"So you think that team is working on something other than what they say they're working on?"

"That's the thing, Kyle. They don't even have a cover story. It would be the easiest thing in the world for them to tell us they're performing some simple experiment or other. But we might ask them how it's going, or offer suggestions. They don't seem to want even that much interaction with the rest of us, so they just don't say anything. But Jenkins and Kauffman see the bills of lading from materials that arrive on every Starfleet vessel, and those materials suggest that there might be some genetic manipulation going on."

"Which is frowned upon," Kyle suggested.

"Which is absolutely illegal." Simon had raised his voice unconsciously, and now he glanced around to see if anyone had noticed. "Illegal," he repeated, more softly.

"Which is why you should report it."

"Yes, yes," Simon agreed. "I should. I will, Kyle. I mean, I have no definitive proof. But I have my beliefs, and those of several other prominent scientists on this base. We can ask that Roone and his crew be investigated—not that they've necessarily done anything wrong, but if they haven't then they have nothing to fear, right?"

"Makes sense to me," Kyle had said.

And report it, Simon had, Kyle remembered. The Federa-tion officials had taken it seriously enough that a hearing had been scheduled, and Starfleet sent a ship out to 311 with an investigative team on board. The team had arrived at the starbase, and the starship—the *Berlin*, an *Excelsior*-class ship, Kyle recalled—had made arrangements to come back in several days to pick the team up.

But the day after the team arrived—the day the scientists were to explain what they'd been working on—was also the day the Tholians attacked. At the time, Kyle thought the attack had been prompted by the *Berlin*'s visit, as if the Tholians, barely able to tolerate a starbase, had been set off by the unexpected arrival of a heavy cruiser, instead of the smaller *Oberth*-class ships usually used to supply the station.

Whatever had prompted the attack, it had come suddenly and without notice, almost as soon as the *Berlin* was too far away to return in time to help. Tholian warship activity in the sector was commonplace, as would be expected so close to their well-defended boundaries, so no one gave much thought to the approach of six ships until they crossed out of Tholian Assembly space and neared 311.

Kyle had been sleeping in his quarters when the Tholians had come close enough to raise alarms. He'd been called to the starbase's command center, and by the time the turbolift got him there a red alert had been issued. Klaxons blared, flashing red lights declared a state of emergency, and Starfleet officers ran to their battle stations. This was precisely why Kyle was stationed here.

But the assumption had been that any Tholian incursion would come after a breakdown in negotiations, or after some aggressive posturing on their part. None of their battle simulations had included a seemingly unprecipitated attack out of thin air. Starbase 311, being primarily science and research oriented, had shields and phaser banks and photon torpedoes, but that was the extent of their defensive systems.

When Kyle reached the command center, the first of the Tholian ships were heaving into view near the starbase. Powerful red lights from their ships shone brightly—Kyle's first thought was that they were already firing, but it turned out not to be weapons fire. He was never sure what it was—just illuminating their target, he guessed. But so much about the Tholians would remain a mystery to him. Whatever it was, when the first one appeared, Commander Bisbee, the ranking officer, looked at the red circle of light and said, "Looks like sunset over the Pacific."

"I don't like the sound of that," Kyle had rejoined. "Sounds too final."

Then the other ships pulled into position. Kyle had immediately started shouting suggestions to Bisbee, and Bisbee had instituted those as orders. Two Tholian ships were quickly knocked out of commission.

Two more, though, had started spinning an updated version of the famous Tholian web around the starbase. This web, instead of being a simple energy construct, had the additional effect of disrupting the station's electronic systems. A message had gone out to the *Berlin* as one of the very first acts when the Tholians approached, but no one was at all sure if it had been received or if further messages were going out. Then other systems began failing—shields, intrabase communications, environment, weapons. As the Tholians began constricting their web, the starbase was rocked violently back and forth, slamming occupants and equipment alike into walls and floors. Sparks flew and control consoles burst into flames, and Kyle saw an ensign he knew cut in half by a computer bank ripped from its moorings and hurled into the young officer, crushing her against a bulkhead.

The two remaining Tholian ships pounded the starbase with phasers and plasma cannons. Kyle watched in horror as those around him died. Commander Bisbee was standing too close to a tactical systems control panel when it exploded, and a shard of tripolymer composite sliced through his carotid, fountaining blood across the room. The same explosion blinded Aikins, the security chief.

Starbase 311 consisted of two main rings built around a

central core, which held power generation facilities. Kyle had often thought of it as two rings on a single finger, with just a little space between them. The upper ring was operational, and included engineering, navigation, and tactical departments, while the lower ring was the province of the scientists and researchers for whom the station had been built. During the attack, when comm systems were coming in and going out seemingly at random, Kyle heard a few moments of absolute panic as the Tholian cannons focused on the lower ring. Someone—he had always thought it was Simon, though he could never be sure—had tried to take control of the situation, though it was already hopeless. *"Take cover!"* the frightened voice had commanded. *"Get behind something and hold on! It'll be over in a few minutes!"*

Other voices had screamed dissent, but the voice Kyle believed was Simon's had overruled them. *"I'm telling you, your best chance is to move into—"*

But then that part of the lower ring had been breached. For a second Kyle heard the screaming of metal and polymers, then a great whooshing sound, and then nothing at all. Everyone in that chamber had been blown out into the vacuum of space.

And still the Tholians came. Kyle thought there might yet be a chance if they could focus the starbase's phaser arrays on the energy generators the Tholians used to create the web, but that would have required scanning the attacking ships to find those generators, and the scanners had all been knocked out of commission by the web. As had the phaser arrays, for that matter.

Even as he ticked through the possibilities in his head, Kyle realized that there was almost no one left alive to carry out any strategy he might create. Then the command center was rocked by a singularly powerful blast and Kyle's feet went out from under him. His head smashed against an ops console and then against something else—bulkhead or floor or ceiling, he had no idea. He saw a brilliant flash of light, then he saw nothing for an indeterminable period of time.

When he woke up, he tasted blood. He pushed himself to a sitting position and blinked his eyes open, spat blood onto the floor, fighting off a wave of nausea. Command was full of smoke; his lungs burned with it.

But at least he could sit up. Everyone else was dead.

On a flickering viewscreen he could see a Tholian ship, its red lights completely washing the starbase, so near that a tiny portion of the ship blocked the entire screen. He tried to ignore the frightening image as he stumbled from one corpse to the next, checking for pulses, listening for any faint breath. It was no good, though. Kyle's heart was the only one that still pounded: so loud he thought the Tholians would hear it from their ships. And he was in bad shape, himself—his left arm and shoulder had been crushed, his scalp lacerated. Burns covered much of his body, and he felt unbelievably thirsty. Something had torn open his right leg almost to the bone.

Giving up on the command center, he left it, limping into the hallways to see if there was anyone alive elsewhere on the ship. He had barely taken a dozen steps when he heard what was unmistakably a human voice. But it was raised in an inhuman scream. Kyle stumbled toward it, drawing a phaser pistol he'd strapped on at the first sign of trouble. As he rounded a corner, he saw Lieutenant Michaud on her knees, tears streaming down her face, and behind her, a Tholian pointing what looked like a crooked stick at her. But it was a crooked stick that spat death in the form of a searing red ray. While Kyle watched, helpless, Michaud's chest exploded, blood and gore spilling onto the floor even as she fell.

Kyle trained his phaser on the Tholian and squeezed the trigger. The Tholian was large, completely enclosed in a thermal suit that would enable it to survive in what must have been, to it, wretched cold. Its helmet was a faceted, crystalline mass of planes that Kyle couldn't even really focus on; it was like trying to pick out one plane of a diamond that was spinning in a centrifuge. But he held his phaser on it, and the creature buckled, emitting a terrible, screeching noise that Kyle thought would surely rupture his eardrums, and died. When its suit burst with an explosive boom it issued a blast of heat so powerful that Kyle could feel it, like a desert wind.

Another Tholian, alerted by the first one's death shriek, appeared at the other end of the hall and took aim at Kyle. But Kyle fired first, and this one fell too. To ease the spatial dissonance that could be caused by living inside a doughnut, the inner hallways of the rings had been constructed as short, straight segments with definite corners. Kyle approached the next corner with caution, and peeked around it, over the corpse of the Tholian he had just shot. His phaser was held in two hands, to steady it against his own shaking. The alien's internal heat, leaking out through the phaser hole in its suit, was already almost unbearable, and as soon as he had determined that the coast was clear, Kyle hobbled, as fast as his broken body would carry him, to the next corner.

And that was when he knew he was doomed. A pack of them loomed at the far end, all bizarre-looking and carrying those sinister sticks. Kyle stayed close to his corner and fired into the pack. He knew he hit several, but the red beams started shredding the wall that was his only protection, and after a moment he turned and ran. He couldn't get near the last corner he had passed—the Tholian was already so hot that the polymer bulkheads were melting around it. Instead, he slipped through a door that led to the central core, the "finger" of the space station.

He tried to run, but he was weakening. Behind him, he heard the Tholians following. He kept listening for voices: human voices, friendly ones, anything but the strident screeching of the Tholians, but he heard none. Instead of running, he took refuge in a Jefferies tube, descending several levels and then tucking himself away, phaser at the ready, and waiting.

It seemed to take hours. He could hear the Tholians moving through the core, blasting through walls, knocking down doors, tearing open the tubes. Every now and then he thought he heard a non-Tholian voice, but each time he did it was screaming in agony, until he no longer wanted to hear them. He began to hope that everyone was already dead so their suffering would end. He began to wonder if he should finish himself, as well: if a phaser blast to the head would be less painful than sitting and waiting and finally succumbing to one of those sticks.

But he couldn't bring himself to do it. He was Kyle Riker, a survivor from way back, from a long line of survivors. His great-great-grandfather, the stories went, had led the residents of a small Wyoming town safely through the grim days of World War III, fighting off the marauding bands of refugees that had combed the nation's wild places in those days, as well as the radiation poisoning that had killed millions. The town had lost two residents, both to exposure during a particularly long, cold winter, but otherwise they had all made it through the worst days. Eventually, of course, Jamie Riker had died of old age, and many of those under his protection had gone as well, of natural causes, mostly. But the legend lived on—a Riker had persevered and kept his town alive when the rest of the world was going mad. Kyle already had failed to live up to that example, though—if the starbase was his town, he had utterly missed the mark.

Even so, he was unable to just give up. It wasn't in his nature.

And finally, they found him again. They breached the tube twenty meters from him, and he started firing as soon as the first Tholian showed his ugly crystalline face mask. At the same time, he tried to stand, to run again, but his injured muscles had frozen up, locked him in place. Stuck where he was, in a half-crouch, he tried to raise his phaser again, but it was so heavy, so heavy. . . .

Just as the red beam from a Tholian stick weapon struck him, he stumbled and fell flat, the beam slicing across his back as he landed facedown on the surface of the Jefferies tube.

Chapter 14

Kyle lost consciousness again, so he didn't see precisely when or why the Tholians left. Maybe they thought they'd killed him. Maybe the *Berlin* had come too near and it was time for them to retreat. At any rate, they'd sent their message, loud and clear. *Don't get too close to us,* they had said. From now on, Starfleet would pay attention.

Kyle had remained comatose through the whole journey on the *Berlin*. He hadn't come around until he'd been transferred to an infirmary in San Francisco, where his care had been taken over by Dr. Katherine Pulaski. She credited his own will to live for his incredible survival, in the face of enough wounds to kill several times over. He had always credited her medical skills. Yes, he had wanted to live, but until she came along he didn't have the tools to fight for life. She taught him those, and more—she gave him another reason to live, one he hadn't had since Annie had died eighteen years before.

Kate Pulaski had brought a unique combination of medical and psychological insights to his case, leavened with good humor and a powerful dose of humiliation. "You can do better than that!" he remembered her barking one day during physical therapy, when he'd wanted to give up after a dozen achingly slow laps around his room.

"I can't take another step," he had protested meekly.

"My niece can walk faster than that, and she's not even a year old yet," Kate countered tartly. "And she does it without complaining, which is something you might think about."

Kyle remembered smiling at her, although that meant lifting his head, which was also painful. "You're the devil," he had insisted. "And . . ." he searched his mind for an adequate insult, but couldn't come up with anything he hadn't already used during that session. "And you're named after a fire-fighting tool."

"It's named after me," she shot back. "Well, an ancestor, on my father's side. He's been dead for hundreds of years and I'm sure he can walk faster than you, too. Now get at least another lap done before you break down and cry like a baby."

He had complained, but he had done the lap. And the next one, and the one after that. Kate had a way to keep spurring him on to new achievements, and the persistence to not let him quit until he really couldn't go on. She had brought him back from the edge of the grave, there was no doubt of that.

Now, thinking about Kate, about Simon and Commander Bisbee and Lieutenant Michaud and Li Tang and the rest of the brave souls who had died on Starbase 311, Kyle felt his eyes threaten to fill with unexpected tears. He blinked them back, glad there was no one here to see this. It was undignified, a man crying for the dead and the lost, all these years later. An observer might see him and assume he was crying because of his memories of himself, wounded and broken, so weak that his doctor, whom he came to love, had to help him take baby steps, had to support his weight and guide him to a window so that he could see that he really had come home. Or that observer might think he was crying for that doctor, whose love he won and as quickly threw away. Their love had flamed hot for a year, a little more, but then, once he had the strength to function without her, he had somehow come to believe that she was holding him back. He wanted a career again, he wanted to matter to Starfleet, he wanted to apply the hard lessons he had learned on Starbase 311 to his craft. Being with Katherine Pulaski could only get in the way of that, tie him down, and so he had driven her away.

He dabbed at his eyes, smiling wryly at his own foolishness, and picked up the padd again. Something he had seen, scouring the records before he had distracted himself with his own memories . . .

He found it. Most of the logs of Starbase 311 had been destroyed in the Tholian attack, but portions had survived, and there was one he had never paid attention to before. A shuttle hangar log showed that in the moments before the red alert, someone had tried to launch one of the shuttles. A mechanical failure had kept it grounded, and then once the attack came, all docking bays and hangars were closed to prevent enemy incursion. There was no record as to who had tried to flee the station moments before the Tholians came, or why. But it was curious, just the same. Did someone know the attack was imminent? Who might have known that, and who would have had good reason to run?

When an idea occurred to Kyle, he tried cross-referencing with the bits of remaining logs he could access. He had also downloaded the inspection reports of the Starfleet Corps of Engineers team that went to the ruins of 311 and decommissioned her, and he checked and cross-checked those as well.

What he discovered surprised him. Heidl, Roone, and Bistwinela had not been near their lab when the attack came. Heidl's body had been found near the shuttle hangar,

Roone and Bistwinela outside the transporter room. More strangely still, when the S.C.E. team had made it into what was left of their lab, it had been dismantled. The Tholians had damaged it, as they had the rest of the station, but none of the apparatus or data that had presumably been in there before the attack was there after. The data, in fact, was never found.

Kyle felt a chill run up the back of his neck. Those three *had* been up to something, he thought. Something bad—something dangerous. Had they conspired with the Tholians, or was the timing of the attack coincidental? They were all dead; at this point, he would never know. But it caused him to wonder how much else he didn't know about Starbase 311, and the rest of the Federation as well.

He set the padd aside and stared toward a rusty patch on the wall opposite his bunk, eyes unseeing. No matter what he learned, or figured out, now, it would be a while before he could investigate further or bring it to anyone's attention.

A long while indeed.

He had just fallen asleep—sleep being one of the few ways of passing the time available to him on the *Morning Star*, in addition to talking now and then with John Abbott, exercising in his room, and his twice-daily runs up and down the long halls, with some ladder climbing thrown in for good measure—when he heard his voice being called. He hadn't even realized that his quarters had a comm system, although it only made sense.

"*Mr. Barrow*," he heard again. The creaking voice could only belong to a Kreel'n.

"Yes, what is it?" Kyle answered, assuming that whoever it was could hear him.

"*This is Captain S'K'lee*," the captain's voice said. "*I thought perhaps you'd like to visit the bridge?*"

Kyle didn't think twice. He could sleep anytime. Anyway, day and night meant nothing on board the ship. In his quarters he could turn the lights up or down at will, and the rest of the vessel was uniformly dark. And he didn't know anyone except Abbott, barely could tell one Kreel'n from the next, so similar did they look to his untrained eye, so he couldn't measure time of day by crew members' shifts. As the weeks had passed, trying to keep track of time had seemed less and less important. He slept when he was tired, he ate when he was hungry, and the rest of the time he tried to keep occupied, mentally, physically, or both. "I would be most interested," he replied, grateful for the diversion.

"Come up, then," S'K'lee told him. *"I will expect you shortly."* There was a barely audible click as she broke the connection. Like most of the other systems on this ship, communications seemed to be operated with fairly ancient technology. Kyle wouldn't have been too surprised to look underneath the *Morning Star* and see a couple of sets of wheels there for landings.

But the door opened when he worked the complicated opening mechanism, so he stepped into the dim, utilitarian corridor and tried to remember where the bridge was. He had only a vague mental image of the ship's layout, even after all his days on board. The ship didn't seem to have anywhere near the clean lines of the Starfleet vessels he was used to, but instead it was bulky, almost boxy, with a massive, squared-off bow, tapering slightly toward the stern. He'd been told that she could move fast when she needed to but he had a hard time believing it.

The bridge, he knew, was in a separate dome section that jutted out from the top, not far back from the bow, breaking the line of the ship like an afterthought. Which meant that Kyle had to work his way in that direction. Assuming the artificial gravity was standard, the ladders would take him up. If, however, that assumption was wrong, he might be going in entirely the wrong direction.

But he was in luck. The ship's gravity was indeed Earth-like, and what felt like up to him was indeed up. After several minutes of searching he found what must have been the topmost deck, and then he ran across one of the more humanoid crew members in the corridor, a female with sleek fur like a panther's, black spots underneath. "I'm looking for the bridge," he said. "Captain S'K'lee invited me up."

She looked at him for a moment as if surprised he could speak at all, then tilted her head toward the ceiling and wandered away. He wasn't sure if she was indicating that he should continue going up, or if it was some form of shrug. At any rate, he was back on his own again, and he roamed through the corridor until he heard a familiar voice behind him.

"Mr. Barrow," John Abbott boomed jovially.

"Mr. Abbott," Kyle said. "I'm looking for the bridge."

"S'K'lee must be having a party," John said. "She's asked me up as well."

"I've been curious," Kyle said. "Have you ever seen S'K'lee pilot the ship?"

"Of course, many times," Abbott replied.

"How does she do it?" Kyle wondered. "You know, being blind."

"That, my friend, is something she'll have to explain to you. It's beyond me. Just follow me, and all will be revealed."

He led Kyle up the corridor he'd been walking down, then fiddled with a gearlike contraption on the wall that Kyle would have had no idea how to use. With a soft hiss, a panel slid open, revealing a wide staircase—its stairs short and close together, like the ship's ladder rungs—leading up to a large, domed space that Kyle knew must be the bridge.

"Guests on the bridge," Abbott shouted when they were halfway up. Kyle was just able to see crew members, mostly Kreel'n of course, moving about the bridge or working at various stations. The control panels he could see looked much as they had on other starships he'd visited, if a little more primitive. The walls and ceiling of the dome were all transparent and the spacescape beyond was quite beautiful.

Captain S'K'lee spun around in her chair, which was positioned in the dead center of the round room. "Welcome," she squeaked.

"Captain," John said before Kyle could even open his mouth. "Mr. Barrow here doesn't believe you can fly this bucket."

Kyle shot the man an angry glance. "That's not precisely the way I put it," he explained quickly. "I just asked how you could pilot, since, as I understand it, ships' captains voluntarily undergo surgical blinding."

S'K'lee made her laughing noise again, long and loud. "Visiting a museum once, when I was much younger, I put on a special helmet that reputedly approximated the visual acuity of humans," she said when she had brought her laughter under control. "I was astonished that you even think you *can* see. By our standards, you're quite blind yourself, even at your optimum."

She could be right, he supposed. With six eyes ringing half their heads, at the very least a Kreel'n's field of vision would be much greater. And he supposed there could be advantages to depth perception, possibly making them more adept at judging distances, and maybe better able to shift from close to distant focus.

"Even so," he said. "At least I can look out the viewscreen and see what's ahead of me." John Abbott, he noted, stood by silently, occasionally nodding to himself. He'd heard all this before.

"Your way of seeing—even our way—just gets in the way when doing complicated flying," S'K'lee said. "My ship's instruments tell me everything I need to know. In a tricky situation, the momentary gap between perception and response could be fatal, if I relied on my vision. But when I rely on the ship's perceptions and responses, the possibility of error is all but eliminated. Seeing would only endanger the ship and crew, making me more likely to trust my own senses instead of my instruments, if they should be at odds. Hence, the blinding procedure."

"Still," Kyle said. "If the ship's crew can see, it must be a bit harrowing to them when you're at the helm in a tight spot."

S'K'lee fixed some of her dead black eyes on him as if she were looking at him. "They trust," she said simply. "They trust."

Kyle glanced about at the ship's officers, going about their routines now. They looked capable enough, and he'd had no problems with S'K'lee's flying when they left the space station. And certainly in his years, he'd encountered much stranger things. "Thank you," he said. "For the explanation."

"I'm afraid I have something else to explain to you," S'K'lee said. Kyle was no expert, but the tone of her scratchy, squealy voice seemed to have changed a little. He couldn't make out what this change might signify, though.

"What is it?"

"You can't see it," S'K'lee said with a grimace that Kyle took to be a smile, "because it's beneath us just now. But we've been hailed by a Starfleet ship—the *LaSalle*, I believe its captain said it was."

Kyle felt his heart slam against his ribcage like a wild beast vying for release. Suddenly dizzy, he reached for the nearest control podium and held on for support. Hoping no one had noticed, he glanced over at John Abbott, who still watched S'K'lee, apparently unconcerned.

"Hailed?" Kyle managed to croak out. "Why?"

"According to its captain, we're harboring a fugitive," S'K'lee said. "I, of course, told them we were doing no such thing and invited them to beam aboard and search us if they chose."

"And their response?" John asked.

"They'll have a security squad here in ten minutes," S'K'lee replied. "I stalled them for a while, but I thought it best to warn you both. Just in case."

"I'm sure it's some kind of mistake," John said.

"Of course," S'K'lee agreed.

"I'll return to my cabin, then."

"As you wish," S'K'lee told him. "And you, Mr. Barrow?"

"I . . . uh, I'll do the same," Kyle said. He felt like his world was turning upside down, like the temporary sense of security he had enjoyed had been suddenly shattered. In a blurry haze, he followed John Abbott off the bridge and down a succession of ladders. Finally, John looked back at him, as if surprised to see that he was still there.

"You passed your deck a while back, Barrow," he said abruptly. He seemed a bit winded now, though Kyle thought that might have been because he'd been hurrying down ladders barely wide enough for his bulk.

"Oh," Kyle said dumbly. "I . . . I guess I lost count."

"Got you a bit nervous?" John asked with a grin.

"Well, you know. The idea that there might be a fugitive on the ship, it's a little frightening."

John touched his chin and nodded. "It certainly is," he said.

"I guess I should go back up then. To my own cabin," Kyle said.

"I suppose. When this is all over, we'll have a drink and laugh about it."

"It's a deal," Kyle agreed. He climbed back up to his own deck and found his own cramped quarters. *But should I bother going in?* he wondered, half-panicked. *Should I run? To where? Surely they've already scanned the ship, they know there are only two human passengers aboard. If I ran, all I could do would be to get myself lost, but I couldn't hide from them for long.*

He sat down on the edge of his bed, breathing deeply and trying to calm his fears. The captain hadn't specified that the fugitive was human, had she? Starfleet might have any number of reasons for seeking out anyone on board such a big vessel. And at least he hadn't begun having Tholian flashbacks again, he realized with some satisfaction. There was that much to be grateful for.

But he couldn't shake the certainty that they had come for him. He was still sitting there, trying not to think about what the Starfleet Security team might have in store for him, when there was a knock at the door to his room. "Come in," he said, and the door hissed open.

Two uniformed security officers, one an average-sized human female and the other a yellow-skinned being so tall he had to stoop his shoulders to avoid hitting his massive, shaggy head against the passageway's ceiling, peered at him through the open door but didn't enter. "Mr. Barrow?" the human woman asked.

"That's right," Kyle said.

"Mind if we ask you a few questions?"

"That depends," he answered, plastering a quick grin on his face to defuse the defensiveness of his response. "What about?"

"Did you know the man who called himself John Abbott?"

Kyle picked up on the past tense reference right away. "What do you mean, 'did' I? Of course I know him."

"How well?"

"Has something happened to him?" Kyle demanded.

The shaggy yellow creature spoke for the first time, his voice deep and rumbling with menace. "Please just answer our questions, Mr. Barrow. It'll be easier on everyone."

The woman flicked her eyes toward her partner, and Kyle got the impression that their working styles were not always in smooth confluence. "I'm afraid that Mr. Abbott took his own life," she explained, sounding sympathetic. "When he heard we had come for him."

"Took his own life? Why?" Kyle asked, already forgetting the tall one's warning.

The woman blew out a sigh. "How well did you know him?" she asked again.

"Just casually," Kyle replied. "We were the only humans on the ship. We had a few drinks together, had a chat from time to time. I didn't know him before we met during the trip, and wouldn't consider him a friend. But I'm sorry to hear that he's dead. Was he in some kind of trouble?"

"You could say that," the tall yellow officer said. "Abbott was a killer. In his cargo, we've found parts belonging to at least a dozen different bodies. But the captain of this ship says that a couple of her crew members have gone missing in recent weeks, and now she's worried that he might have been continuing his spree on board."

"You don't mind if we have a look around in here?" the woman asked. Her tricorder had already appeared in her hand.

Kyle stepped away from the door to let them in. The yellow alien had to bend over uncomfortably far to fit beneath the low jamb, ducking like a palm tree in a hurricane, or a snow-laden fir. "Not at all," he said, his mind racing to determine if there were anything in the room that might point to his real identity. As long as they didn't try to access his padd, he thought he'd be okay.

Both officers ran their tricorders across the room—scanning for body parts, Kyle guessed, though he couldn't be sure if any of their outlandish story had even been true. When they were finished they locked eyes and shared a shrug.

"You're not making this up?" Kyle asked. "About Abbott and the bodies?"

"It's not our job to tell spooky stories," the yellow one said. "Abbott wouldn't have told you any, would he? Maybe let on where he stashed his newest victims?"

Kyle shook his head grimly. "This is the first I've heard of anything like that," he said. "He seemed like a nice enough fellow to me."

"That's what they always say about the worst ones," the woman told her companion. "Thanks for your cooperation, Mr. Barrow. Sorry to disturb you. Enjoy the rest of your trip."

They both stepped from the room, the tall one scrunching himself down again to get out, and the door closed behind them. In the wake of their visit, Kyle found himself at once astonished and terrified. He had known that Abbott was a phony name, of course, but had thought maybe the man was a smuggler or something. Certainly nothing as sinister as a killer.

As he sat back down on the bed, he realized that the other thing Abbott had been was the only other human being he had spoken with on the *Morning Star*. Now there was no one on the ship but the crew, mostly Kreel'n, who had shown no indication of wanting to interact with him at all.

You wanted to be left alone, he told himself. *Congratulations. It doesn't get much more alone than this.*

Where is he?
He's everywhere. He's nowhere.
What does that mean?
No one has seen him. There have been no records of his showing up anyplace—he hasn't been home, he hasn't been to

his office, he hasn't been near Headquarters. But his padd's GPS shows that he's everyplace from Venus to Taipei to Taurus II. Every reading comes from someplace different. It's as if he's completely vanished.

That's impossible!

Exactly my point. We've lost him, or he's lost himself. Either way . . .

But . . . but I want him! I want to see him squirm, see him suffer. I want him crushed! There's a high price that needs to be paid, and Kyle Riker is the one to pay it!

I'm not resting . . . I won't rest, until he's found. And punished.

Yes, punished . . .

PART TWO

FEBRUARY—MAY
2356

Chapter 15

The sun set late on Hazimot, which was one of many reasons why Kyle liked it there. Eighteen hours of sunlight in a row reminded him of the Alaskan summer, that golden time of year when you remembered why you put up with Alaskan winters. Of course, Hazimot was hotter than Alaska, even Valdez in midsummer. It had its sun, technically a star known as Iamme IV, and then it had a secondary sun, Myetra, much farther away but still near enough to cast light and some warmth down on Hazimot's arid surface. The conflicting gravitational fields gave all the system's planets skewed orbits, and there were long winters on Hazimot that were much colder than Alaska's. But the next one wouldn't come around for about twelve earth years, and Kyle didn't plan to stay that long.

Kyle was walking home from work through the twilight streets of Cozzen, one of the largest cities in the nation of Cyre, with Clantis, a Cyrian coworker. The day had been long and wearying and as Kyle walked he felt a heaviness of limbs and a weariness of muscle that left him at once tired, sore, and satisfied. Clantis, taller than him and broad, with a deep chest and massive shoulders that made him well suited to hard physical labor, had skin the color and texture of hammered copper. The months on Hazimot had bronzed

Kyle's as well, but he figured he'd never achieve the look that Clantis had.

When they reached the intersection where Kyle went one way and Clantis another, the Cyrian regarded Kyle with a bemused expression and shook his head slowly. "I can't believe you still live in that hole," he said. "You make enough, don't you, to get a real place? In a neighborhood where you don't have to fear for your life every day?"

Kyle shrugged. He had always had a facility for languages, and Cyrian had been easy for him to learn. "I guess it just suits me."

"Suits the vermin who get into your food and bedding," Clantis argued. "Not you. You're a smart guy, a hard worker. You could do better, easy."

Clantis's own home was a low, domed house in a neighborhood of similar structures, all built in the shadow of one of the great walls that surrounded Cozzen. It had seven rooms and was technologically current. Kyle, on the other hand, still lived in the place he'd found upon first arriving in Cozzen, so many months before. His building was half a dozen stories tall, one of many in its cramped district, a warren of narrow streets and abandoned buildings turned squatters' hovels. Kyle shared his building with a changing cast of characters, twenty or so at any given time. But rent was free and, more important, no one asked difficult questions there or pried into one another's private affairs. Hazimot had a fairly substantial human population, and the natives were humanoid enough that blending in was easy.

"I suppose," Kyle said, noncommittal. "But I'm happy, so why worry about it?"

"Happy?" Clantis echoed. The two had grown fairly close, working side by side on the interminable public redevelopment projects that were so common in the city, and walking home together most days. *Close enough*, Kyle thought, *that he seems to be taking my life choices personally now.*

That's not good. Next thing, he might start wondering about my past.

"I don't see how you can claim to be happy," Clantis continued. "Living down there with the dregs, the losers and maggots that feed on society's droppings."

"It's not quite that bad," Kyle said with a chuckle. "Like you say, I'm a smart guy. I wouldn't put up with it if it was as bad as you describe."

"Everyone has their own standards," Clantis admitted.

"Exactly. I'll see you tomorrow, Clantis."

"See you then, Joe."

Kyle tossed off a casual wave and headed into the neighborhood called The End, because it had, once upon a time, been at the end of a long road that connected several of Cyre's cities. The name had stuck, and now had quite different connotations. Kyle's own name had not passed his lips since he left the *Morning Star* to live here; instead he had called himself Joe Brady, because it was a bland name with absolutely no resonance for him. Except for the fact that he was a mass murderer, Kyle had been a little sorry that John Abbott hadn't lived longer—while it had lasted, their relationship had been an educational one.

Kyle tried to clear his head before venturing into The End. The mazelike streets were unmarked, for the most part, the buildings nearly identical. There were vehicles on the streets, sometimes moving faster than was safe, and few sidewalks, no specially designated pedestrian areas. And, as Clantis had hinted at, it wasn't the safest neighborhood in the city. Kyle had seen dangerous neighborhoods on a number of planets, in fact, and with the possible benefit that there didn't seem to be any Tholian neighbors here, this was one of the worst.

Which made it, of course, perfect. Or as nearly so as he could hope.

Most buildings on Hazimot, it seemed, were round, or at least rounded off. By the time Kyle had been on the planet a few days, he had understood why. Another effect of the dual suns was wind, and lots of it. It slipped around the curved buildings, where more squared-off ones would have resisted and eventually been damaged in the process. When the winds blew on Hazimot, everything bowed to them.

This golden evening, though, the air was still, and The End was quiet as Kyle walked its confusing streets. A few of the locals were out, standing on the streets or sitting on the stairs of their buildings, dodging the sweltering heat that could build up inside. They watched him pass, most without comment, though there was an occasional hand raised in greeting. Poverty was rampant in this neighborhood, and most of those Kyle saw didn't have jobs to take them out of it during the long hot days, or much inside to keep them occupied at night.

After the death of John Abbott, Kyle had studied up on the Class-M planets that the *Morning Star* would be visiting. Hazimot had met his requirements in a number of ways. It was not a Federation planet, nor would it be anytime soon, Kyle was certain. It was politically unstable, with armed and economic conflict among a few superpowers and a host of lesser ones. Within Cyre there was an enormous gap between rich and poor, and the scramble for money was one of the society's most prevalent features. Kyle was reminded of the Gilded Age of the early twentieth-century United States, just before the Great Depression helped even things out.

It was not, by any means, an ideal place to live. But that made it good for Kyle. He was unlikely to run into anyone he knew, and it was unlikelier still that anyone who knew him would look for him here. Since one needed money to buy goods here, he worked, but instead of a military or government job, as he had at home, he worked at menial labor. He was paid in cash daily by contractors working for the city. If he showed up and worked, he was paid, but if he didn't that was okay too. No one sought him out, until he'd made friends with Clantis, which had happened more or less by accident. Now, if he skipped a day, Clantis noticed. Clantis invited him home, asked him over for meals with his family, took an interest in his welfare. That was just the kind of thing Kyle didn't want.

At one point, five streets came together in a starburst pattern, and the most direct route home was straight across the middle of the star. But as Kyle stepped toward the center of the intersection, a two-person transport came hurtling down the street, skating just centimeters above the surface, kicking up dust and small stones as it charged. Kyle dodged, slamming back into the nearest building, and felt the wind tear at him as it passed. He started out again, but saw a police transport coming behind, half a dozen officers inside. Living in The End, Kyle had learned the poor person's instinctive distrust of law enforcement, of police who enforced the laws made by the rich for the benefit of the rich. He hadn't, to his knowledge, broken any of the laws of the city, but still he shied away from the oncoming vehicle.

For that matter, he realized, he hadn't been breaking any laws back home when the Starfleet officers started gunning for him. So maybe that wasn't necessarily a good indicator.

As he stood there, eyes downcast, the police officers cruised past him. A dropfly, attracted by his stillness, landed on his cheek. He twitched a couple of times and the thing flew away without biting. He was glad—raising a hand toward it might have alerted the cops, and in this neighborhood you didn't want to do that if you could help it. When the police had gone from sight, he continued toward the place he had started to think of as home.

"Tough day in the ditches?" Elxenten asked when he saw Kyle climbing the three wide, curving steps toward the front door of their building. He had, in fact, been building walls all day, but the first day he'd met Elx he'd been filthy and bedraggled after a day of digging ditches for a sewage system, and that had been the Cyrian's standard greeting ever since. He shot a grin at the older man, who'd done his share of ditchdigging over the years.

"That's right," he said. "Everything okay on the home front?"

Elxenten scratched his grizzled chin and laughed. "Yeah, no trouble here."

That, Kyle had learned, was Elx's highest praise. "No trouble" was as good as his life got. He had lived on Hazimot for what Kyle estimated would have been forty Earth years, but he looked at least seventy. His hair was pure white, and sparse, and a thin coating of white fuzz covered his chin and cheeks. Like Clantis, he had copper-colored skin, but this was copper that had been tarnished for too long. "Glad to hear it," Kyle said.

"Michelle's grilling up some hesturn, if you're hungry."

"Hesturn?" Kyle echoed. "Must have been a good day." Hesturn was a kind of fish that lived in the local creeks. They were hard to catch, though, and, while considered fairly common in most parts of Cozzen, they were rare enough in The End to be notable.

"Yeah, it was," Elx said. "You should've seen her when she came in, carrying five of the ugly beasts in a bag like it was treasure, a smile as bright as Iamme on her face."

"Sorry I missed that," Kyle replied. Michelle, a human who'd been here for a few years, was a lovely woman, especially, Kyle believed, when she smiled.

"She's probably sorry you did too," Elx told him. "Lady's sweet on you, Joe."

Kyle laughed. "Right," he said sarcastically. "Because I'm such a good catch."

Elx fixed him with a clear-eyed gaze, and rose up from his seat on the steps. "Steady worker. Honest man, far as I can tell. No obvious addictions. Don't get into a lot of fights. What's wrong with that?"

"You'd have to ask Michelle," Kyle answered. "If I was her, I'd go for me in a heartbeat."

Elx clapped a hand on Kyle's shoulder that almost knocked him to the floor. As was typical with Cyrian men, Elxenten was big and powerful, with the overdeveloped shoulder muscles that made him look like he was wearing padding. "Maybe I'll just do that. After I've got a gut full of her hesturn. Let's go on back."

Kyle reached the door first and held it open for Elx, who nodded his appreciation as he passed. The building had been, in its heyday, a mundane apartment building, and still served essentially that same function today with the exception that nobody collected any rent. The front room was a lobby area, its gold paint flaked and peeling. There wasn't a corner in the place; every wall swooped and arced in reflection of the outside curvature. It was, Kyle thought, an interesting contrast to Starbase 311, which went to such trouble to hide its curved nature. Stairways wound up from the lobby to the various apartments above, and through the lobby there was a courtyard, shared with the other buildings clustered around. It was here, on a heavy grating over an open fire pit, that Michelle was grilling her fish. Kyle could see her through the small-paned double doors, the evening's last slanted rays of light slipping through a space between two buildings and striking her honey-colored hair like a fireball bursting into life. She saw him watching her and laughed, waving her tongs at him like an admonishing finger. It had been a long time since he'd known a woman so alive.

"I told you," Elx murmured behind him.

"It's just wishful thinking," Kyle rejoined. "You're too old for her so you want to live vicariously through me. But you can't do that unless I'm living in the first place."

"Got that right."

"Listen, I need a shower before I'm fit company for anyone, man, woman, or child," Kyle said. "Do me a favor, tell her I'll be along in a few minutes."

"Unless I forget about living vicariously and just run off with her myself," Elx said.

"If you do that, more power to you," Kyle offered. He had a strong hunch that Michelle and Elx would still be in the courtyard, with some of the other neighbors, when he came back downstairs. Unless he hurried, though, it was anyone's guess if there would be any of that hesturn left, and when Elx opened the double doors the scent wafted in with a cloud of smoke, sweet and intense. Kyle could almost taste the tender pink flesh of the creature, and he had to force himself to keep heading toward his own apartment and the shower he so badly needed. Between the heat, the hard work, and the wind that blew almost constantly, he came home filthy every day. The winds dried his sweat almost instantly but kept him coated with a layer of the city's dirt.

The squatters who lived in this building tried to keep it clean, but there were limits. They could only rely on the strength of their own group effort to keep out others, who might not be so careful. And no one, having turned to living here when they were unable to afford a place of their own, wanted to then impose exclusivity on it. Anyone who wanted to sleep here was welcome to do so, as long as basic rules of behavior were followed. Fortunately, there were plenty of empty buildings in The End and a few other, similar neighborhoods scattered around Cozzen.

But there was a tendency for trash and litter to build up in the common areas, and Kyle had to walk through some as he climbed the stairs to the third floor, where his place was. He kept his own apartment as clean as any he'd ever lived in, which meant that it would withstand inspection from the pickiest Starfleet admiral there was, and he made a mental note to pick up the refuse on the stairway when he came back down to get some of that hesturn.

On such an arid planet, water was a precious commodity, and it was therefore carefully regulated. Every building had its share, even those that were officially empty, because to deny access to water was tantamount to a death penalty. In return, Hazimot's citizens learned to use it sparingly. In most homes of the middle and upper classes, sonic showers were commonplace. Power derived from sun and wind was cheap and abundant, so even these squatters' tenements had power as well. As Kyle entered, his apartment recognized that the daylight was fading and lights turned on. He went to the flat's bedroom and stripped off his filthy work clothes, then into the bathroom for a quick shower.

When that was done he put on a tunic and some baggy pants of a light, cool local fabric. The clothing was meant to be comfortable in heat and still protect against the winds, and it did a good job of both. He didn't have the build of a Hazimotian, but other than that he looked like he belonged here, and he found that he liked it that way. Kyle was pleased that he had found a niche here and fit into it so well. He worked because he believed in work, believed that a person had to do a job of some kind to contribute to society. He made a little money, and most of that he contributed, anonymously, to local charities, since he didn't need much to live on.

But it still bothered him that he was so far from his real job, from Starfleet. They needed him, he was convinced, needed the services that only he could provide. On the *Morning Star*, during his month of solitude before he had disembarked on Hazimot, he had wracked his brain trying to fathom why he would have become a target. He had made plenty of enemies among Starfleet's foes, but there was nothing—*nothing*—that should have made him an enemy of Starfleet. So there was something more going on, and he couldn't figure out what it might be. He had gone over every job he'd done, every conflict on which he'd advised. And he kept coming up blank. If there was no reason for Starfleet itself to want him out of the way, he reasoned, then that left someone within Starfleet, acting for reasons of his or her own. Which meant, since he was no threat to Starfleet, that there was someone in the organization's ranks pursuing a private agenda. Which, since that agenda ran counter to Starfleet's interests, was treasonous.

Except for being unable to solve that problem, though, as the time had passed, he had felt himself healing more. He wished, from time to time, that he could talk to Kate, could describe to her how he was getting better and seek her counsel for continued improvement. The Tholian attack flashbacks faded, and he realized that there would come a day when he would even forget the details of that terrible event, as it drifted further into the past. The unreasoning fear that had propelled him off-planet had faded too. Now, he stayed away as a strategic ploy, not out of blind panic. But he remained at a standstill—he didn't want to go home until he had a plan, and he couldn't come up with a good plan until he had some sense of what he was facing.

Dressed and dried by the crisp, hot air, he went back downstairs, collecting the trash from the staircase as he went and tossing it into a recycling unit at the bottom. It was a simple chore; he couldn't understand why some folks didn't bother to do it at all.

The odor of the grilled hesturn had filled the lobby now, and other residents were coming down to see what was going on. Kyle nodded hello to a few of them, Templesmith and Blevins and Xuana, and joined the procession through the double doors out of the lobby. The suns had gone down and the firepit provided the only light, casting shadows that danced throughout the circular courtyard. Michelle had pulled her day's catch off the fire and was bent over a table, cutting them into sections, one strand of her long blond hair clamped between her lips as she concentrated.

"Smells delicious," Kyle told her as he approached.

She glanced up at him, tossing him a quick smile, then turned back to her work. "I think it is," she said. "It's just that people keep showing up, and it's getting harder and harder to get the pieces to equal sizes."

"Well, they shouldn't all be equal," Kyle said. "You caught them all, right? You should help yourself to as much as you want."

"I'm just trying to get close," Michelle insisted. "I'll have plenty, Joe, don't you worry about me."

In the light from the fire, he could see that she looked older than he had first thought. Time, work, and worry had etched lines at the corners of her mouth and eyes. But she was beautiful, there was no getting around that. Her eyes were like Annie's had been, blue as an Alaskan lake, her forehead wide and smooth, her rose petal-pink lips full. Occasionally in the time Kyle had known her, a shadow had seemed to cross her face, and her brow furrowed, eyes narrowing and lips pressing together. There was, he felt sure, something troubling her, something dark and private. He found himself wanting to know, wanting to help, and he didn't even know how to ask her about it. But then, most of those living in The End had secrets. He was certainly no exception to that rule.

Instead of prying, he found a chair in the balmy courtyard and, surrounded by the casual conversation and easy laughter of his new neighbors, he joined with the others in eating her fish.

Chapter 16

Drake Kimball, though he had retired from Starfleet a decade before, looked every inch the military officer he had once been. His silver hair was cut short and impeccably

combed, his clothing was as crisp and neat as any dress uniform, and his bearing and posture were textbook perfection.
He sometimes paced as he delivered his military history lec-
tures, for which he never used notes, but his attitude was always formal, as if he were on parade.

"Every battle is brand new," he said as he stood at the
front of the classroom, hands clasped behind his back. "But
the elements that make it up have been around forever. The
flank, the feint, the siege . . . these have been practiced since
the first bipeds picked up sticks and attacked the band next
door. You are not, ladies and gentlemen, likely to invent any
new maneuvers, any new tactics, in the course of your
Starfleet careers. So the key to success is in how you apply
the old ones, how you combine them to new effect. And that
means being thoroughly conversant in them."

This was nothing new to Will. Kimball had said basically
the same thing on the first day of class, expressing the impor-
tance of knowing military history inside and out. For his part,
Will was sure he'd finish this class near the top. He'd studied
the history of strategy and tactics on his own, ever since his father had told him bedtime stories of Napoleon and Alexander
and Hannibal. He had realized early on that he would never
be the biggest kid in school, or the strongest, or the fastest. But
he could still be big and strong and fast enough, and he could
amplify his own skills by the application of strategic thinking.

"You have, ladies and gentlemen, occasionally pleased
me, and sometimes disappointed me, with the essays I expect from you," Kimball continued. "This one will be a little
different than most. Rather than examining a particular battle or the work of a master tactician, I want you to research
an individual soldier. I want you to delve into the life and career of a man or woman who fought on the fields of battle,
famous, infamous, or unknown, and I want you to tell me,
in this essay, what that particular soldier did, right or wrong,
that resulted in victory or defeat. If the soldier you're study-

ing survived, I expect to discover why. If not, why not. Understood?"

There was a chorus of "Yes, sir" from the assembled students. Kimball gave a due date and a few more detailed instructions, and dismissed the class. Will met up with Dennis Haynes on the way out of class. "This should be kind of interesting," Dennis said. "A little different, like the old man said."

"Do you have any ideas yet?" Will asked him. "Anyone you'd like to research?"

"The first thought that came to mind was James T. Kirk," Dennis told him. "But then, I figure he'll get a dozen of those."

"You're better off picking someone less well known," Will agreed. "Less competition for original ideas, less chance that Kimball will have already reached his own conclusions."

"Harder to find source material, though," Dennis said as they walked across the open campus. "If I pick someone who's not well known."

"There are ways around that," Will told him. The sky was the color of lead, and cloudless, and the air carried that metallic, charged tang that it sometimes did when it seemed as if the weather might assert itself.

"What about you?" Dennis asked him. "Got any ideas? You're always so good at coming up with creative twists."

"I've got a couple of possibilities in mind," Will said. This was a lie, though. He had made up his mind as soon as Kimball had described the assignment. He owned, thanks to his father, the diary of an ancestor named Thaddius Riker, who had fought in the American Civil War. That's who he was going to write about—his own kin.

He and Dennis were continuing across campus toward their next class when Will noticed a familiar, dark-haired shape walking toward them. "It's Felicia," Dennis said.

"So it is," Will noted. He hadn't talked to Felicia much since the end of the last school year. He had thought that maybe she was interested in him, during Admiral Paris's survival project. But after the project's disastrous end, he had come out the superintendent's office and she had been gone, halfway across the Quad, lost in conversation with Estresor Fil. He had kind of expected her to be waiting for him, and when she wasn't he became convinced that his typical luck with women was holding, and he had only imagined that she might be attracted to him. Embarrassed by his own ineptitude, and moody and depressed at being, once again, stuck on Earth all summer, he had avoided contact with almost everyone he knew. The longer he had gone without talking to anyone, the more shy he had been when he'd seen them again. With Paul and Dennis and some of the others, he had fallen quickly back into old routines once school started up again. But with Felicia, he had never been able to overcome that double dose of awkwardness. And this year, they had no classes together. The few times he'd run into her it had been with a lot of people around, and he'd managed to avoid having an actual conversation with her.

Now as she approached, he saw on her lovely face a sly half-grin.

"Excuse me," she said, projecting a naivete that he knew was an act, but which he found somehow appealing anyway. "You look a lot like a young man I used to know. His name was Will Riker. Have you ever heard of him?"

Will had to laugh. "Yes, Felicia," he said. "Yes, I'm a big fat loser. I admit it. I'm sorry."

"I was thinking along those same lines, Cadet Riker," she said. "Though a little stronger, perhaps. Hello, Dennis."

"Hi, Felicia."

"I don't suppose you'd mind leaving Cadet Riker and me alone for a little while," she said, still directing her words to Dennis. "Will and I need to talk about how he's going to atone for his foolish and, may I say, ungentlemanly behavior."

Dennis seemed a bit flabbergasted, but she had made it clear that she was demanding this, not really asking, and he responded with his typical good humor. "I . . . uh, sure. I'll leave you two alone. Send Will's pieces back in a bag when you're done with him."

"I'll do that, and thank you for your consideration." She stood with her hands on her hips, watching Dennis get beyond earshot, then faced Will. Her stance was determined, and Will figured he was in for a severe admonishment. *Which I no doubt deserve*, he thought. *Not that that'll make it any easier to hear.* She pointed to a nearby bench, and they both sat down.

"Felicia, I—" he began, hoping to ward off the brunt of her attack with some kind of excuse. But he didn't really have one, and she didn't give him a chance to get it out anyway.

"Be quiet, William Riker, and let me talk. I get the distinct impression that you've been avoiding me, ever since September. I also have the feeling that if I hadn't made a point of 'accidentally' being outside your classroom today, I still wouldn't have seen you. What I'd like to know is what terrible crime I committed to deserve this exclusion from your life, because I must have done something."

"You . . ." Will began, and then he stopped because he didn't know where else to go. "It isn't anything *you* did, Felicia," he said. As he spoke he watched a bird struggle to lift a crust of bread nearly as large as it was. He knew how the bird felt. "I . . . I had a rough summer, I guess. And then that kind of led into a rough year. I've been busy, you know, trying to knuckle down and get my grades up."

"Even so . . ."

Will shrugged. "I guess I'm not always good at understanding women."

Felicia stared at him, open-mouthed, as if he had just emerged from a particularly disgusting cocoon. "Understanding women? It isn't like we're a separate species, much less a nonhumanoid alien life-form, Will. We're just like you, only with some different parts."

He felt duly chastised. "I guess it's those different parts that throw me off."

"You don't have to let them. It's those different parts that make things interesting. Anyway, how would you feel if you knew I had avoided you for the last six months?"

"I didn't realize you hadn't been," Will offered. "I mean, I wasn't so much avoiding you as just not seeking you out. And I thought . . ." He stopped, once again not quite sure how much he wanted to say, or in what direction he really wanted to take the conversation. "I think I thought you weren't interested in me. In being friends with me."

"Well, you were wrong. And I have looked for you, a few times. But after you didn't answer my messages during the summer, and then during the school year you never seemed to be where I could find you. I got the feeling you just didn't want to be bothered. At least, not by me."

Will found that he was smiling for the first time since they'd taken their seats on the bench. "So I'm not the only one who doesn't always understand other people."

"People are hard to understand if they don't communicate," she said. "But yes, apparently I misjudged you as well. Will you forgive me?"

"I think there's going to have to be some mutual forgiving," Will suggested.

"Maybe we should just start over from the beginning," Felicia said. She offered her hand. "Hello, Cadet. I'm Felicia Mendoza, from El Salvador, Earth."

"William T. Riker," he said with a smile. "Valdez, Alaska, Earth."

"Can we be friends, Cadet Riker?"

"I think I'd like that, Cadet Mendoza." He felt like a weight had been lifted from his shoulders that had been there since the end of school last year. The awfulness of the

summer had been compounded, he knew, by his confusion
over Felicia's feelings—or, as he understood now, his mis-
judgment of Felicia's feelings. He still didn't quite know
what had happened, but he thought that it might be better
just to let the details slip away, rather than dredging them up
and having to undergo the discomfort of facing them specifically. For now, the softness of her hand in his, her warm
smile and the light that danced in her brown eyes and the
way a strand of her dark hair rested against her olive cheek,
where it had escaped her ponytail, all conspired to make
him believe that he had come out of a long tunnel into a
glorious day.

When Felicia had dismissed him—and he'd been a little
hurt by then, because, after all, who wouldn't want to be the
other person in that triangle, the one that Felicia sent somebody away in favor of?—Dennis had taken the opportunity
to go back to his room and start searching for a soldier he
could research. But his eyes kept glazing over as he tried to
focus on his computer screen, his attention kept being
drawn to the city beyond the window. The occasional shuttlecraft flashed by, lights blinking in the darkness, and the
nighttime illumination of the city spoke of thousands of lives
being lived out there.

Felicia was a beauty, there was no doubt of that. But it
was to Will, not Felicia, that his thoughts kept wandering.
William Riker had something, some quality, that Dennis
couldn't put his finger on.

It wasn't just that Felicia obviously preferred Will to him,
though they'd both known her for about the same length of
time. Certainly Will was a handsome guy, and Dennis was a
little surprised he didn't have girlfriends all over the place.
But what got to Dennis was that, although Will struggled, he
always seemed to come out fine in the end. He had turned
his grades around, and now seemed to be on course to finish

this year near the top of their class. His other, nonacademic pursuits—athletics and extracurricular activities—were career builders that could take Will far in Starfleet. He was popular, and had made contacts among faculty, staff, and fellow students that would help him immensely in the years to come. He had never made it look effortless, but he made it look *possible*.

Dennis, on the other hand, felt as if he were drowning, like the water got deeper every day and he could barely see the sky above its surface anymore.

He had just turned back to the computer screen, intent now on finding someone he could study up on, of turning at least this one assignment into a success instead of adding it to the pile of work not-quite-done that threatened to swamp him and drown his career before it started, when there was a knock on his door. "Come in," he called.

Estresor Fil opened his door and walked in. He waved her toward his couch, and she sat down, her feet no longer touching the floor when she eased her bottom all the way back into it. "Hello, Dennis," she said as she made herself comfortable.

"Hi, Estresor Fil. What are you up to?"

She seemed surprised by the question. "Visiting," she pointed out.

"Of course," he said. "I meant . . . never mind." He was, in fact, a little surprised by her appearance. They were friends, certainly, but rarely saw one another outside their group.

"Am I disturbing your work?"

He sighed. "If I had been actually working, you might be. But so far, not."

"You would let me know if I were, right?" she asked.

"Yes, Estresor Fil. Don't worry about that. Is there some particular reason for your visit, or is it just a social call?"

She considered the question for a moment, causing Dennis to believe there was something more to it than a simple drop-in. Maybe she was uncomfortable talking about it, though. Which, given her ordinarily blunt nature, probably narrowed down the likely topics considerably.

"Social call," she finally said. "Or possibly not . . . I do, in fact, find myself in need of some assistance. Dennis, how much do you know about love and romance? Earth-style, I mean."

Dennis had had a few casual girlfriends over the years, but hardly considered himself an expert on such things. And then there was the question of why she had come to *him* with such a thing. Did Estresor Fil have a crush on him? He wasn't quite sure how he would feel about that. Complimented, certainly, but she looked just a bit too much like a praying mantis for him to be able to return the compliment. "Not really that much, I guess. I mean, I know the basics, in principle, but when it comes to putting them into practice I'm as useless as the next guy. Why do you ask?"

"It's just all so confusing to me. I try to figure these things out by myself when I can. And there's an episode of *Squirrely Squid* that is really quite helpful, I think." Dennis wasn't sure what a primitive holotoon series for children would really have to say about adult love and romance, but he knew Estresor Fil too well to point that out and he kept his doubts to himself. "But even with that, there are some things I just don't understand."

"Like what?" Dennis asked. He didn't have high hopes, but he'd be helpful if he could.

Estresor Fil crossed her ankles and broke eye contact, another indicator that she was oddly uncomfortable. "How do you tell? If someone likes you, I mean?"

Dennis had struggled with that one his whole life. Who didn't? After third or fourth grade when there was a lot of arm-punching going on—although at the time, he remembered, he had not correctly interpreted the punching either, he had been pretty much lost unless a girl actually came to him and more or less confessed her attraction. "I guess you just sort of have to know it. By the way they talk to you, the way they look at you. If they touch you a lot, you know, just casually. Or sometimes you have to come right out and ask them, I think. And always be prepared to get turned down."

"That's just so silly," Estresor Fil said. "It's so much easier for Zimonians. If we're interested in someone, that way, we simply display ourselves. If they are interested in us, they will come over and say so. If not, they pretend they didn't see the display and there's no more discussion of it. But there is no ambiguity, no wondering or trying to guess."

"By 'display,' you mean . . . ?"

"Of reproductive organs," she said, matter-of-factly.

"Yeah, that's what I was afraid of. I don't think that would go over well here," Dennis warned her. "Especially at the Academy."

"Oh, I know that," Estresor Fil reassured him. "I wasn't suggesting it, just pointing out that our way is vastly preferable to yours. When you leave it all up to guesswork, mind reading, and so on, I think you are just creating barriers to happiness. Particularly since there are so few genuine mind readers among you."

"Maybe so," Dennis admitted. "But the other way might be just a little bit distracting to those around you. Is there . . . some special person you're interested in?"

Estresor Fil still couldn't meet his eyes. "Yes," she admitted after a long moment. "All of you—humans, I mean— looked sort of funny to me when I first got here. So tall, with skin colors that are so bland, and such odd facial features. I think part of why I like your cartoons so much is that there's such variety in the characters, far more than in your actual species. But I have come to see that there is beauty among you, and one person in particular has caught my interest. I think I might be in love, but I'm not really sure how you tell. And I am definitely not sure how to tell if that person loves you back."

"If you could come up with a certain answer to that one," Dennis said, "you'd be the most popular being on the planet."

"I feel . . . shy . . . about telling you who it is," Estresor Fil said, almost in a whisper.

Dennis wanted to put her at ease if he could. Even though she had definitely unsettled him with this whole line of conversation. "Don't feel like you have to, if you're not comfortable."

"But I want to talk to someone, Dennis. Someone who may be able to help answer my questions and concerns."

"And you think I'll be able to do that?" he asked.

"Possibly. But I find myself oddly embarrassed."

Dennis wasn't sure how someone whose idea of the proper way to express romantic attraction involved the public display of reproductive organs could be embarrassed about speaking a name, but decided that was a matter for sociologists, not for him. "I'm not very judgmental," he assured her. "And I promise I won't laugh or anything. If you want to talk, I'm here to talk to."

She took a deep breath, which he found a very human thing to do, and let it out slowly. "Very well. I find myself quite taken with Felicia Mendoza. Do you think that she would ever return my interest, Dennis?"

Felicia? Dennis was in shock. He had always assumed that Felicia and Will would get together at some point, and when she had chased him away to corral Will this afternoon, he thought maybe that point would come sooner rather than later. He'd never really talked to Felicia about her love life, but he had never seen any signs, at least that he recognized, that she was attracted to the diminutive green alien with the huge popping eyes.

He could feel her gaze on him, and now he couldn't bring himself to meet it. "Am I just being foolish, Dennis?" she asked. "Do you think . . ." He could hear the hurt in her voice as she considered the possibility.

"I . . . I really don't know, Estresor Fil." That was the truth, at least. "I don't know what Felicia is looking for, that way, or who. If anyone. I've never really discussed it with her."

"So there's a chance?" Now her voice sounded hopeful, and he didn't want to be responsible for dashing that hope.

"A chance? Of course there is," he promised her. "There's always a chance." *I think.*

Riker?
Nothing. Nothing at all.
But the search continues?
Of course it does.
Friends, family, interviewed? All known prior whereabouts examined?
Except Starbase 311, of course.
Of course.
Otherwise, yes. The son, Will Riker, knows nothing. Neither does the woman.
Pulaski? The doctor?
That's right. She hasn't heard from him. She's not happy about it. They were together only a brief while. He seems to have hurt her badly.
No surprise. It's the kind of man he is. Cold, unfeeling.
It was hard to tell if she was angrier about the fact that he vanished without telling her, or about the fact that she was being asked about him.
She's a good doctor? This Pulaski?
One of our best.
Then let her live.
Are you sure? He might still have some feelings for her.
Her punishment, for caring about Riker, will come when she learns of his death.
Fitting.
It's all fitting. That's the point. It isn't truly justice if it doesn't fit the crime.

That's all I want. Justice.
That's all any of us want. Justice. And Riker's head in a box.

Chapter 17

"The land here is as God-forsaken as ever a man has set eyes upon. It is swampe, most of it, with almost no solid erth to walk on. With every step your boots sink deeper into the muck and fill with brackish water. The swampe stinks and is ful of bugs and even gaters which can bite a man before he sees it coming. Fore the last three days and nights I have never been dry but always wet and misirable. Priv. Rector pulled a leech from my neck, afternoon yesterday, and then found four on his own legs, under his trous., drinking his blood. We are only days from Savanna, they say, where the Navy waits for us. But the days and nights are cold and we are hungry and ready to fight.

"Its a good thing the taste of our victories in Atlanta and since still remain in our mouths, and the cheers of the slaves who follow us from place to place, to drive us on through this because in a long and hard campaign I cant remember the boys ever beeing so unhappy and fed up. We know what we do is importent and Gen. Wm. Sherman, or Uncle Billy as the boys call him, keeps telling us so. I just keep going, try not to complane, and some of the boys have started calling me Old Iron Boots because they say nothing can stop me from taking the next step. Maybe they are right. Anyhow I guess its all a man can do is to keep marching. We havent seen a Johnny Reb to shoot for two days so we just keep pushing threw the swampe trying to keep powder dry and muskets ready."

Will closed the old book and carefully set it down on his

desk. He'd meant to just skim through it, but he found that the stories Thaddius Riker told—despite his rather primitive literary skills—were fascinating. Riker had accompanied Major General William Tecumseh Sherman on his long fight to Atlanta, and at this point in the tale, they had moved on after putting that city to the torch, headed for Savannah and the sea. Will knew enough about military history to realize that Sherman's assault on Atlanta and then Savannah proved more than successful, that it was a turning point in the war, capturing one of the Confederacy's most vital supply centers and cutting Southern rail links. Additionally, by leaving detachments behind to maintain his own supply lines all the way back up to Nashville, Sherman had cut off the South's western states from the capital in Richmond. The move had been bold, brilliant, and extraordinarily effective.

Sherman, it was said, had coined the phrase "War is hell," and Old Iron Boots Riker's diary seemed to confirm that assessment. An earlier entry, about a friend of Thaddius's whose arm had been amputated in a field hospital by a drunken surgeon using a dull, rusted bayonet, had been as good a description of hell as any Will ever hoped to read. Will's ancestor had indeed been through hell, but he had survived it.

Anyway, reading the diary had helped to take Will out of his own life and concerns, which was good because otherwise he'd have been thinking of nothing but Felicia day and night. There was nothing wrong with thinking about Felicia, he resolved, but there had to be limits, even to that. He wasn't opposed to having a social life, even a romantic one, but he was at the Academy to do a job, to prepare himself for service to Starfleet, and even Felicia Mendoza had to take second place to that.

Will found the diary hard to read: its brittle pages flaked and chipped as he turned them, and Thaddius Riker's handwriting was cramped and spidery. Sometimes blotches of water, ink, or something that Will thought might be blood obscured words or even whole sections. But even so, no matter where he dipped in, he found himself lost in his ancestor's exploits, and only occasional mental images of Felicia's radiant smile or the way her strong body filled out her Academy uniform could haul him back to the twenty-fourth century. For the past couple of days he had been turning to the diary as often as he could make the time, in between classes, other work, and little bits of social time.

William Sherman had been the kind of general Will could appreciate, and there were times, reading about "Uncle Billy," that he wondered if his own parents had named him for Thaddius's friend. After taking Atlanta, Sherman had chased General Hood around the South for a while. Tiring of that exercise, he had returned to his original plan for after Atlanta's defeat—the march to Savannah. He moved in the exact opposite direction from Hood, leading his sixty-two thousand troops toward the sea. He left behind him all sources of supplies and communication—completely on his own, behind enemy lines, but with the intention of routing the enemy and showing them why it was a bad idea to continue fighting. All the way across Georgia they marched, torching fields, killing stock, liberating slaves, and generally making Confederate sympathizers curse Sherman's name for years to come. The plan was reckless, foolish, utterly wrongheaded, and absolutely the right thing to do.

Thaddius Riker, at the head of the New York 102nd, was with Sherman for the whole thing. They had fought through the hills and forests of northern Georgia together; before and after taking Atlanta they had fought at Kennesaw Mountain and Allatoona and Rome. Thaddius Riker had taken a minié ball in the shoulder at a battle in a place called Pine Mountain, and had fallen, inside Confederate territory. Only the aid of a mysterious stranger helped him get back behind Federal lines, probably saving his life. "I had never seen this fellow before," Thaddius had written. "But he came along at just the moment when I needed someone. Without him, I would not be here writing these words today. Later I tried to find him agin, to thank him, but he had vanished back into whatever regiment he came from. Whoever he may be, I owe my life to him, and he has my thanks forever."

But it was near another small town called Garner's Ridge that Thaddius showed his own strategic thinking.

Cut off from supply lines, Sherman's men had to live off the land. As Sherman pointed out, if millions of Southerners could do it, his force of several thousand could too. But it meant raiding farmhouses, barnyards, and fields as well as hunting native animals. As an additional benefit, any crops or livestock the Union Army didn't leave behind was food the Confederate Army couldn't eat when they came in pursuit.

To further that end, Sherman sent his troops on foraging missions as they cut their swath to the sea. These foragers had express orders not to loot or pillage civilian homes, but to cause as much damage as they could to supply depots or arms warehouses, to put the torch to crops, to free slaves and to supply the Federals whenever possible. According to Thaddius's diary, these orders were frequently ignored. "I seen three boys come around the bend this morning," he scrawled at one point. "One wore a long white dress with bows and a bustle, over his uniform, with necklaces that looked like gold tied around his head. The next had outfited himself with a fine beaver top hat and a gentleman's coat. The last one was covered in muck, and held a squealing baby pig in his arms."

Thaddius himself, it seemed, had taken Sherman's instructions to heart. He kept the New York 102nd in line and under control. Outside the tiny town of Garner's Ridge, he had led a foraging party of seven, trusted men all. They had come across a large, wealthy plantation, with manicured fields and lawns surrounding an enormous white house. As the men approached the farmhouse, a blonde woman who Old Iron Boots described as "a natural Southern beautey" stepped onto the wide porch with a rifle in her hands, pointing it at the men.

"I reckon you gentlemen are lost," she said bravely. "Y'all are in the Confederacy now, and those blue coats are not very popular."

"No, ma'am," Jim Railsback, a sergeant in Thaddius Riker's regiment replied. "We ain't lost at all. It's just that the Confederacy is shrinking around you."

"Well, this plantation is still a part of it, and I would appreciate it if you all were on your way."

"We can't do that, ma'am," Thaddius said. "We need to have us a look around, see if you have any provisions here that we can use. General Sherman's army is a hungry one, ma'am. We won't come in your house or cause you any grief, we can avoid it, but if you've got a smokehouse or anything in your barn we'll find it and help ourselves. You try to use that rifle you'll find yourself asking for a lot of trouble you don't want."

Thaddius believed she was thinking it over, but then another soldier, called only Frankie in the diary, shouted, "Window, sir!"

Guns were drawn and pointed at a downstairs window, where Thaddius saw only a fluttering of curtain. "Who's inside, ma'am? Soldiers? Children?"

"My children are soldiers," the woman said, and now Thaddius could see that she was older than he had thought at first, but still trim and attractive. "Fifteen and nineteen, and if they don't beat you, their children will."

"You really think the war's goin' to last that long?" Railsback asked.

"Never mind that," Thaddius Riker snapped. "Who's inside the house? Speak up or we'll have to go in and see for ourselves."

The woman shrugged. "It's just the darkies," she said. "They're hiding from you too. They've heard that y'all are tools of the devil, and it's the gospel truth."

Even as she spoke, though, the door opened behind her and Thaddius saw a black man step onto the porch. He was nervous, glancing at the Union soldiers and then at the ground, afraid to meet anyone's eye. "Lucius," the woman said. "Get back in the house and make sure the others do too."

But Lucius ignored her command and came down the stairs, past his mistress and toward Thaddius. He was barefoot, and his pants and shirt had been patched so many times it was hard to tell what color they'd originally been. "Y'all are real," he said. "I been told I'd see devils in blue coats for so long I was expectin' horns and tails. But you men, you look like God's own angels to me. Are y'all men or angels?"

"We're men," Thaddius said. "Just men who are tired and hungry and trying to live through this damn war. Is there anyone else in the house?"

"My family, sir," Lucius said. "My wife and our baby. Rest is in the pen, 'round back."

"No more white men, no soldiers?"

"No, sir. Miz Lily's husband was killed, and her boys are off with General Hood, hear tell. Ain't been around in some weeks."

"And there are more slaves, in a pen, you say?"

"Yes, sir."

"Show me. You have a problem with that, ma'am?"

"Besides the fact that y'all are interfering with my private property?" she countered.

"Where I'm standing, old Lucius looks like a man," Thaddius said. "You're going to have to get over the idea that men are property you can buy and sell."

She shifted the rifle in her grasp. "Not as long as I draw breath."

"You'd best put down that gun," Thaddius said. "Or you

won't have to worry about breathing for much longer. I told you we're not here to hurt you or your kin, or damage your house. But we can't hold with keeping human beings in a pen."

"If I had a dog I suppose you'd take that too."

"That would depend on the dog," Railsback offered helpfully. "Yesterday we shot a hound that was used for tracking escaped slaves."

"Y'all killed old Clarence?" Lucius asked, breaking into a grin for the first time. He displayed a ragged scar on his calf. "I wisht I'd'a been there for that. Dog has left his mark on me a few times."

"I don't know as it was Clarence," Thaddius said. "But if it wasn't, we'll find him too. I'll even give you the pleasure of pulling the trigger. Now let's see that pen."

Miz Lily didn't stand in their way, so Lucius led the others to a low wooden structure behind the barn. It was unpainted, as if the slaves held inside were even less important than the animals in the neat, whitewashed barn. When Railsback broke off the padlock on the door and Lucius pulled it open, the stink washed over Thaddius like a wave. Inside, there were nineteen slaves, men, women, and children, in a space that might have accommodated six. They had wooden pails for toilets, a barrel with some water in it, and straw for beds. The men had been tied to beams with leather straps.

"These kind gentlemen is here to free us," Lucius said. "Miz Lily don't want none of it, but they won't back down from her. It was a sight, I'll tell you."

The people inside burst into laughter and thanks, and some even began to cry, pray, or both. Children ran out into the yard and dashed in wild circles, exuberant at being let out of the pen without a chore assigned to them. One of the women told Lucius that she'd go into the big house to get his family out. He warned her to be careful of Miz Lily, but

Frankie volunteered to go along to make sure she didn't try anything.

"Where we gone go, suh?" one of the women asked Thaddius.

"Anywhere you want, I reckon," he told her with a grin.

"Ain't got nowhere special in mind," she said. "But most places we go, someone will just catch us up again."

"But you're free now," he said.

"You think so, and I might think so," the woman argued. "Are most other folks in these parts gone think so?"

"I see your point," Thaddius admitted. This had become a problem already—freed slaves, with no place better to go and no guarantee of safety anywhere in Georgia, had taken to following Sherman's army around. But that meant more mouths to feed, slower progress, and more targets for Johnny Reb. There was no good solution to the problem, but Thaddius didn't feel right about turning these people away now that he'd rescued them from a slave pen. "I reckon you can stay with us awhile if you've a mind to."

The slave pen had been put to the torch and the smokehouse raided for stores of beef and pork. Livestock was shot and fire set to the edges of the fields and then, with twenty-two former slaves in tow, the foragers went to rejoin their regiment.

The trouble started on a wooden bridge over a slow, narrow river. From a copse of trees on the far side, shots rang out, and Private Joyce, one of Thaddius Riker's men, was hit in the gut. He fell, and the rest flattened themselves, drawing their weapons. Thaddius waved the ex-slaves down. But then gunfire came from behind them, up a hillside that banked down toward the river.

"They got us pinned down here," Railsback muttered. "It'll be like target practice for 'em to pick us off."

"That's because we're on the wrong side of the bridge," Thaddius said.

"But they're on both sides!"

"I'm talking about over and under," Thaddius explained. "We're over. We need to be under. Give 'em some hell, boys!" he shouted. "And let's get wet!"

The men all started shooting then, setting up a covering barrage that drove the rebs back into the trees and those up on the hill into hiding while the Federals dove from the bridge into the lazily moving river. The water wasn't very deep and the men were able to keep their guns and powder above its surface. In the shade of the bridge, they were at least somewhat protected from those on the hill, and the cut of the riverbank kept those in the trees from being able to see them, much less shoot them. But when the freed slaves joined them under the bridge, it became crowded, and the soldiers on the hill were able to pick off the people around the edges. Two of the slaves were hit, and Frankie took a ball in the shoulder, shattering bone and spraying blood into the water.

Thaddius knew this was only a temporary measure. They couldn't stay in this water indefinitely, and the bridge would only offer protection for so long. It was just wood and eventually the Confederate shot would chew through it. Besides, when the men from the trees came to the river's edge they'd be easy targets. He needed a plan, and he needed it fast.

"How many men you think they have?" he asked Railsback.

"Can't be too many. We didn't think they had any forces around here. My guess is this is a small patrol that spotted us and thought they'd make some trouble. A dozen, maybe, six in the trees and six up top."

"That's what I'm thinking too," Thaddius said. "Which means they still outnumber us two to one and have the tactical advantage."

"Unless you count the Negroes," Railsback pointed out.

"They don't have guns, but I was just getting to that," Thaddius said. "How well can you swim?"

"I swim fine, I guess. What do you have in mind, sir?"

"Well, when we go underwater our rifles won't do us any good. So we leave them behind with whatever of those slaves can shoot, and we just take bayonets."

"Bayonets, sir? Against a dozen men? Or what we hope is only a dozen men?"

"I know the odds aren't great," Thaddius Riker said with a smile. "But that's their own fault for joining the Confederate Army."

He recruited another soldier and three of the strongest, healthiest former slaves, including Lucius. Each man was assigned a bayonet, and a secondary hunting knife. Rifles were left with those who would stay behind. At Thaddius's signal, the little force under the bridge began firing up the hill, distracting the rebels up there, and Thaddius, Railsback, Clancy, and three ex-slaves dove under the water, swimming for all they were worth. They swam underneath until their lungs were fit to burst, then came up close to the near bank, where they hoped the men up the hill wouldn't be able to see them. Then they ducked under again, and swam another distance downriver. Finally, they dragged themselves out and up the bank, dripping, cold, and weighted down with all the water they'd taken on.

Thaddius led the men by example and hand signal. They climbed up the far side of the hill, and within a short while were slipping down behind the armed rebels, who had taken up positions behind large rocks and downed trees. But those bulwarks protected them only from bullets fired from below. At Thaddius's signal, his tiny force attacked. There were eight rebels, not six. One of them got off a shot, which tore through the wrist of one of the ex-slaves. But the bayonets did their dirty work, and in a few short moments the Confederates were all on the ground, bleeding into the dirt.

The wounded slave grinned at Thaddius in spite of his injury. "I ain't had so much fun in years," he said. "Y'all get to do this every day?"

"Not quite like this," Thaddius replied. "But if you can handle a gun as well as you do that bayonet you might could find a place in this army."

"Be a little tricky with but one wing," the man said. "But I'll gladly give it a try." He took a musket from one of the Confederate corpses and balanced it on a boulder, sighting down it toward the copse of trees. As Thaddius had hoped, the rebs there had grown restless and were creeping toward the riverbank, where they figured they would have easy pickings at those stuck in the water.

"Let's see what you can do," Thaddius urged. He helped himself to a gun and the other men did the same. The former slave fired first, and his target dropped. The others began firing, and the Confederates, all in the open now, were disposed of quickly. By the time Thaddius and his men came down from the hill, the rest of the Federals and freed slaves were out of the water, wringing out their clothes, stamping their feet, and helping themselves to weapons and ammunition from the rebel corpses.

Will Riker liked the tale because it demonstrated a trait that Thaddius Riker had in common with William Tecumseh Sherman, and one that he hoped he had as well — the ability to look unconventionally at a difficult situation and find a unique solution. Most leaders wouldn't have abandoned their guns and attacked a larger force with lesser weapons. But without that creative response, the story of Thaddius Riker might well have ended in that cold, slow Georgia creek near Garner's Ridge.

Maybe that was what he needed with Felicia, he realized. The two had talked for hours the other night, after they had made their peace. Since then he had seen her a couple more times, but usually in groups. They had touched a few times, hands coming together, but there had been little forward progress in the direction that Will had decided he wanted to go. He still didn't know if it was what Felicia wanted, but he was more convinced than ever that it might be. He just needed to find out. And since he didn't know quite how to go about it, he needed a creative way to force the issue.

As he got ready for bed, and then later in his bed as he tried to find his way to sleep, he worked on coming up with just that.

Chapter 18

Sometimes in the evenings as the suns drifted one by one toward the horizon and the winds churned through the twisting streets, the atmosphere in The End was that of a carnival, loud and joyous and full of color. Kyle walked the streets on one of these long twilights. A couple of blocks from home he encountered a crowd spilling out of buildings, jamming the sidewalk and overflowing into the street. Kyle shouldered through the mob, alternately smelling perfume, sweat, roasting meat from a nearby spit, and alcohol on breath and in bottles. Ahead the laughter was raucous and shouts rang out, whoops of delight and encouragement. He couldn't quite tell what they were shouting about so he kept going through the crowd, past the mostly adult men and women, human and otherwise, who composed it. When he was finally near the front he could see the source of the commotion.

In a small clearing—the crowd was just as dense, or more so, on the other side of it—two Cyrians faced one another, bare-chested, their loose cotton slacks belted at the waist. They were big and muscular, though one had an enormous roll of flesh that hung over his belt, and both were tattooed, with brilliant splashes of color, yellows and reds and peacock blues and a green that reminded Kyle of forested mountainsides back home, snaking across chests and arms and backs. A *fight*, Kyle thought, but the two men were smiling, grinning like drunken fools, and Kyle realized they were drunk but not fighting. This was a different kind of competition altogether.

A streetlight, rare in The End, cast a circle of illumination over the whole scene. The taller of the two Cyrians, the one with the flat stomach, pulled back his own hair, which fell below his shoulders in thick waves. Where his ear was— no, where his ear should have been, Kyle realized—there was instead a flap of skin that looked like a shaven cat's ear, punctured by at least a dozen gold hoops all the way around the rim. Kyle decided the fellow must have surgically altered it, since every other Cyrian ear he'd noticed had looked just like human ears. The crowd loved the ear, though, and responded with gales of laughter and shouts of joy. Kyle wondered what he'd missed so far, before he'd been able to see what all the excitement was about.

The second one, with the gigantic gut, had a bald head and Kyle could see both of his ears. They were studded and pierced but otherwise normal. This man smiled broadly, and then opened his mouth wider, and wider. When it seemed like his head would split open, he stuck out his tongue—*or unrolled his tongue, to be more precise,* Kyle thought. It was at least thirty centimeters long and bright red, and when he wagged it at his opponent it seemed to be prehensile. At the end of it—which was forked into three distinct points—were three silver rings. The man stiffened his tongue and held it at its most extreme distance, then raised his arms. The crowd, understanding the gesture, quieted, and then the man clapped the tiny rings together as if they were chimes. The bell-like tinkling floated over the crowd, and then was lost again in the thunderous roar of approval that followed.

Now, glancing away from the main event, Kyle saw that money was changing hands. He had thought this was a fight, initially, and in fact it was a kind of contest. And these people were betting on it. He didn't understand the rules and couldn't be sure how to tell the winner or the loser, but the man with the tongue had certainly made some points. As he scanned the crowd—many of whom, he realized, were similarly tattooed and pierced—he recognized a couple of faces. Jackdaw, a human who lived in his building, a man with golden brown skin, a thick, long shock of straight black hair and a beard that strangled his neck and chin like a malevolent hand, stood across from him, on the other side of the contestants. Next to him was Cetra ski Toram, a native of Hazimot but from the nation of Muftrih, half a world away. She was ancient, with cobalt blue skin and long white hair and sunken eyes that always seemed to be looking below the surface. Kyle had never seen her smile but she was doing so now, mouth open in a grin that revealed just how few teeth she had remaining. Behind her stooped form was Michelle, who had never told Kyle her last name, if she even had one. She caught Kyle's gaze and waved. He returned the wave, but then she was lost again in a new uproar.

Kyle returned his attention to the combatants in the clearing, and saw that the tall one with the long hair was raising his right shoulder, already huge and bulbous as most Cyrian shoulders were. But this man worked it up, higher and higher, lowering the opposite one at the same time, until his shoulder was higher than the top of his head. The crowd fell silent, awed by the spectacle. There must have been a hundred onlookers now, and not a whisper could be heard.

But the Cyrian wasn't done. When his shoulder could go no higher, the weird muscles that Kyle had never quite understood seemed to bulge and separate, and then his entire arm dropped off. The crowd roared, and Kyle realized it was an illusion, but barely. A thin stalk of gristly muscle still connected arm to shoulder, but that was all. His hand hung almost to the ground, and in fact, his fingers stretched and picked up a pebble, which he then threw at his opponent, bouncing it off the man's round stomach. A chorus of cheers and laughter greeted this act, and the tall Cyrian reeled his arm back in.

Kyle saw money changing hands again. Apparently, from the snatches of conversation he heard, this would be a hard stunt to top. "But wait," some said. "Lefeertsin isn't done yet." Kyle had gathered that the fat man was Lefeertsin, and the thin one Gal. *Their names*, he thought off-handedly, *match their sizes.*

Gal stood, recomposed now, and accepted the congratulations of his fans with a proud smile. He looked like someone who believed he had already won the match. But Lefeertsin apparently disagreed. He stood up to his full height, which wasn't much shorter than Gal, and hoisted his vast stomach up with both hands, fingers digging into the soft flesh there. Then, much as Gal's shoulder had, the rolls of flab seemed to peel themselves away as if each were controlled by its own independent musculature. Kyle was reminded of a flower opening, although only in two directions, with some petals lifting up and others falling away. When the stomach rolls had finished, the crowd fell silent again. There, in the center of the stomach now that the extraneous fat had cleared itself away, was a giant eye, at least the size of Kyle's hand from fingertip to wrist. It was bright green and seemed to have all the parts of a regular human eye. There were gasps from the crowd, but no applause yet, as if something more were expected.

Then Lefeertsin let out a loud belch and the eye winked at Gal.

The crowd went mad with delight. Spectators cheered and laughed and danced, or simply stayed in place and hopped up and down. A cry of "Lef! Lef! Lef!" started up, building and building. More money changed hands, as Lefeertsin was the obvious winner now, but no one seemed chagrined to have lost or especially delighted to have won, beyond the enjoyment they took in the performance itself. People bumped into Kyle, and one Cyrian woman hugged him to her abundant bosom, then released him with a pinch on the rear.

Kyle was starting to push through the mob, trying to get to Michelle and the others, when the mood suddenly turned. There was a hush and smiles were replaced in an instant with scowls. On the edges of the crowd, people began to melt away into nearby buildings. For a moment Kyle didn't know why things had changed so suddenly, but when he looked in the direction nearly everyone else was, he understood.

Rolling down the street toward them was a squadron of police vehicles. Armored officers ran behind the vehicles, shields up, energy weapons at the ready. It looked like a war, like an invasion, more than a police action.

Someone grabbed his arm and Kyle started, so intent was he on the oncoming police. "Joe, come on. Let's go!"

It was Michelle, her brow furrowed with anxiety, her eyes narrow and frightened. "Michelle, what's . . . ?"

"Let's go," she repeated urgently. "Now!"

"But . . . were we doing something wrong?"

She tugged at his arm again, then released it and started to back away. It was obvious that she was leaving, whether he went with her or not. Behind her, Cetra and Jackdaw waited with a couple of others Kyle didn't know. She had given Kyle the chance—more of a chance than the others seemed comfortable with, judging from the worried expressions on their faces—and either he'd take it or not. Michelle met his eyes once more and then turned to run. "Wait," Kyle shouted, but he ran after them.

He had expected Cetra ski Toram to be slow, but the old woman surprised him with her speed and agility. As they rounded a bend Kyle glanced back over his shoulder. Behind them, many of the people in the crowd either hadn't been able to run away in time or had chosen to stand their ground, and the police were tearing through them. Their energy weapons emitted bright blue bursts that vaporized flesh and bone, and everywhere they shot, blood splattered. People were screaming, begging for mercy, but the police showed none. Those who weren't shooting used their shields as rams or clubs, chopping and bashing with them. Some of The End's residents tried to fight back, but they were outnumbered and outgunned.

Kyle stood there, rapt. He couldn't believe what he was seeing. None of those people had been doing anything wrong. Even if the competition had been illegal for some reason, no one had been hurt by it. It had been a party, a street fair, improvisational theater. Michelle tugged on his arm again. "If you stay here, you'll die like those others," she warned him. "Please, Joe, come with us. It's the only way."

He shook his head as if by clearing it he could make the horrific carnage go away. But it didn't. The street ran with red and blue blood, mixing into vibrant purples, black where it vanished into shadow.

"Yes, okay," Kyle said. He felt detached, in shock. As he ran hand in hand with Michelle he expected the Tholian flashbacks to start up again. But they didn't. This fresh horror was bad enough on its own. Out of the light, they kept running, past buildings so dark and silent they seemed already to be mourning the fallen. Finally, Jackdaw led the way into a building Kyle had never seen before, a collapsing wretch of a place with boarded-up doors and windows. Jackdaw entered through a side door, where a flat object Kyle only recognized at the last moment as a bed leaned up against a gaping doorway. Jackdaw and Michelle slid the bed far enough over for them to gain entry, and then they pulled it back into place, disguising the opening from the outside.

Inside, they were met in a small, poorly lit room by a handful of others. Kyle recognized a couple of people who he had noticed in the crowd outside, and who must have run here faster—not bothering to wait for him. The other two he had never seen before. One was human, two Hazimotian, and the last barely humanoid but of no species Kyle had seen before. It had what was recognizably a head and what seemed to be legs in the correct places, but that was all he could make out; the rest was a gelatinous blob that seemed to have other life-forms moving about beneath it, like fish swimming in a thick semi-opaque sea.

Michelle clung again to Kyle's hand. "This is Joe Brady," she said to the others. "He's new here."

"And you brought him with you because . . . ?" one of the Hazimotians asked. She was a female, from either Stindi or Wachivus, Kyle guessed, though without much certainty. Not Cyrian, for sure. Her voice was deep and threatening, and she looked as if she'd as soon shoot Kyle as admit him into whatever inner sanctum this was.

"Because he wasn't part of what happened out there and I didn't want to see him die for no reason," Michelle said. "Besides, I trust him."

Kyle was surprised by that pronouncement. He liked Michelle, but their relationship was superficial at best. She barely knew him, really. As if she could read his mind, she turned to him and said, "I size people up quickly, Joe, and I have a lot of faith in my own instincts."

"What . . . what the hell was all that about?" Kyle asked. He flailed his arm back toward the direction from which they'd come, as if anyone could see the carnage from here. "And what is this place? Who are you all?"

"Easy now, Joe," Jackdaw said. He was a small man, whip-thin and nasally, and his thick mane of black hair seemed like it should belong to someone else. He talked fast, as if trying to get too many ideas out at once. "One point at a time, okay, and we'll get all this cleared up. You're a guest here, you know."

"I appreciate that," Kyle said, still agitated from the attack and wondering what was going on. "I'm just not altogether sure that I'm a guest by choice."

"I had pegged you as a survivor, Joe," Michelle said with a frown. "If I was wrong, I'll be disappointed."

"You have no idea." Kyle tried on a grin but it didn't quite work. "I definitely qualify on that count."

"Well, if you hadn't come with us, you'd probably be dead," she said. "So you should just count your blessings and let us explain things to you."

"Have a seat, all of you," one of the Hazimotians who had been here from the beginning said. This one, a male sitting cross-legged on the bare tile floor, looked Muftrihan, like Cetra, but much younger, with pale yellow hair and tiny black eyes. "You're making me nervous, looming around like that."

The others had been sitting on ramshackle chairs, which were the only furniture in the place. It looked like a meeting room more than a dwelling, but with walls that had been shredded by time and misuse and a rough-hewn floor that squeaked with nearly every movement. The air was close and musty smelling. Jackdaw and Cetra took chairs, while Michelle and Kyle joined the Muftrihan on the floor. Kyle couldn't bring himself to relax—his heart was racing, epinephrine pumping, and he remained tensed to spring up and run at the slightest provocation. Fight or flight—he recognized the sensation well.

Michelle touched Kyle on the knee. "You're upset, Joe, and probably scared. I don't blame you a bit, and I'm sorry

we had to run away from there before I could give you any
kind of explanation."

"Obviously there was a certain urgency to it," Kyle admitted.

"That's right. But now that we're here and relatively
safe, I can do the right thing. First, introductions are in
order. You already know Jackdaw and Cetra ski Toram, I
believe. This," she said, pointing to the Muftrihan on the
floor, "is Baukels Jinython." She gestured in order toward
the first Hazimotian woman who had spoken, the woman;
then the human male; and finally the unidentifiable one.
"That's Melinka, Alan, and Roog. As I told all of you, this is
Joe. He lives in my building, and I believe he can be
trusted."

"He has to be now," Melinka said. "Or killed."

"She's just joking," Michelle assured Kyle.

"No she's not," Melinka responded.

"I can be," Kyle told them all. "Trusted, I mean. But I'd
like to know what I'm being trusted with. And I'd like to
know why the police came in and started killing people."

"The two issues are interrelated," the bulbous creature introduced as Roog said. Its voice was low and phlegmy, but if
it had a gender, Kyle couldn't ascertain it from that. "We
are, you might say, a group that meets from time to time to
discuss certain political issues. And the police were killing
because that's what police do, especially here in The End."

Kyle could hardly believe what she was saying, even
though he had seen it for himself. "The police do that?
Aren't they supposed to uphold the law?"

"They do," Michelle says. "But we're not supposed to be
living here, and congregating inside The End is definitely
against the law."

"So it was okay for them to just move in and start killing?
I didn't see them trying to disperse the crowd, or make any
arrests."

"In other parts of the city they would have, okay, but not in The End," Jackdaw pointed out. The little man moved constantly, his leg twitching, fingers tapping. "Rules are different here. Life is cheap, okay?"

"They're right, Joe," Michelle told him. She sounded sincere, but everything he was hearing was so outrageous he wasn't sure what was real. "They don't like us being here, and they use any excuse they can to try to drive us away."

"Away where?" Kyle wondered. "I thought this was pretty much where people went who don't have anyplace left to go." He'd been living here for many months, and though he'd heard horror stories, none of them had been as bad as what he'd just seen. Police here seemed to have a habit of picking on individuals, but he'd never seen or heard about an organized attack on a whole neighborhood.

"It is, okay, that's the thing," Jackdaw agreed. "But you have to understand the power structure here, Joe. The rich like to be rich, and they don't want a bunch of poor people running around making things unpleasant for them. That's what we are in The End. The lowest of the low, as far as they're concerned. They can do whatever they want, and get away with it."

"So the authorities know about this? Condone it?"

"Joe," Michelle said. "We're giving you the shorthand version here. If you'd like, we can talk all about the socioeconomics of it later. The gist is, the division of rich and poor here in Cyre is an enormous gap, more of a chasm, with less and less middle class all the time. The very poor, which is most of those in The End, are considered disposable in order to make room for the new poor, which used to be the middle. The authorities wouldn't really mind if a plasma bomb wiped us all out, except that it might be a bit of a public relations problem. When they catch us breaking the law, though—even a ridiculous law—they have no problem with killing as many of us as they can."

"'That's crazy," Kyle muttered, shaking his head. "It makes no sense."

"You've been here long enough to know better than that," Michelle reminded him. "You know about the gulf between the rich and the rest of us."

"Yes, yes."

"And you have heard of other altercations. The one last month, when seven teenagers were shot by the cops? Remember?"

"Of course. I just hadn't put it all together into a pattern yet."

"It's a pattern," Alan said, the first time he'd spoken. His handsome, lined face was grave. "Just not a pretty one."

"Can't something be done?" Kyle asked.

"We're working on it, okay?" Jackdaw said. "But we need more time."

Kyle almost laughed, but he realized that would be a bad idea and contained it. "You?" he asked, trying to keep the disbelief from his voice. "What are you, some kind of revolutionary group?"

"A revolution is exactly what's needed," Roog said.

"But . . . you're not very many. Especially against such an entrenched power structure."

"We have friends," Michelle told him. "Supporters. We are more than you see here, many more. Now tell me, Joe Brady. Was I right to trust you?"

Kyle wasn't quite sure how to answer that. He felt certain that they were fighting a hopeless battle, unless their "friends" were far more numerous and powerful than they were. This tiny group couldn't hope to battle Cozzen's authorities on their own, much less the rest of Cyre. There was, though, the flame of righteousness burning in their eyes, the fire of those who believe they're on a sacred quest, and Kyle knew better than to underestimate people who thought that way. These were true believers, and from what he'd seen today there was every chance that their cause was just.

Which still didn't make it *his* cause. He had served Starfleet because he believed in the things Starfleet stood for, which included accepting the basic decency of all beings, and striving for equality and fairness. Hazimot, he had known, had not come close to measuring up in those areas, which made it a perfect place to hide from Starfleet. But he hadn't reckoned on the cost of life in such a backward society making itself known in such a direct and immediate fashion. He had hoped to live on the sidelines until he felt ready to go back and take on Starfleet himself. The sidelines had shifted, though, and suddenly he seemed to be straddling the center, expected to take a position one way or the other.

While he contemplated, Jackdaw had jumped up and run out the doorway. Now he came back in. "It's all clear out there," he announced. "We can go back out anytime."

"I don't think it's fair of us to expect Joe to make up his mind this second," Michelle said. "We've thrown a lot at him in a short time, and it's been a traumatic evening."

"As long as you're sure he won't turn us in," Melinka said, her tone one of warning.

"Will you, Joe?"

"Of course not," Kyle promised. He wouldn't, either. Certainly not before he had amassed a lot more information. Even if he wanted to, at this point any claim he made would be his word against theirs, and they could probably get him locked away for a very long time if he tried to make trouble for them.

Besides, he had no reason to. So far as he could tell right now, they were on the side of the angels.

As if to underscore that idea, Michelle stood up and then offered him a hand, helping to hoist him to his feet. When he was standing, she was very near him, and he could feel the warmth of her body, smell the slightly salty tang of her skin. "Let's go home, Joe," she said. "And I'll tell you whatever you need to know."

He hadn't had a better invitation all day.

Michelle's apartment, like the others in this building of illegal squatters, wasn't luxurious, but she had made it as comfortable as possible. She had brought in what seemed like tons of fabrics and covered the windows, the walls, the furniture, with loose, draped fabric that made the place at once intimate and inviting. Her bed was mounded with mismatched pillows, most of which had ended up on the floor over the space of the last forty minutes or so. Kyle lay back with his head against one of them, his arms behind his head, and Michelle's head rested in the crook of his right arm. One hand trailed across his stomach and chest as they talked, toying with the small hairs there. Candles burned on a nearby table, adding their aromas to the mingled scents of man and woman.

"So I hope this wasn't just a ploy to win me over to your cause," Kyle said softly, stroking Michelle's long, soft hair.

She playfully punched his solar plexus. "How can you even say that?"

"You have to admit the timing is a little suspect. We've both lived here for ages, but nothing like this ever happened until tonight."

"Strong passions run deep in me," Michelle told him. "They get mixed up sometimes. Politics and fear stir things up."

"And I just happened to be available?"

She laughed and slapped him again. "Are you *trying* to be a jerk, or does it really come that naturally to you?"

"I'm just trying to figure out why I'm here," he said.

"You're here because I find you attractive. Because I thought we could bring each other pleasure, and once again, I was right. I told you I trust in my own judgment. Is that too complicated for you?"

"Maybe too simple," Kyle replied. "I'm a pretty complicated guy."

Michelle turned and boosted herself up on her elbows, looking at him. Her lips were soft and pink and the way they felt beneath his was one of his very favorite recent memories. "None of us are here because we're easy cases," she said. "In The End, I mean. The ones who can just go along and get along don't wind up here. Only the interesting ones do. The ones with stories to tell. You've got a story, don't you?"

He chuckled and shook his head. "I've got a story, all right. It's a doozy. But I'm not telling it, not here, not tonight. Some of us have to go to work in the morning."

"Why do you live here? You work pretty regularly, you must get paid okay."

"I guess because I'm not an easy case either," he answered.

"Must be a good story, then."

"Oh, it is."

"Full of love and hate and betrayal and passion? Those are the best stories."

"I think it's safe to say all those elements are present in mine," he said. "What about yours?"

"I don't have a story," Michelle said, closing her eyes. Her lashes were long and thick and, like the rest of her face, perfectly formed. "I'm the exception that proves the rule."

Kyle reached out and touched her perfect chin. "I don't believe you." As he held it, she opened her eyes and it was like staring into the sky on the clearest summer day imaginable. He felt lost, as if he were falling into the vortex of their blue.

"I guess you'll have to stay around for a while," she said. "So you can find out if you're right or not."

"I can think of worse things to do," Kyle said.

"I can think of better things." She pushed herself forward, so that her face was closer, and tilted her chin, bringing her lips against his again. "Much better things."

Chapter 19

There was, Will had always believed, some kind of mystical connection between the night sky and romance. And because he had romance on his mind, he found himself looking forward to a scheduled trip to the moon with more eagerness than he had previously expected. Various squadrons would be going to stay for a few days in Tycho City there and to work on some flying exercises. He was going, which was great, and Felicia was going, which was even better. He figured there would be a chance to get her out under the starry lunar sky and really find out what he meant to her. And to let her know what she had come to mean to him, which seemed to become, with every passing day, all the more urgent. Besides, it was a chance to get off-world, and that in itself was reason to celebrate.

Probably because he was so excited about the trip, the days before it seemed to drag along interminably. He went to classes, he did homework, he played strategema and racquetball and poker and parrises squares. From time to time he went out with friends, but much as he wanted to be alone with Felicia he really wanted to save that until the Tycho trip. It all seemed so numbingly routine. During quiet moments, when he was eating or lying in bed waiting for sleep to claim him, he ran through different scenarios in his head, but they all included him and Felicia.

Tycho City, Will knew, was a populous place—so big that

it could be seen from Earth on a very clear night. But he'd been there once before and he knew there were some spots on its outskirts—not far away from the Starfleet base they'd be staying in—that were still within its atmospheric and gravity fields but were otherwise traditional lunar landscape, as it had existed even before Neil Armstrong had left the first human footprint there. He would take Felicia out there, alone, and they'd sit close together, looking out at the Earth and the stars. He would take her hand in his and look into her warm brown eyes and say something like, "Felicia, I've really enjoyed spending this time with you." Then she would melt into his arms.

Except there were some occasions in his mental motion picture when she would simply laugh, or even shake off his touch and storm away. He wasn't sure what he would do if those came true, but he knew his heart would stop beating. Maybe he'd simply walk outside of Tycho's atmosphere and see how long it took him to suffocate or freeze to death.

When he got to thinking that way he would shake his head and tell himself that he was being stupid. *That's not you*, he thought. *That's some lovesick puppy. Will Riker's a lot of things, but he's not a guy who'd commit suicide for anyone.*

Then again, love changes you, he guessed. *If it doesn't, maybe it was never really there at all.*

Tycho City was everything Will had remembered it being—big, sprawling, bustling, full of bright lights and loud noise and riots of color, as if to chase away the deadly silence of the moon's surface. Everyone who lived there seemed to speak louder than was necessary, and tried to pack more activity into each day than Will did in a week. The pace of life was furious.

For the cadets, the pace was also fast. They woke early each morning, bathed and ate and then went straight to the field for flight practice. Breaking into their squadrons, they flew an assortment of shuttlecraft, mostly ships that would have been mothballed if not for the educational opportunity they offered. On the morning of their last day, Will was at the helm of a twenty-year-old executive shuttle. It was a sleek ship that seated ten, though on this one there were only the four cadets and their flight instructor, a Vulcan named Satek.

Will felt nervous as he eased the ship out of the dock under Satek's watchful eye. He had done this enough times in flight sims and training runs, but he wanted everything to be perfect this time. The ship responded like a dream to his commands, though, despite its age — it was actually pretty lush, compared to what he was used to, since it had been the private shuttle of a highly placed Federation diplomat, and all its systems were in top working order. The shuttle hangar opening looked awfully small as they approached it, and the nose of the ship awfully large. And despite the low speed Will knew they were holding at, he felt like the ship was accelerating much too fast.

"You're doing great," Paul Rice whispered to him as they cleared the hangar bay. "No problems. Give it some power now."

With the last structure safely behind them, Will knew that it was okay to give it some juice. They would fly out to a series of buoys, perform a few maneuvers around them, then return. The only tricky part yet to come would be landing again, which would also be Will's job.

Once at the buoys, each of the cadets in the squadron took their turn putting the shuttle through its paces. They worked on accelerated banked turns, figure eights, hard stops, and other aerial maneuvers. As usual, Paul had the surest hand and best control — he was born to fly, Will was convinced. Dennis Haynes, still in Will's squadron, was uncertain and hesitant, and that showed in his flying. Estresor Fil was workmanlike and by the book, but every move she made felt just a little stiff. She got the job done, though, and Satek seemed pleased with her performance. Jenna Garcia was nearly as smooth as Paul was, impressing Will with her technical acuity and her command of the conn.

Finally, once they had all made a couple of turns, Satek turned to Will. "Very well done, gentlemen. Cadet Riker, please take us back to Tycho City."

"Yes, sir," Will said. Jenna slipped from the helmsman's chair and Will sat down. He glanced over the instrument display. Everything looked shipshape. "Set course for Tycho City, Starfleet hangar bay," he instructed the computer. A quick look at the navigational reference display told him when the course had been confirmed.

A short while later the hangar bay loomed in the front viewscreen as the ship's navigational systems homed in on it. Will kept track of all his displays, and everything looked good for a landing when Satek spoke up. "Computer off, Instructor Satek's command."

Instantly the onboard computer obeyed, switching itself off, and the shuttle was under Will's manual control. "You're in control, Mr. Riker," Satek said. "Bring us in."

"But . . . yes, sir," Will replied. He fought back the sudden wave of panic. He could do this manually, he felt sure, even without a computer. Any pilot worth the name had to know this procedure inside and out. He'd practiced it, run through the steps, simulated it . . . that hangar was rushing up at them fast, though, as they entered Tycho's gravitational field.

"Bring up the nose," Paul said, reading the situation.

"I know, Paul!" Will snapped, already reaching for the manual flight operations control. He brought up the nose a few degrees and slowed the shuttle's descent. Next he powered down the impulse engine and brought the manual thrusters to a half-reverse, slowing the shuttle more and making the descent smoother still. "Landing gear down," he said as he tapped that control pad, more verbally ticking through the checklist than because he expected a computer to do it for him. A slight correction to the X-Y translation control veered the ship to starboard four degrees, and Will continued his steady descent, regulating forward motion through his pressure on the center pad. His breathing was returning to normal now, as he knew he would pull off a smooth landing.

Three minutes later they were docked, with only the slightest bump on contact. "Well done, Cadet," Satek said, stone-faced in his Vulcan way. Even Paul Rice congratulated him, once they were out of the shuttle and safely on the floor of the hangar. "I could have brought it down without that huge bump," Paul added. "But I doubt that you did too much damage."

"Don't listen to him," Dennis said. "You did fine."

"I was nervous," Will said, "when Satek shut off the computer. Even though I knew I could do it."

"Anyone who can't perform a simple manual landing has no business at the conn," Paul said.

"That's true," Dennis countered. "But usually you know more than a few kilometers from your landing site whether it'll be manual or not."

"You can't count on that, though," Will put in. "Satek was right to test me. I'm just glad I passed."

"With flying colors," Jenna said, clapping him on the shoulder. "We're all still here, aren't we?"

At least there's that, Will thought. *We're all still here. And finished with the day's activity in plenty of time for tonight.*

If Will had felt anxious about performing a manual landing in front of his instructor and peers, he was far more nervous about his plans for the evening. He knew he'd be able to grab Felicia after dinner—all the cadets were having a group dinner with some of the officers from the Tycho City

Starfleet base—and he planned to invite her out for a walk at the city's edge, where the lights weren't so bright and the starscape would be vibrant and alive.

It was what would happen at that point that tied his stomach up in knots. Either he would be able to give voice to his feelings, or he wouldn't. If he couldn't then she would probably think him a complete idiot, of course, but that was a chance he had to take. Then the other consideration was whether or not she would return his affections or spurn them. He tried to brace himself for that, but it was like trying to get ready for a kick in the groin—all the mental preparation in the world would be worthless when the foot finally made contact.

During dinner—he barely knew what he was eating, and he was sure he didn't get much of it in him—he kept looking at Felicia, who sat at a different table, across the room from him. Fortunately, she was in front of him, because it would have been even more awkward if he'd had to turn around in his chair to see her, especially since he'd tried to keep his feelings a secret from even his best friends, lest she get wind of his plans. She was just wearing her usual uniform, but her hair was neatly brushed and piled on top of her head, and she was smiling and chatting with the officer seated next to her, and Will was certain he'd never seen a more beautiful sight. When the dinner dishes had been cleared away, an admiral got up to speak to the assembly. As far as Will was concerned, the man's mouth was moving but nothing was coming out, as his attention was fully riveted on Felicia at this point.

Finally, the speech ended, and the cadets were excused. As they began to file out, Will headed for Felicia, who had already been intercepted by Estresor Fil. Before Will could reach them, though, Dennis Haynes cut him off. "Hey, Will. That was a great speech, wasn't it?"

"Hi, Dennis," Will replied off-handedly. "I guess so." He

started to move around Dennis, but his friend blocked his way. "Dennis, I need to see Felicia."

Dennis moved closer to him and spoke in low tones. "Not tonight, buddy. Estresor Fil has big plans for her tonight."

Will felt the floor tilt and drop out from under him. "What?"

"She's—I'm not supposed to say anything, but I guess by tomorrow it'll be settled one way or the other—Estresor Fil has a gigantic crush on Felicia. She's going to tell her tonight."

"You're kidding," was all Will could manage to say.

"No. Pretty sweet, isn't it?" Dennis beamed like a proud father. "Estresor Fil has been coming to me for advice. Not that I'm some great expert or anything. But I think it'll go well for them. At least, I hope so."

"You?" Will demanded, aware that he was reacting too harshly but unable to restrain himself. "You did this? Good move." He stormed away from his friend and out of the banquet room, pushing his way past Starfleet officers who, in other circumstances, he would have been thrilled to meet. *Maybe the Riker men are just cursed*, he thought.

"It's so beautiful here," Felicia said. She still wasn't sure why Estresor Fil had brought her out to Tycho's lunar plain, away from the party and all their friends. But she was awed by the sight of the moon's surface as it had been for so many millions of years, before humanity swept over it, and even more so by the vast array of stars visible once you got beyond Tycho's brilliant lights. She could see the Earth, hanging in the sky like a blue marble, and a dizzying display of white dots representing billions of other stars and planets.

"I hoped you would like it," Estresor Fil said. "I'm not sure why but walking at night seems popular with some humans."

"I think it's just the natural beauty of the night sky," Felicia told her. "Pregnant with possibility, always different and amazing. I never get tired of it."

"I am pleased," Estresor Fil said. She never sounded completely comfortable speaking English, and tonight she seemed even a little more on edge than usual. Felicia wondered if it had something to do with whatever reason they were out here. Estresor Fil obviously had something on her strange alien mind. Felicia hoped she'd get to the point soon. They flew home tomorrow and she had planned to be in the rack early.

"How did your flight go today?" Estresor Fil asked her. Without waiting for an answer she continued. "Ours was uneventful. I wish I were still in a squadron with you."

"I miss you sometimes too," Felicia told her.

"You do?" Estresor Fil sounded surprised, and the smile on her face was so rare and unnatural that Felicia thought for a moment the Zimonian was choking on something.

"Of course I do," Felicia said. "I thought we became pretty good friends last year, and we work together well."

"I agree," Estresor Fil replied. They had reached the first row of warning signs posted by Tycho City officials. There were three sets of signs, and anyone who went beyond the third set was taking their life into their hands. "Very much so."

Estresor Fil stopped near one of the signs, and Felicia came up next to her. Estresor Fil glanced at Felicia, as if measuring the distance between them, and then stepped to the side, halving it. "Are you comfortable?" she asked.

"Yes, I'm fine," Felicia assured her.

"I am sorry, I'm so bad at this," Estresor Fil said. When Felicia looked at her again, the smile was gone and she was afraid the other girl might cry.

"Bad at what? Estresor Fil, what's going on?"

Estresor Fil took a big, wet breath. "I think I love you, Felicia," she said. "I am quite sure, in fact. But I don't know how these things work, among humans, and I so wanted to do it right. But now I've made it all stupid and wrong!"

Felicia felt her heart go out to Estresor Fil, who she had always thought of as a kind of younger sister, even though the Zimonian was actually a little older than she was. She certainly hadn't expected anything like this—well, she had, to be honest with herself, but judging from the way Will Riker had been oh-so-subtly checking her out all evening, she had thought it would be coming from him. But definitely not from Estresor Fil. She supposed, as Zimonians went, she was probably quite attractive. But that didn't necessarily make her appealing to Felicia's eye.

On the other hand, there was a kind of exotic beauty in her finely sculpted features. She was not someone to whom Felicia would be instantly drawn, but she wasn't repulsive, either. And she had a good heart—she was kind and intensely loyal, and she'd been able to summon up the courage to pull this off. That was something a lot of people—again, Will came to mind—never seemed able to do.

"You haven't messed anything up, Estresor Fil," Felicia said gently.

"I haven't?"

"Not at all. You've done just fine. Even humans find this sort of thing difficult with other humans."

"That's what Dennis told me," Estresor Fil said.

"Dennis *Haynes?*"

"Yes. I went to him for advice on human pairing rituals."

"I see," Felicia said. Dennis wouldn't have been the one to whom she'd have turned, but apparently his advice hadn't been so bad after all.

"He suggested that I put my arm around your shoulders," Estresor Fil went on. "But . . . I can barely reach them. It might be awkward."

"It might be," Felicia agreed. "Why not just put it here,

around my waist? Then I can rest mine across your shoulders, like this." When they were in position, Felicia sighed and looked at the Earth. Boy, were things going to be complicated when they got back down there.

Chapter 20

It wouldn't be quite so bad, Will thought, *if only I didn't have to look at them.*

On the ship that took them home from the moon, Felicia and Estresor Fil were together virtually every minute. He couldn't tell if they had become romantically involved or if their friendship had just taken a more intimate turn. They laughed together, they sat close and chatted, now and again they seemed to be holding hands or touching one another's faces. But that might have been an illusion, just normal touching magnified in Will's mind by his own dark mood.

By the time they disembarked at the Academy in San Francisco, Will had come to an understanding with himself. It was stupid to even think that he should get involved with a woman in the first place. He had his Academy career to worry about, and after that his Starfleet career. Maybe once that was on track he could start to think about women, maybe getting married and starting a family at some point. But not until then. A girlfriend now would just set him back, cost him time and energy he needed to spend studying and working. There was no room in an active, ambitious career for romance, and thinking that there was had been simply delusional.

When he saw Estresor Fil and Felicia walking to their dorm together, Felicia's head bowed so she wouldn't miss a word of whatever the little Zimonian was saying, he didn't begrudge them their happiness at all. He didn't, he decided, feel a thing.

Chapter 21

Roog seemed unhealthy at the best of times, and one misshapen foot in the grave at the rest. Kyle had ascertained that she was a female because Michelle referred to her as "her," but that was all he knew about her beyond her political beliefs, which were strident, and her patience for fools, which was virtually nonexistent.

He and Michelle stood at the back of a large room in the labyrinthine bowels of The End, a room that might once have been a banquet hall or a ballroom. Today, it contained maybe two hundred people, mostly residents of The End and other impoverished neighborhoods, individuals of every race and description. On a raised dais made from construction scraps that afternoon, Roog, Cetra ski Toram, and Melinka sat. They had taken turns addressing the crowd, alternating between describing detailed political and economic scenarios and doing some pure rabble-rousing, trying to direct the audience's anger at the Cyrian government. When Kyle had suggested that Michelle should also be on the dais, she had colored and waggled her hand in the Cyrian gesture of negativity. He was getting used to conversing with her in English with touches of Cyrian thrown in, like that or the back and forth hand wobble that indicated assent or agreement. "I'm just a foot soldier," she protested. "Not a general."

"I know a little bit about strategy," he admitted. "And I know that generals aren't worth much if they don't have footsoldiers they can count on."

"I get the feeling you know about a lot of things, Joe Brady," she replied. Then she hushed him, because Roog was talking and those near them were shooting them dirty looks.

"No plutocracy can survive indefinitely," Roog was saying, "because, by definition, the majority of its citizens are shut out of power. And when a majority understands that it's being used and abused by the powerful for the sole benefit of the powerful, then that majority rises up and takes back its proper role."

This pronouncement was met by cheers and warm applause from the audience. Roog waited for it to finish and went on. "The Cyrian plutocracy is at that point now. They are willing to kill us—kill the majority—because we are inconvenient to them. That's always—always—a sure sign of a plutocracy that has lost its way, with a leadership that has lost its collective mind. Individual members of government may still be sane, but the government itself is insane. Unsound. Mad. The time has come to stop fighting back with words— words can only influence those sane enough to hear and understand them. The time has come for action!"

A much louder roar of applause went up this time, and Kyle found himself hoping the government didn't have spies in the neighborhood. This room was deep inside a large building that might have been a luxury hotel, in its prime, but to have contained the noise this bunch was making, he hoped it was still well soundproofed.

"I can't promise you that victory will be easy," Roog said when the applause had abated. "It won't be. I can't promise you that it will come without sacrifice—and you, of everyone in this nation, have already sacrificed plenty. It will not. I can't promise that you will all be here to taste the fruits of your efforts—the fresh taste of freedom, of self-governance, of economic possibility. You won't be.

"We are talking about a struggle, and in a struggle there are casualties, and some will die, and others will be injured, and along the way there will be dark days when you wonder if it's worth the pain and the loss and the heartbreak. So I say to you today, look at yourselves. Look at those next to you, behind you, all around you. Look at your families, your young. It's for them that we must fight. For yourself, of course. But also for your neighbors, your loved ones, and your offspring. For everyone that you know, and everyone you are ever likely to know. Because we fight for justice, and there is no justice if justice is selective. Justice must stand for all if it is to stand for any!"

When the crowd broke into more sustained cheers, Kyle turned to Michelle. "She's good," he said.

"She knows how to work a crowd," Michelle agreed. "If she could address thousands, or tens of thousands, all at once, we'd have a revolution today and economic justice tomorrow. But she would be killed before she could get a word out, if the government knew she was doing this. As long as the struggle has to remain secret, it'll be a hard road. As it is we need to rely on these people spreading the word to friends and neighbors, but doing so discreetly."

"And that's really what you think will happen? Revolution?" They had talked about this several times in the weeks since the police attack, but he kept pressing her on the point. He knew the success of such a movement was a long shot, and the more he got to know her the more he didn't want to see her hurt or killed.

The rally over, the audience began to stream from the building, out into the glare of midday suns. Michelle and Kyle went with the flow, but as the crowd dispersed, they found themselves alone on one of the winding streets. "Of course it is," she replied as if he had just asked the question. "We're both from Earth, Joe, and we're both from the United States. We know that revolution can succeed when the cause is just and the people are behind it."

"We also know how rare it is to have both of those elements in the right balance," he countered.

She took his hand and squeezed it. "That's why we need the right people in the right positions, Joe. Like you said, you know something about strategy. I haven't asked you any questions about your background, your history, and you haven't asked me any. I appreciate that about you, and I respect your privacy. But I think it's time we came clean. If we're going to succeed—and I mean the revolution, but I also mean us, you and me—then we need to know each other. We need to understand what we can each contribute."

She stopped walking and turned to face him, taking his other hand and holding them both in hers. "My name really is Michelle. Last name Culhane. I . . . broke some laws. Not on Earth, I only lived there for a few years, as a girl. My parents were rovers, wanderers, and I lived on a dozen worlds by the time I was twenty. After that, I struck out on my own and did pretty much the same. But I didn't always run with the most reputable company. There was an incident, on Blue Horizon. Lovely place, but bad things can still happen in nice surroundings. I killed a person—two people, actually. It was justified, but that doesn't mean it wasn't illegal. I ran. I can tell you more about it if you want to know."

"No," Kyle said, somewhat taken aback by the unexpected confession. "I mean, maybe someday, if you want to talk about it. If it'll help you. But I trust you, I don't need the details."

She kissed him tenderly on the cheek, and then on the lips. "Thanks," she said, drawing away. "For the trust. I like that."

"You taught it to me," he replied.

"So what's your story, Joe? That's not your name, is it? It doesn't quite fit you, it's like you're wearing someone else's shirt."

Kyle shook his head. "No, no, it's not my name." He felt a moment's hesitation, but then, emboldened by her confession and by his own growing feelings for her, he decided to tell her the truth. "My name is Kyle Riker," he revealed. "I work—or used to, anyway, for Starfleet. I'm a civilian but I serve as a military strategist for them."

"That's perfect!" Michelle blurted out. "I mean, a trained military strategist. You could do wonders for the revolution." She looked at him, a smile on her face. "Sorry, I interrupted, didn't I? I do that."

"That's perfectly okay," Kyle said. "That's pretty much the story."

"You're here for a reason," she prodded. A wind blasted down the street, flaying them both with her hair, and she laughed. Over their heads, a purple skray winged by, shrieking at them. They were, as far as he could tell, the local version of pigeons, and every bit as unappetizing.

"Someone was trying to kill me—well, either ruin my career or kill me, I guess. Someone associated, in some way, with Starfleet. I've had some pretty traumatic experiences in recent years, and I guess that one was the topper. I more or less flipped out and ran. I still intend to go back, but before I do I want to figure out who I'm up against, and why. So far I keep coming up blank, which is why I'm still here."

"Maybe it's not something you can find out from a distance," Michelle suggested. She squeezed his hands again. "Maybe you just need to be there. Not that I want you to leave, of course. Especially not now."

"I understand, Michelle. And you could be right. You probably are. But now . . . now you're here. I've screwed up before, and it's like some kind of second chance. Fourth or fifth chance, maybe."

She smiled once more. "I'm glad that matters to you, Joe. Or should I say, Kyle?"

"Stick with Joe," he urged. "It's safer that way."

"I like Kyle better," she told him. "That is a name that fits you. It's stronger. Joe is nondescript, and you're anything but. I'll call you Joe, but in my heart you'll be Kyle. Is that okay?"

He couldn't help feeling glad that events had conspired to send him to Hazimot, where he could meet such an exceptional woman. That made three amazing women—Annie, Katherine Pulaski, and now Michelle Culhane—who had opened their hearts to him. How did a man get to be so lucky?

At the same time, he recognized that, while illness had claimed Annie, he alone had been responsible for the fact that he wasn't still with Kate. He'd have to take care not to make the same mistakes again, because Michelle seemed like the kind of woman he could spend a lifetime with.

"That'll be fine," he said finally. "Just fine."

"And will you help us?" she pressed. "You don't have to fight if you don't want to, but will you advise us? Help with strategy?"

"Let's keep talking about that," he suggested. "Give me time to come around. From what I've seen so far, you have more passion on your side than you do prospects."

"That may be true," she said. "But passion counts for a lot too. And we have some good minds working on it. Native Hazimotian minds, and others. With you, several good human ones as well."

"Who else is human among the leadership?" Kyle asked. "Jackdaw? Alan?"

"They are, but they're not really leadership," Michelle suggested. "But I am, and of course Roog—"

"Roog's human?" he interrupted. He pictured her indistinct, amorphous form with what seemed like other beings moving about beneath semi-translucent skin, her lumpish head and barely functional limbs. "How . . . what happened to her?"

"Cyre happened," Michelle said, an explanation that didn't explain much. When Kyle just stared at her, she elaborated. "You might have noticed that body modification is kind of a hobby, or a fetish, of many of the locals. Especially here in The End, where it's the only kind of art one can expect to keep when one is forced to move from one hovel to another."

"But I thought that was just among the Hazimotians," Kyle said.

"For the most part, but not completely," Michelle replied. "Roog has been here for a long time, and she's gone native in most ways. Including that one. She's had a lot of work done, not all of which turned out exactly as she'd hoped. But she's still human inside, where it counts. She still has the experience of revolution in her genetic memory. And she's as dedicated as you'll ever find, on our home world or this one."

"I guess you just can't trust appearances," Kyle offered.

"You never have been able to," Michelle agreed. "Why start now? You can only trust hard facts, like this one. When I tell you that I love you, Kyle Joe Brady Riker, I mean it. That, you can trust."

What is the report on Kyle Riker?

The report is that there is no report. Still no news, no information. He cannot be found.

How is this possible? We have at our disposal the most far-reaching information gathering technology in the history of the galaxy. We have fingers everywhere. And one simple man can elude all of this? It simply isn't possible.

It may not be possible, but it seems to be the case. There has been no sign of Riker since the day he vanished. We may need to accept a potential scenario that we have not wanted to . . .

That he's already dead. That he killed himself, perhaps, to avoid his certain fate at our hands. Yes, I have considered that. But it doesn't seem like his way . . .

But when a man is pushed too hard—

Too hard? How could anything be too hard? After what he's done to us . . .

It's only a suggestion, not a fact. We need to be open to all possibilities.

Agreed. I will entertain that one, but will not accept it as an excuse to stop looking. The search continues. Kyle Riker, or his bones, must be found. And in the meantime . . .

The boy?

Yes. The son. What of him?

He is easily at hand. At the Academy. He thinks he's going to Saturn for the summer.

Keep him here. I want him nearby. Just in case. If we can't find the father, there is a certain poetic irony in targeting the son instead. Or in addition, even better . . .

Yes, in addition. I like that.

I thought you might . . .

PART THREE

MARCH—JUNE
2357

Chapter 22

Senior year brought Academy cadets more privileges, but also many more responsibilities and a heavier workload than ever before. Will, strangely, found that he thrived under the pressure. Each year had been harder than the one before, but conversely, he had done better each year. The difficulties of his first year had been largely gone by the end of his second, but he was still finding his way then. Third had been a time of emotional upheaval that had sometimes interfered with his performance. This year, though, he had been focused on the work. Attending Starfleet Academy was at the same time a great honor and a very difficult job. By paying more attention to the job part, he found that he was able to maximize his results. The more he put in, the more he took out. His grades reflected that new philosophy.

But with the new rigors and responsibilities sometimes came hard truths. And one of them had just hit home. The famous Vulcan science officer who had served on the *Enterprise* with James T. Kirk, Ambassador Spock, was coming to Starfleet Academy to give a lecture. His topic was to be "The Philosophy of Diplomacy, or Why Giving In Isn't Always Giving Up."

It would be fascinating, Will knew. Most of his friends were going. They would get an invaluable experience out of it. They might even get to meet Spock himself, who was as close to a living legend as existed in the galaxy today. And the information he would impart would be beyond helpful to anyone considering a Starfleet career. For all these reasons, Will wanted very much to attend.

But he couldn't. Because by the time Ambassador Spock would be in San Francisco in two days, he would be—finally—on Saturn. Two summers in a row, his assignment to Saturn had been scotched at the last minute. This last summer, there had never even been an explanation forthcoming, just a simple change in orders, keeping him on Earth yet again. But now, he would definitely make it to Saturn. A flight exercise run among Saturn's moons was taking him and an assortment of other cadets away, and they'd be gone for the duration of Ambassador Spock's visit to Earth. The exercise was an important part of his grade, and couldn't be missed, even for a once-in-a-lifetime opportunity like the Spock lecture.

The whole situation ticked him off. Ultimately, the Spock lecture would be more educational than flying patterns he knew in his sleep. *There has to be a way to make it work*, he thought. *There just has to.*

And of course, he realized, *there is.*

It took him a while to figure out just who would be the most helpful, but finally he came up with Trinidad Khalil. Trinidad, a third-year student, was a terrific pilot, skilled and comfortable at the conn of any ship he encountered. And Will remembered that he had been present when Spock's visit had been announced, but he had shown little interest.

Will found Trinidad in the dorm and took him out to an off-campus saloon called the Ready Room. After a few minutes of idle chatter, he brought up the issue there, over tall glasses of Aldorian ale. "So it didn't seem like you had much interest in Ambassador Spock's lecture this week," he said bluntly.

Trinidad shrugged. He was a darkly handsome young

man, about Will's size. "I'm not a hero worshipper or anything," Trinidad said. "I mean, Spock has made some great contributions, you know? But I've read about them. I don't feel like I need to see him talk about them too."

"I'd sure like to be there," Will admitted. He kept his voice low, as there were plenty of students and faculty in the place. Despite the implication of its name, the saloon was styled after the lounge on board a Starfleet vessel, not a captain's ready room. It was decorated with lots of grays and blues, in sleek lines and stylish curves, and was popular with cadets as well as personnel from Starfleet Command.

"Is there some reason that you can't be?"

"I'm part of that Saturn exercise. We leave tomorrow. I'll be flying maneuvers the whole time Spock is here."

Trinidad's face brightened. "You got picked for that run? Congratulations, Will. That'll be such a blast."

"You really love to fly, don't you?" Will asked him.

"More than anything. I don't ever want to make captain, that's for sure. They hardly get to have any of the fun."

"It's too bad," Will said, trying to sound sincere when things were playing right into his hands. "I want to be here, and you want to be there. And yet, our positions are reversed."

They sat in silence for a few moments while Trinidad processed the idea that Will had planted. "But do they have to be?" he asked.

Will casually took a sip of his ale and arched an eyebrow. "What do you mean?"

"What if there was a way to trade places? If I could go to Saturn and fly, and you could stay here and see Spock."

"I don't know if they'll just swap out our orders like that, especially this late," Will hedged.

"Maybe they don't need to. We don't look a lot alike, Will, but we're about the same build. And no one on Saturn knows you, right?"

"Not that I know of," Will replied.

"So if I borrowed your identity for a while . . ."

"The people going to Saturn to fly with me know me," Will pointed out. He hadn't been able to get over this hurdle, though he hoped maybe Trinidad could come up with something.

"But they're friends of yours, right?" Trinidad offered. He seemed even more excited by the prospect than Will was. "So maybe they could be encouraged to go along with the gag."

"It's possible, I guess," Will relented.

Trinidad raised his glass and held it out toward Will's. "Come on," he said. "A toast. To getting what we want."

Will lifted his glass and clinked it against Trinidad's, watching the amber liquid catch the light as it sloshed around. "To getting what we want." He liked the sound of those words.

He wondered what it actually felt like.

After leaving Trinidad at the Ready Room—fortified, he knew, by his success at persuading his friend to take a dangerous chance as well as by several glasses of strong Aldorian ale, Will decided that he wasn't ready to stop getting what he wanted. His trip back to campus was kind of a blur, but he eventually found himself standing outside Felicia Mendoza's door. He raised a hand to rap against it, but the door suddenly moved a little farther away than it had been. Looking down, he realized that the whole floor was moving—turning in a slow circle and pulsing up and down at the same time. He thought at first that it was an earthquake, but realized a moment later that it was far more likely the full effects of the ale kicking in. His stomach was making similar motions.

He had come this far, though, so he steadied himself and knocked at the door. It was only after he had done so that he considered the possibility that Estresor Fil might be here, and the embarrassment that might ensue.

But Felicia was alone when she came to the door, in blue

cotton pajamas. "That's not regulation uniform," Will observed.

"Nor do regulations require me to be in uniform at oh-two-hundred," Felicia shot back. "Will Riker, are you drunk?"

"There is a very distinct possibility that I am, yes."

"Get out of here."

"But, Felicia . . ."

"Will, I would be perfectly happy to have you visit my room at virtually any other time. Although waking hours are, of course, preferred. But not when you're too drunk to think straight. Much less stand up straight."

What she was saying probably made sense. But Will couldn't really concentrate on it because the floor was moving faster now, dipping and rising like a thrill ride, and she swam in and out of focus, and his stomach. . . . "Felicia, I . . ." he got out, and then he pitched forward and the world went dark.

When he opened his eyes again, he thought the movement would kill him.

"I see you're up," Felicia's voice screamed at him.

"Shhh!" he insisted with a giggle that pierced his brain. "You'll wake Felicia."

"Are you still drunk, Will?"

He realized several things at once. He was on the floor of Felicia's room, which he determined because he could see Felicia standing across the room looking at him, and he recognized the art on her walls. Someone—presumably she—had put a blanket over him while he slept. His brain was on fire, his mouth tasted as if a Klingon had been herding *targs* in it, and he had hopelessly humiliated himself. But he was no longer drunk.

"No," he managed. "Because if I was, then I wouldn't be in pain. Feeling no pain, that's what they say, right?"

"Sometimes they do," she agreed. "But you're feeling it now, aren't you?"

He tried to push himself to a sitting position. It didn't

work very well. He reached out and steadied himself against her bed and did it again, and this time he was able to sit up, as long as he leaned against the bed. His head throbbed blindingly and his stomach churned. "Yes," he admitted. "I'm feeling it."

"You do know where you are?"

"I'm in your room. I came here . . . to talk to you."

"You didn't seem interested in talking. Snoring, maybe."

"I'm sorry, Felicia," he said. "I hope I didn't keep you up."

"After you woke me up in the first place, you mean."

"Sorry about that too," he said. The words were coming a little easier, but some water would make it easier still. She had already figured that out, it seemed, and she brought him a glass.

"You're dehydrated," she said. "You need to drink this. Slowly and carefully."

He took a sip and felt his stomach lurch. He waited for it to settle, then took another sip. "I really messed everything up," he said. "I am so sorry."

"You're a Starfleet Academy cadet," Felicia said with a shrug. "It's practically a graduating requirement."

"You hardly ever mess up."

"I am unique in my brilliance and self-possession," she said, laughing.

"That's kind of what I wanted to talk to you about." Will drank some more water and felt a little stronger.

"If you came to compliment my good qualities, I'm sorry you were unconscious the whole time," Felicia replied. "But now I have to get to class—as do you, although I doubt you'll make it. So we'll have to reschedule my praise."

"But . . . no, Felicia." He forced himself to his feet, made it for a second and then fell back to the edge of her bed. Progress, though. "You know what? I've put this off too long. I know I've blown it, probably ruined whatever chance I might ever have had. But I still have to say it. So stick around, please. For a little while."

"Will, this class is important to me."

"But *you're* important to me!" *There,* he thought. *It's out.*

"I appreciate that, Will," she said, apparently not quite getting what he'd meant. "And I like you too. But I don't want to miss this class."

"Felicia," Will said, hanging his head and gripping it with both hands as if to keep its halves together. His outburst had been truly excruciating. "Just . . . wait. Bear with me a little, okay? We've known each other for a long time."

"Yes, we have." She sat down on a chair facing him and waited. "So what did you want to talk about?"

"This made a lot more sense last night," he began. "Or at least I thought it did. But . . . well, us. I wanted to talk about us."

"There's an us?"

"I always wanted there to be," Will said. "I guess after last night, I can see that there never will be. But as long as I've known you I've wanted to be with you."

"And of course I was supposed to know this by the fact that you never once mentioned it."

"Yes," Will said. Then, "No. I mean . . . you couldn't have, I guess. I kept hoping you would just figure it out. And I wanted to tell you, several times. But things kept getting in the way."

"What kinds of things?" she asked him. She seemed a little dismayed by this whole conversation, and he couldn't blame her a bit.

"Different . . . things. Like when we were on our survival project, I wanted to say something. But we ended up being arrested and sent to Superintendent Vyrek's office, and by the time I got out, you were already gone."

"I waited for you to come out," Felicia corrected him. "But it took so long, and the others were leaving. And then when you did come out, you went the other direction. You didn't even try to catch up to us."

"I thought if you wanted me around, you'd wait," he said. "I guess maybe I was wrong."

"Maybe," she echoed, nodding her head.

"And then, on the moon. After that dinner, remember? I wanted to take you out under the stars and tell you then. But you went out with Estresor Fil instead. And after that, it seemed like you two were doing so well together, I didn't want to get in the way."

"Estresor Fil is sweet and kind and was gutsy enough to say what she felt," Felicia told him. "Which you're a couple of years late with. We've had some good times, she and I. We enjoy each other's company. We like to be together. But what we have isn't a romance, and it won't ever be."

"I thought . . ."

"I know what you thought, Will. Or I think I do. I also think you're emotionally stunted. You don't know what you want, and once you figure that out you don't know how to pursue it."

"I thought we were here to talk about your qualities, not mine," he said with a weak grin.

"There's a time for everything, Will," she shot back. "You're making me miss my class, I get to tell you how I feel. Fair's fair."

"Okay," Will relented. "Go ahead. Let me have it. I deserve it, I know."

She took to her feet again, as if this would be easier standing up, and started pacing before him. "Will, you're a nice guy. You're smart, you're funny, you're frequently very sweet. You're easy to look at. I like you a lot. But you're so dense sometimes I can't stand it."

Will knew he was opening himself up, but he had to ask. "Dense?"

Felicia laughed so hard she actually snorted. Will would

have enjoyed it if the sound didn't make his head hurt so much. When she had composed herself, she wiped a tear away with the back of her hand and stood in front of him. "Look at me, Will. Am I unattractive?"

"Not at all," he answered truthfully. "You're the most beautiful girl I've ever known."

"Do I have any kind of objectionable odor? Any unsanitary or unsightly habits you know of?"

"Besides the snorting thing when you laugh?" he teased. "Of course not."

"So it's safe to assume that if I had wanted a boyfriend or a girlfriend during my time here at the Academy, I could probably have had one."

"I suppose."

"Especially since I'm not too emotionally naïve to go out and look for one, if that's what I wanted."

"You could put it that way," Will admitted.

"And yet I don't," she pointed out.

"No, you don't seem to. Not if Estresor Fil doesn't count."

"She doesn't count."

"Then I guess the answer is that you don't. What was the question again?"

She lowered herself to her knees, now, in front of Will, and put her hands on his knees, looking right into his eyes. "The question, Will Riker, is just how long did you expect me to wait around for you?"

"For me?"

"Did I say 'dense'?" Felicia asked, smacking his knees with her palms. "I meant impenetrable! The planet's crust isn't as thick as you, Riker!"

"Wait," he said, slowly catching up. "You were waiting for me?"

Felicia covered her face with her hands. "Just don't ask me why!"

"But that means . . . you . . ."

She pushed herself up on his knees again, bringing her face level with his. "I'm crazy about you, Will. I always have been. But you kept walling yourself off, closing yourself away from me. You hid from me for, what was it, six months? I would have said something but I knew you weren't ready. I had to wait until you could make up your own mind, or you'd spend the rest of your life wondering if I'd pushed you into something. I wonder if there's a Starfleet medal for extreme patience in the face of idiocy."

A sudden vision of Trinidad clinking glasses with him at the bar flashed into Will's mind. "Oh, no," he said. "Speaking of pushing people into things . . . oh, no."

"What is it, Will?"

He held he face between his palms. "I've got to find Trinidad Khalil," he said urgently. "And then I've got to go to Saturn."

"Today? You're leaving today?"

"If they haven't left without me," Will said. "Oh, no."

"Will, what is it?"

"Just another bad mistake in a whole series of them," he told her. He pulled her face closer and pressed his lips against hers. He liked the way that felt, a lot, and he did it again. "You've waited this long, you can wait a few more days, right?"

"I guess so, Will, but . . ."

"I need to go." He kissed her again, twice, then twice more. "I really need to go." He kissed her one more time. "I'm going now."

"Will, if it's that important," she said, her lips caught under his, "then you should really go. I'll be here."

"You promise?"

"I promise."

Will caught Trinidad as he was leaving his room, his duffel packed for the trip to the Saturn base. "Trinidad," he said, breathlessly. "You can't do this!"

Trinidad eyed him. "You look awful, Will. What happened to you?"

"I know," Will assured him. "I slept on a floor. But I feel wonderful."

"What do you mean, I can't do this? Last night you were trying to make me think it was my idea. Almost worked, too."

"Look," Will said. "There's a certain diabolical cleverness to the idea. But it's doomed to fail. Everyone knows you're not me. Someone would accidentally call you Trinidad in front of the instructors and it would all be over. Or they'd call out 'Will' and you'd forget to answer. Or there would be a DNA scan or a retina scan at some point. There are too many ways for it to go wrong, don't you see? If we got caught—and we would—we'd both be in serious trouble." Will had had enough close scrapes at the Academy. If a Starfleet officer broke the rules with a good enough reason, that was one thing. But before he actually got into Starfleet, he knew it was important to play it safe—or he might find himself out before he ever got in.

"But . . . you wanted it," Trinidad said. He sounded mournful, and Will was sorry he'd ever brought it up. Trinidad loved to fly more than anything, and this must have seemed like the adventure of a lifetime.

"I know. I would love to stay and see Spock. But I can't, and you can't go to Saturn. You're just third year, though, and already a better pilot than me. You'll go next year, for sure."

"You think so?" Trinidad asked, brightening a little.

"Definitely," Will said. "I know it."

"Well, if you're going," Trinidad suggested, "you'd better hustle. The shuttle's leaving in twenty minutes."

Will groaned. He had known it was late, but he hadn't realized it was that late. "Give me your duffel," he said.

"What?"

"Your duffel. You don't need it. We wear the same size uniform. I don't have time to pack."

"Are you sure you've sobered up?" Trinidad asked him.

"I'm as sober as I need to be," Will said. "Come on, quick. I need to go."

Trinidad shrugged and handed over his duffel. "Have a good trip," he said. "Don't drink the Aldorian ale."

"Never again," Will promised him.

Borrowed duffel in hand, Will turned and dashed toward the lift. Less than twenty minutes to make the shuttle. With every step he ran, his head pounded, like someone opening and closing a vise on it.

And yet, in a different way, he had never felt better.

Chapter 23

Cyre was governed by a ruling council made up of seven members, each representing a different geographical region of the nation. Cozzen was in the largest region, an inland area dominated by that city. There were also two coastal areas, a mountain region, and three smaller inland areas, all making up a nation that was more or less rectangular, bounded on the north and west by seas, on the south by an enemy, and on the east by two separate but allied smaller states. The council members purported to represent the entire population of each region, so that the whole council would support the interests of the nation.

It didn't work that way, Kyle had learned.

Instead, the council members really represented a small minority of the wealthiest and most powerful citizens in each region. New council members were chosen by existing council members, for terms of nine Hazimotian years, so there was little chance of anyone who genuinely represented the population finding a seat at the council. Each council member also served as the chief executive officer of his or her region, with another, similarly chosen council at that level under his or her rule.

The main function of the council seemed to be—at least as Michelle and her friends described it—the raising of revenue through taxes, various fees, and fines for criminal behavior. That revenue, however, rarely came back to the citizens in the form of services, but instead seemed to be spent on a never-ending litany of important government contracts—awarded to council members and their allies, of course—that rarely had any real impact on the nation. At the local level, at least, some of the money eventually filtered down, as Kyle had learned. He'd been employed since arriving on Hazimot as a laborer for a perpetual series of municipal repairs. But the money budgeted toward those repairs seemed to be many times what went out in salaries and materials, so it was obvious that the local councilors were padding their pocketbooks the whole time.

The public, squeezed from the top and with no relief in sight, began to object, and so the fires of discontent spread. But the council, isolated from its populace, remained ignorant of how fast and wide their actions fanned those flames. And the population as a whole, though embittered and impoverished by the council's decisions, didn't know the full extent of their own unhappiness. Public displays of dissent were banned, the press strictly controlled. There are enemies at our borders, the council said. We'll take care of you, but you have to be silent and let us do our jobs.

What the revolution needed was a public action, a Boston Tea Party, a storming of the Bastille, a barrage of Station Salem One. Something to show the nation that there was an opposition, that it was organized and strong and determined.

That's where Kyle came in.

He sat with Michelle and her friends, with Cetra and

Roog and Melinka, with Alan and Jackdaw and Baukels Jinython, and with the others who formed the extended planning leadership of Cozzen's revolutionary cadre. From other cities, including the Cyrian capital of Coscotus on the northern shore, others came. They met, they ate and drank, they talked incessantly. Proposals were put forth, debated, and usually discarded. Others were massaged and kept for further consideration. With Michelle vouching for him, Kyle was accepted into the highest levels of the group. He appreciated the intent of their effort but he was not, by nature, a political activist, and he served as a kind of devil's advocate for them, poking holes in their ideas to see where the air leaked out.

Finally, the time came to put talk aside and take direct action. Their first attack was meant to be primarily one of public relations, not military. Too many of Cyre's vast underclass had already died in combat, drafted and sent to battle the unending supply of enemies in other lands. The goal was to oust the council with the least amount of military action, the fewest deaths. But that could happen only if an overwhelming number of the nation's populace rose up at once.

Mahaross Ka Elstreth was the council member for Cozzen, and on this day he was in the city, officiating over the induction of Cozzen's newest councilor, his third son, Mahaross Ka Ennis. A parade was planned, and spontaneous displays of patriotic pride were not only encouraged, but had in fact been orchestrated in advance by commercial allies of the councilors. A great many citizens would be watching, and the day's events would be broadcast live throughout Cozzen and across the land. Two of Elstreth's fellow council members would also be on hand to greet his son into the ranks of privilege.

The parade would not, if Michelle's friends had their way, go precisely as expected.

On the day of the action, Michelle dressed quickly, anxious to get into position. But when Kyle tried to follow her out the door she pushed him back into a chair, palms flat against his chest, head wagging. "No," she said. "You stay here. This isn't your fight and you can't get involved."

He had to laugh. "Seems like I'm already pretty involved."

"Among those of us on the committee," she pointed out. "But not on the streets. The rest of them, the people who will be doing the dirty work, don't know you—they don't know anyone by name, so if any of them are arrested they can't implicate anyone on the committee. We've all used *noms de guerre.*"

"That's a good idea," Kyle said. He knew that she had met with various planning committees while he worked—that while he had helped with the broad strokes planning, he hadn't been around for much of the detail work. "But still, if you're going to be out there I want to be next to you."

Michelle shook her head again. "Absolutely not. Probably nothing will happen to me, and I'll see you when it's over and make passionate love with you. If, on the other hand, something does happen, the movement will need your skills to carry on."

"My skills only go so far without someone like you to put my plans into action," Kyle protested.

"Exactly my point," Michelle said. "Someone needs to put this into action, and that's me. If you object to me going out and acting, then we've got a problem."

Kyle could see that arguing with her was going to be fruitless. In fact, he realized, in all the planning for today's activities he had never been assigned a specific role. He'd thought that he would simply be accompanying Michelle, but now he realized it was because she knew he would object if she let him know ahead of time that he was being left behind. "All right," he said, giving in for now. Another thing he knew was that when Michelle had made up her mind there was no budging her. "But you be careful."

"Don't worry," Michelle promised him. "I love you too much to not come straight back here when it's over."

"I'll be waiting," Kyle said. "And watching."

"You do that." Michelle kissed him several times, and then dashed out the door, her face flushed with the excitement of the day. Kyle felt a surge of disappointment that he wasn't going with her, combined with worry that he wouldn't be around to watch her back. But the plan was for a nonviolent action today, more street theater than revolution, so there shouldn't be much danger.

In a way, this was what Kyle was used to. In his Starfleet role, he was the adviser, the civilian who stayed back while others executed his plans. He had, he was fully aware, been responsible for the deaths of thousands, over the span of his career—Starfleet personnel as well as aliens he would never meet or even see in person. It wasn't something he thought about very often, because it was a difficult burden to bear. Because he was good at compartmentalizing, that was an aspect of his life that he kept tucked away and didn't take out to examine very often. When he did, he just accepted that it ran in his family.

His father had been a military man, as had his grandfather. His grandfather, he remembered with displeasure, had also been a tyrant at home, a martinet, running his household as he would have a starship if he'd ever held a command position. But probably because of his violent temper he never was put in charge of troops, so he had taken his aggressions out on his family instead. As the oldest son, Kyle's father was first in line when his purple rages came upon him.

Kyle's father, in his turn, had sworn never to lay a hand on his family in anger, and had kept that vow. From his military service he took a different lesson, that of self-discipline, of keeping his emotions in check, of leading the fragmented unit of his family into functioning as a whole. Kyle had, he hoped, put more of his father's lessons into practice than his grandfather's. To a certain extent, he supposed, he was genetically doomed to a military career and all the attendant difficulties. There had been very few generations of Rikers, as far back as he'd been able to research, that hadn't included soldiers. And while, of course, not every military person had emotional problems, he guessed there was probably some correlation. The traits that made for a good soldier—the ability to follow orders, to sublimate the individual for the unit, to kill without undue anguish—didn't necessarily lend themselves well to getting along in a domestic situation. Will—poor, innocent Will—had had to pay that price as well, and that, as much as losing Annie and letting Kate go, was the central heartbreak of Kyle Riker's life.

He didn't want to let it happen again, ever.

After a quick dash through the hot, dusty morning streets, Michelle met her unit at a designated spot near the fringes of The End. Those who were taking part in today's parade disruption had split into nine teams of seven each. Michelle's unit consisted of six people she'd never met before, who knew her only by her *nom de guerre* of Kyle Riker, which she had taken in honor of the man who had done more for her, in a relatively short span of time, than all the men she had ever known. He'd inspired her, he'd guided and encouraged her activism, he'd offered brilliant strategic advice, and he had touched her, emotionally and physically, in ways she hadn't believed she could be touched. The strangest part was, he seemed almost totally oblivious to it all, as if he couldn't quite believe he offered all these gifts and kept wondering what hook it was that kept her near him.

Her unit was all Cyrians, except for her. That was fine, they'd blend in better with the crowds around the parade. Security was always tight around public events, especially when multiple council members were present, but unless there had been leaks, it wouldn't be any tighter today than usual. Which meant there would be openings, and more would become available once things started to happen.

"I brought the reels," one of them said. Her *nom de guerre* was Alstatis, the name of an ancient Hazimotian hero whose exploits had entered the realm of myth. She opened a bag and showed off seven reels of extremely fine metal wire.

"That's excellent," Michelle said. From several blocks away they could already hear cheers and jubilation, either from the parade itself or one of the "spontaneous" demonstrations of support for the council. She didn't really care which it was—both would serve their interests, which involved getting the largest audience possible for their action. "Everybody take one."

The Cyrians, evenly split between males and females, obeyed her instruction without question. None of them knew who she was but they knew she was the leader here, a member of the cadre that had planned the action, and who would be in charge once the revolution began in earnest. They didn't mind that; they knew they were the ground troops, the ones who would execute the committee's plans, and that was fine with them. Michelle noted some shaking hands and dry swallowing as they divvied up the wire reels.

"We're all nervous," she told them. "It's not just you guys, but everyone who's participating today. After this, everything changes. There will be no backing down, no fading back into the shadows. After today, we overthrow the council or we die trying. So if any of you want to change your mind and give up, now's the time to do it. Your last chance."

They watched her as she spoke, their faces rapt or frightened or both. A couple of them said, "I'm staying in," and one, who Michelle knew only as Cividon, said, "It's about time." No one chose to withdraw, for which Michelle was glad.

"Let's get into place, then," she suggested. The others agreed and they moved out, toward the parade route.

The parade was slated to run for twenty blocks, or about two kilometers, with a couple of right angles along the way and then a last sweep up the wide, gently curving arc of Epindeis Way, named for one of Cyre's most famous military victories over its longtime foe Taleraa. Michelle's group went to the last right turn before the final march up Epindeis, arriving just as the parade passed that point. They saw soldiers marching in full uniform, with helmets on and weapons in hand, and among the soldiers various armored ground vehicles. Behind the soldiers were bands playing uniquely Hazimotian instruments—since arriving here and deciding to stay, Michelle had tried and tried but had never quite been able to comprehend what the Hazimotians considered musical, and the racket they made just seemed like an assault on the ears. Various minor officials brought up the very rear. At the end, far up on Epindeis Way, there was a reviewing stand from which the council members and other luminaries watched the proceedings, and where the induction ceremony would take place as soon as the parade ended.

Now the parade, nearly eight blocks long in total, was entirely on Epindeis Way, which meant it was almost time for the fun to start. Police lined the parade route but after the marchers passed, their attention waned and spectators were allowed to cross the street. Nothing to do now but wait. Michelle felt her own knees shaking with anxiety now, as the moment to act grew ever nearer.

The minutes dragged by.

Finally, there was a commotion at the end. She could barely see what was happening, but they'd been over it often enough in the committee that she knew it anyway. One unit of counter-marchers had suddenly confronted the parade's head with signs bearing slogans like "The Council's Corrupt" and "Feed Your Children, Not Council Greed," and chanting. Another unit had activated smoke devices and hurled them under the reviewing stand—even now,

Michelle could begin to see gray and yellow plumes swirling up from the crowd. Yet another on that end exploded noise-making devices—not bombs that would do any damage, but that would leave people's ears ringing for a good long time. Finally, the last group, already shackled together, would chain themselves to the reviewing stand so that the induction ceremony couldn't begin until the police had, very publicly, arrested them and hauled them away.

Michelle and her unit were responsible for the finishing touch. As soon as she knew that things had started on the far end of Epindeis, she ordered her troops into action. Three of them squatted on the ground at the parade route's edge, a wire reel in each hand. The other three grabbed the ends of the wires and ran across the street, trailing wire behind them. Once they'd reached the other end of the street, they also squatted, so six threadlike, nearly invisible wires were strung across the parade route at about knee height. As expected, when the commotion began near the reviewing stand, the minor officials and bands and many of the police officers and soldiers on this end tried to turn and run the other way, distancing themselves from the trouble. But the first ones who ran—the politicians, mostly—found themselves tripped up on the wire. Michelle laughed out loud at seeing so many hated politicos going ass over teakettle onto Epindeis Way.

And the more who came this way, backtracking or retreating from the fireworks at the far end, the greater the pileup. The musicians, carrying their bizarre instruments, tripped over downed politicians. Soldiers and police officers fell over both, trying not to shoot themselves or anyone else as they did so. By this point, Michelle's teammates had released the wires, which spun silently back into their reels, their work done. No one would know why so many had fallen, now, but they'd look like a bunch of buffoons to the spectators. Buffoons and cowards, for running in the first place.

The council had been publicly embarrassed, and the world would now know that there was an organized opposition. Things would turn ugly now, and blood would spill, but that would be the council's doing, not theirs. They had begun with a comedy, and the government's response to it would launch the tragedy.

From such a small seed, a revolution would grow.

Chapter 24

Kyle had never seen Michelle quite so jubilant. It looked good on her; but then, there wasn't much that didn't. Maybe the gloom that descended on her like lowering storm clouds sometimes, when she came face-to-face with those parts of her past that were too painful to recall, the things she had come to Hazimot to run away from. But those moods were rare. She had not, Kyle decided, let tragedy destroy her. She used it, even now, to spur her on to action, as she had done today. He'd watched the whole thing in a neighborhood tavern just outside The End, where the interruption of the parade had at first drawn horrified gasps but then acceptance and finally raucous laughter as the city's minor, unloved officials fell all over each other trying to run away.

He had gone home after that, arriving just a few minutes before Michelle burst in wearing a smile that involved her entire body, from the spring of her step to the way she shook her head, whipping her hair out to the sides. "It was fabulous!" she gushed. "Did you see, Joe?" Even in private, she still called him Joe, to make sure she didn't slip up with others around.

"I saw," he assured her. He held out his arms and she rushed into them, laughing. "You were great. All of you."

"We were, weren't we?" A momentary glimmer of dread passed over her face. "Some got arrested, though."

"They were supposed to," Kyle reminded her. That had been discussed, in great depth, at some of the meetings. Arrests were certain at this early stage. It was when the government stopped arresting and started killing that things would get really difficult.

"No, I mean of the ones who weren't supposed to. At least, one was, from my group. Maybe others I don't know about."

"We knew that could happen."

"Yes, we did, didn't we?" The smile was back. She was so charged up, holding her was like hanging on to a live wire. "I am sorry they were caught, but even so . . . even so, it was a huge success, wasn't it? Wasn't it?"

"I believe it was," he told her. "You did what you set out to do. It doesn't get much better than that."

"One thing could make it better," she said, holding his gaze with her clear eyes.

He didn't know what she meant, and said so.

"This," she whispered, and kissed his chin, then his cheek, then his lips. At the same time, she began to move her hands all over his body. "I feel so . . . so ready. So hungry," she said.

Now that he thought about it, so did he.

Much later, they went back into the streets. There was a notable difference now that Kyle could feel with all of his senses. It might pass again, he knew, but for the moment people seemed excited, optimistic. They greeted one another as they passed, exchanging grins that seemed fraught with the promise of better things to come. They passed clusters of people standing together, talking about the morning's events, discussing what they might mean in the short and long term. Michelle and Kyle strolled, hand in hand, not engaging anyone in dialogue but simply soaking up the atmosphere. The mood was celebratory and it fed into Michelle's already elevated state.

After they had walked for a while Michelle leaned into his arm. "This might be real," she said. "It really, truly might."

"Isn't that the point?"

"Yeah, but . . . it's always seemed like kind of a pipe dream, you know? Like something we wanted to happen but not necessarily something that would. Or something that I could help bring about. But now, it seems like it's all those things."

"You definitely helped bring it about," he assured her, happily inhaling her scent.

"I know. It feels funny." She laughed, then released him and did a pirouette in the street. "I'm a star."

"A star of the revolution," Kyle agreed. "George Washington, Thomas Jefferson, and you."

"Wrong revolution," she said, wrinkling her nose at him. "But right idea." The smile vanished from her face again. "What if it's a bad idea?"

"What, revolution?" Kyle asked. He had struggled with the concept many times himself. Maybe armed conflict wasn't the way to change social conditions here.

"What if history is effectively over?" she wondered. "I mean, maybe the time for revolution was hundreds and hundreds of years ago. The universe is a different place now. What impact might an upheaval on Hazimot have on intergalactic trading partners, on the Federation?"

"Well, Hazimot's never going to be accepted into the Federation without some serious changes," Kyle pointed out. "As for the timing—I think each planet has to move forward on its own timetable, regardless of what's going on elsewhere. Obviously conditions in Cyre are egregious, and the rest of the planet's not much better, if at all. If it's time for revolution here, then it's time. You can't worry about how people who've never set foot on the planet are going to feel about it."

"Good answer." Michelle beamed at him. "That's why I love you, Joe," she said. "You're always thinking."

"It's what I do best."

"Second best," she corrected, leaning in for a kiss.

She broke the kiss when they both felt the ground shudder, and not in the good way. They froze in place and listened. A low rumbling sound infiltrated their consciousness now, growing nearer. "What is it?" Kyle asked.

"I'm not sure, but I don't like it," she replied. "It sounds like . . . like trouble. At the least."

The mood of the neighborhood changed as the sound increased. Over the rumble they could hear a voice now, broadcast through some kind of loudspeaker, repeating the same brief message over and over. People came running past them, fear glinting in their eyes. Kyle grabbed one by the shoulders, stopping him from his mad dash. "What is it?" Kyle demanded. "What's going on?"

"Troops," the Cyrian said, his eyes wide with fright. "Lots of them." He broke away from Kyle's grasp and kept running.

"No . . ." Michelle's lower lip began to tremble. "They can't . . . it's too soon."

"They can," Kyle countered. "It's not what I would do because it'll increase public resentment against them. But if they can put an end to the revolution immediately, before it gets off the ground, then they might not care what the populace thinks."

"But we're not ready," Michelle said. "Nobody is."

"That's precisely the point of it," Kyle told her. "To make sure nobody gets ready."

The closer the troops came, the louder the sound of their machines of war. The ground was literally shaking now, buildings vibrating. A bit of stone fell off one nearby and exploded into dust on the ground.

"What are we going to do?" Michelle asked. "We need to find the others."

"No," Kyle said. "Not just now. Not with those soldiers nearby. The last thing you want to do is to congregate in one place. Then they can simply take out the leadership all at once."

"You're right," Michelle said. "Let's just go home and wait it out."

With no better plan coming to him, Kyle agreed to that, and they started back toward the building in which they both lived. As they reached their street, though, the first troops were coming into view, around a bend. They wore full battle armor, black and gray with gold trim, and carried rifles. Locals stood on the streets and watched them march. Behind them, the vehicles hove into sight, massive troop carriers and battle tanks. Unlike most Hazimotian vehicles these didn't float a short distance off the ground but rolled forward on gigantic wheels that tore up the old streets of The End as they came.

And now Kyle could make out the words coming over the loudspeakers. "Remain in your homes," the voice instructed. "Do not attempt to hinder our advance in any way. Stay inside and out of our way. We are looking for a few troublemakers. If you deliver them to us, then the rest of you will not be harmed. These are the individuals we want."

Kyle felt his veins go cold at the announcement, but he and Michelle remained on the side of the road, arms around one another.

"Kiana ser Totkis," the voice went on. "Gisser Struitt. Melifin Pate Brionn."

"Those are all the fake names," Michelle said, breathing a sigh of relief. She smiled nervously. "They don't really know who they're looking for."

The soldiers were closer now, the first rank of them almost even with Michelle and Kyle. They let their gazes wander across the buildings, carefully looking at everyone on the sidewalks. They looked young and nervous. From what Kyle had seen, this was the same kind of force that Cyre would have sent into battle against its enemy neighbors.

Suddenly Michelle tensed in Kyle's arms. "Except . . . oh, no."

"Cass wis Tinerare," the loudspeaker voice continued. "Kyle Riker. Senager Millish."

"I guess I should have had a *nom de guerre* too," Kyle observed.

"For now, we want those individuals only," the voice said, almost too loud to make out now as the vehicles came closer. "And if they are not delivered to us within the hour we will start knocking down The End, building to building, until the whole area is flattened."

A rush of conflicting emotions coursed through Kyle. The End was, literally, the end of the line for most of its residents, the place they lived only because there was no place else that would have them. For him, it had been a hiding place, somewhere he could find the anonymity he sought. But it had become more than that—in so many ways, it had become the first real home he'd had in a long time.

But the soldiers had his name, his real name. And if he kept quiet, those who had taken him in would be displaced, or killed.

The worst that could happen, he figured, was that he'd be arrested. When he was able to prove that he had spent the day watching the parade at a tavern, he would likely be released. Possibly, because his name had come into it, Starfleet would hear and he'd be released into their custody. But he'd spent long enough evading them anyway—it was, he had been starting to think, time he straightened that mess out once and for all.

Michelle stood fast beside him, holding tightly to his arm. The troops continued their slow, inexorable march down the street, their vehicles shredding the pavement as they went. The loudspeaker voice started up again. Kyle glanced at Michelle and freed his arm from her grasp. At the questioning look in her eyes, he turned away and stepped into the street.

Immediately, a dozen rifles were pointed at him, and the march halted.

"I'm Kyle Riker," he said.

The soldiers held their weapons on him but didn't speak. One of the troop carriers opened up, though, and an officer emerged, followed by the head of a Cyrian male Kyle had never seen. The Cyrian looked at Kyle, then at the officer, and waggled his hand. *No*, that meant.

The officer scowled at Kyle. "Stop this foolishness," he said. "Proceed!"

"But I *am* Kyle Riker," Kyle insisted.

"No," Michelle said, pushing past him before he could stop her. "No, he's lying. *I* am Kyle Riker."

The officer looked back toward the head sticking up from the troop carrier's bowels like a turtle's. The Cyrian wobbled his hand back and forth in affirmation.

"Cividon, you bastard," Kyle heard Michelle mutter under her breath. He knew that Cividon must have been part of Michelle's unit, the one who had been arrested after the parade. Cividon had turned on his movement's leaders easily, Kyle realized. He knew only the false names, but Michelle's false name had been real enough to cause this trouble.

She couldn't have known that any of this would happen, or that a single other soul on the planet knew Kyle's name wasn't Joe Brady. If he had just kept quiet, there would have been no trouble.

If he'd kept quiet, though, The End would have been razed, its residents slaughtered.

He couldn't have kept quiet then. Michelle wouldn't have either. There really had been no other choice.

The weapons trained on Kyle shifted, aiming at Michelle. Kyle felt himself trembling. Michelle had been there, and visible, at the parade. Cividon had fingered her. She was in serious trouble, and he couldn't figure out how to get her out of it. Even if he started something, there were too many soldiers, too many weapons, to fight.

"Michelle . . ." he started.

"Don't, Joe," she said urgently. "Old Earth expression. I've made my bed."

"But . . ."

The officer pushed Cividon back into the troop carrier and climbed in himself. When only his own head remained outside, he barked an instruction to the troops. "Kill her!"

The soldiers didn't hesitate. A dozen energy beams blasted at Michelle, all at once. One moment she had been standing there, and the next she had dissolved into a fine spray which coated Kyle. Watching open-mouthed, he tasted her on his tongue and knew that she was on his skin and clothes and hair, in his eyes and nose. What was left of Michelle he and the street and the wall behind them had absorbed.

Blinded by fury and the Michelle-mist, Kyle threw himself toward the soldiers. He didn't have a chance against them, with their armor and weapons, and he knew it, but he didn't care. He battered them with fists and feet, tears streaming down his face as he took their blows in return. Finally, one brought the stock of a weapon down against his head and he staggered back a few steps, the world spinning crazily away from him, and he fell down in the street, unconscious.

Chapter 25

This is no fun at all! Will thought.

It had started out looking as if it might be. The flying exercises were, as Will had expected, mundane, even boring.

He knew his stuff by now, and so did the rest of the cadets selected for this journey. It was almost a punishment rather than a reward, particularly since he knew he was missing the chance to listen to Spock.

But Paul Rice, maybe looking to add some spice to the trip, had challenged Will to a friendly race. He'd done it in front of their friends, and he'd pressed it even when Will had tried to laugh it off.

"I thought you were a flyer, Riker," he'd said. "I thought maybe you had some nerve. But I guess your by-the-book attitude has killed that, huh? Stolen your courage along with your skills?"

"I can outfly you anytime," Will said, though he knew it wasn't true. Paul was still one of the best natural pilots he'd ever encountered. "I don't need to break the rules to know that."

"Funny," Paul said, gesturing toward the other cadets who had gathered in a circle, watching them. "They don't know that. I don't know that. Seems like maybe you're the only one who thinks so."

"If you think that matters to me in the least, Paul, you're sadly mistaken."

"My only mistake was thinking you had any guts at all," Paul shot back. "Remind me not to accept a posting on any starship that's got you on it. I want brave officers on my team, not cowards."

Will knew that Paul didn't mean it. Despite appearances, they were still good friends. Paul was just trying to wheedle him, to push him into playing along with his stunt. The problem was, even though Will knew that, it was working anyway. And when some of the other cadets started piling onto Paul's side, he knew it was hopeless.

"Yeah, Riker," Donaldson jeered. "What are you afraid of?"

"Okay, okay," Will relented. "If it means that much to you, I'll do it."

This drew a round of approval from the gathered cadets, and Will felt his stomach sink even as he agreed to it. What Paul wanted was a race, one against one—*mano a mano*, as he put it. But they had completed their flights for the day, and they didn't have personal ships to race in. Which meant they would have to—Paul had used the term "borrow"—two shuttles from the Academy Flight Range orbiting Saturn. There would be some security, of course, but that was mostly geared toward keeping outsiders from coming in, not wayward cadets from leaving. Liberating the two shuttles could be done. Flying them would raise an alarm, though, and returning unnoticed would be impossible.

The trip would be relatively short, just around Phoebe, one of Saturn's many moons, and back. Once Will had agreed to it they had suited up, made sure the two Type-6 shuttles were prepped, and with some other cadets distracting the shuttle-bay crew, they'd made their getaway. Will recognized the stupidity of his action—he had come here instead of letting Trinidad take his place because he didn't want to break a comparatively minor rule, and now here he was smashing a huge one. But he'd still thought they would be able to get away with it, and if they flew well, they might even get away with just a minor talking to instead of a real punishment.

But that had been before things started to go wrong. Now he knew that he'd be lucky to avoid expulsion. If he even lived long enough to be expelled.

Will had been first out of the bay, but not by much. He thought he was coaxing every available ounce of speed from the shuttle, but somehow Paul found more and pulled ahead. Will had stayed close behind, though, as they neared Phoebe. Circling the moon and whipping back would require the most careful flying—she was large enough to have a faint gravitational pull, and the trick was to get in close enough to make a narrow turn without getting so close it bogged you down. Paul was, Will thought, going in closer than was necessary or wise. He'd been tempted to follow suit, but then had noticed his instrument panels reacting violently and had pulled back.

This is trouble, Will thought. Unless he misread his instruments, Paul was caught in an ion storm near the moon's surface. That was when Will decided that he was not, in fact, having any fun at all. He tapped his combadge. "Paul! Are you all right?"

What he heard back was static, and then Paul's voice, fragmented and breaking up. "*. . . trouble . . . storm is making . . . can't pull . . .*"

Paul's ship disappeared from his viewscreen then, though he could still follow its progress on his instrument panel. It seemed to be diving toward Phoebe's surface. "Paul, get out of there!"

He heard only static in reply.

"Emergency, Starfleet Academy Flight Range," Will called out, "this is shuttle—hell, I don't know what shuttle I have. Do you read me?"

"*We have you,*" a voice answered. "*Where's the other one?*"

"You need to make an emergency transport," Will insisted. "He's going down on Phoebe."

"*We can't even see him, Cadet,*" the voice reported. "*We can't get a lock. There seems to be some interference.*"

"It's an ion storm," Will told the voice. "That's why he's lost control of his shuttle."

"*He lost control because he tried to fly a shuttle that was in for repairs into an ion storm,*" the voice said. "*We'll send an emergency evac team out after him, but we can't transport him off there with the storm going on.*"

Damn it! Will thought. He'd known better than to let Paul egg him into this stupid game, and now it had all gone sour, as he'd somehow known it would. He made a quick decision and hoped it was the right one. "He'll never live long enough on the surface for your team to get there," Will said. "I'm going in to pick him up."

"Negative, Cadet," the voice instructed. *"Don't try that. Just wait for us."*

"Riker out," Will said, and broke off communication. "Computer," he said out loud, as much for his own benefit as for the computer's, "we're going in."

"Inadvisable," the computer argued. *"Atmospheric conditions are too severe."*

"Nevertheless," Will explained. "We're doing it. Shields at full power."

The computer is obviously smarter than I am, Will thought. It knew this was a fool's errand. But it complied with his commands, and he started the pitched descent toward Phoebe's icy surface. As the shuttle entered the ion storm, Will felt it buffeted about in spite of the presence of the shields, and he knew that without the shields he'd be a dead man for sure. *Of course, it's early yet,* he thought.

But something happened as he piloted the small craft down, through the battering of the storm and the entry into Phoebe's thin atmosphere. Where flying had been mechanical for Will, something at which he was skilled but which he had to think through, now, suddenly, he was doing it all almost unconsciously. His hands made the right moves across the control pad, manipulating the pitch and yaw of the ship as it dropped closer and closer to the surface, controlling the direction and speed, following the locator beacon that Paul had, at least, managed to deploy. He did it all smoothly and without hesitation, as if he'd been flying all his life, and even when he realized what he was doing he was able to keep doing it. Concern for Paul had taken the self-consciousness out of piloting the ship and the abilities that had become ingrained through hours and hours of practice and training had taken over.

Phoebe grew enormous in the viewscreen, its surface rugged and terrifying. Vast chasms of ice whipped past beneath him, and tall jagged cliffs. If he had to land on this moon, he realized, they'd both be waiting for the emergency team from the flight base, and the chances were that neither of them would survive. He would try to avoid landing, even though that left only one option, and it wasn't much better. But as he neared the locator beacon he prepared himself to take it.

He tapped his combadge again. "Paul, can you hear me?"

There was no response. Maybe this was all moot, he knew. Still, he had to take the chance. "Paul, do you read me?" No answer.

That didn't matter. He was closing fast and his best shot, maybe his only shot, was coming up. Leaving the ship's control on autopilot for the moment, he turned to the transporter controls. Scanning for Paul, he was almost surprised when the transporter got a lock almost immediately. He was very near, then—otherwise the ion storm would have interfered. But he couldn't transport Paul on board with the shields up, and lowering them during an ion storm, this close to the moon's surface, was virtually suicidal.

It was also the only thing he could do. With Paul's coordinates locked, he braced himself as best he could. "Shields down," he said, following it with "Energize."

As soon as the shields went down the shuttle was pounded by the storm, driving it into a downward spiral. Will fought for control, but the moon's harsh surface spun sickeningly toward him. "Shields up," he muttered, struggling to find voice with the g-force pulling at him. The deflector shields returned to full power, or as much as they had left to give after being bombarded by the storm, offering Will a modicum more control of the shuttle. But he was still dropping fast, spinning like a top.

So instead of trying to fight the spin, he decided to go with it. He turned into the spin, and pointed the nose down instead of attempting to pull up. For a moment, the surface was right there in front of him and he was certain he'd mis-

calculated. But in the next moment his maneuver paid off—
he had turned completely away from the surface and was
skimming above it upside down. His stomach lurched but
he knew that he would live for at least a few more seconds.
Now he pointed his nose down farther, except down was up.
Once he was a safe distance off the surface he righted the
shuttle. Getting out of Phoebe's atmosphere and away from
the storm was a relatively simple matter now. He blew out a
sigh of relief, and then remembered why he had gone down
there in the first place.

"That's some nice flying," Paul Rice said from behind him.

"Paul!"

"Now I suppose you're going to expect me to slavishly devote my life to you or some such nonsense," Paul said. He
sat down in the chair next to Will's, hardly looking the worse
for his experience. "Well, you can forget about that."

"I could beam you back down there," Will warned with a
smile.

"And miss your own medal ceremony?" Paul asked. "I
can't see it. Not you, Riker. Or should I say, golden boy?"

"Golden boy?" Will repeated. "We'll both be lucky if
we're not expelled."

"If I had died, you'd be expelled," Paul ventured. "Since I
didn't, we'll probably get by with a reprimand."

"A *reprimand*? You broke their ship!"

"Wasn't much of a ship," Paul countered. "I think it was
broken to begin with."

"Well, yeah," Will admitted. "It was. Good choice, Rice."

"I was still winning, wasn't I?" Paul asked. "Bum ship or
no."

"That's true, you were ahead," Will said. "I was going to
pass you on the home stretch, though."

Both cadets laughed then, and kept laughing most of the
way back to the Flight Training Base.

* * *

"It was amazing, Will," Felicia said when she saw him. She'd greeted him with a hug and a big kiss, which Will found pretty amazing in itself. "Ambassador Spock was brilliant, of course. And so nice!"

"You got to meet him?" Will asked her, full of envy. They were in her room, and she was beaming as if she had just now finished shaking the ambassador's hand.

"Yes, at a reception afterward. He was warm and friendly and even a little bit funny."

"Funny?" Will echoed. "We are talking about Spock the Vulcan, right? Not some other Spock?"

"Well, you know, not the kind of funny that you see in Estresor Fil's cartoons, but wry."

"I guess I can see wry," Will said. "I'm glad you had such a good time."

She hugged him again, and then sat him down on her bed, with one hand clutching his arm and the other resting across his thigh. "I did, Will, I really did. I just kept wishing you were there. You've got to watch the speech, though, even if you don't get to meet him yourself."

"Well, maybe one of these days," Will said. "Assuming I don't get kicked out of the Academy."

Felicia's beautiful lips made an O shape. "Kicked out? What do you mean?"

"I'm surprised you haven't heard," he said. "Bad news usually travels fast around here."

"I haven't heard anything, Will. What's going on?"

He told her about the unauthorized race, the theft of the shuttles, and Paul's misadventure on Phoebe. He didn't leave out any details, and when he was finished she had a look of total shock on her face.

"Will, you stupid dumb idiot! I am so glad you're okay. But how lame can you possibly be?"

"How many degrees of lameness are there?" he replied. "Because I guess I'm pretty far down the list."

"And you don't know yet what your punishment is going to be?"

"I'm supposed to report to the superintendent in . . ." he looked at his chron. "Twenty-two minutes. With Paul. I guess we'll both find out then."

"Can I go with you?" she asked, stroking his arm solicitously.

"Better not," he suggested. "Guilt by association, you know. Save your own career."

"I'll wait outside," she said. "But I want to know what happens as soon as you get out."

"Deal," Will agreed. "If I get thrown out you can make me dinner to console me. If I don't, you can make me dinner to celebrate."

"There are . . . various ways we could celebrate," she said with a sidelong glance.

"If you're suggesting what I hope you are," Will said, "I don't want to think about it until after I'm out of Superintendent Vyrek's office. I swear that Vulcan can read minds. Even without a mind-meld."

"Then I'm not going to tell you what I'm suggesting," Felicia declared. "Until after."

Twenty-seven minutes later, Will and Paul were standing at attention in the superintendent's office as she paced in a circle around them, hands clasped behind her back. Captain Pendel, their flight instructor, and Admiral Paris were also in the room, but both men stood back and let the superintendent have the floor. "You are lucky that I am a Vulcan, gentlemen, and not a human. Because a human, at a time like this, would have a very difficult time controlling her anger. You are both, for the most part, excellent cadets, with admirable records. But you are both headstrong, impulsive, and apparently lacking in any kind of what you call common sense and what I call reason. You stole—*stole*—vehicles from the Academy's Flight Training Base. One of those vehicles was in for repairs, but you somehow were not even aware of it. You, Mr. Rice, managed to crash that vehicle into one of Saturn's moons without killing yourself. You, Mr. Riker, disobeyed a direct order and flew into an ion storm in order to rescue the foolhardy Mr. Rice. The fact that you are both standing here is an affront to the laws of probability, not to mention the regulations of Starfleet. Does that about sum it up?"

"It seems to, sir," Will said, suitably chastened by her monologue.

"Yes, sir," Paul agreed.

"You are both in your last year," Superintendent Vyrek continued. "I should put you back a year. But Starfleet can use your skills sooner rather than later. And I would have to put up with you both for another year, and that aggravation, I assure you, is more than I can bear. Therefore, I will not punish myself and my instructors in such a fashion. Instead, I will put a strongly worded reprimand in each of your permanent files. And I will advise you not to be brought back to this office again, for any reason, during your final months at this Academy. If you are, I will not even take the time to talk to you, but will summarily expel you. Am I understood?"

"Loud and clear, sir," Paul said.

"Mr. Riker?"

"Yes, sir," Will answered. "Understood, sir."

"The fish incident was bad," Superintendent Vyrek said. "This is far, far worse. Do not let it happen again."

"Yes, sir," both cadets replied in unison.

"I have nothing more I care to say to either of you," the superintendent said dismissively. "But I believe Admiral Paris does."

Owen Paris stepped to the center of the room and stood in front of the cadets, looking them up and down as if on an inspection tour. "Gentlemen," he said. "That was quite a stunt you pulled. You should be ashamed of yourselves."

"We are, sir," Paul said.

"As Admiral Vyrek says, you are lucky you're not both dead. You do realize that, right?"

"Yes, sir," Will replied. "We do."

"You went down on one of Saturn's frozen moons, Rice. And you went after him, Riker, even though it meant flying with no shields in an ion storm, less than a kilometer from the surface."

"That seems to be an accurate description, sir," Will said.

"Stupid. Incredibly stupid."

"Yes, sir."

"I docked both your grades the last time we were here together, didn't I? After what Admiral Vyrek so astutely refers to as 'the fish incident'?"

"Yes, sir, you did," Paul said. "And my squadron had to repeat the class."

"The second time you took it, your grade improved, correct?"

"Yes, sir."

"Well, it just improved again. Both of you. Out of a possible one hundred points in my class, you both score one-fifty."

"I'm sorry, sir?" Will said, not quite understanding.

"You were stupid, both of you," Admiral Paris explained. "By all rights your frozen corpses should be up on Phoebe. But you survived. I teach a survival class. I haven't had any students show me what you two have, ever."

"Yes, sir," Paul said. Will was still at attention, eyes front, but he could hear Paul's smile in his voice.

"But, sir—" he began.

"Just say 'yes, sir,'" Paul instructed him.

"Yes, sir," Will repeated, catching on. "And thank you, sir."

"Don't thank me," Admiral Paris said. "Just stay out of trouble. A few more months, okay? I think even you two can do that."

"Yes, sir," both cadets responded.

"You are dismissed," Superintendent Vyrek said from her desk. Her voice was weary. Will suspected he'd be weary too if he had to deal with cadets like himself all the time.

Outside, Felicia waited for him. She ran to him when he exited the building, arms wide, and he caught her in his own and scooped her up. "A reprimand in my file," he said. "And Paris raised my survival grade."

"So it's celebrating and not consoling?"

"That's right," he affirmed.

"Oh, goody," Felicia said. She nuzzled against Will's neck and nipped the flesh there with her teeth. "Then I can tell you what I was suggesting earlier."

"I'm not sure we need to really talk about it," Will said, his lips urgently seeking hers. "In fact," he mumbled against her mouth, "talking may even be counterproductive."

Felicia broke away from him and started to run. "Oh, we can talk," she shouted back over her shoulder. "Until we get back to my room. After that, I think we'll be much too busy."

And she was right.

Chapter 26

The last couple of months, Will had learned, were definitely the hardest. He had heard about schools where students could basically skate through their last year, but Starfleet Academy was not one of those. Here, course work got progressively more difficult from the beginning to the end. When he was finished at the Academy, a cadet needed to be able to step from the campus onto a starship or starbase, where the lives of others might depend on his knowledge, experience, and reactions. There could be no slacking off.

So he saw Felicia when he could, but mostly he bore down
and worked. He closed himself in his room when he wasn't at
classes, usually alone—because when Felicia was there, they
found it hard to focus on their work—and studied. He had, for
the time being, set aside most other activities. Outings with
friends, athletics beyond a minimal daily workout . . . those
were important but not as important as making up the grade
handicap that had been with him from his first year. He had
made great progress, he knew. His grades had improved every
year, and he'd become much more confident in his own abilities. But he still had those lousy first-year grades on his record,
and if he was to be satisfied in his own performance he
wanted to balance them out with exceptional grades this time.

He was in his room, as usual, the night Dennis Haynes
knocked on his door in something like a panic. The rapid-
fire pounding startled Will, who was deeply immersed in a
text on the geological specifications of Class-G planets of the
Ophiucus sector. He pushed himself away from the desk,
still caught somewhere between two worlds, his eyes not
wanting to leave the computer screen because he didn't
want to have to find his place again in the discussion of the
effect of cooling magmas on crystallization processes. Finally he forced himself to abandon the screen because he
knew the door was locked. *Specifically so I wouldn't be bothered,* he thought, *so how well did that work?*

When he opened the door Dennis stood there, his face
flushed as if he'd been running, his brow wrinkled, mouth
turned down in a frown. "I can't do this, Will," Dennis said
without preface. "I just can't do it."

Will, tempted to simply close the door and go back to his
work, instead waved Dennis in. "Can't do what?" he asked
reflexively, thinking, *Don't ask, because he'll only want to tell
you and then you're stuck.*

"This. The work. The Academy. Any of it." Dennis's
words gushed out of him like water from a broken pipe.

"Calm down, Dennis. Have a seat." Will closed the door and ushered Dennis to the couch. He put his hands on Dennis's shoulders and pushed his friend down, then pulled up the chair he'd been using at the computer, turned it around, and straddled the back of it, facing Dennis. "What's the problem?"

"I am so far behind," Dennis said. "I'm so stuck, and I just can't seem to understand anything anymore. I can't catch up with anything. I can't grasp whatever it is we're supposed to be learning, and the more I try the more I worry that I'm not getting it. And if I don't get it, then I don't belong here."

"Can't argue with that," Will said with a smile, hoping to cajole Dennis back into making some kind of sense. "But it's probably not as bad as you think. You're just getting nervous."

Dennis shook his head vigorously. "I'm beyond nervous, Will. Nervous was months ago. I'm way past that. I'm into terrified now. Petrified."

"You need to relax, that's all," Will said. "When was the last time you went out and had some fun?"

"There's no time for fun, Will," Dennis insisted, shaking his head again. "I need to work every waking hour or I'm just not going to make it. And I can't do that, because there are classes, and then if I forget to eat, then I get weak, and . . ."

Will found himself saddened and appalled at the same time. "Dennis, you've got to eat. You've got to take care of yourself. You can't possibly keep up with the work if you're not in your best physical condition. You can't skip meals."

"I have to, Will," Dennis said. "It's easy for you—"

"No it's not."

"Easier, then. For you and the others. For Estresor Fil, the course work is a breeze. Even Felicia. But for me, I don't know, it just doesn't sink in. This stuff doesn't come naturally. My dad's a farmer, you know? Maybe I've got dirt in my veins."

"You have blood, same as everyone else," Will replied. Then, remembering some of the more alien types around, he amended himself. "Well, nearly everyone."

"It doesn't seem like I have much in common with anyone," Dennis continued. Will didn't think he was even listening anymore, just venting. "It's so much harder for me than for anyone else. There's so much of it that I just don't get. I wish I did—I want to serve. I want to be out there, you know, exploring new worlds. I have so much curiosity about the galaxy—"

"Then you have what you need," Will interrupted, his own work forgotten for now. "You can pick up the rest. You have the drive, the courage, the desire, Dennis. The learning and experience can be taught, but the things you have, that'll make you an asset to Starfleet, are the things that can't be taught. If you didn't have those I'd agree that you're a hopeless case, but you do."

"*You* think I do. I used to think so. Now I'm not so sure."

Will threw up his hands. "I don't know what you want, Dennis." He rose and paced around the room. "You want me to tell you that you're doomed? That you should just drop out now? Because I'd be lying if I did that. I don't believe that."

Dennis's gaze followed Will as he walked, his face crestfallen. "I'm sorry, Will. I shouldn't even have bothered you." He glanced at the computer. "I know you're busy too."

"You're my friend, Dennis," Will said. "There's no such thing as too busy for a friend."

"Thanks, Will."

"So is there any way I can help you?"

"Well, that's the thing," Dennis said. "I was hoping you could tutor me."

"Tutor?" Will echoed. His first thought was just how time-intensive that would be, if Dennis was really as far behind as he claimed. "I don't know if I'm the best guy for that."

"You're the only one I'd even ask, Will," Dennis implored. "You're my best friend here. You know me better than anyone, and you have a knack for explaining complicated stuff in ways that makes it all seem so simple."

"But—"

"I know it'd take a lot of your time, Will. Too much, probably, to catch me up. You could tutor somebody smart in no time at all, but I'm a losing proposition."

"That's not what I said," Will objected.

"I know. And I do have one other idea. Something that'd take less of your time. It'd hardly put you out at all."

"What's that?"

"You could let me cheat off you," Dennis said.

Will didn't even know how to answer that. Never mind that it was impractical. It could be done, he supposed, for some courses, though it'd be tricky and would require quite a bit of advance work. But it was so clearly unethical. . . .

Dennis watched him like a dog waiting for a scrap of food from the dinner table.

"Dennis, that's . . ."

"I know it's a lot to ask, Will. Believe me, I know it is. I wouldn't if I had any other choice. I'm going to fail, Will. I've never failed before, really, not at anything important. But I will this time, I just know it. And I don't know how to handle that. I don't know how to deal with it." He paused and angled his head toward the floor. "I'm afraid."

Will would have liked to have made a snap decision, which he knew would be the right one. He felt like he owed Dennis a bit more consideration, though. They had been through a lot together. In large ways and small, Dennis had helped him get through the rigors of Starfleet Academy. Turning down a friend who had done all that for him just didn't seem right.

But neither did the alternatives. Giving Dennis the kind of tutoring help he was asking for would mean sacrificing most of his own study time. Instead of finishing near the top of his class, and countering those bad early grades with strong late ones, he'd be lucky to pass everything. He would squeak by, but his record would not be nearly as impressive as he'd hoped, and it might actually affect his starship posting.

And helping Dennis cheat would be even worse. Starfleet stressed fairness and honesty, and cheating was neither. It ran against everything Starfleet stood for. And that was only a problem if they didn't get caught. If they did, they'd both be booted out of the Academy, and any chance of ever serving in Starfleet would vanish. Will didn't know what he'd do then. Go back to Alaska? Remain a civilian like his old man? Eventually marry, then abandon his family later in life to pursue a dream he'd abandoned years before?

No, it didn't take much thought to dismiss the idea of cheating. But the tutoring thing, now, that was harder. Because that made a certain amount of sense, at least from Dennis's perspective. Tutoring could actually help Dennis master the material. He would come out of the Academy more educated and a better asset to Starfleet. He would get passing grades, instead of flunking out. There was no downside.

For Dennis, that was. For Will, the downside was the time it would require. Way too much of it, he knew. If Dennis was as bad off as he said—and Will was pretty sure he wasn't entirely exaggerating his position—then he would need massive amounts of work. Will could probably do it, but only at the expense of his own grades and his own future.

This was a situation, Will knew, in which there was no way to win. There were only bad options, and the problem he faced was, which option was the least bad of the bunch? He resented Dennis more than a little for even putting him in this position, though he understood that Dennis would not have done it if he'd seen any other way out.

As he paced around the room thinking about these things, he knew Dennis was watching him again. He looked out the bay window at the San Francisco skyline, a million lights glittering against the darkness, like the starry skies he yearned to travel. What he did, the decision he made in these next few moments, could determine whether or not he ever traveled those spaceways.

"Here's the deal," he said at last, turning back to Dennis. "I'll tutor you." Dennis broke into a grin, but Will cut him off before he could express gratitude, knowing that his good cheer would only last a moment. "But I can only afford the time to offer you very limited tutoring. I can help out in the classes that we're in together, because helping you understand those will help me get a better grasp of the material. But for the others, for the older work ... I don't know, maybe you can try Estresor Fil or something. I just ... Dennis, I really can't spare the time. Not without killing my own chances."

Dennis's smile had vanished as quickly as it appeared. "I know, Will. Believe me. I'm so sorry I had to even ask you." Will thought that would be the end of it, and was relieved that Dennis was taking the news with such good grace. But then Dennis dropped the anvil. "But I'm begging you, Will, to reconsider. Limited tutoring won't help me. I'm too lost. I need major help. Or I need to cheat. I can get this stuff, I'm just not as smart as everyone else and I need more time, a lot more. Cheating is wrong, I know that. But it'll buy me time to really understand everything. That's what I need."

"Dennis, don't ask me for that," Will said sadly. "I can't. I just ... I can't."

Dennis stared at him with eyes that had gone cold. Will was surprised. It was like looking at someone he didn't even know. "You could, Will," he said, his voice glacial. "If you wanted to. To help a friend, you could."

"What?" Will said, astonished at Dennis's sudden sea change. "You're saying I'm not your friend because I won't help you cheat?"

"I'm just saying that if you really considered me a friend, you'd help me in some way."

"I offered to tutor you—"

"In a very limited way," Dennis reminded him. "An hour here, an hour there. And at the end of it, you feel good about yourself and I flunk out anyway. No, thanks. If you don't care to offer some real help, then I guess we know what this friendship is."

"What?" Will asked him, still bewildered by this turn.

"A lie," Dennis said. "Nothing but a lie." He lurched to his feet and stomped across Will's room, headed for the door. "Thanks for nothing, Will," he said. He let himself out.

In stunned silence, Will watched him go. *Maybe it's the stress,* he told himself. *It's making Dennis act in ways he wouldn't ordinarily. He'll come back and apologize in a few minutes. Or tomorrow, first thing, he'll feel so bad he'll beg me to forgive him.*

But even as those thoughts bounced around in his head, Will knew that he was probably wrong. The hateful look in Dennis's eyes, at the end, the set of his jaw . . . maybe this Dennis was the real Dennis, and the one Will had thought he'd known was the imposter. Maybe Dennis Haynes was someone who would befriend you as long as he thought you could help him, and then cut you off as soon as you were no longer useful. He didn't want to believe that, but he knew that it was possible. The way Dennis had glared at him brought that home.

Taking his place at the computer again, Will realized that he had probably lost a friend, for good.

But on the bright side, it gave him that much more time to study.

Chapter 27

The next day dawned clear and warm over San Francisco. This was the kind of day that, before the advent of climate control technology, had been so rare here that it brought the residents outside in droves. Even now, when everyone knew that the weather could be manipulated to a large extent, there was something about such a lovely late spring day that people were tempted to skip their responsibilities and lounge about in the sun.

Will Riker was not one of those people. He appreciated nice weather as much as anyone—growing up in Alaska made one particularly appreciative of warm, sunny days—but at this point in his Academy career nothing could tempt him away from the tasks he had set for himself. He had lunch with Felicia, and their concession to the weather was to eat at an outside table. The table was in a kind of alcove sheltered by a stand of bamboo which rustled in the gentle breeze, with a winding brook on the other side. Felicia had told him that this was one of her favorite spots on campus.

Over lunch, he recounted Dennis's visit to his room the night before. As he told the story he saw her face darken with anger, until he regretted having brought it up at all.

"Will!" she exploded when he finished. "He's your friend! I can't believe you treated him like that!"

Will shrugged. "What was I supposed to do, Felicia? Throw away my own career for his? Cheat for him? How would that help?"

"You could have helped him out in some way," she insisted.

"I offered. He didn't want it. It was everything or nothing, as far as he was concerned."

"Still . . ."

"Are you going to tutor him?" Will asked.

"He hasn't asked me to."

"But he might. What if he does? And you could always volunteer, you know. Are you willing to spend hours every day helping him catch up?"

"Maybe it won't really take that long," she said. "Maybe he's exaggerating the situation."

"Maybe," Will admitted. "But I don't think so. It seems like he knows what his own position is, and it's pretty precarious."

"Even so," Felicia said, anger still simmering in her voice and body language, "you ought to do what you can to help him out. Friendships are important, Will. Relationships are important. You can't just turn a friend away like that."

"Felicia," Will said, feeling suddenly helpless. "I told you, I offered to do what I could. It just wasn't as much as Dennis wanted."

She nodded. "And then, instead of negotiating something in between, you just let him walk out the door. Have you seen him today?"

"No," Will replied.

"Don't you think you should find him? Make sure he's okay?"

"If you had seen him last night, Felicia . . . he turned into an iceberg, like our entire friendship rested on that one question, and when I said no, then it was just over. I don't feel like it's my place to track him down. If he wants to find me and apologize, he knows where I live."

Felicia had folded her arms across her chest and looked toward where the brook cut through a sward of grassy lawn, instead of at Will. "You disappoint me, Will," she said. "Truly." She rose, then, and walked away from the table, leaving Will with the remains of their lunch. "I guess I'll talk to you later," she called back as she left.

Will genuinely didn't know what he was supposed to say

to that. Hadn't he made the best offer he could to Dennis? Didn't he need to keep his priorities straight in order to graduate with the best grades he could? He cleaned up the lunch mess, checked the time, and headed toward his next class.

Professor Knudsen was, Will believed, one of the best lecturers he'd had during his time at the Academy. She paced the front of the room as she talked, a slight, blonde figure in tailored civilian clothes, speaking with a heavy Scandinavian accent, stopping from time to time to accentuate a point with a jabbing finger or a fist punching the palm of her other hand. She knew her material, which was the history of the Federation's first contacts with alien races, inside and out, and never needed notes when she lectured. Normally Will took pleasure in watching her. Her utter command of the subject matter was inspiring and she made it seem important and valuable.

But today he couldn't even focus on what she was saying. He kept running through his conversation with Dennis in his head, and the argument with Felicia that it had precipitated. She hadn't come right out and called him a jerk, but her tone of voice and the way she'd carried herself had done that job for her. He couldn't think of anything he might have done differently, that was the problem. He couldn't accede to Dennis's demands; they were unreasonable. They would put his own standing in jeopardy, maybe even threaten his whole career. It just didn't make sense to take a chance like that for anybody.

And then Felicia's response had seemed out of proportion as well. It wasn't as if his relationship with Dennis would necessarily affect her. She knew Dennis too, they were friendly. But if Will's friendship with Dennis had come to an abrupt end, why did that have to change her own association with Dennis? It didn't—she was just blowing things up for no reason. Maybe she was upset not because her connection with Dennis was impaired but because her own impression of Will had been challenged. Not that her impression had always been a favorable one.

He shook his head and tried to concentrate on what Professor Knudsen was talking about.

He was aware of his lack of focus, and hoped that this particular lecture would be one he could afford to miss most of. But that pointed to a larger problem: Even without agreeing to Dennis's ridiculous demands, his own academic work was being affected. Dennis, and now Felicia, were threatening his career simply by being part of his life and having expectations that he couldn't necessarily live up to. If this sort of thing—disagreements with friends and lovers—could draw his mind away from one of his favorite lecturers, then it was dangerous. He couldn't afford to let his concentration lapse. His priority had to be getting the highest grades he possibly could and doing his best work in these remaining few weeks. As hard as it was now, when finals hit it would be harder still. He needed to be mentally and psychologically available for himself at that point, ready to take on whatever academic challenges were thrown at him.

His decision made, he tried to tune in Professor Knudsen.

He found Felicia after his last class of the day, in her room. Estresor Fil was in there with her, studying, but when she saw the look on Will's face—Will wondered just how bad he must look—she quickly gathered her things and excused herself. Felicia regarded Will with a blank expression. Pointedly, she did not get up to hug or kiss him. Will sat down in the chair that Estresor Fil had just vacated.

"I've been doing a lot of thinking," Will began.

"I'm glad to hear that." Felicia's voice was as flat as her face, as if she had pushed all emotion to the side.

"Yeah, well, it's not always easy for me," he said. She didn't smile at the joke, and he decided not to try that again.

"But what I keep coming up against, Felicia, is this. The school year is almost over. I had a rough first year, and some snags in my second too. If I want to get the best possible posting after the Academy, I have to really shine this year. That's why I couldn't devote the time to helping Dennis—because I need to devote it to helping myself. I have to push myself as hard as I possibly can."

"Career isn't everything, Will," she said. "Friendships are every bit as important."

"Friendships may be important," he admitted. "But not 'every bit as.' Nothing is, not to me. The way I see it, there's no reason to go into Starfleet unless I'm willing to give it my all. It needs a hundred percent of me."

"That seems pretty narrow-minded," Felicia responded. "What's wrong with giving it seventy? Eighty? You need some of you left over for you."

"I don't agree. I mean, sure, that's good enough for some people. But not for me. I've been trying to do this for as long as I can remember. Getting into Starfleet, moving up the ranks, becoming a senior officer—those have been my goals since I was a kid. Now they're within range—I can almost close my hands around those gold pips. I can't afford to lose my momentum. I can't let anything get in the way of that goal. Not now."

"And by 'anything,' you mean . . . ?"

"You know," he said, still unwilling to say out loud what had really brought him to Felicia's room. "Dennis and his crazy schemes. Helping him cheat. That's a sure way to get kicked out, to guarantee that I'll never have a Starfleet career at all."

"But tutoring isn't against the rules."

"We've been over that," Will reminded her. "The degree of tutoring he needs is more than I can handle and still keep my own grades up. I can't really spare any time for him, much less the amount he's looking for."

"So what you're saying is that your career takes precedence over your friends," she translated.

He paused, understanding that he was about to go over a waterfall without so much as a barrel to ride in. "That's right. It has to."

"All your friends?"

Will swallowed but answered quickly. "That's right."

"I had a feeling," she said. "At lunch, when you just let me walk away."

"I really am not sure how I'm supposed to stop everyone from walking away," Will said. "Flying tackles? Is that better?"

"Usually a simple word or two will do it," Felicia told him. "But you have to want to say them."

"What words? You know I'm not good at this, Felicia. You want me to tell you that I love you? I do. Or I think I do, and if there's a difference I don't know what it is. But that's not really what this is about, is it?"

"Not really," she said, keeping her steady gaze fixed on him. "Not whether you can say it, anyway. More whether you can mean it."

"I do mean it," he tried to assure her. "As much as I have ever loved anyone, I love you."

"Are you sure about that, Will?"

"But obviously," he went on, ignoring her question, "that's not enough. For either of us. You want more than I can give. And I feel like I'm already too committed—like just being in a relationship with you is costing me too much. I can't concentrate on my work, I can't separate my personal life, my emotional life, from the things that I need to do to reach my goals."

Now he realized that her eyes had gone liquid. She sniffed once. "I had hoped that you were different, Will," she said. "I saw—I still see—a great person inside you, a wonderful, loving man who is driven and ambitious but also kind and generous and giving. It's those qualities, in combination, that make you the man I want to be with—the man I've wanted to be with since I met you, even though I had to wait so damn long for you to figure it out. And these past few months, when you've actually been that man, have been amazing. I've felt things, being with you, that I could barely have imagined in my wildest fantasies."

A tear escaped her eye and trailed down her left cheek. She ignored it and kept talking. "Your problem, Will, is that you haven't yet figured out how to be the whole person you really are. You think you can only be one part of you at a time, and that's not true. So even though you really *are* the man I love, you can't seem to give yourself permission to *be* that man." She turned her head away, finally releasing him from the withering assault of her nearly unbearable scrutiny. "Funny how I've always known you better than you know yourself. That's backwards, William. You don't have to let it be that way."

"But maybe I do," he countered. "If that's the way I am. You may be right, but I can only be the person I am now, at this time, in this moment. If I can change that in time, fine. But that still doesn't help us right now."

"Apparently there is no help for us now."

"It doesn't look that way," he agreed.

"Well," she said, sniffling and trying on a smile. "Fun while it lasted, right?"

"Yeah," he said. "I am sorry. Really, really sorry."

"Me too, Will. Me too."

He sat there a moment longer, feeling impossibly awkward. There was nothing to say or do that was the right thing, in this situation. He wanted to touch her, to throw himself at her, to scoop her into his arms and apologize, to tell her that he'd been stupid and he'd be different now. But he knew that wasn't true, and he wouldn't fool her for a second. He was right, he could only be the person he was. And the person he was put his career ahead of everything else.

There would be plenty of time for relationships after he had achieved what he needed to professionally. For now, he had to prioritize.

"I guess it's my turn, then," he said at last. "To walk away."

"Looks like it," Felicia agreed. "Since it's my room and all."

Nothing left to say, Will rose and went to the door. He caught a final glimpse of Felicia, the most beautiful, loving woman he had ever known, sitting curled up on her couch, knees pulled against her chest, arms wrapped around her legs, and he walked out.

And she didn't say anything to stop him.

Chapter 28

Even at the time, those last months, weeks, and days of Starfleet Academy ran together in a kind of watercolor blur for Will Riker. By the time a couple of years had passed, he was almost completely unable to remember the precise sequence of events that had transpired. As he was living it, he couldn't see any rhyme or pattern, just work and more work.

He got up in the morning, forcing himself out of bed even though he didn't feel like he'd had nearly enough sleep. Usually, he hadn't. But when he rolled from his bed, the first thing he did was to check the computer, to make sure that any notes he'd made the night before—he had, in recent weeks, developed a habit of waking up at various times during the night with fresh ideas and inspirations—were, in fact, comprehensible. Then he quickly scanned the material he'd studied before going to bed. After a rushed breakfast, he dashed off to his first class. A series of classes interspersed with brief study breaks followed. In late afternoon, after his last class, he went to the gym for a hurried workout, then showered and had dinner. After dinner it was up to his room for more studying until he either dozed off at the computer or could no longer retain what he was working on. That was when he finally allowed himself to go to bed, only to begin the whole process again in a few hours.

But somehow, he got through it, and his grades, when he saw them, were the highest he had ever received. Around campus there was mixed relief and concern at grade time, as those who had done well hurried to call friends and family and share the news, and those who had not agonized over their missteps and the possible cost to their future careers. Will didn't have any family to contact, though, if you didn't count his father who, he was pretty sure, was still missing someplace. And he hadn't seen much of his friends lately— some, like Dennis and Felicia, wanted nothing to do with him, and the rest had been more or less abandoned in the mad rush toward finals and graduation.

Now that it was over, Will could exhale and start working on mending some of those fences, he figured. But his relief turned out to be a little premature. With graduation looming, that meant, he had every reason to believe, posting to a starship, and there was work to be done in preparation for that. He spent what seemed like hours filling out the documentation necessary for a Starfleet assignment, and he had to pack his personal items, some of which he simply gave away, or recycled, on the theory that a starship berth wouldn't give him a whole lot of personal space. And then, before he knew it, graduation day was upon him.

"I'm no Federation president or galactic celebrity," their graduation speaker began, his plain, folksy voice amplified to fill the cavernous space of the Academy's vast auditorium. "I'm just a country doctor who has become sort of important, if at all, simply because I've managed to outlive all of my enemies." Admiral Leonard H. McCoy looked out across the ocean of cadets, and Will could see the blue of his eyes even from his seat midway back. His tuft of hair was as white as the dress uniform he wore. "And some of my friends, too, I'm sorry to say. And I guess that's what I'm here to talk to you all about today.

"You've finished your time at the Academy, which is a hell of an accomplishment, and you've every right to be proud of yourselves. But don't sprain your arms pattin' yourselves on the back, because what you've really done is just the first step in a long process. From here, you become Starfleet officers. Like a lot of Starfleet officers before you, including my best friend in the world, James Tiberius Kirk, some of you will be asked to give your lives in the service of Starfleet. Nobody wants to make that sacrifice—nobody wants to ask you to make it, either—but when they do, when the time comes, if it does, I hope you'll do it in the spirit of the great Starfleet officers who went before you.

"Your chosen career is one in which violence sometimes plays a part. As a doctor and I hope some kind of humanitarian—though if you ever call me that to my face I'll knock you on your keister—I abhor violence. I detest it, and I have always tried, and will always try to find a way to avoid it, like a barn mouse tryin' to keep away from the farmhouse cat. But I also recognize that there are times when it's necessary, and when it has been, then I've tried to face it head-on. I hope you'll do the same."

Will listened to McCoy, enjoying the old doctor's thoroughly informal presentation. The graduates were seated alphabetically in the front section of the auditorium, with family, friends, and observers filling out the rest of the room, and Will sat between Paul Rice and an Andorian named Ritthar. On Paul's other side was a guy he knew only in passing named Vince Reggiani. Will could see the back of Felicia's head, a couple of rows in front of him, but she never seemed to turn around. Will's achievement had been better than he'd dared hope for—he had finished eighth in his class, and that knowledge filled him with satisfaction and a little bit of anxiety, as if he had raised his own bar and would now have to continue to perform at that level. He thought he could do it, but if it meant pushing himself as he'd been doing for the last months of Academy work, he would either burn out fast or simply fall apart trying.

"I started out saying I was just a country doctor," McCoy was saying. "And that's true. But unlike some others, I'm a country doctor who has seen incredible sights. I've seen sunrise on Jupiter and sunset on New France. I've danced with a woman who was born on Rigel VI, and I've listened to an orchestra made up entirely of nonhumanoid, energy-based life-forms whose instruments were part of their own anatomy. I've set foot on close to a hundred planets, and been nearly killed, kidnapped, or knocked in the head on almost half of those. For all the trouble I've seen, all the war and strife and danger, I wouldn't trade my life for anyone else's, anywhere, country doctor or no. I trust, when you've reached the end of the career that you're just beginning today, you'll be able to say the same thing, and mean it.

"Keep that in mind as you take your next step, as you become Starfleet officers, and as you grow into the men and women that you will be. The best thing to say at the end of your life is that you don't regret a thing. Tomorrow, that new life will start, for each of you—you woke up this morning students, and you will wake up tomorrow officers. It's a big change, don't kid yourself into thinking it's not. And I only have one more thing to say about that." McCoy threw his hands into the air. "Congratulations, graduates of 2357! You've earned yourselves a party!"

This was met by a wild chorus of applause and cheers from the assembled graduates, and Admiral McCoy left the stage amidst the tumult. As was traditional, after that, each graduate was called to the stage by name to receive a diploma, and when the last one was handed out the graduates burst into a new round of cheering, before dispersing to find friends and family members with whom to celebrate their accomplishment.

Will was momentarily lost in the noise and chaos. He had no one to seek out, and his friends had all vanished toward the back of the big room. But as he turned in a slow circle, he saw Dennis Haynes, face flushed, walking nearby.

Hoping that maybe his former friend had cooled off a bit, Will stopped him. "Hey, Dennis, congratulations," he said with all sincerity.

"Thanks," Dennis said. He faced Will but there was no hint of a smile on his ruddy face. "Heard you were at the top of the class."

"Eighth," Will corrected. Kul Tun Osir had been first. "Not all the way."

"You know where I finished, Will?" Dennis asked. He made it sound like a challenge.

"I really don't," Will admitted.

"Dead last," Dennis told him. "That's quite an accomplishment, isn't it? *Nobody* was able to do worse than me. When it comes to being bad, I'm the best." He glared at Will, who simply watched him, straight-faced.

"You may have finished last," Will said finally. "But you still finished. You're here, the same as the rest of us."

"I sure am," Dennis said. "I'm here, and I did it by myself. No help from you, obviously, and none from anyone else either. Just my own efforts, my own two hands, and my own barely adequate brain."

"I think you're being a little hard on yourself, Dennis," Will said. "On yourself and everyone else."

"If you'd been in my shoes, you wouldn't necessarily think that," Dennis shot back. "But, luckily for you and Starfleet, you didn't have to find out."

"I'm sure your contribution to Starfleet will be an important one," Will suggested.

"Maybe if I was going into Starfleet," Dennis said. "But I'm not."

"But . . . you graduated from the Academy!" Will was dumfounded. "Even if you don't want to join Starfleet—and I can't imagine why you wouldn't—you kind of have to now, don't you?"

"You'd think so, huh?" Dennis asked. "But it turns out there's a kind of special dispensation for cases like mine. It's possible to do just well enough to make it through the Academy but still bad enough that they won't make you enlist if you choose not to. They don't really want me, any more than I want them."

People were streaming around them now, graduates and family members alike, and Dennis had raised his voice to the point that people cast sidelong glances at them and tried to give them wide berth.

"I guess I just don't understand," Will said. "I thought the whole reason you put yourself through this was that you wanted to be in Starfleet."

Finally, Dennis smiled. "I thought that too," he said. "But you know what happened, Will? I met you."

"Me?"

"You, Will. I think you'll have a brilliant Starfleet career. You'll be some big hotshot senior officer, probably a captain someday, or an admiral. And that's exactly why I want nothing to do with Starfleet. Because the system rewards people who are willing to turn their backs on their friends, who will sacrifice friendships for advancement and accomplishment. You'll thrive in that kind of atmosphere, Riker. But I want no part of it. I'm going home, back to the farm. At least there when you're up to your ankles in manure, you know where you really stand."

Will felt anger overtake him. "I feel like I want to say I'm sorry you feel that way, Dennis," he said. "But really, I'm not. Whatever problems you think you have with Starfleet you really have with yourself. How you did in school is no one's fault but your own. You can't blame anyone else for that. You could have asked for help at any point, and you could have accepted help when it was offered. You could have pulled your own weight like the rest of us did. You chose not to, well, those are the choices you make. But then don't go trying to blame others, or the 'system,' for your shortcomings. As Dr. McCoy might have said, that dog don't hunt."

Dennis shot Will a look of anger much like the one he'd left him with the night he'd demanded help. "Leave it to you to kiss up even when you don't have to, Riker," he said. "McCoy can't hear you now. But it's perfect for a Starfleet drone like you. Have a good life, Will. I'll think of you every time I swamp out the barn or feed the hogs."

Dennis turned and shoved his way through the crowd, leaving Will standing there watching him go. Dennis had really ticked him off—refusing to accept responsibility for one's own actions was something Will hated, and Dennis seemed intent on making a lifelong pattern of it. But part of him couldn't help feeling hurt, wounded, by Dennis's accusation, and by the bitter tone in his one-time friend's voice. And underneath the anger there was another feeling—a vague idea that maybe Dennis was right about more than Will wanted to admit. Felicia had implied many of the same things about him.

Will was excited about getting posted to a starship and seeing some action, but at the same time, he thought, a change of scenery might be a good opportunity to take a long, hard look at his own life. *It might just be*, he thought, *that it's time to make some changes.*

Chapter 29

More than a year had passed since Kyle Riker had last seen Earth, and the sight of his home planet filling the shuttle's viewscreen filled him with a sense of joy that took him by surprise. He knew there were still dangers ahead, and difficult times, but he would meet them on his home turf and face them in a way that he hadn't been equipped for when he had let them drive him away before.

Getting to this point had been a challenge, to be sure. The night Michelle died had ranked right up there with the worst nights of his life. The police had been out in force that night, he remembered, clustered together in groups on street corners, armored and tense. They had stared at him as he passed by, a ragged-looking man with what might have been blood sprayed across his face and clothing, but they hadn't stopped him. He figured he looked too beaten down to be much of a threat.

Kyle knew that when things went downhill they would happen fast, but even he was unprepared for the velocity and brutality of the next morning's events. Instead of waiting for Cetra and the others to give themselves up, the army simply returned to The End in full force, with far more soldiers and machines than they had used the day before. The tanks rumbled into the old part of Cozzen five abreast, not paying attention to where the roads wound. They made their own roads. The ancient buildings barely slowed them down. When they approached one that looked more substantial than the rest they simply fired upon it before they got to it, their energy beams lancing across the early morning landscape and blowing huge chunks from the walls. Then the tanks rolled forward, their sheer mass finishing the job their guns had started. Soldiers, on foot and in troop carriers,

came behind, using their handheld weapons on any who
survived the destruction of their homes. Smaller and weaker
structures were merely ground into dust by the big machines.

Kyle had finally fallen asleep in an alley, but the thunder
and crash of the army's advance woke him up early. It took a
few moments to get his bearings—he felt hungover, though
this hangover had only to do with grief, not with drink—but
once he figured out where he was, he ran through the
chaotic streets to Cetra's place to warn her. When he got
there, he saw that a police unit had already raided her place.
As Kyle watched, helpless to stop it, Cetra was led out of the
building with her hands in shackles by five uniformed police
officers, the shortest of whom towered over her by half a
meter. Another dozen stood outside the building around an
armored vehicle, as casually as if this were any other day,
any other job.

"Cetra!" Kyle cried, oblivious to the risk this raised for him.

"It's okay, Joe," she said, tossing him her most gentle,
motherly smile. "You can't worry about me. You take care of
what you can." The police led her into the vehicle and
slammed the doors.

Taking care of what he could was his intention, although
he thought it might sadden Cetra to know that his goal had
nothing to do with Cyre, or Hazimot. Michelle had come to
the conclusion long ago that her future was here on Hazimot—*such as it was*, he thought bitterly—but that Kyle belonged back on Earth. He never had told her any details of
his troubles there, but she insisted that the time would come
when he'd have to go back and face them. "You'll never be
really at peace until you do," she said. "Even with me, you'll
always be unhappy, unfinished. I'd hate for you to leave me,
but you need to return there someday."

He had remembered that conversation, last night, even
through the anguish he felt at her death. He had decided

that she was right, that he needed to go back and take care of things at home. Only by accomplishing that could he be the kind of man Michelle deserved. And even though she would no longer know it, that was the kind of man he meant to become.

Seeing that to try to act against the police who had taken Cetra was purely suicidal, he turned and ran toward home. There were things hidden in his apartment that he would need, if only he could get to them before the building was flattened. Michelle had helped him acquire authentic identification papers in the name of Joe Brady, and a second set in the name of Henry Blue in case the Brady name became compromised somehow. And there was some cash set aside there, since Hazimot operated on a largely monetary basis, and he would need that as well.

The streets were almost impassable now. Everywhere, buildings Kyle had grown accustomed to were burning. Fire licked at the edges of windows or spat high through broken roofs, all accompanied by a crackling roar. Instead of dissipating the smoke, the omnipresent winds just fanned the flames and spread smoke everyplace. Kyle inhaled great hot lungfuls of it and began coughing before he even reached home. Refugees, driven out of their own last-resort housing, clogged the streets, clutching infants and threadbare belongings to their breasts, holding children and lovers by the hands. Many were weeping openly, others angry and scared, readying weapons or looking for an escape route. The thunder of heavy artillery filled Kyle's ears, and the concussive shock of explosions rattled his bones. He felt much as he had that day on Starbase 311—terrified, overwhelmed, and bordering on hopeless. However, he was not experiencing any flashbacks. None of the crowd turned into Tholians, the noises around him sounded like artillery, not those awful Tholian hand-weapons. Under other circumstances, he might be pleased by this, but not right now.

After working his way through the crowd, clenching his lips against the grit and smoke and dust that filled the air, he finally made his way to the building in which he'd lived these many months. The building in which he'd met Michelle, and loved her so powerfully. It stood there, dun colored through the thick smoke, its few remaining windows shattered by the blasts and gaping dumbly at him, and he ran for it as if it offered shelter from the insanity that surrounded him.

Of course, it didn't.

Inside, he couldn't see any of the residents, just a pack of looters, youthful Cyrians, mostly, who were busily trying to make off with what few possessions of value had been left behind. Kyle felt he should challenge them, but then common sense won out. Anything not already claimed would be rubble anyway, soon enough, when this building was flattened like the rest of The End. Instead of confronting the looters, he just shoved past them and dashed up the stairs, hoping they hadn't yet raided his apartment.

In fact, when he burst through his door there were three muscular Cyrian males ransacking his place. "Get out!" he snarled at them. They spun around to face him, one dropping an armload of his clothing on the floor.

"This one's ours," he said, almost calmly. "There are plenty of other places you can pilfer."

"No!" Kyle shot back. "This one's mine. All that stuff is mine. Like you say, there are plenty of other places—leave my things alone."

One of the Cyrians laughed out loud. "Yours? You lost any claim to this place when you walked out the door. You don't defend what's yours, it's not yours any longer." He bunched his huge hands into fists.

Kyle normally didn't care much about material possessions—he had left behind an apartment full of them on Earth, almost two years ago now—but this was quickly becoming a matter of principle as well as survival. "You know what?" he asked, feeling the tension flow out of him and a remarkable sense of peace take its place. "I'm having a bad day. A very bad day, in fact. The woman I loved died, my neighborhood is being taken apart piece by piece, and all my friends are either under arrest or missing. There's nothing I'd love more right now than to tear you all apart, one by one."

"We got what we need," one of the Cyrians said with some reluctance. "Let's go."

The others grumbled, but that one seemed to be in charge, and they finally indicated their assent. They all dropped what they held and made their way to the door, trying to give Kyle as wide a berth as they could. He knew they'd destroy him in a fight, of course—he was just one man, and although he was strong and athletic and driven by fury, Cyrians in general were bigger and more powerfully built than even the biggest humans. But he figured anyone who'd loot the homes of people driven out by invasion wasn't the bravest guy on the block, and even with numbers on their side, these looters would rather have easy pickings in uninhabited apartments than risk injury or worse at his hands.

When they were gone, he went to the hiding place where he had stashed his money and false identification papers, under a loose floorboard concealed by his bed. He shoved the bed aside and pried up the board, and everything was still where he'd left it, wrapped in a cloth bag. He scooped it all up and pocketed it, then did a quick scan to see if there was anything else he needed. Clothing and toiletries would be nice, but he could always acquire more, and he didn't want to look like a man who was traveling. He ended up grabbing a holoimage of Michelle and stuffing it into a pocket, and then he left the rest for the looters.

The first barrage hit the building while he was still running down the stairway. The whole structure shook under the assault. Plaster flew, and a wall opposite him imploded into dust. The staircase groaned and swayed. Kyle gripped the banister to steady himself and continued down, hurtling five and six steps at a time. He heard screams and shouts from elsewhere in the building—probably the looters, he suspected, since he hadn't seen any of the residents around. At least, he hoped it was them—poetic justice if they were trapped inside the building when it came down.

Another wave hit and this time more walls blew in. Dust and debris rained down on Kyle. Above, he saw powerful energy beams lance through the walls, leaving further destruction in their wake. He leapt the last flight of stairs and landed awkwardly on the lobby floor, his feet slipping out from beneath him on the slick, dust-coated tiles. But he caught himself on his palms, righted himself and sprinted for the door.

Outside, he saw machines of war rolling toward the building, already loosing another fusillade against it. Infantry troops supported the tanks. They spotted Kyle running from the building, but ignored him; just another homeless refugee. When he was almost a block away he heard another, still louder boom, and glanced back to see most of his building collapse in a massive cloud.

The rest of the day had passed, like the building, in the cloud of dust and smoke—mostly obscured, always uncertain, never far from danger. He worked his way out of The End, joining the throngs of other refugees trying to escape the morning assault. Once beyond the boundaries of the neighborhood, the castaways scattered into every direction. The Cyrian authorities didn't seem to have developed any kind of a plan except for the attack. There was no one except the soldiers to provide any direction for the refugees, and they didn't seem to have a clue, which meant no order to the evacuation. The newly homeless drifted wherever they chose. Some keened or wailed in their sadness, but most simply wept quietly or were silent, faces caked and streaked with tears, eyes wide and haunted. Most didn't seem to have any plan or goal, which was the main thing that set them apart from Kyle.

He very definitely did. Much as he'd done more than a year ago back on Earth, he made his way to the nearest shuttle port. Security was tight because of all the military activity at The End, but it was nothing that some carefully applied bribery couldn't overcome. He wound up booking passage on the next departure from the planet—traveling, in fact, with the families of some of Cyre's richest inhabitants, being sent off-world until things calmed down there. That ship took him to an orbital spaceport where he was able, after a couple of days' wait, to find a berth on a passenger and trading ship headed for Tau Ceti. From there, he knew, he could catch a ride back to Earth.

The journey had taken weeks, and put Kyle back in the uncomfortable position of having to tell a brand new set of lies to everyone he met. But his return, he knew, probably wouldn't be quite as discreet as his departure had been. He was pretty sure that enough time had passed that Starfleet Security wouldn't be combing every incoming ship for him, and that his fake identification was good enough to get him back to San Francisco safely. From there, though, he'd have to come up with a new plan—he couldn't afford to believe that whatever plot had forced him away had simply collapsed on its own. But he had also come to understand that working out his troubles from such a great distance just wasn't going to be effective.

He had combed through all the records on his padd. He had examined every interaction he could remember ever having had with another individual—and that had been painful indeed, at times. He had even recalled as much as he could about his family's history, in case this was some ancient grudge rearing its head. None of that had proven particularly helpful. Kyle came from a long line of soldiers, all of whom, by definition, had enemies. He also came from a long line, he realized, of taciturn men who kept their own confidences. Riker men weren't the type to share their feelings or their fears with others. If any of them had made an enemy who hated them enough to chase down their descendants, they would have tried to battle it themselves, but they would not have talked about it.

As a result, Kyle had come up empty, and he felt that emptiness tug at him with new urgency. Earth blossomed below, closer with every passing minute. As it did, he felt his stomach tighten with anxiety. He had, for a long while, escaped his problems, even though he had found new ones along the journey. But now he was returning to the root of it all, no better off than he had been before.

With one exception. Now, he felt ready to face it. No more Tholian flashbacks, no post-traumatic stress disorder, no more physical or mental weakness relating to Starbase 311. He was as fit as he'd ever been. He was still in mourning over Michelle, but that just made him madder, sharpened his edge. Kyle Riker was walking into unknown trouble, but he would be ready for it when it came.

Chapter 30

Captain Erik Pressman cut a commanding figure on the bridge of his ship, the *U.S.S. Pegasus*. Will realized that it might have just been because he was still feeling slightly awed by even being on board a starship—being posted to a starship as an officer, that was, rather than simply visiting as a cadet. But the captain seemed to feel so comfortable there. He gave the impression of a man who knew his way around the ship, and his crew was appropriately deferential to him. The man stood straight and though he was not a conventionally handsome man, he radiated command and authority. His uniform hung nicely on his slender but powerful frame. He had a broad, gleaming forehead, and his mouth and jaw were set and determined. All in all, he looked every bit the military man that Will had hoped to serve under.

Pressman was standing behind the captain's chair looking toward the turbolift doors when Will, in the company of First Officer Barry Chamish, stepped onto the bridge of the *Pegasus* for the first time. He looked at Will appraisingly, just the hint of a smile playing at the corners of his wide mouth.

"Captain Pressman," Commander Chamish said, "I'd like to introduce your new helm officer. This is Ensign William T. Riker."

Will saluted. Captain Pressman returned the salute, and then extended his hand. Will stepped forward and took it. "Welcome aboard, Ensign," the captain said, shaking Will's hand firmly and then releasing it. "Outstanding Academy record. I look forward to having you on the team."

"I look forward to being part of it, sir," Will said, with all sincerity.

"Has Number One shown you the ship?" Pressman asked.

"Not much of it, sir. We came straight here."

Pressman glanced around him. "A bridge is a bridge, more or less," he said. "You don't get the personality of a ship from the bridge. You get that from the crew quarters, public areas, lounges. The bridge is functional, that's all. Anyway, you're not on duty until tomorrow, correct? Why don't you take some time and see the rest of her, and then report back here?"

"I'd like that, sir," Will agreed.

"Number One, Mr. Riker needs to continue his tour. Perhaps Mr. Boylen can show him around."

"Yes, sir," Commander Chamish said. He touched his combadge. "Lieutenant Boylen, to the bridge."

Captain Pressman, seemingly immersed in other business, sank into his seat and began studying the status display screens built into the chair's armrests. A few moments later, the turbolift door whooshed open and a tall, sandy-haired officer appeared. He looked like an athlete, with arms that strained his gold uniform sleeves and a jaw that looked like it could cut steel. "Sir?" he said as he entered the bridge.

"Lieutenant Boylen," Chamish said. "This is Ensign Will Riker. He's taking over as helm officer, and the captain would like him to get a full tour of the ship."

Boylen fixed Will with an appraising stare. "Yes, sir," he said. Then, to Will he added softly, "Let's go, rookie."

Will obeyed. As they stepped onto the turbolift, he caught a glint of mischief in the taller man's eyes. "You sure you're old enough to be an Academy graduate?" Boylen asked.

"Yes, sir," Will replied, understanding that he was being set up for something but not comfortable responding to an officer in any other way.

"Because I don't want any kids getting in the way around here," Boylen continued. "There are enough kids as it is, what with the families on board. Chamish has three, all by himself."

"I'm no kid, sir," Will answered.

"Kind of a babyface, though, aren't you?" Boylen needled. "You shave yet?"

Will allowed himself a smile. "Yes, sir. Once in a while, sir."

Boylen laughed at that. "That's good," he said. "I like an officer with a little sense of humor. I think you'll do just fine around here, Ensign Babyface. You can call me Marc."

"Thank you, sir. Marc." Will said. "You can call me Will."

"No thanks," Marc Boylen responded with a smirk. " 'Ensign Babyface' works for me."

They started Will's tour at the starboard warp nacelle. "All right, Will," Marc said when they arrived there. "This is where you'll get to know your new home. *U.S.S. Pegasus*, NCC-53847. How much do you know about her?"

"*Oberth*-class starship," Will recited. "Primary assignments are science and exploration. Named for the flying horse." Will paused. "That's about it, I guess."

"That's about all you need to know," Marc told him, suddenly more serious than Will had seen him before. "Because a ship's history, distinguished as it might be, doesn't really have an impact on your life. What matters is where she goes from here, and what you can bring to it. What you care about is the ship's future, not her past, and rightfully so."

"Makes sense," Will observed.

"Of course," Marc went on, "it's a lie, but then that might apply to anything I tell you, so you'll have to stay on your toes. You need to know a lot more about the ship than that if you're going to fly her. But most of what you need, you already know if you've flown starships before. The rest you can learn." They walked along the length of the warp nacelle. "I don't need to describe the propulsion system to you, do I? Or general starship construction?"

"No, sir," Will told him.

"That's good, because if I did, I'd get you booted off this ship so fast your head would spin."

"What's your position again, Marc?" Will asked.

"You don't know because I didn't tell you, Ensign Babyface. I'm a tactical officer."

"So you couldn't actually boot me off the ship yourself."

"But I know the captain much better than you do," Marc pointed out. "So watch your step."

"Yes, sir," Will said with a chuckle.

"Now, an *Oberth*-class ship has a pretty unique construction," Marc continued, as if he hadn't interrupted his own lecture for a gag. Will took what he said to be the truth, for the most part, since it agreed with what he knew about *Oberth*s. But he tried to stay alert for any lies. "The saucer section, which contains the bridge, is connected to the port and starboard warp nacelles. The warp nacelles are connected to the long engineering hull. But the saucer itself is not connected to the engineering hull, except via the nacelles." He drew a diagram in the air to illustrate his point. The long, narrow engineering hull ran horizontally underneath the saucer section, and the large spar that stuck out behind the saucer, with the warp nacelles out to the sides holding the whole thing together.

"But you can beam between the saucer and engineering," Will speculated.

"Of course, if you need to get there in a hurry. We don't, right now, so we're walking. You can also get there by turbolift, although because the lifts need to be shunted off to the nacelles before going down to the engineering hull, there is a momentary delay. It's not long but it might seem long compared to turbolift operation on other ships."

They reached a narrow, steep passageway where they had to descend on ladders. "We're inside the struts now," Marc said. "There's not much functionality here, except for connecting the various parts of the ship. It's an interesting design, but you can see why it didn't really catch on for other classes of ships."

He led Will through the engineering section, which looked much like every other engineering section Will had ever seen, and introduced Will to an assortment of engineering staff whose names he knew he wouldn't remember until he'd met them all again a few times. That didn't take long, and then they were climbing up, instead of traveling via turbolift, the port strut to the port warp nacelle. The ship, as far as Will could tell, was in excellent shape. If she'd had any problems or damage at any point, it had been thoroughly repaired and patched. When they finally made their way back to the saucer section, Marc showed Will the crew quarters, including his own berth. As a junior officer, Will had a single room, with a bed that tucked into the wall until a control panel was pressed and a washbasin hidden away beneath a shelf. The walls themselves were a soft pastel off-white, with blue-gray trim and accessories here and there. The replicator was built into the wall opposite the bed, and there was a tiny, curved worktable in one corner. Compared to his Academy quarters it was a little cramped, but it would serve his needs. A crew member had already dropped off his belongings, he saw.

"Home sweet home," he said as he looked at the room.

"Until you get promoted, anyway," Marc told him. "Then you get a place big enough to turn around in."

"Good incentive."

"You can personalize it to your heart's content, though," Marc assured him.

"I don't own much," Will said, pointing to the duffel he had brought on board. "A couple of books, some uniforms, that's about it."

"That's good," Marc said with a grin. "If you had any more, you'd have to borrow space from someone else who owned even less than you. And frankly, that person would just be pathetic."

Leaving his quarters behind, Will followed Marc around the saucer section. He saw the holodeck, the shuttlebay, the transporter rooms, the observation lounge, and perhaps most importantly, he thought, suddenly realizing that it had been many hours since breakfast, the mess hall and lounge. In this area he also saw quite a few civilians walking around. As Marc had suggested, families were common on the ship, and he guessed that some of the people out of uniform were the spouses and children of the crew.

"When are you supposed to be on duty?" Marc asked him as they watched the parade of humanity pass by.

"Not until tomorrow morning," Will said. "I was to report to the ship today, but my first shift is tomorrow."

"That'll give you some time to get acclimated," Marc said.

"That's what I was thinking too. When do we push off?" He had boarded the ship at Starbase 10, after shuttling there from San Francisco the day before.

"Push off?" Marc echoed. "We've been under way for the last hour." He swiveled and led Will back to the observation lounge, but this time he opened the door and they went inside. Will peered through the large windows and saw the starscape drifting past them.

"Indeed we are under way," he observed. "Smooth."

"Nothing's second-rate on the *Pegasus*," Marc told him. "Tomorrow morning it'll be your turn to fly smooth. Think you can do it, Babyface?"

Will swallowed once. He wouldn't have been assigned the job if Starfleet hadn't had faith in his abilities. *Unless,* he thought, *Superintendent Vyrek just wants me far away from her.*

"I can do it."

Marc Boylen nodded. "That's good. You keep thinking that way." He drew back one of the chairs and sat down at the long, shiny table. "Have a seat, Ensign."

Will did as he was told. Marc looked serious again. Will had only known the man for a short time, but he knew these serious moments were rare and should be taken, well, seriously. He waited.

"You're going to be on this ship for a long time, Ensign Babyface," Marc said. "Years. You ready for that? That's the hardest part of the job, for some."

Will had given a great deal of thought to this aspect of

the job. What was he leaving behind on Earth, though? He had no family, except a father who had abandoned not only him but also, apparently, his career and everyone who had depended on him. He had no girlfriend, and the few friends he had left that he felt close to were all scattered on their own postings. Of the class that had graduated with him, there were only two other cadets he knew who had wound up on the *Pegasus* with him, and neither were especially good friends.

"I'm ready," he said finally.

"You won't miss Earth?"

"Sometimes, I guess. Not a lot."

"Where'd you live, before the Academy? I'm from Vermont. Stowe. Not much skiing around here, except on the holodeck."

"Valdez, Alaska," Will said. "So I guess we're both used to plenty of snow."

"You ski?"

"Cross-country," Will said. "Downhill's okay but it's not really my thing."

"We'll have to go out sometime," Marc said. "What else are you going to miss? Got a lover?"

Felicia's face flashed through Will's mind but he forced the image away. Ancient history. "No, not now."

"Family?"

"No."

Marc scrutinized him. "You have a life at all, outside the Academy?"

"I guess not much of one," Will admitted. "I'm kind of career-oriented, I guess."

"You'll do fine, then, on this ship. Just remember, there will be times when you'll get homesick, no matter what kind of home you left behind. There'll be times when you miss having terra firma under your feet. If it gets bad, you can talk to the ship's counselor, or you can talk to me."

"What will you do about it?" Will challenged.

"Laugh in your face," Marc said. "Won't do much for you, but it'll make me feel a whole lot better."

"I appreciate that, Marc," Will said, chuckling. "It's nice to know you're looking out for me."

"I'm a tactical officer," Marc reminded him. "I look out for everyone. I'm only looking out for you because you're such a rookie, and because I don't want you to run us into anything when you've got the helm."

"I'll try not to," Will promised.

Marc pushed back his chair and stood up, and Will did the same. "Think you can find your way back to your quarters?" Marc asked him.

Will looked around, orienting himself. "I think so."

"Good. You know where the mess hall is, or you can eat replicator food in your quarters. I was you, I'd go to the mess hall so you can meet some more folks and start learning names. Show up on time for duty tomorrow—if there's one thing Captain Pressman hates, it's lateness. Watch out for Shinnareth Bestor. She's the operations officer. Good at her job, but with a foul temper, especially in the mornings. She's become addicted to coffee, I think."

Will tried to absorb all this. "Any other advice?"

"Don't run into anything. Don't break the ship. You'll be fine." He turned and started to leave, but then stopped after a few steps and looked back over his shoulder. "And when you start having to shave every day, be sure you do. The captain also hates unkempt officers on his bridge."

Then Marc was gone, and Will was, for the first time, really alone on his new ship. His new home. It was big and strange and he knew virtually no one, and first thing in the morning strangers would be depending on his ability to do his job.

But if there was one thing Will was confident about, it was that. He knew he could do the job.

Chapter 31

"I've known you a long time, Owen," Kyle said. "You've always been straight with me. That's why I've come to you now. No matter what's going on, I can't believe you're involved."

Owen Paris looked at Kyle, his mouth still agape, eyes wide, and shook his head slowly. "You can't believe?" he replied. "I can't believe you're standing there. It's been two years, hasn't it?"

"A little more," Kyle admitted. "I'm sorry I didn't say anything before, Owen. I didn't know who to trust. I was scared. Not in my right mind, I guess."

Owen turned his gaze toward the top of his desk. "I thought you were dead, Kyle. I think after a while, we all did."

"Not an entirely inappropriate conclusion, considering someone was trying awfully hard to kill me."

"So it seemed," Owen said. "And then you vanished. What else were we to think? We tried to find you—Starfleet Security was knocking on doors and interviewing people all over the place. But you were simply gone. Where were you? Where have you been all this time?"

"That's not important now, Owen. It was a bad place, and I lost someone I cared about there. Tell you the truth, I'm still grieving for her. But I'm back now, and I want to get to the bottom of this thing once and for all. I don't want to be looking over my shoulder for the rest of my life, wondering who the next killer is. And I'd like for the rest of my life to last more than just a few days."

"We all would," Owen assured him. "I know Starfleet investigated the attempts on your life, the ones we knew about, anyway, for a while. But they didn't turn anything up, and then you were gone, so I think the investigation petered out after a while. No body, no evidence, no witnesses. It's still an open file, I'm sure, but with nothing to go on, they had to give up the hunt at some point."

Kyle had contacted Owen's office shortly after landing in San Francisco. He'd been nervous about approaching Starfleet Command, and after trying to think of a safe way to approach, had finally sent a message to Owen asking him to meet at the wharf. Kyle had arrived a little early, and the ten minutes or so he'd had to wait for Owen to show up had been anxious ones—hoping Owen, and he alone, had received the message and would comply. Now they stood on the wharf in gathering fog, looking out at the choppy gray water. "So if they'd like to get busy again, they're welcome to. As for evidence, I don't have any more than I did then. But now that I've returned, if the attempts start up again there'll be plenty, I imagine."

"If the attempts start up again after this long, it means someone really holds a grudge," Owen said. "You still don't have any idea who it might be?"

"Not a clue," Kyle informed him. "Or rather, too many ideas. Anyone in my position has a lot of enemies. Anybody that has been beaten in combat thanks to my advice and strategies. Even other Starfleet personnel who might feel that they were ignored, or passed over, because of me. Sure, I've got enemies. I just don't know who they are."

"I've got to bring security into this," Owen told him. "I'll help where I can, but it's really not my bailiwick."

"I know that, Owen," Kyle replied. "I didn't come to you because I thought you could fix it. I came because you were the one person I was sure I could trust."

"What was the final straw?" Owen asked him. A hovercraft chugged by on the water before them, bristling with fishing rods. "Was there some incident, some attempt, that prompted you to go into hiding? Maybe they can start there."

Kyle had to think about it for a moment. So much had happened since then, it was sometimes hard to keep the sequence of events straight in his head. "After the last attack you know about, the bomb transported into my apartment? I was at Starfleet Command, in the infirmary. I ran into a friend, in the hallway, and went into a private room for a moment. While we were there, we heard some security officers outside claiming that they had an arrest warrant for me, and—"

"An arrest warrant?" Owen exploded. He rubbed his smooth forehead vigorously. "How is that possible? What would you have been charged with?"

Kyle shrugged. "Treason, according to Admiral Bonner's source, right?"

"That's another investigation that seems to have stalled out," Owen said. "Again, with you gone, it hardly seemed worth pursuing. I haven't heard anything about it from Horace."

"I'd like my name cleared, Owen, if there's genuinely a question about it."

"Bonner had a source," Owen said, his tone dismissive. "His source seemed to have some pretty good information. But the conclusion—that you were somehow responsible for the Tholian attack—seemed exceedingly far-fetched to me." Owen shook his head. "I guess I wouldn't have blamed you if you'd stayed away forever, considering all the crap you've got to put up with here."

Kyle nodded, reflecting. "I might have," he answered. "If not for this woman I met. She was amazing, Owen. She would not accept injustice. Just wouldn't put up with it. Taught me a thing or two, I can tell you. And after I lost her, well, I guess I felt like I ought to carry on her ideals. I could have done it there, where I was—they have a fight on their hands, to be sure. But I realized that this is my home, and that what happened to me here is a form of injustice that I need to deal with before I'll be any good to anyone else."

Owen examined him carefully. "So when you solve the situation here, are you going back there? Wherever there is."

Kyle shrugged. "I don't know yet. I don't plan to. But that could change. Plans, I've learned, are liquid. They adapt to fit the circumstances, or they're worthless. More than that, really, because if you rely on a plan that can't change you might as well have no plan at all."

Owen Paris chuckled. "Sounds like you've become a philosopher since you've been gone."

"I've done a lot of thinking. I don't know if that's philosophy, or a fool's errand. But for a long time, I didn't have much else to do. And then when things happened, they happened all at once. If a cat has nine lives, Owen, then I don't know how many I've got, but I must be just about out of them."

"We'll keep your return as quiet as we can, Kyle," Owen promised him. "Some people will have to know, because, as I said, security is going to have to reopen the investigation. But you watch your step until we figure this thing out."

"I'll watch my step," Kyle said. "But I want to come back to work."

Owen looked at him like he'd gone insane. *Maybe I have,* Kyle thought. *Maybe insane is the only way to counter insanity.* "Back to work? Are you sure? Then it'll be no secret that you're back here."

"That's right," Kyle said. "If they're going to come at me again, whoever they are, I want them to do it in the open. I want everyone to know I'm here. I want to flush them out. If my presence is a secret then any attacks on me will be a secret too. I want to force their hand, make them sweat a bit. They'll play the cards I deal them this time, and not the other way around."

Owen shot him a smile, the first Kyle had seen on him since he'd arrived at the wharf to see his long-since vanished friend. "Did you spend your time thinking, or playing cards?" he asked. He put a friendly hand on Kyle's shoulder.

"I don't necessarily agree with your plan, but I'll go along with it. You deal the hands; I'll back your play as best I can. And I'll make sure my friends in security do the same."

"I appreciate that, Owen," Kyle said. "That's the best I can ask for."

Lieutenant Commander Dugan glanced up from the computer screen, sleepy-eyed but alert. "There's no record of any arrest warrant for Kyle Riker, Admiral," he said. "Not two years ago in June, not ever."

"I didn't think so," Owen Paris said. Kyle had left him at the wharf a couple of hours before, promising to get in touch when he'd found a place to stay in the city. His apartment had long since been occupied; his belongings put into storage. "But I had to check. What about the other thing?"

"That's a strange one," Dugan said. He'd been promoted a little more than a year ago, and Owen had absolute faith in his trustworthiness. "A security officer named Romesh McNally was on duty that night. He was approached, he said, by a fellow officer, Carson Cook, to help serve a warrant on Riker. McNally never saw the actual warrant, it turns out. Cook had it, he said, and McNally was just along as backup. They went to the infirmary to serve it. McNally says Cook was acting strangely—fixated on this one task, serving this warrant, and unable or uninterested in engaging in any conversation or activity that was not directly related to the job. It was, McNally says, like he was obsessed with it. McNally describes him as tense, too, as if he expected trouble."

"Isn't there always the possibility of trouble when a warrant is being served?" Owen asked him.

Dugan touched his silver hair, smoothing it down even though it wasn't out of place. "Sure," he said. "You never know what might happen, what the response might be. You're tense, ready to go for your sidearm if necessary. But at the same time, in spite of that tension it's kind of a routine thing. You joke around, you talk about sports, women, whatever. You don't focus on it like it's the only thing in the world. Cook was an experienced officer; he had been through it plenty of times. I knew him—not well, but a little. He was a good man."

"Was?" Owen asked. "Clarify, Commander."

"Yes, sir," Dugan said, and Owen realized that he had slipped into admiral mode without even realizing it. "I had only a vague memory of this, but I checked the records. And McNally, of course, remembered it all fairly well, when I interviewed him about it. Both officers showed up for their next shift, after failing to serve the warrant, and McNally had asked Cook what had happened. He assumed that someone else had taken over the warrant, maybe serving Riker at his home or office the next day, or, failing that, if an investigation into Riker's whereabouts had been launched. But Cook couldn't remember what he was talking about. He claimed not to know who Kyle Riker was, didn't recall the trip to the infirmary. It was like the whole event, the whole shift that night, was gone from his memory."

"That must have been disturbing."

"I'm sure it was. Nobody's quite sure if that set off what happened next, or if it was just symptomatic. But Cook's mind seemed to deteriorate rapidly. Not quite overnight, but according to the records, within weeks his memory was completely gone. Every known therapy was used to try to restore it. Counseling, hypnosis, holotherapy, data extraction. Nothing helped. His mind, again according to the records, had been wiped clean. He couldn't remember how to pull on a pair of boots. He didn't know his own name, or recognize his immediate family."

"I remember the case," Owen said. "I just didn't realize it was the same person. Of course, I didn't know about the 'warrant' then, or I might have made the connection."

"Almost no one knew, except for McNally," Dugan explained. "He talked about it with a few people, including his immediate superior. But soon enough, Cook's deterioration overshadowed any puzzle about a nonexistent warrant for a guy no one could find anyway. The mystery of the warrant went into the databanks and was largely forgotten, until you brought it up again today."

"And the one man who claimed there was a warrant isn't available to ask about it."

"You could ask him," Dugan corrected. "He's here, in a private care facility in San Francisco. The thing of it is, you just wouldn't get an answer."

Ensign Tanguy Messina looked in on his charge several times a day. The poor guy had been Starfleet, just like he was, and even though he could no longer serve, he was still entitled to the respect due the uniform he had once worn. Now he didn't wear a uniform at all, unless a loose white robe counted. They made sure he was comfortable, at least as far as one could determine the comfort level of a person who couldn't tell you how he felt. Carson Cook could have stood outside in a blizzard, naked, and except for involuntary responses like shivering and turning blue, he'd have seemed every bit as content as he was inside this temperature-controlled environment with his every physical need catered to. The room was light and airy, the furniture soft and comfortable, and soothing music played in the background. Calming holoimages, rotating at random intervals, were displayed on the walls.

"People asking about you today, Cars," Ensign Messina said casually. "That doesn't happen too often anymore, does it? But today, everybody wants to know how you're doing. Funny, huh?" He watched Carson closely, but there was no evidence that the guy understood a single word he was saying. As usual. He talked to the guy sometimes just because it felt weird not to. He was completely mindless, as far as Messina could tell, but he was still a human being.

"How you doing today?" he continued. "Same as always?"

Carson's gaze flitted across him as if he wasn't even there. It was strange, he knew. Modern medical science could cure just about anything, it seemed. He knew that historically, mental health care had been largely hit-and-miss. Some people could be put right again, others suffered forever, their conditions sometimes mitigated by drugs, talk therapy, electroshock, or other treatments. Messina had made a study of the dysfunctions of the mind, and he volunteered at this care facility, which had only the occasional "hopeless" case, where in centuries past it had been full to overflowing, while he worked on his medical training as a graduate student at the Academy.

He had glanced away from Carson, but when he looked back, it seemed as if something had changed. Maybe a little tensing of the muscles, which was rare. Carson sat in a chair most of the time; though he was capable of almost full mobility, he just didn't seem to have anywhere he wanted to go. He was in that chair now, but he seemed a little more wound up than he had been just a moment before, almost coiled. And his eye movements were different. Rather than drifting aimlessly about the room, they seemed to dart.

This was definitely a change, Messina realized. He had to alert the director. Something was going on with Carson Cook, and that had never happened. He started for the door.

"Wait," he heard.

He didn't recognize Carson's voice because Carson had never spoken, not in the whole time he'd been cared for here. But the room was otherwise empty; there was no one else it could have been. Messina turned around, and Carson was trying to get out of the chair. His muscles, atrophied by inactivity, didn't seem to be cooperating. "I . . . can't . . ." he muttered.

Messina rushed to help him. "Carson, hold on. Don't push it," he said. "Let me—"

As soon as he was close, Carson lunged from the chair, no atrophied muscles holding him back at all. He caught the unsuspecting Messina in a headlock, powerful arms encircling Messina's throat. Messina tried to cry out an alarm but he couldn't make a sound. He felt Carson's arms shifting, and then his world turned black.

Carson dropped the red-shirted man on the floor, his neck snapped. That was not the man he wanted, he knew. That was just a man who was in his way. The man he wanted was in the city, though. Not far away. He would find that man, the one he wanted, and he would snap his neck too. Or do something else; he would decide when he found him. The means wasn't important. It was the goal he cared about.

The man was in the city, at last, and the man had to die.

Chapter 32

"Ahead warp five," Captain Pressman instructed.

"Ahead warp five," Ensign Riker echoed. He touched the control panel and imagined he could feel the burst of speed, the g-forces pressing him into his seat, as the *Pegasus* accelerated dramatically. It really was just his imagination. The g-force of a warp five acceleration would smear everyone on the bridge against the rear bulkhead if it could truly be felt, and those who were standing remained in place, just fine, even as the stars outside seemed to blur and stretch. He remembered a tidbit of old Earth history, at the advent of railroads; some people believed that trains would never work because at the speed they hurtled along nobody would be able to stand up.

After a few days of slow and steady progress into space, this was the first time they had traveled at warp, and Will couldn't help being excited. Space travel had already begun to feel routine to him. He realized he wasn't the most patient guy in the world, but he'd started to wonder when something would happen. Then, today, it had.

Captain Pressman had received a call that he'd taken in his ready room, and when he'd come back onto the bridge, his entire attitude had changed. He was brisk and efficient at the best of times, but now he was all business. "We've been sent on an emergency mission," he said. "Go to yellow alert, full enable status."

"Is there a threat, sir?" Marc Boylen asked.

"Not that we know of," the captain answered. "Yet. But there will be." He turned his attention to Will. "Set a course for Candelar IV, Mr. Riker."

Will had relayed that instruction to the ship's computer, which had set the course automatically. Then Captain Pressman had dictated the speed, and Will knew that this really was a matter of some urgency. Warp five was somewhere around a hundred times the speed of light, a concept that simply boggled Will's mind when he really thought about it. Warp technology was a fact of life, and always had been. But the idea that he, a kid from Valdez, would be at the conn of a spacecraft traveling so fast that if he'd been watching it from Prince William Sound would have been gone before he could even see it, was hard to imagine.

And yet, here he was. Traveling at warp five to a destination he'd never even heard of, much less considered visiting. He wanted to know why they were headed to Candelar IV in such a rush, but he didn't want to be the one to ask.

Finally, though, Commander Barry Chamish did. "What's the emergency, Captain?" he wondered.

"It seems that Endyk Plure has been captured," Pressman said simply.

"*The* Endyk Plure?" Marc Boylen asked. "Wanted for war crimes on at least a half dozen planets?"

"That's the one, Mr. Boylen," Pressman replied. "Hundreds of thousands dead, thanks to his predacity. At a bare minimum. On worlds throughout the Candelar system."

"Sounds like a good thing to me," Barry said.

"It is a very good thing," Pressman agreed. "But the Federation wants him to stand trial in a Federation court. They want the trial to be fair and above reproach."

"They don't believe he'll get a fair trial there?" Shinnareth Bestor asked from ops.

"They don't believe he'll live to see his trial date," Pressman said. "He's being held at the most secure facility on Candelar IV. But there are already mobs surrounding the prison, calling for his head. It's positively medieval, apparently. The locals are desperate for someone to get Plure off the planet and into Federation custody as quickly as possible. We're the nearest Starfleet ship, so we're elected."

"Which will make us very unpopular when we arrive," Marc observed. "Hence the yellow alert."

"That's correct," Pressman noted. "If they get wind of our approach, the Candelarans may even try to intercept us. Not the authorities, but the citizens."

Will felt an unfamiliar tension squeeze his gut at this discussion. He had wanted to do something—anything. He hadn't wanted to simply cruise around space without apparent purpose—"exploring" for the sake of exploration. Now they had a purpose, a mission, and it sounded like a dangerous one. There was an element of excitement to it all, but also a nagging fear. His life had been in danger before—certainly when he'd followed Paul Rice onto Saturn's moon, it had. But he hadn't had a lot of time to think about it then. This time, he was in control of the ship, intentionally flying them right toward certain trouble.

He smiled, though he tried to hide it from the rest of the bridge crew. *This is it*, he thought. This *is what I signed on for*.

"Mr. Riker," Captain Pressman said sharply. "My office. Mr. Chamish, you have the bridge."

"Aye, sir," Barry said.

Will gulped and followed the captain to his ready room, just off the bridge. He wondered if he'd done something wrong. He couldn't imagine what. He'd brought the ship into orbit around Candelar IV, outside visual range from the surface, as instructed. They had made good time and arrived without incident.

When he entered the ready room, Captain Pressman was already sitting down behind a large desk. The door shut as soon as he walked through. This was the first time Will had seen inside it. The walls were a warm beige, set off by a cool blue carpet. Over the captain's right shoulder was a large window, through which Will could see Candelar IV's ocher sphere. Directly behind him was a shelf on which stood a small bronze sculpture that Will recognized as a Frederic Remington bronze, an old-fashioned Earth cowboy trying to hang on to a horse that reared up to avoid the strike of a rattlesnake. As if to demonstrate that he was not entirely old-fashioned, Pressman had put a model of an *Ambassador*-class starship on the shelf next to his Remington bronze.

"Sir?" Will asked, standing at attention.

Pressman fixed him with an unwavering gaze. "Nice flying, son," he said. "I know it wasn't particularly difficult, but you did what you were told to do without asking a lot of questions, and you got us here. Now we just have to get Plure off the planet and get out of here again."

"Yes, sir," Will said.

"At ease, Will," Pressman said. "You prefer Will, correct? Not William? That's what your file said."

"That's what I'm used to, sir," Will answered, relaxing his stance a little.

"I make snap judgments about people, Will," Pressman said. "Sometimes I'm told that I shouldn't. That it's a bad thing, a dangerous thing. Trouble is, more often than not, I'm right. My judgments are borne out in practice. So I keep doing it."

"If it works for you, sir, I don't see the problem."

"There it is, Will, in a nutshell. It works for me. And I have to say, my judgment about you has been formed from precious little evidence. You've sat on my bridge for a few days, you've flown my ship, and you haven't said much. The few times you have opened your mouth have been to ask intelligent questions or to offer opinions, most of which make sense to me. I've read your file, of course, and I know you had some rough times at the Academy, but I also know that you graduated near the top of your class and were quite an accomplished cadet."

"I did my best, sir."

"I'm sure you did. So here it is, Ensign Riker. I'm sending an away team to the planet to pick up Endyk Plure. I want you to be part of that team."

"Me, sir?" Will asked, realizing even as the words passed his lips how stupid it sounded. The captain hadn't been talking to anyone else.

"You, Will. I have a good feeling about you. I think you'll prove to be a smart, capable Starfleet officer, destined for accomplishment. I don't know what it'll take to turn you from a raw rookie helm jockey into the kind of officer I think you can be, but my guess is that you need experience. Lots of different kinds of experience. An away mission like this one is something that doesn't come along all that often, so I want you to be part of it. The way I see it, if you're going to start collecting experience, there's no time like the present, right?"

"I suppose that's true, sir."

"Do you see the statue behind me, Will? The cowboy?"

Will didn't know how anyone could miss it. "Yes, sir."

"The popular myth is that cowboys were loners. The rugged individual. Do you know what that is, Will?"

He didn't know what the captain meant, precisely. "No, sir."

"It's a load of hooey," Pressman declared. "Maybe they were, to some extent, in the sense that it was hard for a cowboy to marry and settle down, since he was out on the range for several months of the year, going off on six-month long cattle drives and the like. But the fact is, every cowboy worked as part of a team. They worked for a ranch. One cowboy can't control a herd of cattle, or string an entire fence, or do much of anything else by himself. Cowboys were team players, and they all had to pull their weight. That's why I keep that statue behind me—to remind everyone who stands where you are that we're all part of a team here."

"Makes sense, sir."

"And the ship next to it, in case you're wondering, is the *Zhukov*. First vessel I served on. Captain D'Emilio is the one who taught me the value of team play. We're all in this together, is what he used to say. The two statues pretty much sum up my philosophy of command."

"I see, sir."

"Not yet, you don't," Pressman argued. "But you will. And you'll start the process today, when you go down to Candelar IV. Be careful down there—when you get back, you'll need to get us out of here fast."

Will beamed down to the prison on Candelar IV with a trio from security: Florence Williams, Marden Zaffos, and the chief, Lt. Teilhard Aronson. Hendry Luwadis, the director of the prison, was waiting for them anxiously, and practically wept with relief when they materialized in his office.

"What took you so long?" he wanted to know.

"We came as quickly as we could," Lt. Aronson assured him. "We were the nearest Starfleet ship, but we were still quite a distance away."

"When we joined the Federation," Luwadis said, "I thought we'd be better served by our membership. But this . . . leaving us with this killer on our hands . . ."

"Sir, we're here to take him off your hands." Lt. Aronson spoke with a soothing tone, but Luwadis was not easily soothed.

Glancing at the surroundings, Will began to understand his problem. This was not a highly developed world. Advanced enough to qualify for Federation membership, but probably just barely. The structure they were in, the main prison administration building, was made of stone. The office was full of uniformed, armed guards, but their weapons looked relatively primitive compared to the phaser rifle in Will's hands. Even Luwadis's clothing, a coppery suit a few shades darker than his skin, looked rough-hewn, as if it had been made by hand, by someone not particularly skilled or imaginative.

"You can understand how they feel," Luwadis went on, waving a hand toward the large glass doors that led out onto a balcony. "The mob, I mean. Plure has killed more of us than anyone wants to think about. The mob wants him dead. So do I, for that matter. But we've agreed, by joining the Federation, to abide by Federation standards of justice. Plure should have a trial, and then he should be punished. Without that, there will be no guarantee that he is, in fact, the one responsible for all the crimes he's been accused of. I'd rather have certainty than a quick death, even in this case."

"You made the right decision," Aronson said. "He'll have a fair trial. If he's guilty—which, on the face of it, seems pretty evident—he'll be punished appropriately."

"Appropriately?" Luwadis echoed. "Can he be killed seven hundred thousand times?"

"I don't know much about his physiology, sir," Aronson replied. "But I'd guess he can only be killed once."

"Yes, yes, which is why you've got to get him out of here."

Will noticed that Zaffos, probably made curious by Luwadis's gesture toward the balcony, had edged closer to the doors there. Will started to move, as subtly as he could, to intercept Zaffos if he should decide to go outside. But the continued conversation between Luwadis and Aronson had distracted him, and Zaffos took two quick steps before Will could stop him.

"Wow," he heard Zaffos say. "He's not kidding."

Will lunged onto the balcony. He spared only a glance toward the prison walls. Beyond them, what looked like thousands—tens of thousands, maybe—teemed, pressing up against the walls as if trying to knock them down by sheer weight of numbers. Will grabbed Zaffos's gold-sleeved arm and tugged him toward the door. "Get back inside," he urged. "We're supposed to stay out of sight, remember?"

"Here, here!" Luwadis shouted from inside the office. "Don't go out there! If they see you—"

Will and Zaffos stepped back inside and Will pushed the doors closed. But it was too late. A deafening cry rose up from the crowd on the other side of the walls. Will couldn't make out many words, but he thought sure he heard "Starfleet" among the furious din.

"I . . . I'm sorry," Zaffos said quickly. "It's my fault. I wanted to see."

Luwadis scowled at him. "You wanted to see? You wanted to touch off a riot, that's what you wanted to do!"

Will risked another glance outside. Luwadis was right. The mob's angry cries had grown louder, and now he could see that some of them had gained the top of the wall. Prison guards were rushing to quell them, but they were vastly out-numbered and maybe even outgunned.

"Get out," Luwadis insisted. "Get out of here, and take Plure with you, or we're all dead!"

Four guards approached through an open doorway, sur-rounding a prisoner. Endyk Plure was as dangerous-looking as his reputation implied. He was a big, beefy individual, with coppery coloring similar to Luwadis's. His muscles strained at the sleeves of the plain prison-issue tunic he wore. His face, unshaven for at least a week, was solid, jaw square, mouth cruel. His eyes were small and did not reflect much intelligence, Will thought, but maybe a vicious cun-ning. He stared defiantly at the Starfleet team that had come to collect him, but didn't speak. Will knew that appearances could be deceiving, but in this case he was pretty sure that he could have picked Endyk out as a mass murderer in any lineup.

"You're coming with us, Plure," Aronson said. "To stand trial in a Federation court for war crimes and mass mur-der."

"Sounds like fun," Plure growled, his voice every bit as unpleasant as the rest of him. "Maybe you'll introduce me to your family. The meals they serve here stink, and you look like some good eating."

Aronson ignored the taunt and touched his combadge. "*Pegasus*," he said, "five to beam aboard."

As Will dematerialized, to arrive a moment later in the transporter room of the *Pegasus*, he thought he heard the ter-rible mob break through the prison walls. He hoped Luwadis could calm the mob before he and his guards had all been killed.

Chapter 33

There was little security in the psychiatric facility. Carson Cook wasn't considered a danger to himself or anyone else. One had to have some kind of mental process to be dangerous. Carson was just a blank slate, and no one had written menace onto it. And psychiatric science was such that very few people needed to be confined. So Tanguy Messina was alone in the building with Carson Cook, and once Tanguy was dead, there was no one standing in his way.

Carson walked away from the building rapidly, partly in order to put distance between himself and Messina's body, but mainly to find and kill his next victim. There was menace in him now, certainly. He personified danger. He didn't have a conscience—had he been asked, he wouldn't have been able to define the word. He didn't have a moral code or a set of ethical standards. All those things had been left behind in the man he had once been, but was no longer.

Now, he was a targeted missile.

At uneven intervals he received new information, helping him lock onto his target. As he walked, some people stared at him, he noticed. Eventually he figured out that it was his robe. He was naked underneath, and it wasn't what they were wearing. When he came to that conclusion, his mind told him that he should do something about it. He needed to blend in if he was to reach his goal. He watched a man about his size enter a house, and as the man was just passing through the doorway, Carson rushed up the walk and hurled himself at the man. His momentum carried them both inside. The man cried out but Carson slammed a fist into the man's throat, effectively silencing him. The man flailed at him. He was no soldier, though; he was weak, and soft. Carson smashed his head against the wall a few times, and it left a thick red smear when the man sank to the floor.

The man's clothes were torn and bloody now, but Carson understood that he was inside the man's home. He went upstairs, found a closet full of similar suits, and put one on. With a tunic and pants of the same color, a pleasant royal blue, and a pair of actual boots, Carson figured he would look enough like anyone else on the street to withstand casual scrutiny. He looked around for a few more minutes, to see if there was anything else here that might be useful to him. He didn't find anything, but so attired, he went back out into the city and waited for more instructions.

A night passed, and a day, and then, as if he had always known it, he knew the location of his target. He knew what his target looked like, how he might be dressed, what the sound of his voice was. He went to his target's approximate location, and he waited.

And finally, his target showed.

As promised, Kyle reported his new address to Owen Paris as soon as he'd secured an apartment. And as Owen had promised, he relayed the information to Starfleet Security, to personnel, to records—to virtually every department he could think of, short of writing it on the walls of Starfleet Headquarters in giant red letters. If there were going to be more attacks against Kyle, they would happen soon.

They'd have to. Kyle had been feeling low-grade anxiety ever since he'd entered Earth's orbit. He wanted to get this over with, once and for all, so he could go back to living his life.

He spent the next day trying as best he could to put his affairs back into some kind of order. He retrieved his abandoned belongings from storage—his books, his maps, his clothing, some artwork, some sentimental items that reminded him of Annie, or Kate. To these, in his new home, he added the holoimage of Michelle. The three women he hadn't proved worthy of. But maybe it wasn't too late to try.

His new apartment had a food replicator, but he was back in San Francisco, which was still one of the best places in the galaxy to get a fine meal. So that evening, instead of eating by himself in his apartment, he went out. He had his heart set on Italian—some capellini pomodoro, maybe, with a nice bottle of Saint Emilion, a favorite wine he'd introduced Owen Paris to over dinner a few years earlier.

Notwithstanding his generalized anxiety and the grief that still clawed at his heart, Kyle felt better overall than he had since before the attack on Starbase 311. Even with all the horror he experienced there, the time on Hazimot had been healing and restful. He felt sharp, alert, and clearheaded. The hard manual labor he had done there had left him strong, with stamina he hadn't enjoyed since he was much younger. And being back in San Francisco helped, too. He loved the city; always had. Its cool breezes, crazily diverse architecture, and almost uniquely polyglot population sang to him. As he walked down the street, confident that whatever Italian restaurant he came to first could provide an excellent meal, he felt almost happy again. He felt, at least, the possibility of happiness; no, the inevitability of it.

Inevitability. He liked the sound of that. He even tried saying it out loud. He repeated it, almost like a mantra, inside his head as he approached a small storefront restaurant called Paolo's, its sign glowing golden and inviting in the twilight.

But before he reached Paolo's, he saw a man coming toward him in an ill-fitting blue suit, a glazed expression on his face. This, he was pretty sure, was it. Maybe the first of many, but definitely an attack. *You should have armed yourself,* he thought bitterly. *A phaser would make short work of this guy.* He hadn't wanted to be overly impulsive, though. Maybe the man was just lost, a stranger in town, confused and looking for a hand. The way Kyle had been feeling lately, he might have fired first, leaving San Francisco with one less tourist and himself with an even bigger problem.

His muscles tensed, his heartbeat and respiration quickened. Still the man came toward him, not deviating from his path. His hands were clenching and releasing, and Kyle knew then that he was not wrong. He glanced around himself, rapidly, trying to determine whether or not this person was alone. It appeared that he was, so Kyle froze in position and let the man come to him.

As he neared, steel flashed in his hands. The man carried a Ligonian knife, its blade wickedly curved, in his right hand. Kyle barely had time to register that when the man in blue sprang at him.

Kyle dropped to a partial crouch, minimizing his target area and bringing his arms in front of himself for defense. Now Kyle recognized him: Carson Cook, the supposedly comatose security officer; Owen had sent over an image of him last night. Cook moved in fast, blade slashing wildly toward him. Kyle blocked the first attack with a blow to Cook's forearm. Cook almost dropped the knife, but he recovered it and brought it down below Kyle's waist level, then stabbed up, aiming for the ribs. Kyle caught Cook's wrist, the knife's point just nicking his own forearm as he did. With his other hand he reached for Cook's throat. Cook dodged the arm, so Kyle, still gripping the wrist, kicked at Cook's knee instead. The kick connected, hard, and Cook lost his footing. He fell to one knee and Kyle jerked his arm skyward, twisting as he did. Cook's hand spasmed and the Ligonian knife went flying, landing on the street with a clatter.

As soon as Kyle released his wrist, Cook lunged forward again, this time from his kneeling position. His mouth opened and he snapped at Kyle's stomach. Kyle brought a knee up, smashing it into Cook's jaw. Cook's teeth crunched sickeningly and he swayed backward. Blood appeared at the corners of his mouth and he spat bits of tooth into the street, but he didn't go down.

Rather than wait for the next attack, Kyle doubled his fists together and swung them like a baseball bat, catching the side of Cook's face. Cook's head snapped sideways and the fight went out of him. He slumped to the street.

Before Kyle could catch his breath, two Starfleet security officers ran up to him, phasers out and pointed at Cook. "You're a little late," Kyle said. "I thought you were supposed to protect me, not just clean up the mess afterward."

"Sorry, sir," one of the security team said. Her hair was a mass of tight blond coils and her uniform sleeves bulged at the biceps. "We were trying to stay out of sight, to draw out your attacker. And then, well, it looked like you had things under control."

The other officer, a male with dark hair and a somber face, knelt down next to the body in the street. "It's Carson Cook," he said.

The blonde nodded. "He escaped yesterday from the mental care facility he's been living in," she explained to Kyle. "Nobody thought he could so much as open a door."

"Apparently he's better."

"Doesn't look like it from here," the male officer said. He held up Carson Cook's head. Cook's eyes were open but there was no spark of life in them. His mouth was slack, a mixture of blood and saliva running down his chin. The officer waved his hand in front of Cook's eyes but they didn't track, didn't even blink. "He looks just the same as ever."

"But you saw him attack me," Kyle insisted.

"Yes, we saw it," the blonde said. "Doesn't make sense, does it?"

"Not a bit," Kyle agreed. "But then, a lot of things about

this whole situation haven't made sense for a long time. That's the only consistency, in fact."

"Well, maybe this will put an end to it," the blonde officer suggested.

Kyle shook his head. "No, it won't. Cook's just one man. He's a tool, somehow, but he's not what this is all about."

The officer shrugged. "One thing at a time, I guess. We'll get him picked up and put back into custody. In a more secure facility, this time—he's a murderer, now. And we'll stick a little closer from now on."

"Sounds good," Kyle said. "I was just going to Paolo's there for some dinner. That shook up my appetite a bit but I think I can still eat."

"Let me have a look inside first, sir," she said. "Just in case."

"Fine," Kyle said. "Go ahead."

He glanced back at the male officer, who had just used his combadge to call for help removing Cook's comatose body. But as Kyle watched, Cook—his eyes animated again—snatched the phaser from the officer's holster and triggered it. The beam caught the male officer full in the torso. He screamed once and then fell onto the sidewalk, his uniform shirt smoldering.

Cook turned the phaser toward Kyle, who dropped flat on the sidewalk just in time to miss the beam that shot over his head. Cook tracked him down and fired again. Kyle rolled to the side and the beam missed again, but not by much. Before Cook could aim again, a phaser blast caught him in the head. Cook twitched once, dropped the stolen phaser, and was still.

"Damn!" the blonde said as she rushed to her partner's side. "How do you keep up with that? One second he's basically an empty shell, and the next he's alert and deadly."

"I wish I knew," Kyle admitted.

She held two fingers against her partner's neck. "He's

gone," she said, her eyes filling with tears. "Mack's a great guy. Nice wife, terrific kids, the whole package, you know?"

"I'm very sorry," Kyle said. He wanted to be sympathetic, but at the same time he didn't take his eyes off Cook, just in case.

When the female officer spoke again, there was a new edge in her voice, of anger, even rage. "I don't know what you're mixed up in, sir, but it's getting pretty expensive. First the attendant at the care facility, and now Mack."

Kyle put a hand on her shoulder, but kept an eye on Cook. He had hoped to be able to question his attacker— whoever it turned out to be. But even if Cook had survived the phaser blast, wherever his mind was, he was beyond interrogation. "I know it is," he said softly. "It's been expensive for a long time. If there's a way to finish it, I'm going to find it, though. You can count on that."

Chapter 34

Will was exhausted.

The away party had taken more energy out of him than he'd anticipated. He hadn't had to do much of anything, but the level of tension had been draining, and now that his shift was over all he wanted to do was hit the rack and sleep until he had to report for duty the next morning. The last hour or so on the bridge, flying out of the Candelar system, he'd barely been able to stifle his yawns. Captain Pressman, though, looked alert and crisp as ever, and Will hadn't wanted to let on how tired he was.

It was funny, he thought, how different the pace of life onboard was compared to the Academy. At the Academy, the day was broken up more—different classes, different faces, and different activities—so there was always variety. When he was on duty he was on the bridge most of the time, with the same crew and the same responsibilities, and at the end of the day he was almost always beat. He guessed he'd get used to it, and once he had a chance to start an exercise regime he'd have more energy. So far, though, that hadn't happened, and it wouldn't tonight.

As he made his way down the corridor to his quarters, nodding to crew members whose names he was trying to keep straight in his head, he was stopped by a hand gripping his shoulder. "Will," a voice said, "I just wanted to thank you."

Will turned to see Marden Zaffos looking intently at him. The security guard, a couple of years older than Will, had a thick mass of dark curly hair, and around his eyes there were dark smudged rings that reminded Will of a raccoon.

"No problem," Will replied. "I don't know if you heard, but Luwadis was able to quell the riot before too many were hurt. The mob is probably still mad at him for calling us in, but my impression is they're even madder at us."

Marden nodded, his hands folded across his chest. "Can't really blame them," he said. "But I know I should never have gone out onto that balcony. That was a stupid mistake. I just wanted to see . . . to get a glimpse of Candelar."

"We all make mistakes," Will said, biting back another yawn.

"Some are worse than others." Marden eyed the ceiling for a moment, and cleared his throat. "Can I talk to you, Will? Someplace more private?"

Will hoped this wouldn't take long. He could almost hear his bed calling to him. "Sure," he agreed, not wanting to turn away a fellow crew member, and potential friend, who clearly had something important on his mind. "I'm just around the corner, if that's okay."

"That would be great," Marden said. "If you have something else you need to do, we could talk another time . . ."

"No, now's fine," Will said. "I don't have any plans except for sleeping." He led the way to his quarters and opened the door. Marden followed him in. Once inside, Will lowered the bed and sat on it, his back up against the bulkhead. He offered Marden the desk chair.

"I should never have gone on that mission," Marden said. "My mother's father was from Handihar."

"In the Candelar system," Will observed.

"That's right. Her mother, my grandmother, was human, and my father's family is all human. So I just have that little bit of Handiharian in me. But my grandfather always told me these great stories about his homeworld, when I was a boy. I never thought I'd see the place. Candelar IV isn't exactly the same thing, but I figured it was the closest I'd ever get, and I just couldn't resist taking a look. I didn't think it would be a problem, but I guess I wasn't really thinking it through. I put us all in danger, and I'm sorry."

"We were never really in danger," Will pointed out. "We always had the option of beaming out before there was trouble."

"That's true," Marden agreed. "But still—it was a stupid thing to do."

"I won't argue with that."

"But at the same time," Marden went on, "I couldn't help sympathizing with them."

"With the mob?" Will asked, slightly surprised. "They wanted to lynch Plure."

Marden nodded. "And Handihar is one of the worlds he plundered," he reminded Will. "A hundred thousand dead, there, more or less. Basically so he could extort a payment from them to make him go away. And the payment has almost utterly destroyed their economy. Handihar is a backward place, Will. Tribal, low-tech. Not wealthy. And not able to stand up to a heavily armed madman like Endyk Plure on their own."

"Well, he's in Starfleet hands now. A Federation trial will be fair, and he'll be appropriately dealt with when it's over."

"Luwadis was right about that," Marden argued. "There's no fair way to deal with such a person. The best he should be able to hope for is a slow, agonizing death."

"I understand how you feel, Marden," Will assured him.

"I don't think you do, Will. Those were my people. Distantly related, but still. Endyk Plure has to die for what he did, and I'm afraid that Federation justice won't do the job."

"So what do you propose?" Will asked. He wasn't at all sure what Marden was driving at.

"I've got full access to the brig," Marden said. "And I know the shift schedule. I can take care of it tonight, before we reach the transfer point."

"No!" Will was shocked that Marden would even suggest something like that. "Marden, you can't. You're Starfleet. We have rules. Principles. You can't just abandon those."

"Yes, we have principles," Marden said, leaning forward in the chair now. "But don't you agree that some principles outweigh others? The idea that Endyk Plure's life might be spared, in spite of all the deaths he's caused—I just can't take that. It's repugnant to me."

"But to take it all into your own hands . . . how is that better?"

"It's better because I would be killing one man, the killer of thousands. It's just simple math, Will. One for many."

"It's more than math," Will countered. "It's what's right and wrong. You can't just decide for yourself that he's guilty and decide his punishment."

Marden stood up and paced around Will's small room. "His punishment seems obvious to me. How could it be otherwise? Someone who is responsible for so many deaths . . ."

"I'm just saying, there's a system to determine that. When you put on the uniform of Starfleet, you agreed to enforce that system."

"But, Will . . . he . . ." Marden looked down at Will, still sitting back on his own bed, and his face was full of anguish. Will felt bad for the man, but not so bad that he could agree with his plan. As tired as he was, he realized that if he could just keep Marden here, talking, maybe they'd get to the point where they were to transfer Endyk Plure to another vessel before Marden could throw away his own career. He could almost kick himself for the inspiration, but he felt he had to try.

"Tell me about Handihar, Marden. What did your grandfather tell you about it?"

Marden smiled for the first time, a little wistfully, as if remembering pleasant times with his grandfather. He drifted back over to the chair and sat down again. "Like I said, it's mostly a tribal society," he began. "Close to the land. It's a big planet, huge, I guess, according to him, and his part of it is densely forested. Junglelike. They live in wooden structures, not much more than huts, I think. The air is so humid that the buildings have to be replaced on a pretty regular basis. My grandfather left there when he was a young man, but from what he has told me it's still mostly that way."

"Sounds pleasant," Will said, just to keep Marden talking.

"I've always wanted to visit," Marden told him, smiling a little as he thought about it. "He makes it sound kind of like paradise. But . . . there's one story he told me, Will. I think maybe it especially applies, in this case."

Will had just wanted him to reminisce about the planet, trying to keep him away from the subject of Endyk Plure. But he guessed that sitting here talking was still better than seeking the guy out in the brig and killing him. "What story?" he asked.

Marden took a deep breath. *Apparently it's going to be a long one,* Will thought. He hoped he could stay awake for it.

"Have you ever heard of a *gralipha*?" Marden asked by way of beginning.

Will racked his brain but couldn't recall that he had.

"It's a huge, wild beast," Marden explained. "Many legged, and with a massive, heavy skull, horned on the top. Almost like some kind of Earth dinosaur, I think. Anyway, this story that my father's family passed down, for generations, was about the time a *gralipha* attacked his family's village. Just came in out of the jungle and ran around in a blind rage, berserk, smashing huts, killing with abandon. The people were taken by surprise—they lived with *graliphas* in the jungle all the time, but none had ever charged the village like this. They couldn't do much to fight back—it was all they could do to try to stay out of its way. It cut a swath through the village and then left, back into the jungle it had come from."

"Sounds kind of like those stories of rogue elephants," Will suggested. "How they'd sometimes attack Indian villages."

Marden nodded. "Very much like that. Except this thing was at least twice the size of any elephant. Or, that's how my grandfather tells the story, anyway."

"What did they do? The villagers."

"They picked up after the attack. They buried their dead, they tended to the wounded, they rebuilt their homes and fortified the log wall around the village. Then they went into their culturally prescribed mourning period. For days, they mourned the dead, weeping and laying offerings at their graves. This was, grandfather said, how his people honored their dead.

"What they didn't do was go after the *gralipha*. And six days later, it came back. It tore through the brand new fence like it was paper, and ran amuck again. More homes fell, more people died. Children and the elderly and those hurt in the first attack, especially, because they couldn't dodge it in time."

"That's terrible," Will said.

"It was. My grandfather can barely hold back the tears when he tells the story. Some of his ancestors—mine too, I guess—died in these attacks.

"But this time, the villagers reacted differently. They left the rebuilding and the mourning for later. They organized into hunting parties and they followed the path the beast made when it left the village. They tracked it. When they caught up to it, there was a terrible battle. More lives were lost. The thing swung its head and its horns gouged and tore at the villagers. Their weapons were just primitive spears and arrows and slings—they could barely penetrate its tough hide.

"They didn't give up, though. They continued the fight. Eventually, their weapons found tender spots—the eyes, the roof of the mouth, the base of the neck. They brought the mad *gralipha* down, and they killed it, even though the cost was high. Because this was the only way they could guarantee that it would not return to their village later."

Will understood. He shifted his position, sitting cross-legged on the bed with his spine straight. "So Endyk Plure is your *gralipha*," he said.

Marden nodded. "He's rampaged through the village once too often. If he's not stopped at the first opportunity— that means now, tonight—there's still the chance that he'll escape and come back. His forces might be closing in on the *Pegasus* even now. The authorities on Candelar IV said they wanted the Federation to take him so he'd get a fair trial, and so the mobs wouldn't storm the prison, but I'm convinced that they were just as worried about Plure's troops coming to his rescue."

"You could be right," Will admitted. "Although I doubt that Plure's forces would want to risk an attack on Starfleet.

Against the Candelar system—and I don't mean to be dismissive, just realistic—they were tough guys. But that's a pretty backward system. Against Starfleet, they'd be schoolyard bullies facing down real adults with real firepower. They wouldn't have a chance. And the thing about bullies is, they only like to fight the weak. They usually leave the strong well enough alone."

"Possibly," Marden said. "But even if they don't come for him, I won't be convinced that he'll never escape until I see him dead with my own eyes. And it wasn't just ancient ancestors that he killed on Handihar, but family. My grandfather's two sisters, and their entire families. There are just too many reasons for him to die, and none that I can see to let him live."

"Except your career, and the oath you swore to uphold Federation law," Will pointed out.

"That's one argument, Will," Marden said. "I'm just not sure it's a good enough argument."

Will had felt something nagging at him while Marden told his story, and now he remembered what it was. A story of his own, from his younger days, that might also be applicable. He closed his eyes for a minute, knowing that to do so was to risk falling right to sleep, but wanting to get the story straight in his mind before he started telling it. And when he did, it all came rushing back to him, as clear as if it had been yesterday.

It had been his fourteenth summer, he recalled. Valdez, still a small town, sat at the edge of one of the greatest wilderness areas in North America, but even so, he was beginning to feel constricted, limited, and impatient to see more of the world. But halfway through the summer, there was an event that promised diversion, and he welcomed it.

A campsite in the nearby wilderness had been attacked by a grizzly—a rogue, one of the campers said, enormous and vicious. The bear had torn though the tents, upending food lockers, and maiming one of the campers. The remaining campers—there had been, Will recalled, eight in all—had survived, and determined that someone needed to kill the bear before someone else was hurt. Some of the local people in Valdez volunteered to find the animal, agreeing that a rogue grizzly could be bad for their community and needed to be put down.

Will's father was one of the volunteers. Will insisted that he should be allowed to go along. His father argued, but not very energetically, and he changed his mind more easily than Will had even anticipated. So they each got a phaser rifle and they joined the hunting party leaving from the campground early on the morning after the attack.

As they walked through the forests and meadows of the wilderness area, weapons at the ready, alert for any signs of the bear, Kyle Riker was more talkative than usual. "This is nice," he had said. "I mean, not the idea that we have to kill a grizzly before it kills one of us. But being out here in the sunshine and the trees, with a blue sky over our heads, a father and son together . . . we don't do this sort of thing often enough, Will. We never have. My fault, I guess, and I'm sorry."

He had stopped in the middle of the trail then, and laid a hand softly on Will's shoulder—the kind of physical contact that was rare between this father and son. "I'm sorry for a lot of things," he had said. "More than you can imagine. I hope one day you'll understand why I've done things the way I have. I hope I've made some good choices, even when they haven't seemed like it. A day like this, being out here with you—Will, you're a man, look at you! I'm sure there are still things you need to learn, but I'm not so sure that I can teach them."

He had gone quiet then, more like the father that Will was used to, the one who kept his feelings bottled up inside as if they were poison, and they had continued tracking the bear. When they'd lost the trail for a while, Will had found it by scouting in ever-wider circles until he cut across it, and Kyle had clapped him on the back. "You'll be fine, Will. You'll be just fine," he had said. Will hadn't realized then— hadn't realized until just this moment, sitting in his quarters on the starship *Pegasus* with Marden Zaffos, what Kyle had meant by that. He had known then that he was going to leave, going to abandon Will to his fate. The way Will handled a gun, the way he cut bear track—those were pretty meaningless skills, in the greater scheme of things, but somehow Kyle Riker had decided that they meant Will was mature enough to make his own way in the world.

They had, later that day, found the bear. She had a den, and when the hunting party approached she had growled ferociously and lunged at them. But several of the hunters fired at once, and the bear fell without any human casualties.

Inside the den, though, they found something that cast a different light on things. There were three cubs inside the den—dead cubs, bearing wounds that could only have been made with phasers. None of the campers had claimed to be hunters, and indeed none of them had joined this hunt. But they'd been the only ones out in this area that any of the townspeople knew about.

The hunting party returned to the campground and ransacked the tents until they found the hidden phaser rifles. The campers protested, denied, and then finally, faced with the evidence, admitted their guilt. They had tracked the bear for sport, finding her den and killing her cubs just because they could. It hadn't occurred to them that the animals were an endangered species, that they had done something stupid and shameful, until it was too late. And when the bear came to their campsite, she was only seeking revenge for her loss.

Will told Marden the story in as much detail as he could remember, and when it was over Marden looked puzzled.

"Are you saying revenge is never legitimate?" he asked.

"Not at all, Marden. I'm just saying it's something you have to be careful with. It's more complicated than it looks, sometimes. If you kill Plure, are you the hunters? Or are you the bear?"

Marden shook his head. "Will, that story doesn't even make any sense."

"Who said life has to make sense?" Will shot back. "It's just something that happened. Whatever you want to take away from it is up to you."

"Well, what do you get from it?"

Will considered for a moment. "Something really unexpected," he said. He described what his father had said, and what he now thought it meant. "It was my father's good-bye speech," he said. "It wasn't much of one, but it was the best one he could bring himself to give."

The hours passed as Will and Marden talked. Will battled sleep, and eventually reached a point beyond tiredness, where he became more alert, and might not have been able to sleep if he'd tried. Later, they'd made some coffee and sat in silence, drinking it. Finally, Marden looked at the time.

"We're there," he said. "Unless the schedule has been thrown way off for some reason. Plure is being beamed to the starship that'll take him back to Earth for his trial, or he will be soon."

"Probably so," Will agreed.

"I know what this was all about, Will. I know you just wanted to keep me talking so that I wouldn't get my shot at Plure. I wanted my revenge, and you kept it from me."

"I can't apologize for that, Marden," Will said. He felt different, somehow, after the long night and the unexpected revelations. Maybe it was just lack of sleep, but maybe it was something more. Maybe it had to do with a new kind of maturity making itself felt. He hoped that was it, in fact—he had wondered if he'd ever grow up, and now it seemed that he might after all.

"You don't need to. I appreciate it. I'm mad as all hell—but I appreciate it anyway. You stopped me from making a fool of myself, from throwing away my career and maybe my life. More than that, though, you corrected my course even when I couldn't. I'm not a vengeful person, I'm not a judge and a jury, and I'm damn sure no executioner. If I had let myself become those things, it would have been a terrible mistake."

Will was as pleased as he was surprised by this response. "I think you're right, Marden," he said. "But if it's all the same to you, now that you're on to me, I'm going to kick you out of here. I need a shower. I'm on duty in a little while, and I need to wake up."

"On duty?" Marden asked, shocked. "I guess you're right. We've been at this all night, haven't we? I'm sorry, Will, honestly."

Will stifled yet another yawn and stretched his arms behind his head. "Don't sweat it," he said sleepily. "I'll be fine." But as he prepared himself for another duty shift, after his most exhausting day on the job and without a wink of sleep, he couldn't help remembering what Marc Boylen had said on his first day here. "Don't run into anything."

If he was going to, today would be the day.

Chapter 35

Cook failed.
Failed? What do you mean, failed?
He made an attempt. It went bad. He's dead.
Well, that's some consolation, at least. And Riker?

He's fine. Unhurt.

He's been gone for, what, two years? And now that he's back we still can't manage to get him?

To kill him. His career is in tatters. And we've been watching his son; we can move against him anytime we need to.

Still . . . sweet as that might be, Kyle Riker is the main goal. He has to be. What he did out there must be avenged.

I can't argue that. But the way things happened . . . at least there were some positive results.

How can you even think that! Are you—

Insane? Don't even bring up the idea.

Then what?

It made us . . . closer . . . than we ever had been. Than we could ever have expected. And we know the research bore . . . certain fruits.

I suppose. Still . . . had it never happened—

We needed it to happen, remember? For that matter, we pulled the trigger. We created the situation . . .

Because there was no other way. Starfleet would have found out.

That's a risk we ran, knowingly. And with the backup measure in mind. That's why we chose 311 in the first place, because of its remoteness, and because of the possibility, if we needed it, of using them. It was just the schedule that went a little . . . haywire.

Yes, haywire. But Riker survived it. And you didn't. Which is why he has to pay the price. But . . .

Yes . . . ?

Since we know, for the first time in quite a while, where the father and the son both are, how much more delicious would it be if Riker had to watch his son die before he drew his own last breath?

I do like the way we think.

Kyle passed a few days in San Francisco, enjoying the

feeling of being back home. Except for the hole in his insides every time he thought of Michelle, he was already beginning to feel like his time on Hazimot was a dream, half-remembered, some of the details already fading as real life went on. *Not that this is anything like real life,* he thought. He wasn't working yet, still hadn't even entered the Starfleet Command complex.

He was bored already and growing more so by the hour. Now he stood on the crest of a long hill, wishing someone would attack him just to provide some diversion. When he heard footsteps approaching rapidly from behind him, he whirled, half-expecting and, he realized, almost desiring some kind of assault.

But it was Ensign Halalaii, one of the guards assigned to protect him. She was panting, as if the climb had taken more out of her than him. "Sir," she said, "Admiral Paris would like you to report immediately to Starfleet Headquarters. There's an emergency of some kind."

The thought of going back to Headquarters—the lion's den, as far as Kyle was concerned—was still a bit unnerving. But Owen had done a lot for him, and if he could help out the admiral, he had to do it. "I'll catch an air tram right away," he said.

"No time for that, sir." She tapped her Starfleet insignia badge, which she wore on her chest in spite of being out of uniform for this assignment. "Three to beam in."

Kyle braced himself for the momentary vertigo that always overtook him when he was transported, and then it was over and he was standing in Owen Paris's office.

"Thank you for coming, Kyle," Owen said, rising from behind his desk.

"I'm not sure that I had a choice," Kyle answered. "The ensign said there was an emergency."

"That's right," Owen said. He excused the two security officers, asking them to wait in the hall. They would continue to keep their distance from Kyle, but would stay alert just the same. "Come on," Owen said to Kyle. "I'll explain as we go."

"Go where?" Kyle asked, rushing to keep up with Owen. The admiral had already started down the hall, his strides long and purposeful.

"Situation room," Owen replied. "We'll be met there by the others."

"What others?" Kyle queried. "What's happening, Owen?"

Owen slowed a moment to give Kyle a chance to catch up, and when he explained he did so in low tones, so that not even the security officers following behind could hear him. "It's a ship, the *Pegasus*. Captain Erik Pressman in command."

"I don't know him," Kyle said. "What's he like?"

"He's a good officer. A bit too ambitious for my tastes, but otherwise I have every faith in him."

"So what's the problem with the *Pegasus*?"

"We'll be there in a moment," Owen said. "And you'll see."

He led the way through a door guarded by yet another gold-uniformed security officer. Inside, a long, curved table stood in front of a vast display screen. In addition to the seats around the table, there were a dozen workstations, and beyond those, auditorium-style seating for a couple dozen more. No one else was in the room when they arrived, but there was an image on the screen. Two planets, one reddish and the other predominantly green, but with orange splotches here and there. Arrayed around the planets were fine-lined spherical grids that intersected one another. In the area of intersections was a blinking red dot.

"That's Omistol," Owen said, pointing to the planet on the right. "And Ven, on the left. Heard of them?"

"I think so, but not recently. I've kind of been out of the loop recently."

"I know you have, Kyle," Owen said. "But we're going to ask you to catch up fast now."

"You still haven't told me what's going on," Kyle reminded him. "Or what this has to do with the *Pegasus*."

"Omistol and Ven have been at war for almost three years," Owen said. "A vicious, bloody, terrible war. Each side has lost more lives than it can afford. We keep thinking the war will end because one side or the other will realize that they're both committing suicide. So far, though, that hasn't been the case. They're still at it."

Kyle nodded. He could follow this, all right, but he wanted Owen to get to the real point.

"Those grids on the display show each planet's claimed sphere of influence. As you can see, there's an overlap. That's a big part of the problem, right there—they both want to control that section of space, which is a main shipping lane for their system. It's not the whole problem, but it's kind of symptomatic of the greater issues. They both claim that space, and neither will relinquish that claim. The red dot in the middle of the disputed territory? That's the *Pegasus*."

"What's it doing there?" Kyle asked. As he did, the door opened again and more Starfleet officers filed in. Kyle recognized Vice Admiral Horace Bonner and Admiral J. P. Hanson, but none of the others, a mix of captains and some of their staff people.

"Captain Pressman was responding to reports that a pirate—one that has been preying on Federation ships, not too far from Omistol and Ven—had taken refuge in the disputed zone. He went in intending only to investigate the report and capture the pirate vessel if it was, in fact, inside there, and to leave immediately if it wasn't."

"And was it?"

"The *Pegasus* was unable to locate the pirate. What it located instead was trouble."

"Why?"

"Because the fleets of both Omistol and Ven were moving toward one another, in force. Omistol's ships were cloaked. They were on the *Pegasus* before Captain Pressman knew they were coming."

"Cowardly bastards," Kyle growled. "I hate cloaking."

"So does every civilized people," Vice Admiral Bonner put in, joining the conversation. "Welcome back to the fold, Mr. Riker."

"Thank you, Vice Admiral," Kyle said. They shook hands. "It's nice to be back, I think."

"As you can see, we've brought you back at the best possible time. For us. Maybe the worst for you, I'm afraid."

"What do you mean?" Kyle asked.

Bonner looked a little surprised. "You haven't told him, Owen?"

"I've been trying to fill him in on the whole picture," Owen Paris said. "Not just the details."

"If the details are important," Kyle said, "then I'd like to know them as well."

"Very well, Kyle," Owen relented. He looked like he was sorry to have to say it. "One of the bridge officers on board the *Pegasus* is your son, Will."

Chapter 36

Will had tried every trick Starfleet Academy had taught him, and a few new ones he'd made up on the spot, trying to break the grip of the graviton beam that held them in place. The Omistolian warship was gigantic, half again the size of the *Oberth*-class *Pegasus*, and its tractor beam powerful beyond even the experience of Captain Pressman. Beads of sweat appeared on Will's upper lip and at his temples, not from the heat but from the exertion and concentration he applied to the problem. And still nothing worked.

The worst part was, they had come here for nothing—chasing a shadow, a ship that wasn't here in the first place. Captain Pressman had warned them of that possibility before they'd entered the system. But they had all agreed that it would be worth the risk if they could find *Heaven's Blade*, the pirate vessel that had been making this region decidedly unsafe for Federation freighters. The *Blade* hadn't been here at all, though. If by chance it had passed this way, it hadn't stayed long.

The word that it might be here had come in from Starfleet Command shortly after they'd transferred Endyk Plure to the ship that would carry him to Earth. After a brief conference with his officers, during which the phrase "suicide mission" had come up a few times too often for Will's liking, Pressman had given the orders to move into the war zone between Ven and Omistol. And so they had. They had still been in the disputed zone, looking for the elusive *Heaven's Blade*, when the Omistolians had decloaked. There had been a brief verbal exchange between Captain Pressman and the leader of the Omistolian force, but no shots were fired. And then, when Captain Pressman gave the order to Will to get them out of here, now, the tractor beam had been engaged. They had gone, since then, exactly nowhere.

"We could try blowing them out of the sky," Marc Boylen suggested. He'd already suggested it, a couple of times, with no luck.

"Mr. Boylen," Pressman reminded him. "The ship holding us in its beam is just one of many. It's far larger than we are and far more heavily armed. We're a scientific exploration vessel, not a warship. Even if we could beat that one ship, they have many more. We would be begging for them to wipe us out."

"May I speak frankly, sir?" Lieutenant Commander Rungius asked. Bethany Rungius was the ship's chief of security, a hard-nosed officer with a reputation for making hard decisions quickly.

"Of course," Captain Pressman said.

"While I would never suggest that we 'beg' to be wiped out, I can't really see the difference. They're not holding us because they want to play catch. If they don't destroy us now they'll destroy us later."

"They want us for something," Will argued, "or they'd have done it already."

"Exactly, Mr. Riker," Pressman agreed. "We just need to wait until they tell us what it is they want from us."

"But meanwhile, sir, the Ven fleet continues to approach," Rungius pointed out. "If we're still here when they arrive, then we're stuck in the crossfire and we're dead anyway."

"Maybe that's why they're holding us," Marc offered. "To use as a shield, or a hostage, against the Ven?"

"The Ven have no more reason to like us than the Omistol do," Rungius countered. "We'd make a pretty poor hostage. Neither world seems to be all that fond of the Federation."

"All we can do," Pressman told his crew, "is wait. When they want us to know, they'll tell us."

The wait wasn't long. The bridge had fallen into an uncomfortable silence, everyone watching the implacable advance of the Ven fleet and the maneuvering into battle position of the Omistolians on their display screens, when Dul Dusefrene, the ship's communications officer, spoke up. "There's a hail from the Omistolians, sir," she said. "It's Oxxreg." This, everyone knew, was the commander of the Omistolian fleet and the one who had carried out the short and unproductive dialogue with Captain Pressman earlier.

"On the screen," the captain ordered. A moment later, the image of the Omistolian appeared on the big main screen. His face was flat, an unpleasant shade of dark olive. Will was reminded of toads back home.

"I have a proposition for you, Captain Pressman," Oxxreg said, his voice sibilant and oddly mellifluous. *"You'll want to discuss it with your superiors."*

"This is my ship," Captain Pressman replied. "I am fully empowered to make decisions regarding her safety." Nonetheless, Will noticed that he put his hands behind his back and, so hidden from Oxxreg, gestured toward Lieutenant Dusefrene. She nodded, almost imperceptibly, and her hands flashed across her control board. Starfleet had already been alerted to their situation here, and she was opening a channel to headquarters so that they'd hear whatever Oxxreg's proposal was.

"Not this decision, I would wager," Oxxreg said. *"But have it your own way."*

"I will," Pressman said, standing firm. His jaw was set and he looked as determined as he sounded. Will hoped it was convincing to the Omistolians.

"I'm offering an extremely simple deal," Oxxreg went on. *"Your ship's safety, in return for a very small favor."*

"We're not in the habit of negotiating with those who make unprovoked attacks on us," Pressman replied.

"You were inside our zone of influence with no prior authorization," Oxxreg shot back. *"A zone currently the subject of a rather bitter dispute. For all we know, you are working with the Ven."*

"I've already explained our mission to you."

"Yes, chasing a ship. Which your Command, all the way back on Earth, claims was here, but which none of our instruments have located any sign of. Surely you understand that this explanation is not terribly convincing or believable."

"Nonetheless, it's the truth."

"*Be that as it may,*" Oxxreg argued. "*You're in restricted space. You have not received, or even asked for, permission to be in this space. We are fully within our rights to destroy you as a trespasser and a spy. I'm offering you a way to avoid that fate.*"

Pressman moved his shoulders a little. "Say we were to accept that negotiation is an option," he said. "What would your offer be?"

"*We would release your ship and grant you safe passage out of our vicinity,*" Oxxreg replied.

"In exchange for . . . ?"

"*In exchange for Starfleet arms and assistance,*" Oxxreg said. "*This war has been brutally expensive, in terms of lives and finances. Both our planet and the Ven—*" This word he said with a sneer, almost as if it were the worst curse he could think of. "*—have nearly bankrupted ourselves waging it. We need but a few solid victories, though, to turn the tide. Starfleet could provide the necessary armaments to destroy Ven's fleet, and maybe their entire planet.*"

"And you think that they'll give you these weapons, just to save us?" Pressman laughed at the screen. "You obviously don't understand Starfleet."

"*Your superiors do not value you and your crew?*" Oxxreg asked.

"Of course they do," Pressman objected. "But they have priorities, and standards. Both of those require that they not interfere in wars that are none of their concern. Particularly in petty little skirmishes like the one you have going with the Ven."

Oxxreg exploded at this. "*Petty? I have lost my father in this war, and three sisters. Others of us have lost their whole families. We willingly give our lives because our cause is just.*"

"Your cause is nonsense," Pressman told him, pushing,

Will knew, as hard as he dared. "You don't like the Ven. They don't like you. So instead of agreeing to be neighbors who just don't get along, you pick this sector of empty space and decide that one of you must control it. If neither of you did, what would happen? Ships would still use it as a trading lane. Your war, sir, is idiotic."

"*I take it, then,*" Oxxreg said, his voice newly dripping with hatred, "*that you're turning down our offer?*"

"I'll take it to Starfleet," the captain said. "As you suggested. Just don't expect to get the answer you want. Pressman out."

Dusefrene broke the connection and the viewscreen went blank.

"At this point," Marc Boylen put in, "I think the answer he wants is that Starfleet won't cooperate, simply so he can shoot you."

"You're not seriously considering their offer," Lieutenant Commander Rungius said. "Starfleet would never—"

"Of course they wouldn't," Pressman assured her. "I'm just buying time, that's all. Besides, Starfleet heard the whole thing. If they want to weigh in, they will."

"They must be insane if they think we'll go along with that!" Vice Admiral Bonner exclaimed. His face was red with anger, white blotches showing up on his cheeks and forehead. Kyle thought his reaction was a bit extreme, and he, not Bonner, was the one with a family member on the vessel in danger.

"It would be a serious violation of the Prime Directive," Owen Paris agreed. "I hate to see a war allowed to go on unchecked, particularly one with the potential to utterly devastate two different worlds. But if that's their choice, we can't interfere with them. We certainly can't take sides in their fight."

"It's just a first offer," Kyle pointed out. "They'll likely agree to something more reasonable later."

"Any agreement we should come to would be a bad idea," a captain named Jensen observed. "It would be a signal that we're willing to deal with those who threaten us."

"We've done it before," Kyle noted. "I'm not saying it's a good idea. But I wouldn't rule it out without some consideration."

"I agree with Captain Jensen," Bonner said. "We can't cave on this one. We'll have ships all over the galaxy held for outrageous ransoms. If the price we pay is the *Pegasus*, well, that's just the way it has to be. Captain Pressman and his crew knew the risks when they took the job. I'm sorry, Mr. Riker, I know it's hard to hear that."

The room fell silent as everyone digested this. Kyle knew that it was true. He couldn't say that he was close to Will anymore, or knew what was in his son's heart, but he was still a Riker and he had put on the uniform of Starfleet, so there was every indication that he was aware of, and willing to accept, the dangers that went with it.

Kyle looked at the others, lost in their own contemplation, their faces different mixtures of rage and sorrow. Being a Starfleet officer, it seemed, didn't require leaving one's emotions behind, but rather learning to work through one's feelings, to ignore them when appropriate, but not to deny them. Everyone in the room felt the pressure, understanding that the lives of everyone on the *Pegasus* were dependent on the decision they reached.

"How much time do you think we have?" someone asked.

"Not much," Bonner replied. "The way the Ven fleet is closing in, the Omistol is going to want a quick decision." He cast a sudden glance at Kyle. "I doubt there'll be time for a lot of back and forth. Like when the Tholians attacked Starbase 311, I expect we're looking at minutes, not hours."

The statement struck Kyle as odd. What did Bonner

know about 311, outside of the stories he'd heard and the official record? And why bring it up now, as if it had been on his mind? Didn't they all have plenty to think about with the current crisis? He nearly replied, but then decided not to. His attention had to be on the *Pegasus*, on coming up with a solution to the problem that didn't involve giving any arms to the Omistol but still could help save the ship.

Owen Paris approached and sat next to him, heaving his bulk into the chair with a tired sigh. "Kyle," he said softly. "I've got something I need to tell you."

"What is it, Owen?"

Owen looked at him with a weary expression. "I've had it with the sedentary life," he said. "Teaching is great—I love the young people, the open, eager minds. But the rest of it, sitting behind a desk . . ." He nodded toward the display screen, where the steadily blinking red dot reminded Kyle of the urgency of their task. "I can serve better out there."

"Out there?" Kyle echoed. "You want to leave the admiralty?"

"I've already got a ship," Owen told him, smiling a little. "The *Al-Batani*. It's being overhauled now, and I'm gathering a crew. Maybe it'll only be for one five-year stint, but I feel like it's important. Things aren't so complicated out there. I feel more alive. Here I'm just getting old. Used up."

"This is a strange time to tell me about it," Kyle observed.

"This is the best time I could think of," Owen said. He rubbed his face briskly with both hands, as if to restore circulation. "That's what I'm talking about. They're taking all the risks. I can't stand sitting down here and sending them out to face danger, without putting myself in the same position. It's just not right. Why should the young ones die so we old-timers don't have to?"

"I see what you're getting at, Owen." Kyle said. "It's a very courageous stand."

"It's got nothing to do with courage," Owen insisted. "It's got to do with being able to look at myself in the mirror. It's got to do with sleeping well at night. It's fairness, not courage, I'm talking about."

"Well, congratulations, then," Kyle said. "Sounds like you know what you want, and I'm glad you were able to make it happen."

"The one good thing about seniority," Owen Paris declared. "When you want something bad enough, it's hard for Starfleet to find an excuse not to give it to you."

"Not to change the subject," Kyle said, intending full well to change the subject anyway. "But we've got to make a decision about the *Pegasus*."

"I thought it had been made," Owen said. "Bonner's right, we can't bargain with them."

"I'm not suggesting that we do," Kyle said. "But I think I might have another option to suggest. Before I do, though— and believe me, I understand that Will is on that ship and time is of the essence—do you have someone on your staff that you trust absolutely? Preferably someone who's already in the room but who might not be missed if they leave for a little while?"

Owen pursed his lips together. "That's a tall order, but I think I know just the person. Wait here."

Owen rose and crossed the situation room to where a small knot of his staffers were working through some computations. He leaned in close to one of them, a young woman with auburn hair swept up on top of her head, a few locks fallen to her cheeks as she worked. She glanced over at Kyle, who nodded subtly to her. Then, as Owen went to consult with another group, the young woman approached Kyle.

"Admiral Paris said you wanted to see me, sir?" Her voice

was unexpectedly husky, and her green eyes flashed with barely contained mischief. She held out a hand. "My name is Ensign Kathryn Janeway."

Chapter 37

"Yes, sir. I think we understand."

Captain Pressman had been discussing their situation with Admiral Paris. Will was glad that Admiral Paris was involved—he had a lot of respect for Owen Paris, and he trusted the man's survival skills. If they needed anything right now, it was a plan that would help them survive. He knew, though, that the *Pegasus* was not the most important thing on the table—it was Starfleet's resolve that mattered most. Like everyone else on the bridge, Will understood that if they backed down and dealt for their lives, others would take advantage of the example they set.

But Admiral Paris, living up to Will's trust, had offered them a plan that might just get them out of this. The other alternative, of course, was that it might get them killed. Doing nothing would accomplish that same goal; this would just speed things up a bit. Will didn't see a reason not to try, and he hoped the captain would agree.

"Thoughts, people?" Pressman asked.

"I don't like it," Barry Chamish said. "Suicide never seems like a good idea to me, not when there might be another solution."

"Is there another solution?" Shinnareth Bestor asked.

"Not that I can think of," Chamish admitted. "But I also don't want to admit defeat, and that's what the admiral's plan sounds like to me."

"It just might work," Will countered. "I think it has a better chance of working than anything else we've come up with."

"You'll be the one doing the heavy lifting, Will," Captain Pressman said. "Most of it, at any rate. So if you're comfortable with that . . ." He left the sentence unfinished. As the freshest face on the bridge, Will knew that a decision of this magnitude wasn't really up to him. He appreciated being made to feel like he was part of the process, though.

"I can handle my end," Will assured the captain. This earned him one of Pressman's rare smiles. For such a rotten day, this one had its fringe benefits. He only hoped he might live long enough to look back on them fondly one day.

"I'm for it," Rungius said.

"Same here," Boylen put in.

Chamish looked horrified. "You're asking us to kill ourselves!" he insisted. "How is that a good idea?"

"It's a chance, at least," Rungius argued. "One chance is better than none."

"Agreed," Bestor said simply.

"Very well, then," Captain Pressman said. "This is a starship, not a democracy, and the majority of us are in agreement anyway. Mr. Dusefrene, hail Oxxreg, if you please."

Will noticed that Dul Dusefrene's hands quaked as she moved them across her control board. Since each of her hands had seven fingers, Will was reminded of a spastic spider when they shook. He wondered how many of the bridge crew had gone along with the plan because they didn't want to appear cowardly, and how many genuinely were scared. Or if there was a difference.

And if there was, which camp he fell into.

When Oxxreg's amphibianlike face appeared on the main viewscreen, Captain Pressman faced him, shoulders square, hands again clasped behind his back. "We have considered your offer," the captain said. "And I'm here to tell you that there will be no deal."

Oxxreg arched what would have been an eyebrow, had

he possessed them, wrinkling his forehead. "*Your superiors don't care what happens to you?*"

"They care," Pressman argued. "But they care more about upholding Starfleet regulations. We are a neutral party, as far as your war is concerned, and we will remain so. I hereby demand, once again, that you release us and let us be on our way. Starfleet is no threat to you."

"*I'm sorry you have to so humiliate yourself, Captain.*" Oxxreg sounded almost disappointed. Will supposed he probably was—he had probably been congratulating himself on the brilliance of his plan, and now faced having to explain to his own superiors why it wasn't going to work. "*But very well,*" he went on. "*You'll have a few more minutes to live, then. We'll see how willing the Ven are to fire on a Starfleet ship when they get within range.*"

This time, Oxxreg broke the connection. Pressman turned toward the bridge crew. "So we're to be a shield, apparently."

"Maybe the Ven are more reasonable," Dusefrene suggested.

"We're one ship—a small one, compared to the Omistol ships," Will noted. "We won't make a very good shield. And when the shooting starts, I doubt anyone will make a special effort to miss us."

"Mr. Riker's right," Captain Pressman said. "So let's put the admiral's plan into motion, see what happens. Are you still with us, Admiral?"

"*I'm here,*" Admiral Paris's voice replied after a few seconds. Communication by susbspace radio was far from immediate, but it was pretty fast. "*I wish you the best of luck, Captain.*"

"We'll need more than luck," Pressman said. "Let's see if we've got it. Mr. Riker, commence."

"Yes, sir," Will said, trying to sound as sharp and military as he could. He knew what they were proposing was risky, so he wanted to try to keep everyone's morale up as best he could. The only morale he could directly influence was his own, though, so he focused on that.

He tapped at the conn controls, reversing the thrust of the *Pegasus*'s engines. Where before they had been burning fuel trying to escape the tractor beam, now he began to gently nudge the ship closer to the Omistol vessel that held them.

"They're on the move," Captain Jensen pointed out.

There was increased tension in the situation room, but also a growing sense of elation. At least something was being done. No one knew if it would work, but it was movement.

To Kyle, the success or failure of the plan had even greater significance than it did to the Starfleet officers in the room. Sure, it was their ship, their personnel. But his son was on that ship. He'd been a lousy father, and he wasn't likely to change now. The last couple of years had taught him some hard lessons, though, and one of those was that his standard approach to life—duty first, all other considerations a distant second—was perhaps not the healthiest way to live. It had cost him too much. He knew he couldn't simply waltz back into Will's life, even if the boy survived the next few minutes. But at least Will would still be out there, and maybe somewhere down the line he'd be able to find it in his heart to forgive his old man for the stupid mistakes he'd made.

"I hope this works," Admiral Paris muttered.

"It *has* to," one of the other officers fired back.

"It may not," Kyle said, always willing to play devil's advocate to his own tactics.

"We'll know soon enough," Bonner observed. "There's nothing we can do now except wait."

"They're getting closer," Jensen said, as if he were the only one who could see the screen.

Over the subspace radio relay, Kyle heard the words he'd been waiting for—the words that would make this plan work.

Or fail miserably.

"This is Captain Erik Pressman," the captain's voice said. *"Initiate auto-destruct sequence."*

There was a pause, and Kyle knew the next voice he heard should be the first officer's. When it finally came, it quavered with fear and uncertainty.

"This is Commander Barry Chamish . . . Captain, I can't. I won't."

"Number One, I must insist," Captain Pressman said.

"You can't make me," Chamish replied. To Kyle, he sounded more like a petulant child than a Starfleet officer.

"It's your duty," the captain urged. *"To this ship and this crew."*

"That's exactly why I won't do it," Chamish said. *"I think it's the wrong decision for the crew. I refuse to give my authorization."*

"You're relieved, Mr. Chamish." Kyle could hear the fury in Pressman's voice as he did so.

"Sir, I'll do it," another voice broke in. *"If I can."*

Kyle thought the voice sounded familiar. It was not a voice he'd heard often, certainly not recently. It was deeper, more mature than he remembered it. But the sound of it, the valor he heard in those few words, filled him with immense pride.

Will felt every eye on the bridge burning into him. Captain Pressman regarded him levelly, as if trying to fit a new perception around the old ones he had already established.

"You can't, Ensign," Pressman said. "It would have to be the third-in-command of the ship."

"Well, it's got to be soon, sir. We're already within range."

Before Will finished his sentence, the officer to his immediate left said, "This is Lieutenant Commander Shinnareth

Bestor." The operations officer's voice was flat, betraying no emotion at all. "Initiate auto-destruct sequence."

"*Verbal confimation requested,*" the computer replied. "*Captain Pressman?*"

"Confirmed," Pressman stated.

"*Lieutenant Commander Bestor?*"

"Confirmed," the operations officer said.

"*What is the desired interval until destruction, Captain Pressman?*"

Pressman glanced at Will, who checked his instruments quickly and then held up three fingers. "Three minutes," the captain said.

"*Auto-destruct sequence initiated,*" the computer intoned. "*Destruction in two minutes, fifty-eight seconds.*"

Will wiped at his forehead. His heart pounded in his chest and the rush of blood in his ears almost drowned out the other noises on the bridge. Everything except the computer's soulless voice, counting down the last few seconds until the ship blew itself up. The force of the explosion, he remembered from the Academy, would be roughly the equivalent of a thousand photon torpedoes.

At least it'll be quick, he thought. *Probably fairly painless. Probably even a relief after sitting around waiting for it for three minutes.*

"What's going on up there?" someone asked plaintively.

"You can hear as well as the rest of us," Bonner responded. "They're waiting."

Kyle knew it wasn't that simple. The delay inherent even in subspace radio meant that the *Pegasus* might already be destroyed. He wondered what they'd hear on this end—static? An electronic hum? Or would they first, momentarily, hear the thunder as the explosions ripped through his son's vessel?

"The Ven are getting awfully close," Admiral Paris observed. "They're right there—definitely within firing range."

One more thing to worry about, Kyle thought. He had hoped the *Pegasus* situation would be resolved before the Ven showed up and further complicated matters. Maybe if that first officer hadn't chickened out . . .

"*Destruction in forty-five seconds,*" he heard. He swallowed hard. This was getting too close.

"They've cut the tractor," Bestor said excitedly.

"Will, engines on full," Pressman ordered. "Take us out, now."

"Yes, sir!" Will shot back, already implementing the command.

"*Destruction in fifteen seconds,*" the computer announced.

"Computer, this is Captain Erik Pressman. Abort auto-destruct sequence." He swiveled about in his chair. "Commander?"

"Computer, this is Lieutenant Commander Shinnareth Bestor. Abort auto-destruct sequence." Will noted that the operations officer sounded relieved. He was feeling a little better about things himself, but he knew they weren't out of the woods yet.

"Sir, they're firing on us!" Bethany Rungius said.

"All power to shields," Pressman replied. "Don't worry about returning fire."

"Shields are up, sir."

The first volley from the Omistolian ship hit them astern. The bridge rocked, lights flickered, but the shields held.

"They didn't want us to blow up right next to them," Captain Pressman noted. "But they have no problem letting us get a little farther away and then blowing us up themselves."

Will concentrated on putting distance between themselves and the Omistolian ship. He knew their greatest danger had been with the Omistolians themselves—if they had not been scanning the *Pegasus* closely enough to notice when their auto-destruct sequence started, they would never have shut off the tractor beam. But now they were one little science ship in the middle of a war between two enemy fleets, so their chances still didn't look that promising.

"Sir," Rungius reported. "The Ven ships are firing."

"Brace yourselves," Pressman commanded. Everyone did, but no barrage landed.

"Sir," Rungius corrected. "The Ven are firing on the Omistolian ship that held us — on Oxxreg's ship!"

Will blew out a sigh of relief. The kilometers were passing by the second, thousands upon thousands of them. They weren't out of range yet, but apparently Oxxreg had bigger problems right now. Captain Pressman ordered that Oxxreg's ship be put on the main viewscreen, and the whole bridge watched as four Ven ships fired upon it at once, green beams lighting up the sky. Then the Omistolian ship exploded, parts of it spiraling out into space, trailing smoke. The concussion wave from the blast caught up to them a few moments later, pushing them even farther away from the battle.

"Mr. Riker, ahead warp six, if you please," Captain Pressman said.

Will laughed. "I do please, sir. I please very much. Warp six it is." He moved his fingers across the control panel like an experienced hand, and reveled in the fact that he, a kid from Valdez, was at the conn of a starship.

And that it could fly really, really fast.

Chapter 38

Kathryn Janeway came back into the situation room just as the cheers were dying out. She walked straight to Kyle's side, barely sparing a glance for anyone else. "It looks like I missed something," she said. "Is everything all right?"

"Everything's just fine," he told her with a grin. He patted the back of the chair next to him. "Have a seat, Ensign, and tell me what you found out."

She spoke quietly into his ear for a couple of minutes, and Kyle felt his gaze drawn to the person of Vice Admiral Bonner, who, alone among the individuals in the room, seemed not to be celebrating the *Pegasus*'s escape.

Admiral Owen Paris came over to Kyle, giving Janeway an inquisitive look but saying nothing, and clapped Kyle on the back. "Congratulations, Kyle," he said. "It looks like you've still got the touch."

"Thank you, Owen," Kyle said. He spoke louder than was strictly necessary, but he did it on purpose, wanting to attract attention. "I'd like to ask you something, though."

"What is it?" Owen said. He looked a little taken aback, though he must have known that Kyle had been using Janeway for some private purpose.

"I'd like to know who it was that ordered the *Pegasus* into that space in the first place. I understand they went in looking for the pirates, but I believe they were acting on intelligence supplied by Starfleet Command. Was it Vice Admiral Bonner?"

Owen hesitated for a moment before answering, as if unsure what can of worms he might be opening. "Yes," he said finally. "Yes, it was. How did you . . . why do you ask?"

"I thought it might have been," Kyle said. He noticed that by now he had the attention of everyone in the room, including Bonner, who stared at him with undisguised contempt.

"I don't know if I appreciate this line of conversation," Bonner objected. "This man is a civilian; what business is it of his whether or not I ordered that? Anyway, we had no reason to doubt the intelligence."

"He's right, Kyle," Admiral Paris said. He still sounded

hesitant, as if he didn't want to shut Kyle down, but he needed to maintain the proper protocols. "Is this going somewhere?"

Kyle rose from his seat. He trusted Owen, and because he did he trusted Ensign Janeway. But he sure hoped her information was accurate.

"It is, Owen, and I'll ask you to let me finish this."

"Absolutely not!" Bonner exploded. "What is this, some kind of civilian tribunal?"

"Nothing of the sort," Kyle assured him. This was his second strategic ploy of the day. He hoped it played out as well as his first. "But my son's life was in danger today, and he helped save a lot of other lives. I think I'm entitled to a few questions and answers, here."

"You have no official status here, Kyle," Owen reminded him. "You've been missing for nearly two years. You are here as a favor to me, and I'll ask you not to push things too far. That said, I agree, you are entitled to some answers."

"I most strenuously object," Bonner blustered. He lurched from his seat, face red and blotchy again, scalp dripping with sweat.

"Horace," Owen said. "Sit down and shut up."

Bonner glared at him, but noticed that everyone else in the room was staring, and finally returned to his seat.

"Kyle, you'd better explain yourself," Owen suggested.

"Thank you, Owen. I will. Vice Admiral Bonner sent the U.S.S. *Pegasus* on a wild goose chase into disputed, dangerous space, even though, in fact, there was no information that *Heaven's Blade* was anywhere in the vicinity."

There was an audible gasp from some in the room, and murmured conversation among others that quickly stopped when Kyle continued. "That part is just speculation, though I suspect if we examine the Vice Admiral's logs we'll see that it's true. Something else is definitely true, though, confirmed for me just moments ago by the very capable Ensign

Janeway. Vice Admiral Bonner had a stepson on Starbase 311 with me—a young man named Charles Heidl. Mr. Heidl was a scientist, not a military officer. Although Vice Admiral Bonner and Mr. Heidl were very close—as close as any father and son, I would guess, from what I've been able to learn—the relationship between them has been kept very secret. Possibly because Vice Admiral Bonner had, on numerous occasions, arranged for Starfleet favors for Mr. Heidl. Chief among these was helping to arrange funding, transportation, and a facility on Starbase 311 for some of Heidl's experiments."

Bonner looked at Kyle, his mouth opening and closing soundlessly, like a fish in a tank. Owen addressed Janeway, still seated next to where Kyle had been. "Is this true, Ensign Janeway?"

"Yes, sir. Once Mr. Riker told me precisely what to look for, it wasn't hard to find the details."

"We know that the Tholians attacked Starbase 311," Kyle went on. "We know, through intercepted communications, that the Tholians did so because of intelligence, which they deemed believable, that Starbase 311 was to be the launching point for an incursion into Tholian space. Further, we know through hard experience what kind of response that would surely generate among the Tholians— precisely the kind that it did. A swift and vicious assault. That intelligence—again, this has been confirmed in the past few minutes by Ensign Janeway—came from the starbase itself."

"Someone on the base signaled the Tholians and invited attack?" Captain Jensen asked, incredulous.

"That's correct, Captain," Kyle replied calmly. "There's one more piece to the puzzle, but this one I haven't yet been able to confirm. Even Ensign Janeway isn't a miracle worker, it seems, and we'll need a bit more time to study this. But I recall that Starfleet or the Federation was planning an investigation into experiments on Starbase 311—to be specific, whatever experiments Mr. Heidl was engaged in. Becoming aware of this investigation, Vice Admiral Bonner contacted Heidl and ordered him to shut down the experiments and destroy the evidence, according to their prearranged plan. The best way to ensure that the experiments would never be investigated in depth, of course, was to arrange the destruction of the starbase. So the Tholians were contacted. And they came, and all of us on board—all except me, by the merest twist of fate—were killed."

Kyle had moved closer and closer to Bonner as he spoke. Bonner couldn't take his eyes off his accuser, and his face seemed almost to be collapsing in on itself as the truth of his crimes was revealed. His gaze was full of hatred, and his hands seemed to have taken on a life of their own, twisting and wringing one another as if they were possessed.

"What was it, Bonner?" Kyle demanded, bending close to his prey. "Genetic experimentation? Something banned by the Federation, at any rate. Something that couldn't be done closer to home, where the authorities might stumble across it."

"I can't . . . I can't tell you!" Bonner cried. "He'll . . . he'll . . ."

"You'll be telling a court martial, soon enough," Owen Paris said. "You might as well come clean."

"Actually, I think I can guess," Kyle said. He glanced over at Janeway, who understood the signal and rose from her seat. "Based on what's happened since. It was some kind of mind control experiment, wasn't it? If we run a check, I suspect we'll find that the crew members who have attacked me were all, at one point or another, stationed at Starbase 311. Long before the Tholian attack, of course—probably long before I was there. But while Mr. Heidl was there, running his experiments. And even after it was all over, they remained susceptible to suggestion."

"But . . . isn't Heidl dead?" Owen asked. "Or did he make it off the starbase in time?"

Bonner was simply shaking his head now, tears beginning to run down his cheeks. Kyle couldn't bring himself to feel sorry for the man, though.

"No one made it off in time," Kyle said. "The last thing Ensign Janeway checked for me was a travel log. Vice Admiral Bonner was in deep space when the Tholians attacked. He was, in fact, not too terribly far from Tholian space. I believe he went there to help his stepson eliminate evidence, and to provide a ride home for Mr. Heidl. For whatever reason, though, Mr. Heidl missed the boat."

"He went back," Bonner mumbled, his face buried in his hands. "I . . . we went there to bring him home." He dropped his hands and turned his head slowly, facing everyone in the room, as if they were all his accusers. "We came to my ship, but we had forgotten to make sure some of the records were destroyed. So we went back."

Kyle noted the change in subject pronoun, and realized that Bonner's problems were even deeper than he had thought. And he had thought they were pretty bad indeed.

"What was it, Bonner? Am I right?"

Bonner nodded and answered wetly. "Mental control and manipulation. Limited range, but very . . . effective. We made . . . remarkable progress. But then, we went back and . . . we talked, via closed-channel communications. 'They're here!' we shouted, and then we could hear the noise of the Tholian torpedoes, and the explosions. We didn't . . . didn't hear Charles anymore, but the channel stayed open and we heard the rest of it. The Tholians, when they boarded the starbase and searched it, destroying every survivor. Except one. Except Riker."

"Horace," Owen said, his voice gentle. "You're saying 'we.' What do you mean by that? Who?"

"He's . . . he's in here, with us. Charles. We can't explain . . . maybe our mental powers were so well developed, by that time . . . that we were able to make the jump across space."

And maybe, Kyle thought, *you're just nutty as a fruitcake.*

"Horace, we can get you some help," Owen said.

"No!" The word was an explosion. "We don't need **your** help!" Bonner leapt from his chair, sending it flying backward behind him, and whipped a phaser from his belt holster. He aimed it at Kyle and pulled the trigger.

Chapter 39

Kyle had expected something like this, though he wasn't at all sure what form it would take, and he had warned Ensign Janeway to get ready for it. At his signal she had taken up a place at the light panel for the room, and as soon as Bonner drew his weapon, she slapped at the panel, plunging the room into utter darkness. Kyle threw himself to the floor, underneath the solid conference table. He heard the phaser discharge, saw the room briefly illumined by its beam. Shouts rang out all around the room.

Kyle rolled out from under the table, close to where Bonner had been standing. He willed himself to be calm, collected. He breathed slowly but shallowly, trying to keep his breath and his heartbeat quiet. Kyle Riker had played a lot of anbo-jytsu in his time. He didn't need to be able to see to fight.

Bonner, for his part, wasn't a difficult target. He sobbed once and drew in his breath, and Kyle charged him. In the dark he misestimated Bonner's height, slightly, and hit him higher than he'd wanted, his shoulder colliding with the vice admiral's chest instead of his ribcage. Even so, they both fell back. But Bonner crashed against a wall and didn't go down. The phaser discharged again, its beam jetting harmlessly into the ceiling, sending down a cascade of sparks but injuring no one.

Kyle grabbed for Bonner's wrist, but the man was strong in spite of his insanity—or maybe because of it, Kyle thought. He took a couple of hard blows to the head as he wrestled Bonner in the dark. He wasn't sure how many more of those he'd be able to shrug off. He needed to take Bonner down, fast.

The lights came back on. "See here, Bonner," Kyle heard Admiral Paris saying once he could see what was happening. Bonner ignored him, and Kyle tried to ignore everything. Bonner's madness had indeed given him strength—or else he was right, and there were two people in him, each contributing his own strength. In spite of Kyle's best efforts, Bonner had managed to angle his wrist so that his phaser was pointed directly at Kyle's head.

"We'd like to see your precious strategy get you out of this," Bonner snarled. His finger tightened on the trigger.

Kyle released Bonner's wrist suddenly. Since Bonner had been fighting against the pressure Kyle had been putting on it, the sudden action made his arm drop precipitously. Kyle sidestepped the phaser blast, which tore a hole in the floor, and moved in with a left jab at Bonner's middle. The left was a feint. When Bonner moved to block it, Kyle instead threw a right that connected hard with Bonner's chin. Kyle thought he might have broken a knuckle, but he didn't care. Bonner's head snapped back, blood already trailing from his mouth, and slammed into the wall behind him. Kyle followed up with another left, a real one this time, but Bonner was already sliding down the wall, unconscious. Kyle caught his wrist and worked the phaser from his hand, then let the vice admiral fall to the floor.

"Sometimes, Vice Admiral Bonner," he said in reply to the man's final statement, "all the strategy in the world isn't worth as much as a good right hook."

"Is he insane, do you think, Kyle?" Owen Paris asked him later. "Even with all of our science, all our knowledge, there's so much we don't know about the human mind. We can't build ships that can go in and explore it like we do outer space. We're only guessing at so much of it. Is it possible that Heidl really is, somehow, in there with Bonner?"

They were in Owen's office. They had eaten some lunch, and Kyle felt better, more relaxed and contented, than he had in a very long while. He took a sip of excellent coffee. "I'll leave it to people smarter than me to figure that out," he said. "As far as I'm concerned, he's just nuts. He had to listen to his stepson die. The *Berlin* came to drop off the team that was to investigate Heidl's experiments, then it left. Bonner was on that ship, keeping it just far enough away to not be able to help when the Tholians came, but trying to keep it close enough that Heidl could escape to it. Heidl went back, as Bonner said, but then the attack came and no one could beam off the starbase anymore. He tried to launch a shuttle—our records prove that someone tried to—but he couldn't do that either. He was trapped on the starbase, and Bonner was stuck listening to him die. Then he couldn't tear himself away from listening to the rest of the invasion either. It must have been then that he went insane, or started to."

Owen steepled his hands and tapped his fingertips against his mouth. "You're probably right," he said. "At least, that story fits the facts that we know. The other facts—what Heidl and his friends were working on, why Bonner went on that trip and why he couldn't save Heidl—we'll just have to speculate on. Or take Bonner's word for."

"I'm not sure I'd do that," Kyle suggested. "Bonner's word probably isn't good for much."

"What amazes me," Owen said, "is how long he was able to function here. We'll go through his records thoroughly, and maybe we'll find that he wasn't really functioning all that well. But he seemed to be. He passed. Except that he was also busy planning his revenge on you, for surviving when Heidl couldn't."

"And on Will," Kyle reminded him. "It's no coincidence that it was the *Pegasus* he tried to sabotage."

Owen's eyes widened. "I hadn't even thought of it that way," he said.

"Your mind isn't devious enough," Kyle said. "You sure you want to go into space again?"

"I hope a devious mind isn't a necessary prerequisite," Owen replied. "From listening to the *Pegasus* today, though, it sounds like courage is."

Kyle simply nodded, and Owen continued. "Who do you suppose that was," he asked, "who spoke up, volunteering to initiate the auto-destruct since the first officer wouldn't? The voice sounded awfully familiar to me."

Kyle just looked at Owen, sitting across the desk from him. "You know who it was," he said.

"I know who I think it was. And his name's Riker."

"Of course it was Will," Kyle confirmed.. "Who else but a Riker? He was willing to blow up his own ship to pull off a bluff—moving close enough to the enemy to guarantee that if the ship did auto-destruct, it'd take both ships with it. Given that the phrase 'self-sacrifice' didn't seem to be in their vocabulary, the Omistol *had* to cut their tractor. Will's a chip off the old block, that's for sure."

"He's the image of his old man," Owen said with a friendly smile. "I hope I have a crew full of young people just like him on the *Al-Batani*. I hope Tom grows up just as gutsy."

"If you have a crew like that Ensign Janeway," Kyle told him, "you'll be in good shape."

"She's a peach, all right," Owen agreed. "Kyle, I just can't wait to get out there."

Later still, Kyle walked alone alongside the bayfront, enjoying the cool snap of the wind as it blew off the water. For a change, there were no security officers following him, and he did not miss their presence. He was convinced that his ordeal was finally over, that there would be no more attempts on his life now that Horace Bonner was in custody.

Instead of worrying about his own safety, though, he thought about Will, so far away, one little person on one little ship in the vastness of the universe. There would be dangers untold in Will's future, he knew. As he'd told Owen, Will was a Riker, through and through. *Of course* he had volunteered to blow up the ship. He put duty before his own fears, his own feelings. That's what Rikers did.

But when he thought of Will, so far away, acting like a Riker, he did so with a great sense of melancholy. The Rikers had a way about them, that much was undeniable. Kyle Riker looked out across the bay, then up at the sky, where a single star appeared above the horizon. He felt a kinship with that star, alone in the sky. Acting like a Riker had put him here, he knew. Being a Riker had made him alone. He had never really seen it before, had learned this lesson much too late to do him any good, or to save any of the possible futures he might have had, with Kate or with Michelle.

Or with Will.

He just hoped his son could learn the lessons he had more easily than he had. He hoped that Will could become a different kind of Riker, could become unlike his old man, who loved him dearly but couldn't find a way to tell him so.

And he hoped it would happen for Will before his life was screwed up, for good. Like his old man's was.

But as he watched the sky, standing there with the wind picking up, whipping his hair and stinging his skin, another star appeared in the night sky, and then another, and then ten, thousands, millions.

And Kyle understood then that it wasn't too late, not even for him. Alone now didn't have to mean alone forever. If he'd had a glass in his hand, he'd have raised it, but instead he just turned his face to the sky.

"Another lesson, son," he said softly. "We Rikers may be stubborn as hell, but eventually we learn from our mistakes. You'll do fine out there, I know you will."

He turned away from the bay and the wind and the stars and started to walk home. "You'll do fine," he repeated. And as he did so, he knew, somehow, that he was right.

ABOUT THE AUTHOR

Jeff Mariotte is the author of many novels, including several set in the universes of *Buffy the Vampire Slayer* and *Angel*, as well as *Charmed*, *Gen13*, *Gene Roddenberry's Andromeda*, and the original dark suspense novel *The Slab*. Previous encounters with *Star Trek* include writing the S.C.E. novella *No Surrender* and editing *Star Trek* comics for DC Comics/WildStorm. He's also written more comic books than he has time to count, including the Stoker award–nominated horror/Western series *Desperadoes*. With his wife Maryelizabeth Hart and partner Terry Gilman, he owns Mysterious Galaxy, a bookstore specializing in science fiction, fantasy, mystery, and horror. He lives in San Diego, California, with his family and pets, in a home filled with books, music, toys, and other examples of American pop culture. More about him can be gleaned from www.jeffmariotte.com.

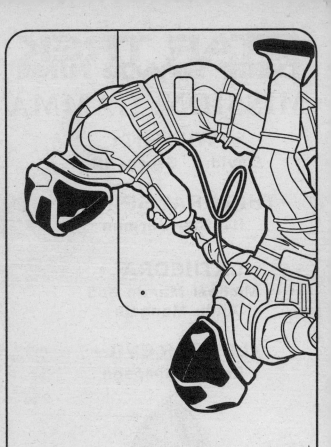

STAR TREK®
THE STARFLEET
SURVIVAL GUIDE
AVAILABLE NOW... FOR THOSE
WHO PLAN AHEAD.

STSG